BLACK SKIES

Arnaldur Indridason worked for many years as a journalist and critic before he began writing novels. Outside Iceland, he is best known for his crime novels featuring Erlendur, Elínborg and Sigurdur Óli, which are consistent bestsellers across Europe. The series has won numerous awards, including the Nordic Glass Key (both for *Jar City* and *Silence of the Grave*) and the CWA Gold Dagger (for *Silence of the Grave*). His most recent novel is *Strange Shores*.

ARNALDUR INDRIDASON

Black Skies

TRANSLATED FROM THE ICELANDIC BY
Victoria Cribb

VINTAGE BOOKS
London

Published by Vintage 2013

2 4 6 8 10 9 7 5 3 1

First published with the title *Svörtuloft* in 2009 by Forlagið, Reykjavík

First published in Great Britain in 2012 by
Harvill Secker

Vintage
Random House, 20 Vauxhall Bridge Road,
London SW1V 2SA

www.vintage-books.co.uk

Addresses for companies within The Random House Group Limited
can be found at: www.randomhouse.co.uk/offices.htm

The Random House Group Limited Reg. No. 954009

A CIP catalogue record for this book
is available from the British Library

ISBN 9780099563365

This translation has been published with the
financial assistance of NORLA

Typeset in Minion by Palimpsest Book Production Limited,
Falkirk, Stirlingshire

Printed and bound in Great Britain by Clays Ltd, St Ives PLC

BLACK SKIES

1

He took the leather mask from the plastic bag. It had not turned out as he had intended; in fact, it was a bit of a botched job. But it would serve its purpose.

His greatest fear had been of running into a cop on the way, but in the event no one had paid him any attention. In addition to the mask, the plastic bag contained two bottles from the state off-licence and a suitably heavy hammer and metal spike bought from a DIY shop.

The materials for the mask had been purchased the day before from a wholesaler who imported leather and hides. Since he had known exactly what he needed he had no problem in acquiring the necessary leather, thread and strong wedge needle. He had made an effort to shave beforehand and put on the least shabby clothes he owned.

Realistically, there was little danger that he would attract any unwanted attention as it was early in the morning and there was barely a soul about. Head down, making sure not to catch the eye of any passer-by, he strode up to the wooden house on Grettisgata where he hurriedly descended the steps to the basement, opened the door and slipped inside, closing it carefully behind him.

Once inside he paused in the gloom, though by now he knew the layout of the flat so well that he could find his way around it in pitch darkness. It was not large: there was a windowless toilet to the right, off the hall, and the kitchen was on the same side with a big window that faced the back garden, which he had covered with a thick blanket. Directly opposite the kitchen was the sitting room and, beside that, the door to the bedroom. The sitting-room window faced on to the street but had heavy curtains drawn across it. So far he had only taken one quick glance into the bedroom, which had a single window, high up in the wall, blacked out by a bin bag.

Instead of turning on the lights he fumbled for the candle stub that he kept on a shelf in the hallway and lit it with a match, before following its eerie illumination into the sitting room. He could hear muffled cries coming from the old man tied to a chair with his hands bound behind his back and a gag over his mouth. Being careful to avoid even a glimpse of his face, especially his eyes, he put the bag down on a table and took out the hammer, mask, spike and bottles. Next he tore the seal off the *brennivín* and began eagerly gulping down the lukewarm spirit that had long since ceased to burn his throat.

Then he set the bottle down and picked up the mask. Only the finest materials had been used: thick pigskin, and seams double stitched with waxed sailmaking twine. He had cut out a round hole in the forehead to accommodate the galvanised-iron spike, then sewn a thick rim around it so that the spike would stand up unsupported. The sides of the mask had slits for a broad leather strap which could be tied tightly round the back of the head. There were also slits for the eyes and mouth. The top of the mask extended to the crown of the head and had a leather strap attached that could be tied in turn to the strap at the back of the neck to make sure the mask did not slip. He had not bothered to take precise measurements, working mainly from the size of his own head.

He took another swig of the spirit, trying not to let the old sod's whimpering get to him.

There had been a mask like this on the farm when he was a boy, though it had been made of iron rather than leather. It was kept in the old sheep shed, and despite being forbidden to handle it, he had once managed to sneak a look. The iron, which was rusty in places, had felt cold to the touch, and he had noticed that there were dried bloodstains around the spike hole. He had only seen the mask used once, when the farmer destroyed a sick calf one summer. The farmer was far too hard up to own a gun, but the mask did its job. It was almost too small to fit over the calf's head and the farmer explained that it had been designed for sheep. The farmer had picked up his big hammer and struck the spike a single heavy blow which drove it deep into the calf's head. The animal collapsed on the spot and did not move again.

He had been happy there, in the countryside, where nobody ever told him he was a pathetic little wimp.

He had never forgotten what the farmer had called the headpiece with the spike which jutted out like the reminder of a quick and painless end. A death mask.

It was a chilling name.

He stared for a long time at the spike which protruded from his own ham-fisted effort. He had worked out that it would penetrate five centimetres into the skull, and he knew that this would be enough.

2

Sigurdur Óli let out a heavy sigh. He had been sitting in his car outside the flats for nearly three hours now. Nothing had happened: the newspaper was still in its place in the postbox. A few residents had come or gone but no one had so much as glanced at the paper, which he had purposely left sticking halfway out so that any passer-by could easily snatch it if they had a mind to. If they were a thief, in other words, or had some reason for wanting to upset the old woman upstairs.

As cases went, it was not exactly a challenge; in fact, it was the most trivial, tedious affair that Sigurdur Óli could remember since joining the police force. His mother had rung and asked him to do a favour for a friend who lived in a block of flats on Kleppsvegur, near Reykjavík's northern shore. The friend had a newspaper delivered but when she went to fetch it on a Sunday morning she kept finding that it had vanished from her postbox in the communal lobby. She had had no luck in discovering the culprit herself, as her neighbours all swore blind that they had not taken it. Some even sneered that they would not touch such a crappy right-wing rag with a bargepole. In a way she agreed; she only really stayed loyal to the paper for the obituaries section that sometimes made up as much as quarter of its contents.

The friend had identified various suspects on her staircase. On the floor above, for example, there was a woman she believed to be 'one of those nymphomaniacs'. There was a constant stream of men to her door, especially in the evenings and at weekends, and if not her, then no doubt one of them was the culprit. Another neighbour, two floors up, did not have a job but lounged around at home all day, claiming to be a composer.

Sigurdur Óli watched as a teenage girl entered the block, evidently on her way home from an all-nighter. She was still drunk and could not immediately find her keys in the small purse that she took from her pocket. She swayed, grabbing the door handle for support. She did not give the paper a second look. No chance of any photos of her in the Social Diary section, thought Sigurdur Óli, as he watched her stagger up the stairs.

He still had a touch of flu that was proving stubborn to shake off. No doubt it was his own fault for getting up too soon but he simply could not face languishing in bed, watching films on his 42-inch plasma screen any longer. It was better to be busy, even if he still felt grim.

His thoughts wandered back to last night. There had been a reunion party for his sixth-form class at the house of a guy known as Guffi, a conceited lawyer who had annoyed Sigurdur Óli almost from the day they met. It was typical of Guffi – the kind of prat who used to turn up to school in a bow tie – to invite them round to his place, ostensibly for the reunion but really, as he revealed in a breathtakingly pompous speech, to announce that he had recently been promoted to director of some division at his bank, and that this was as good an opportunity as any to celebrate that *as well*. Sigurdur Óli did not join in with the applause.

Looking discontentedly around the group, he wondered if he had achieved the least of all of them since leaving school. It was the kind of thought that preyed on him whenever he bothered to attend these reunions. The gathering included other lawyers like Guffi, as well as engineers, two vicars, three doctors who had completed lengthy training as specialists, and even an author.

Sigurdur Óli had never read any of his stuff but they made a fuss of him in literary circles for his distinctive style that bordered on the 'irrational', in the jargon of the latest pseudo-intellectual school of criticism. When Sigurdur Óli compared himself to his former classmates – his life in the force, the sort of investigations he was involved in, his colleagues Erlendur and Elínborg, and all the human dross he was forced to deal with every day – he could find little reason to be cheerful. His mother had always said he was too good for *that*, meaning the police, though his father had been quite pleased when he joined and pointed out that at least he would be doing more good for society than most.

'So, how's life in the force?' asked Patrekur, one of the engineers, who had been standing beside him during Guffi's speech. He and Sigurdur Óli had been friends since sixth form.

'So-so,' Sigurdur Óli replied. 'You must be run off your feet, what with the economy booming and all those hydroelectric projects.'

'We're literally up to our eyes,' Patrekur said, with a more serious air than usual. 'Look, I was wondering if we could meet up sometime soon. There's something I'd like to discuss.'

'Sure. Will I have to arrest you?'

Patrekur did not smile.

'I'll be in touch on Monday, if that's OK,' he said, before moving away.

'Yeah, do,' Sigurdur Óli replied, nodding to Patrekur's wife, Súsanna, who, though partners did not usually show up, had accompanied him. She returned his smile. He had always liked her and regarded his friend as a lucky sod.

'Still upholding the law?' asked Ingólfur, coming over, beer glass in hand. One of the two vicars in the group, he was descended from priests on both sides of his family and had never harboured any other ambition than to serve the Lord. Not that he was the sanctimonious type; quite the opposite: he liked a drink, had an eye for the ladies and was already on his second marriage. He used to argue with the other vicar in the class, Elmar, a very different kettle of fish; so pious that he bordered on the puritanical, a fundamentalist who was deeply opposed to change, especially when it involved homosexuals wanting to overturn the country's deep-seated Christian traditions. Ingólfur, on the other hand, could not care less what kind of human flotsam washed up on his doorstep, adhering to the one rule his vicar father had impressed upon him: that all men were equal before God. He enjoyed riling Elmar, however, and was always asking him when he was going to form his own breakaway sect, the Elmarites.

'And you? Still preaching?' Sigurdur Óli asked.

'Of course. We're both indispensable.' Ingólfur grinned.

Guffi appeared and gave Sigurdur Óli a hearty slap on the back.

'How's the cop?' he boomed, full of his new importance.

'Fine.'

'Never regretted quitting your law studies?' Guffi went on, conceited as ever. He had put on quite a bit of weight over the years: his bow tie was now gradually disappearing under an impressive double chin.

'No, never,' Sigurdur Óli retorted, though actually he did occasionally wonder if he should leave the police and go back and complete his degree so that he could get a proper job. But there was no way he was going to admit this to Guffi, or the fact that Guffi was something of an inspiration to him when he was in this state of mind: after all, he often reasoned, if a buffoon like Guffi could understand the law, then anyone could.

'You've been marrying queers, I see,' said Elmar, joining the group and giving Ingólfur a reproachful look.

'Here we go,' said Sigurdur Óli, searching for an escape route before he got caught up in a religious debate.

He turned to Steinunn who was walking past with a drink in her hand. Until recently she had worked for the tax office and Sigurdur Óli used to call her from time to time when he ran into difficulties with his tax return.

She had always been very obliging. He knew she had got divorced several years ago and was now happily single. It was partly on her account that he had made the effort to come this evening.

'Steina,' he called, 'is it true that you've left the tax office?'

'Yes, I'm working for Guffi's bank now,' she said with a smile. 'These days my job consists of helping the rich to avoid paying tax – thereby saving them a fortune, according to Guffi.'

'I guess the bank pays better too.'

'You're telling me. I'm earning silly money.'

Steinunn smiled again, revealing gleaming white teeth, and pushed back a lock of hair that had fallen over one eye. She was blonde, with curly shoulder-length hair, a rather broad face, attractive dark eyes and brows that she dyed black. She was what the kids would call a MILF and Sigurdur Óli wondered if she was aware of the term. No doubt; she had always known that sort of thing.

'Yeah, I gather you lot are not exactly starving,' he said.

'What about you? Not dabbling yourself?'

'Dabbling?'

'In the markets,' Steinunn said. 'You're that kind of guy.'

'Am I?' Sigurdur Óli asked, grinning.

'Yes, you're a bit of a gambler, aren't you?'

'I can't afford to take any risks,' he said, grinning again. 'I stick to safe bets.'

'Like what?'

'I only buy bank shares.'

Steinunn raised her glass. 'And you can't get safer than that.'

'Still single?' he asked.

'Yes, and loving it.'

'It's not all bad,' Sigurdur Óli conceded.

'What's happening with you and Bergthóra?' Steinunn asked bluntly. 'I heard things weren't going so well.'

'No,' he replied, 'it isn't really working out. Sadly.'

'Great girl, Bergthóra,' said Steinunn, who had met his former partner once or twice at similar occasions.

'Yes, she was . . . is. Look, I was wondering if you and I could maybe meet up. For a coffee or something.'

'Are you asking me out?'

Sigurdur Óli nodded.

'On a date?'

'No, not a date, well, yes, maybe something like that, now you come to mention it.'

'Siggi,' Steinunn said, patting him on the cheek, 'you're just not my type.'

Sigurdur Óli stared at her.

'You know that, Siggi. You never were, never will be.'

Type?! Sigurdur Óli spat out the word as he sat in

his car in front of the flats, waiting to ambush the newspaper thief. *Type*? What did that mean? Was he a worse type than anyone else? What did Steinunn mean by her talk of types?

A young man carrying a musical-instrument case went inside, took the paper from the postbox without breaking his stride and proceeded to open the door to the staircase with a key. Sigurdur Óli just made it into the lobby in time to shove his foot in the door as it was closing, and pursued him into the stairwell. The young man was astonished when Sigurdur Óli grabbed him as he started up the stairs and yanked him back down, before relieving him of the newspaper and whacking him over the head with it. The man dropped his instrument case, which banged into the wall, lost his balance and fell over.

'Get up, you idiot!' Sigurdur Óli snapped, trying to drag the man to his feet. He assumed that this was the layabout who lived two floors up from his mother's friend; the waster who called himself a composer.

'Don't hurt me!' cried the composer.

'I'm not hurting you. Now, are you going to stop stealing Gudmunda's paper? You know who she is, don't you? The old lady on the first floor. What kind of loser steals an old lady's Sunday paper? Or do you get some sort of kick out of picking on people who can't stand up for themselves?'

The young man was on his feet again. Glaring at Sigurdur Óli with a look of outrage, he snatched the paper back from him.

'This is *my* paper,' he said. 'And I don't know what you're talking about.'

'*Your* paper?' Sigurdur Óli broke in quickly. 'You're wrong there, mate; this is Gudmunda's.'

Only now did he cast a glance into the lobby where the postboxes hung in rows, five across and three high, and saw the paper jutting out of Gudmunda's postbox just as he had left it.

'Shit!' he swore as he got back into his car and shame-facedly drove away.

3

He was on his way to work on Monday morning when he heard the news that a body had been discovered in a rented flat in the old Thingholt district, near the city centre. A young man had been murdered, his throat slashed. The CID were quick to arrive on the scene and the rest of Sigurdur Óli's day was spent interviewing the young man's neighbours. At one point he ran into Elínborg, who was in charge of the case and appeared as calm and unflappable as ever; rather too calm and unflappable for Sigurdur Óli's taste.

During the day he took a phone call from Patrekur reminding him that they had planned to meet, but as he had heard about the murder he said Sigurdur Óli should forget it. Sigurdur Óli told him it was all right; they could meet later that day at a cafe he suggested. Shortly afterwards he received another call, this time from the station, about a man who was asking after Erlendur and refused to leave until he was allowed to see him. The man had been informed that Erlendur was on leave in the countryside but would not believe it. Finally, he said he would talk to Sigurdur Óli instead, but eventually left after refusing to give his name or state his business. Lastly, Bergthóra rang and asked him to meet her the following evening, if he could spare the time.

Having spent the day at the crime scene, Sigurdur Óli went to meet Patrekur at five at the appointed cafe in the city centre. Patrekur was there first, accompanied by his wife's brother-in-law, whom Sigurdur Óli knew vaguely from parties at his friend's house. There was a beer in front of the man and he had apparently already emptied a shot glass.

'Bit heavy for a Monday,' Sigurdur Óli commented, looking at him disapprovingly as he took a seat at their table.

The man smiled awkwardly and glanced at Patrekur.

'I needed it,' he said and took a sip of beer.

His name was Hermann and he was a wholesaler, married to Súsanna's sister.

'So, what's up?' asked Sigurdur Óli.

He sensed that Patrekur was not his usual self and guessed that he was uncomfortable about having arranged this meeting without warning Sigurdur Óli that Hermann was coming along; as a rule he was the easy-going type, quick to smile and always cracking jokes. They sometimes went to the gym together early in the morning and grabbed a quick coffee afterwards, or to the cinema, and had even holidayed together from time to time. Patrekur was the closest thing Sigurdur Óli had to a best friend.

'Are you familiar with the term "swinging"?' Patrekur asked now.

'No, what, you mean dancing?'

Patrekur's lips twitched. 'If only,' he said, his eyes on Hermann, who was sipping his beer. Hermann's handshake had been weak and moist when Sigurdur Óli greeted him. He had thin hair, small, regular features, and, in spite of being smartly dressed in a suit and tie, had several days' stubble on his chin.

'So you're not talking about the swing – that forties dance?' Sigurdur Óli asked.

'No, not a lot of dancing goes on at the parties I'm talking about,' Patrekur said quietly.

Hermann finished his beer and waved to the waiter to bring him another.

Sigurdur Óli looked at Patrekur. They had founded a neoconservative society known as Milton in the sixth form and produced an eight-page magazine of the same name, singing the praises of individual enterprise and the free market. They had booked well-known right-wing speakers to come to the school and address thinly attended meetings. Later, much to Sigurdur Óli's surprise, Patrekur had turned against the magazine, developing left-wing sympathies and starting to speak out against the American base on Midnesheidi, calling for Iceland to leave NATO. This was around the time he met his future wife, so it probably reflected her influence. Sigurdur Óli had struggled on alone to keep Milton going but when the magazine dwindled to four pages and even the young conservatives no longer bothered to turn up to the meetings, the whole thing died a natural death. Sigurdur Óli still owned all the back issues of *Milton*, including the one containing his essay: 'The US to the Rescue: Lies About CIA Involvement in South America'.

He and Patrekur had started university at the same time and even after Sigurdur Óli had abandoned his law degree in order to enrol at a police academy in the US, they continued to write to each other regularly. Patrekur had come out to visit him, bringing his wife Súsanna and their first child, while he was still on his engineering course, full of talk of soil mechanics and infrastructure design.

'Why are we talking about swinging?' asked Sigurdur Óli, who could not make head nor tail of his friend's hints. He flicked some dust off his new light-coloured summer coat that he was still wearing, in defiance of the onset of autumn. He had bought it in a sale and was rather pleased with it.

'Well, I feel a bit awkward raising this with you. You know I never ask you favours as a policeman.' Patrekur smiled uneasily. 'But the thing is, Hermann and his wife are in a tight corner thanks to some people they hardly even know.'

'What kind of tight corner?'

'These people invited them to a swingers' party.'

'You're on about swinging again.'

'Let me tell him,' interrupted Hermann. 'We only did it for a short time and stopped after that. Swinging is another term for . . .' He coughed in embarrassment. '. . . it's another term for wife-swapping.'

'Wife-swapping?'

Patrekur nodded. Sigurdur Óli gaped at his friend.

'Not you and Súsanna too?' he asked.

Patrekur hesitated, as if he did not understand the question.

'Not you and Súsanna?' Sigurdur Óli repeated in disbelief.

'No, no, of course not,' Patrekur hastily reassured him.

'We weren't involved. It was Hermann and his wife – Súsanna's sister.'

'It was just an innocent way of livening up our marriage,' Hermann added.

'An innocent way of livening up your marriage?'

'Are you going to repeat everything we say?' asked Hermann.

'Have you been practising this for long?'

'Practising? I don't know if that's the right word.'

'Well, I wouldn't know.'

'We've stopped now but a couple of years back we experimented a bit.'

Sigurdur Óli glanced at his friend, then back at Hermann.

'I don't need to justify myself to you,' Hermann said, bridling. His beer arrived and he took a deep draught, then, looking at Patrekur, added: 'Maybe this wasn't such a good idea.'

Patrekur ignored him. He was studying Sigurdur Óli with a sombre expression.

'Please tell me you're not involved in this,' Sigurdur Óli said.

'Of course not,' Patrekur repeated. 'I'm just trying to help them.'

'Well, what's it got to do with me?'

'They're in a spot of bother.'

'What kind of bother?'

'It's all about having fun with strangers,' Hermann chimed in, apparently revived by the beer. 'That's what makes it such a turn-on.'

'I wouldn't know,' said Sigurdur Óli again.

Hermann took a deep breath. 'We got involved with con men.'

'You mean they conned you out of a shag?'

Hermann turned to Patrekur. 'I told you this was a mistake.'

'Will you listen to him?' Patrekur admonished Sigurdur Óli. 'They're in deep shit and I thought you might be able to help. Please just shut up and listen.'

Sigurdur Óli obliged his friend. Hermann and his wife had been involved in wife-swapping for a while two years previously, inviting people over for swingers' parties and accepting invitations to similar gatherings at other people's homes. They had an open relationship, which worked well for them, according to Hermann. The sex was exciting; they only went with 'nice' people, as he put it, and they soon became part of a club consisting of a small group of like-minded couples.

'Then we met Lína and Ebbi,' he said.

'Who are they?' Sigurdur Óli asked.

'A couple of total shits,' Hermann said, emptying his glass.

'Not "nice" people, then?'

'They took photos,' Hermann said.

'Photos of you?'

Hermann nodded.

'Having sex?'

'They're threatening to post them on the Internet if we don't pay up.'

'Súsanna's sister is in politics, isn't she?' Sigurdur Óli asked Patrekur.

'Do you think you could talk to them?' Hermann said.

'Isn't she an assistant to one of the cabinet ministers?' Sigurdur Óli asked.

Patrekur nodded. 'It's a nightmare for them,' he said. 'Hermann was wondering if you could talk some sense into these people, get the pictures off them, scare them into coming clean and handing over everything they've got.'

'What exactly have they got?'

'A short video,' Hermann said.

'Of you having sex?'

Hermann nodded.

'You mean you didn't know you were being filmed? How could you fail to notice?'

'I can't really remember – it was two years ago,' Hermann said. 'They sent us a photo. It looks as if they had a camera installed in their flat that we didn't spot. Actually, I do remember seeing a camera of some kind

– a very small one – on a bookshelf in the sitting room where we were at the time, but it didn't occur to me that it was switched on.'

'It wouldn't require a particularly sophisticated set-up,' Patrekur pointed out.

'Were you at their place?'

'Yes.'

'What sort of people are they?'

'We don't know them at all and haven't seen them since. I expect they recognised my wife because she sometimes appears in the media, so they decided to try a little coercion.'

'With considerable success,' Patrekur put in, his eyes on Sigurdur Óli.

'What do they want?'

'Money,' said Hermann. 'Far more than we've got available. It was the woman who made contact with us. She told us to take out a loan and said we mustn't talk to the police.'

'Do you have any proof of their claim to have pictures of you?'

Hermann looked at Patrekur.

'Yes.'

'What is it?'

Hermann glanced around the cafe, then reached into the breast pocket of his jacket and took out a photo which he slid across to Sigurdur Óli. The quality was poor as it had apparently been run off on a home printer, but it showed a group of people having sex, two of them women whom Sigurdur Óli did not recognise from the grainy image, and Hermann, who was instantly identifiable. At the moment the photo was taken the party seemed to have reached its climax, so to speak . . .

'And you want me to sort these people out?' Sigurdur Óli asked, looking at his friend.

'Before things turn nasty,' Patrekur said. 'You're the only person we know who could possibly deal with scum-bags like these.'

4

He had stalked the bastard for several months before finally taking action. Had stood outside and spied on the dump in Grettisgata, whatever the weather, at all hours of the day and night, taking care to remain at a discreet distance and keep a low profile. It was risky to loiter too long in the same place in case he attracted the attention of passers-by or residents. They might call the police and that was the last thing he wanted. It would not be the first time he had been in trouble with the law.

The houses in this neighbourhood were all much of a muchness. Here and there new houses had sprung up, built according to the prevailing fashion at the time, while others blended in better with the original appearance of the street: humble, low-rise, wooden buildings, clad in corrugated iron, and standing one or two storeys high, on raised concrete basements. Some had been lovingly restored, others neglected and allowed to go to seed, like the dump where the old man lived. The roof was in a dilapidated state, there were no gutters on the side facing the street, the light blue colour the house had originally been painted was almost worn away and large patches of rust marred the roof and walls. As far as he could tell, the floor above the basement was unoccupied; there were curtains drawn across all the windows and he had never seen anyone set foot inside.

The years had not been kind to the old man; he must be well into his seventies by now, stiff-legged and stooped, with grey hair straggling from under his woollen hat, an old anorak, and an air of threadbare neglect. There was little about him to remind one of the past. His routine was more or less fixed: every other day he went to the old swimming pool early in the morning, so early that he sometimes had to wait for it to open. It was possible that he had been awake all night, because he would go straight home afterwards and not stir again until evening, when he would re-emerge to visit the local shop and buy milk, bread and a few other groceries. Occasionally he would drop by the off-licence. He never spoke to anyone on these journeys, never greeted anyone and only ever stopped briefly, just long enough to do what was strictly necessary before continuing on his way. He never received any visitors either, except the postman now and then. His evenings were spent at home, apart from two occasions when he had walked down to the sea by the coast road, continuing along the shore as far as the fishing docks, then home again through the western part of town and the old Thingholt district.

On the second occasion it had started to rain in the middle of his walk and the old man had crept under cover of darkness into the garden of a two-storey period house, where he had peered through the ground-floor windows at the family with several children who lived there. For more than an hour he had lurked behind a clump of trees in the cold rain, at a safe distance from the house, watching the family get ready for bed. Long after all the lights had been turned out, he stole over to the window of one of the children's rooms and gazed inside for a long time before resuming his journey home to Grettisgata.

All that night, ignoring the lashing rain, he himself had stood outside, his eyes fixed on the basement door of the house on Grettisgata, feeling as if he had to stand guard over all Reykjavík's innocent little children.

5

It was evening, and peace had descended over the city with the coming of dusk, when Sigurdur Óli rang the doorbell of Sigurlína Thorgrímsdóttir, also known as Lína, alleged blackmailer. He was keen to get his conversation with her over as soon as possible. She lived in a terraced house in the leafy eastern suburbs, not far from the Laugarás cinema, with her husband Ebeneser, nicknamed Ebbi. Sigurdur Óli looked over at the illuminated frontage of the cinema and remembered watching some great films there back in his teens when he used to be a keen moviegoer. Not that he could call any of them to mind just now – he had always been quick to forget films

– but he knew that the cinema itself would always occupy a special place in his heart thanks to a memorable date there when he was in the sixth form. He had gone there with a girl who had subsequently got away, but he could still remember the long kiss they had exchanged afterwards outside her house in his car.

He did not have a clue how he was supposed to help Hermann and his wife but thought he might as well read the riot act to Lína and Ebbi, threaten them with police involvement, and see if that did the trick. Judging from what Hermann had said, they were not very experienced blackmailers, but then it was not exactly a common occupation.

On the way to Lína's house he had been thinking about the phone call that had interrupted him the night before, when he was lying comfortably ensconced on the sofa at home, watching an American sports channel. As a student in the US he had started following two all-American sports that had previously been a closed book to him – American football and baseball, becoming a major supporter of the Dallas Cowboys and Boston Red Sox respectively. After returning home, he invested in a satellite dish in order to watch the big games live, which he did with great dedication, though the time difference meant that some games took place in the middle of the night in Iceland. Sigurdur Óli had never needed much sleep, however, and rarely missed his morning session at the gym, in spite of his sports obsession. On the other hand, Icelandic sports like football and handball left him cold; the standard of play seemed embarrassingly low in comparison to top international leagues and he regarded domestic competitions as unworthy of being televised.

These days he lived in a small rented flat on Framnesvegur, a quiet residential street in the west of town. When he had moved out after living with Bergthóra for several years, they had divided up their possessions – books, CDs, kitchenware and furniture – in a civilised fashion. He had coveted the plasma screen, she the painting by a young Icelandic artist given to them as a present. She had never watched much television and could not understand his passion for American sports. His new flat still felt rather bare as he had not yet had time to furnish it properly, perhaps hoping deep down that his relationship with Bergthóra could be salvaged.

They had quarrelled over and over again until they could barely speak without losing their tempers and descending into mutual recrimination. Towards the end she had accused him of failing to give her enough support when she suffered her second miscarriage. They had been unable to have children and their attempts to solve the problem medically had ended in miserable failure. Afterwards, when she broached the subject of adoption, he had been ambivalent, before eventually coming right out and saying that he did not want to adopt a child from China as she had proposed.

'What's left then?' Bergthóra had asked.

'The two of us,' he had replied.

'I'm not so sure,' she had said.

In the end the decision to separate had been mutual; their relationship had run its course. They both recognised the fact and knew that the blame lay on both sides. Once the decision had been taken, things seemed to improve; the strain they had been living under eased noticeably and their interaction was no longer as fraught or filled with anger. For the first time in ages they could have a conversation without it ending in bitterness and silence.

When the phone rang he was lounging on the sofa in front of the big screen, drinking orange juice and absorbed in the American football. Glancing at his watch, he discovered that it was past midnight, and peered at the number that flashed up on his phone.

'Hello,' he said.

'Had you gone to bed?' his mother asked.

'No.'

'You don't get enough sleep. You should go to bed earlier.'

'Then you'd have woken me.'

'Oh, is it that late? I thought you might call me. Have you heard from your father?'

'No,' Sigurdur Óli replied, trying not to miss what was happening on-screen. He knew his mother was perfectly aware of the time.

'You remember he's got a birthday coming up.'

'I won't forget.'

'Are you going to drop round and see me tomorrow?'

'Well, I've got a lot on but I'll see if I can make it. Let's talk later.'

'It's a pity you didn't catch the thief.'

'I know. It didn't work.'

'Perhaps you could try again later. Gudmunda's quite distraught about the whole thing, especially the unfortunate business with that musician on her staircase.'

'Yes, well, we'll see,' Sigurdur Óli said, reacting less than enthusiastically to the suggestion. What the hell did he care about Gudmunda's feelings? he thought, though he did not say this aloud.

Once his mother had rung off he tried to concentrate on the game again but with only partial success. The call had upset him. Short though it was, and innocuous though it had seemed, it had left his whole body racked with guilt. His mother had a peculiar knack of expressing things in a manner designed to ruin his peace of mind. It was the tone of concealed accusation, the hint of bossiness. He did not get enough sleep, therefore he was not taking proper care of his health; he had not been in touch with

her, either by phone or in person, and all this was under-
lined by her mention of his father, whom he also neglected.
And to cap it all she had drawn attention to the fact that
he had failed to catch the newspaper thief and was therefore as ineffectual in that as he was in everything else.

His mother had a degree in business studies and
worked as an accountant at a large firm with an
impressive-sounding foreign name. She held a position
of some responsibility, took home a good salary and
had recently embarked on a relationship with another
accountant, a widower called Saemundur, whom
Sigurdur Óli had encountered several times at her house.
Sigurdur Óli had been at primary school when his
parents divorced and had grown up with his mother.
She had been restless during those years and kept moving
to new neighbourhoods, which made it difficult for him
to settle and make friends at school. She had also struck
up short-term relationships with a number of men,
some no more than one-night stands. His father, on the
other hand, was a plumber with fixed political views; a
staunch socialist who loathed the conservatives and the
vested interests they defended tooth and nail – the party
his son always voted for, in spite of him.

'No one has stronger or more legitimate political
convictions than the far left,' his father would claim.
Sigurdur Óli had long ago given up trying to discuss

politics with him. When he refused to change his views, the old man used to say that he had inherited his right-wing snobbery from his mother.

His concentration ruined by the phone call, Sigurdur Óli gradually lost interest in the game until at last he switched off the television, retired to bed and went to sleep.

Now he heaved a sigh and pressed Lína's doorbell again. The accountant and the plumber.

He had never managed to find out what had brought his parents together. Why they had parted seemed far more obvious, though neither father nor son had ever received a proper account. It was hard to imagine a more mismatched couple than his parents. And he, an only child, was their offspring. Sigurdur Óli understood that his outlook must have been coloured by the upbringing he had received from his mother; his attitude to his father for example. His sole wish had long been to be as different from him as possible.

His father never tired of bringing up another snobbery-related trait that Sigurdur Óli had inherited from 'that woman', and that was his arrogance, his tendency to look down on people. Especially the unfortunates at the bottom of the social heap.

Since no one was answering the bell, he tried knocking on the door. He still hadn't a clue how he was supposed to persuade Lína and Ebbi to give up their absurd attempt at blackmail, but at least he could start by hearing what they had to say. Perhaps the whole thing was a misunderstanding on Hermann's part. If not, perhaps he could scare them into abandoning their plans; Sigurdur Óli could be quite intimidating when the situation required it.

In the event he did not have much time to wonder. The door gave way under his knock, opening inwards. After hesitating, he called out to see if anyone was at home. There was no answer. He could have turned round and left but something drew him into the house; innate curiosity, perhaps, or innate lack of consideration.

'Hello!' he called, entering the short hallway that led from the front door, past the kitchen to the sitting room. A small framed watercolour hung askew on the wall by the kitchen door and he automatically straightened it.

Inside, the house was dark, lit only by the faint glow of the street lights, but this was enough to show Sigurdur Óli that the sitting room had been trashed. Lamps and vases lay smashed on the floor, the ceiling lights were broken and pictures had been knocked off the walls.

Amid all the chaos and destruction, Sigurdur Óli caught sight of a woman lying on the floor in a pool of blood, with a large gash in her head.

This, he assumed, must be Lína.

6

He checked for signs of life and could find none, but being no expert, he rang for an ambulance before it occurred to him that he would have to explain his presence in the house. He considered some plausible lie; an anonymous tip-off, perhaps, but then decided to tell the truth; that friends had asked him to go round in connection with a foolish attempt at blackmail. He was anxious to keep Patrekur and Súsanna out of the matter, as well as Súsanna's politically ambitious sister, but knew it would be tricky. Their connection to Lína and Ebbi would come to light as soon as the investigation got off the ground, and another thing was certain: the moment

Sigurdur Óli explained why he had been at the house, he would be taken off the case.

The thoughts chased each other in quick succession through his mind as he was waiting for the ambulance and police to arrive. At first glance he could see no sign of a break-in. The assailant appeared to have entered and left by the front door, not bothering to close it properly behind him. It was possible that the occupants of the neighbouring houses might have noticed something; a car, for instance, or a man who looked capable of attacking Lína and smashing up her home.

He was just bending down to her again when he heard a noise and sensed movement out of the corner of his eye in the dark sitting room. In a flash he glimpsed what looked like a baseball bat swinging towards his head and instinctively dodged, with the result that the blow landed on his shoulder instead, knocking him to the floor. By the time he had clambered to his feet again his assailant had disappeared out of the open front door.

Sigurdur Óli shot out of the house and into the street where he saw a man sprinting away in an easterly direction. Taking out his phone, he called for assistance as he ran. The distance between them widened. The suspect, showing an amazing turn of speed, flung himself into a garden and vanished from sight. Sigurdur Óli dashed after him, leapt over the fence, rounded the corner of the house, bounded over another fence and across the next street and into another garden where he tripped over a wheelbarrow that suddenly blocked his way, hurtled into a currant bush and rolled along the ground in his new summer coat. It took him precious seconds to get his bearings when he stood up again, but then he resumed the chase. He saw that the man had gained a considerable lead as he ran hell for leather across Kleppsvegur and the coast road, before descending into the Vatnagardar district near the container docks, heading in the direction of the mental hospital at Kleppur.

Summoning up his last reserves, Sigurdur Óli plunged into the traffic on the coast road and the drivers slammed on their brakes and honked their horns violently. The phone started ringing in his hand but he did not slow down to answer. He saw the man turn towards the hospital and disappear behind a hill. The hospital itself was floodlit but the area around it was hidden in darkness. He could see no sign of the police cars that he had called out before the chase began and slowed his pace as he approached the hospital, taking the time to answer his phone. It was an officer from one of the patrol cars who had been given the wrong directions and was searching for him around the Hrafnista retirement home. Sigurdur Óli directed him down to the mental hospital and requested further backup, including a dog team. He jogged down to the sea at Kleppsvík where the darkness was total, then halted, peering south towards Holtagardar and the Ellidavogur inlet. He stood quite still, listening, but could not hear or see anything. The man had vanished into the night.

Sigurdur Óli ran back to the hospital where two police cars were just pulling up and directed the officers to the area around the retail centre at Holtagardar, and the Ellidavogur inlet. He gave them a brief description of the man: medium height, leather jacket, jeans, baseball bat. Sigurdur Óli had been keeping a close eye on the weapon and as far as he could tell the attacker had still been holding it when the darkness swallowed him.

Under his orders the police fanned out over the area. He summoned more officers and before long the firearms unit had also joined the hunt, the extra manpower enabling them to expand the search area until it extended all the way from the coast road to the nature reserve at the head of Ellidavogur.

Having commandeered one of the patrol cars by the hospital, Sigurdur Óli drove back up to Lína's house. It was some time now since the ambulance had taken the woman to hospital and he was told that she was still clinging on to life. The street outside the house was filled with marked and unmarked police cars, and the CID forensic team was already busy inside.

'How do you know these people?' asked his colleague Finnur, who was standing outside the house. He had heard all about Sigurdur Óli's emergency call.

'Do you know anything about her husband?' asked Sigurdur Óli, no longer sure if he should tell the whole truth.

'His name's Ebeneser,' Finnur answered.

'Yeah, right. What kind of weird name is that?'

'We don't know where he is. Who were you chasing?'

'Almost certainly the woman's assailant,' Sigurdur Óli replied. 'I imagine he bludgeoned her over the head with a baseball bat. He got me as well, the bastard. Knocked me off balance.'

'Were you in the house?'

'I'd come to have a word with her and found her lying on the floor. Next thing I know this bastard jumps on me.'

'You think he was a burglar then? We can't find any sign of a break-in. He must have entered by the front door. She must have opened it to him.'

'Yes, the door was open when I arrived. The bastard must have rung the bell, then jumped her. This is more than a burglary – I don't think he was here to steal. He trashed the house, hit the woman over the head – no doubt we'll find out soon if he hit her anywhere else.'

'So . . .'

'I think he was a debt collector. We should round

some of them up. I didn't recognise this guy, but then I didn't get a good look at him. I've never seen anyone run so fast.'

'It sounds plausible, given his description – the baseball bat and so on,' Finnur said. 'He was probably here to call in a debt.'

Sigurdur Óli accompanied him into the house.

'Do you think he was working alone?' Finnur asked.

'As far as I can tell.'

'What were you doing here? How do you know these people?'

Sigurdur Óli lost his nerve. Of course, in the long run he would not, even if he wanted to, be able to conceal that the attack on Lína was probably connected to her and Ebbi's ludicrous attempts to extort money. For all he knew, Hermann could have sent the thug round, but he could hardly believe that his friend Patrekur was capable of such a thing. Deciding to leave names out of it for the time being, he explained that he had been following up a lead that implicated Lína and Ebbi in a trade in dubious photographs.

'Pornography?'

'Something like that.'

'Child porn?'

'Conceivably.'

'I wasn't aware of any lead,' Finnur said.

'No,' Sigurdur Óli replied, 'it only came in today. It may be a case of blackmail, which would explain the presence of a debt collector, if that's what he was.'

Finnur eyed him, as if not fully convinced.

'So you just went round to hear what they had to say for themselves? I'm not sure I quite follow this, Siggi.'

'No, it's very early days.'

'Yes, but –'

'Anyway, we'd better track him down,' Sigurdur Óli said firmly, dismissing the subject. 'Scrooge, I mean.'

'Scrooge?'

'Or whatever his name is. Her husband. And don't call me Siggi.'

7

Sigurdur Óli dropped into the police station on his way home to Framnesvegur and discovered that Elínborg had gone home some time earlier. There was a young man sitting on a bench out in the corridor. Forever in and out of trouble for violent behaviour and a variety of minor offences, he was the product of an abysmal home life; his father in prison, his mother a serious alcoholic. Reykjavík was full of such stories. The boy had been eighteen when he first came to Sigurdur Óli's notice for a break-in at an electrical goods store. By then he already had a string of convictions to his name, and that had been several years ago now.

Still angry with himself for letting the debt collector slip through his fingers, Sigurdur Óli paused on the way into his office, his eyes on the youth, then went over and sat down beside him on the bench.

'What is it this time?' he asked.

'Nothing,' the youth said.

'Breaking and entering?'

'None of your business.'

'Did you beat someone up?'

'Where's the twat who's supposed to be interviewing me?'

'You're such a fucking idiot.'

'Shut your face.'

'You know what you are.'

'Shut up.'

'It's not exactly complicated,' Sigurdur Óli said. 'Not even for a moron like you.'

The youth ignored him.

'You're nothing but a pathetic loser.'

'Loser yourself.'

'You'll never amount to anything,' Sigurdur Óli said. 'And you know it.'

The boy sat there, handcuffed to the bench, shoulders hunched, head hanging, eyes on the floor, hoping to get the interview over with as soon as possible so that he could go. As police officers like Sigurdur Óli were all too aware, he was not alone in exploiting a system that specialised in releasing offenders as soon as their case had been solved, which meant he had only to admit to the crime in order to be released to go out and break the law again. Later, he would get a suspended sentence, or if he managed to tot up enough convictions during the period, he would be sent down for a few months, never any more, and even then he would only serve half his sentence because the prison authorities connived in the pampering, as Sigurdur Óli called it. The boy and his mates could tell any number of jokes about judges, probation officers and a life of leisure, courtesy of the Prison and Probation Administration.

'I bet no one's ever told you that before,' Sigurdur Óli continued. 'That you're a loser, I mean. No one's ever told you that to your face, have they?'

The youth did not react.

'Even you've got to realise sometimes what a contemptible specimen you are,' Sigurdur Óli went on. 'I know you probably blame other people – you lot all do, you all feel sorry for yourselves and blame other people. Your mother must be high on the list; your father too, both benefits scroungers like you. And your mates and the school system and all the committees that have ever taken on your case. You've got a million excuses and I bet you've used them all one time or another. You never think about all the boys who've had a much tougher time than you, whose lives are total shit but who don't waste time pitying themselves like you do, because they've got something inside them that helps them to rise above their circumstances and turn into decent members of society, not pathetic losers like you. But then they've actually got a grain of intelligence; they're not complete morons.'

The youth remained impassive, as if he had not heard a word of Sigurdur Óli's speech, keeping his eyes trained down the corridor in the hope that his interview would begin soon. Then he would be released from custody; yet another crime cleared up.

Sigurdur Óli rose to his feet.

'I just wanted to make sure that for once in your life you heard the truth from someone who doesn't need to dirty his hands with scum like you. Even if it's only this once.'

The youth's gaze followed him into his office.

'Cunt,' he whispered, looking down at the floor again.

Sigurdur Óli rang Patrekur. The attack on Lína had been the main item on the late-news bulletin and on all the online news sites. Patrekur had been watching TV but Sigurdur Óli had to tell him three times before he could grasp who was involved.

'You mean it was her?'

'It's Lína,' Sigurdur Óli confirmed.

'But what . . . was she . . . is she dead?'

'She's still alive but it's touch and go. I haven't mentioned you or Hermann by name yet, or Súsanna and her sister, but I don't know how much longer I can get away with it. I was outside the house when the attack took place. I was on my way to have a word with the woman on your behalf, so I've had to explain my presence and now I'm in the same shit as you, Patrekur.'

On the other end of the phone his friend was silent.

'I shouldn't have dragged you into this,' he said at last. 'I thought maybe you could sort something out, but I don't really know what I was thinking of.'

'What kind of guy is Hermann?'

'What do you mean what kind of guy?'

'Has he got any links to debt collectors – would he set someone like that on Lína and Ebbi?'

'I don't think so,' Patrekur said thoughtfully. 'I find it hard to imagine. I'm not aware that he knows any debt collectors.'

'I know you wouldn't do anything stupid like that.'

'Me?'

'Or the two of you together.'

'I introduced you to him, that's all I've done. You have to believe me. In fact, it's probably best if you keep me out of the whole affair. Talk directly to Hermann if you need to speak to him again. I don't want to go anywhere near this. It's nothing to do with me.'

'Is there any particular reason to protect Hermann?'

'You do as you think fit. I'm not going to try and influence your actions.'

'Fine,' Sigurdur Óli said. 'Do you know any more about this than Hermann has told us? Do you know anything I don't?'

'No, nothing. It was my idea to come to you. I'm just the middleman. Was he a debt collector? The man who attacked her?'

'We don't know,' Sigurdur Óli replied, being carefully non-committal, as he wanted to reveal as little as possible about the investigation. 'What were they after? Kinky sex with strangers? What's it all about?'

'I don't know. Súsanna and I got wind of it a couple of years back when her sister started dropping hints. It's just some kind of game to them. It's not something I have any experience or understanding of. I've never even discussed it with them – it's none of my business.'

'And Súsanna?'

'She was shocked, naturally.'

'How did Lína and Ebbi first make contact with Hermann when they started threatening him with the photos?'

'I think Lína rang him. I couldn't say exactly.'

'So if we examine Lína and Ebbi's phone records, it's possible that Hermann's name will crop up?'

'I imagine so.'

'All right, I'll be in touch.'

On his way home, Sigurdur Óli stopped by intensive care at the National Hospital in the suburb of Fossvogur. A police officer was stationed outside Lína's room. Her parents and brother were sitting in a small visitors' lounge, waiting for news, but as yet no one had managed to reach Ebbi. Sigurdur Óli learned from the doctor on duty that Lína had not recovered consciousness and that the outlook was very uncertain. She had received two heavy blows to the head, one of which had fractured her skull, the other had crushed it, causing a brain haemorrhage. No other marks were visible on her body except on her right arm, which indicated that she had tried to protect her head with her arms.

There had been no progress yet in the hunt for her assailant, although the police had widened their net to cover the area around the mental hospital and nearby container port, as well as the Ellidavogur inlet and the residential districts above the coast road. The man had managed to get clean away, leaving nothing but the evidence in Lína's house to help the police establish his identity.

Sigurdur Óli watched a baseball game for a while before going to bed. He thought about the incriminating photos that Lína and Ebbi were holding, which may well have been the attacker's objective. If the man had been searching for the pictures, it seemed likely, from the violent treatment Lína had received, that she had not given up their whereabouts, which meant that the pictures were either still at the house or else in another safe place known only to Ebbi.

Just before he fell asleep, Sigurdur Óli remembered that a man had been asking for him again down at the station. He had appeared around supper time and the duty officer had recognised him, though the man had obstinately refused to reveal his name or business. From what the officer could recall, the man's name was Andrés and he used to be a regular among the Reykjavík down-and-outs, picked up by the police at various times for theft and affray.

8

He had not prepared himself with any great thorough-
ness, nor did he know exactly how he would go about
it, only that the timing had to be right. He had some
idea of what he wanted to achieve by the attack but
none at all about how he was going to manage it. In the
end it was the hatred, so long impotent, that had spurred
him on.

The police wanted to talk to the old man; he had
dropped hints to them about him last winter but the case
had come to nothing. It had been sheer coincidence that
their paths had crossed – he had not even been on the
lookout for him, just happened to see him one day, out

of the blue. It was decades since the bastard had disappeared from his life but then there he was, walking through his neighbourhood. It turned out that the bastard lived there, in his very neighbourhood! After all these years he had moved in virtually next door.

It was hard to find words for the tumult of emotions he experienced when it dawned on him who this was. Surprise, certainly, since he had long ago concluded that there was no chance of their ever meeting again. And the old fear too, for he still dreaded the brute more than anything in the world. But then rage had flared up inside him, for he had forgotten nothing, in spite of all the years that had passed. All these emotions churned within him when he spotted the man in the distance. The bastard may have been old and bent but he still had the power to fill him with fear, with the terror that came crawling out of its hiding place to claw at his heart.

Perhaps it was an ingrained reaction, but from the beginning he took care that the man should not see him. He kept an eye on him but did not have the nerve to do more, did not know what to do with his knowledge. When the police had started asking questions, his instinct had been to say as little as possible, to be enigmatic and contradictory, for his relationship with the police had been at best an unhappy one. In reality, though, he did not have any very clear recollection of what had happened because he had been out of his mind on booze and drugs at the time. Since then he had pulled himself together and come up with a plan for revenge. After learning that the police had been asking after him, the old man was keeping a low profile and had moved house, hiding himself away in the basement flat on Grettisgata.

The last thing he wanted was to feel self-pity. He could never and would never do that. He took full responsibility for his crimes – not the ones that others wanted to pin on him but his own. No, he would not feel sorry for himself, though it was fair to say that he had never known any happiness in his life because of what happened. His parents had been a dead loss; his drink-sodden father used to beat the living daylights out of the kids for the most minor misdemeanours, not that he even needed that excuse. He would use a leather belt for the hidings, and used to beat their mother mercilessly too.

He avoided dwelling on that, could not bear to think about the years before their family was finally broken up and he was sent to live with strangers in the countryside. There, in spite of himself, he had been content. Not that he was ever really happy; he did not know what happiness was. He had a perpetual knot of anxiety in his stomach, a feeling of fear that he could never shake off. Perhaps he clung to it because it was all he knew, and he would be at a loss as to what to put in its place.

One night he had stood out of sight of the house on Grettisgata, thinking that it was time to stop spying on him like this; wearing out his eyes staring at the basement all night but doing nothing about it. He reckoned he could easily take the bastard on, reckoned he could over-power him without much difficulty. He remembered the adventure stories he would read as a boy, all those tales of heroics, and recalled how important it was to take one's enemy by surprise. There was no question of attacking the old bastard outside in the street; it would have to be done in his house. But it would hardly do to knock on his door in the middle of the night when nobody was about – that would immediately put him on his guard. The attack would have to come when he least expected. First thing in the morning would probably be the best time, when he emerged to go for his swim.

The morning he broke into the flat the weather was cold and damp, there was a stiff northerly breeze and he was frozen to the bone after lurking outside for hours, his shabby anorak and woollen hat offering little protec-tion. Not a soul had passed along the street all night. As morning approached, he inched his way towards the house and was within a stone's throw when suddenly the basement door opened. Reacting quickly, he raced down the short flight of steps and met the old man just as he was closing the door, swimming bag in hand.

Without hesitating, he shoved him back indoors, into the little hallway, and shut the door behind him. He heard the man objecting and received a knock on the head from the swimming bag. Grabbing hold of it, he tore it away. Realising the situation was hopeless, the man tried to flee into the sitting room, but he caught him, knocked him to the floor and flung his weight on top of him.

Bringing the bastard down proved much easier than he had anticipated.

9

Hermann wanted to avoid meeting Sigurdur Óli at work, where he managed a business supplying machinery and other equipment to the building industry. Instead, they agreed to talk at the cafe where they had met the day before with Patrekur. Sigurdur Óli understood the reasons for Hermann's wariness but had no intention of treating him with kid gloves. If Hermann knew anything about the attack on Lína, he would get it out of him.

Her condition remained unchanged; she was still lying in a coma in intensive care and the doctors were not optimistic. Ebeneser had turned up, however. He had returned home that night, walking straight into the forensics team who were still at work in his house, and had become extremely distressed when he heard what had happened. They had taken him to the hospital where he was still sitting beside his wife. Finnur had gone to take his statement and learned that Ebbi worked as a guide in the highlands and had been out with a small group of French tourists at the Landmannalaugar hot springs. Another guide had taken charge of the party at Hótel Rangá in the evening and Ebbi had driven back to town. Finnur had his alibi checked and received immediate confirmation. Ebbi claimed that he had no idea why anyone would hurt Lína or who her attacker could possibly have been, but thought a burglar the most likely explanation. He was so distraught that the police decided to postpone his interview.

It was eleven fifteen when Hermann entered the cafe and took a seat beside Sigurdur Óli. They had agreed to meet at eleven.

'Do you think I have nothing better to do than hang around waiting for you in cafes?' Sigurdur Óli asked irritably, looking pointedly at his watch.

'There was something I had to finish,' Hermann said. 'What do you want?'

'The woman who's trying to extort money from you came this close' – Sigurdur Óli held up his pinched thumb and forefinger – 'to dying last night. Even if she survives, she may never be more than a vegetable. Someone smashed her skull in.'

'Was that the incident that was all over this morning's papers?'

'Yes.'

'That was Lína? I just read the news. They didn't mention any names. It said something about a debt collector.'

'We have reason to believe it was a debt collector who beat her up.'

'And?'

'Are you acquainted with anyone like that?'

'Me?'

'Yes, you.'

'You think I did this?'

'I can't think of anyone with a better motive.'

'Hang on, this was yesterday evening, the same day I talked to you. You think I attacked her the very day I talked to you about sorting the matter out for us?'

Sigurdur Óli stared at him in silence. Earlier that morning he had taken his summer coat to the dry-cleaner's; it may have been ruined yesterday evening when he fell into the bushes during the pursuit.

'You know,' he said, 'it's always better for a man in your situation to answer the question directly instead of trying to beat about the bush and twist people's words. I couldn't give a monkey's what you believe I think or don't think.

I couldn't care less about you and your wife or your sleazy sex lives. If you don't want to be banged up right now just answer the question.'

Hermann straightened in his chair.

'I haven't laid a finger on her,' he said. 'I swear it.'

'When were you last in contact with her?'

'She rang me three days ago saying she wouldn't wait any longer for the money. She threatened to circulate the photos. I begged her for more time. She said she'd give me two more days, but she wouldn't talk to me again. I was to deliver the money to her house or else the photos would be posted on porn sites all over the world.'

'So the material was supposed to be published yesterday, the day she was attacked?'

'We didn't set anyone on that bitch,' Hermann said. 'Anyway, how do you go about finding a debt collector? Do they advertise? I wouldn't know where to begin.'

'And you never spoke to Ebbi?'

'No, only Lína.'

'Do you know if you're their only victims?'

'No, I don't. Though it seems unlikely, doesn't it – that it should be just us?'

'So you were supposed to go round to their house with the money, collect the photos and that would be the end of it?'

'Yes, it wasn't very sophisticated, but then they're not very sophisticated people. They're sick.'

'But you weren't intending to pay up?'

'You were supposed to straighten it out,' Hermann said. 'Did you find any pictures at their place?'

Sigurdur Óli had attempted to conduct an unobtrusive search but the presence of the other officers had made it impossible to do a thorough job. He had found nothing, not even a camera.

'You were at their place when the pictures were taken?' he said.

'Yes. It was about two years ago.'

'Was that the only time?'

'No, we went there twice.'

'Yet they only started blackmailing you now?'

'Yes.'

'Because your wife's face is in the media and she has political ambitions?'

'It's the only explanation.'

'Classy,' Sigurdur Óli said. 'What classy people.'

Ebeneser was sitting at his wife's bedside in intensive care when Sigurdur Óli turned up to interview him. Finnur, who was in charge of the investigation, had said he needed to talk to Ebeneser again, but when Sigurdur Óli offered to save him the effort, Finnur had accepted since he had far too much on his plate already. Ebeneser was a lean, vigorous-looking man of medium height, with a slightly weather-beaten face, sporting several days' worth of beard. He was wearing thick-soled hiking boots as one would expect of a highland guide. He rose when Sigurdur Óli entered the room and greeted him with a dry handshake, avoiding eye contact. Lína was lying in bed, hooked up to all kinds of monitors and drips, her head swathed in bandages. The couple were both around thirty, perhaps a decade younger than Hermann and his wife, and appeared to be reasonably good-looking, though Sigurdur Óli found it hard to gauge with Lína in her current state. Could it have been their youth that had attracted Hermann and his wife?

'Are you planning to leave town again?' Sigurdur Óli asked, eyeing the man's footwear once they were seated in the visitors' lounge. Given the circumstances he had been prepared to treat Ebeneser with sympathy and understanding, but was not sure if he and his wife really deserved such consideration.

'What? These? No, not for the moment. I just like wearing boots, even in town.'

'We've received confirmation that you were on your way back from the highlands when your wife was attacked,' Sigurdur Óli said.

'I find it bizarre that you should think I did it,' Ebeneser retorted.

'Whether something's bizarre or not has no bearing as far as we're concerned. Were you and your wife seriously in debt?'

'No more than most people. And we're not married. We're living together.'

'Any children?'

'No, none.'

'Were you in debt to parties who might be prepared to resort to violent methods to recover their money? Like debt collectors, for example? Anyone like that?'

'No,' Ebeneser said.

'So you're not short of money?'

'No.'

'And you haven't been involved with debt collectors before?'

'No. I don't know any debt collectors myself and I don't know anyone who's in contact with them. Wasn't it just an ordinary burglar?'

'Did he take anything?'

'I gather he was interrupted by a cop.'

'I've never come across a burglar who began by smashing up the house he was intending to burgle, then hit the owner over the head with a baseball bat,' Sigurdur Óli said. 'I suppose such a thing may have happened some time, some place, but I'm not aware of it.'

Ebeneser was silent.

'Did anyone know you'd be out of town yesterday evening?'

'Yes, lots of people. But they're all people I know, who would never do anything like this, if that's what you mean.'

'And you don't have money troubles?'

'No.'

'Are you sure?'

'Yes. I should know.'

'What about your sex life – is that good?'

Ebeneser had been sitting opposite him in the visitors' lounge, legs crossed, swinging his free foot gently up and down, evincing little interest in Sigurdur Óli's questions. But at this he stopped, sat up in his chair and leaned forward.

'Our sex life?'

'Your sexual relations with other people,' Sigurdur Óli clarified.

Ebeneser stared at him. 'What . . . are you joking?'

'No.'

'Sexual relations with other people?'

'Let me spell it out for you: do you think that the attack on Lína can have had anything to do with the fact that you both have sex with other people?'

Ebeneser was flabbergasted. 'I don't know what you're talking about,' he replied.

'No, of course not,' said Sigurdur Óli. 'So you've never heard of swingers' parties either?'

Ebeneser shook his head.

'Where swinging is another word for wife-swapping.'

'I've no idea what you're on about,' said Ebeneser.

'So you and Lína have never taken part in wife-swapping?'

'That's disgusting,' Ebeneser said. 'We've never done anything like that. How dare you!'

'I'll make a deal with you,' Sigurdur Óli said. 'You give me the photos that you and Lína took of yourselves having sex with other people and I'll try to pretend I never heard anything about it.'

Ebeneser did not respond.

'Other people,' Sigurdur Óli said, as if struck by a new idea. 'Who were these other people? I only know of the one couple but of course you've been blackmailing people all over town, haven't you?'

Ebeneser stared at him again.

'Someone's had enough of your shitty little games and meant to intimidate you with a debt collector. Is that it, Ebbi?'

Ebeneser decided not to put up with this any longer. He stood up.

'I've no idea what you're talking about,' he said and stormed out of the visitors' lounge, back down the corridor to Lína's room.

Sigurdur Óli watched him go. Ebeneser needed time

to absorb how much he knew and to consider his offer. Sigurdur Óli smiled grimly to himself. He was a pretty experienced police officer but could not immediately recall having met such a consummate liar before – nor one more adept at getting himself into deep water.

10

Bergthóra had already arrived and was sitting at the table, reading the menu, when Sigurdur Óli turned up a few minutes late. She had chosen an Italian restaurant in the centre of town and he headed straight there after spending the day assisting Elínborg, who was bearing the brunt of the inquiry into the Thingholt murder. He would have liked to have gone home first for a shower and a change of clothes but there had been no time. Although he usually enjoyed eating out, he was rather dreading this encounter.

He kissed her on the lips and took a seat. Bergthóra looked tired. The last few months had been hard on her. The IT company she ran, in which she owned a large stake, had recently gone through a rocky patch, resulting in a great deal of extra work for her. Their separation had taken its toll too, on top of their failure to have children.

'You look well,' she said to Sigurdur Óli as he sat down.

'How are you?' he asked.

'Oh, fine. Meeting in restaurants like this feels like dating again. I can't get used to it. You should have come round to mine; I could have made us something.'

'Yes, it does feel a bit like the old days,' Sigurdur Óli agreed.

They pored over the menus. It was not like the old days and they both knew it. They were weighed down by the awareness of their failed relationship, of the wasted years, of the feelings that were no more, of the shared life that had unravelled. They were like weary receivers winding up a bankruptcy; all that remained was to tie up the loose ends and settle the final claims. Because Bergthóra had a tendency to become emotional about the way things had turned out, Sigurdur Óli had chosen to meet her at a restaurant.

'How's your father?' she asked, her eyes on the menu.

'OK.'

'And your mother?'

'Fine.'

'Is she still with that bloke?'

'Saemundur? Yes.'

They chose what they were going to eat and agreed to share a bottle of Italian red. There were few other midweek diners. Soothing music emanated from somewhere over their heads, interspersed with the sounds of clattering and laughter from the kitchen.

'How's life on Framnesvegur?'

'OK, though the flat's still half empty,' Sigurdur Óli said. 'Has anyone been round to view our place?'

'There were three viewings today. One man said he'd get in touch. I'll miss the flat.'

'Naturally. It's a great flat.'

Neither of them spoke. Sigurdur Óli wondered if he should tell her about Hermann and his wife, and decided to give it a go in the hope that it would lighten the atmosphere. So he told her about his meeting with Patrekur who had unexpectedly brought along his brother-in-law Hermann, and described how the couple's former hobby had landed them in trouble. Then he described the attack on Lína, the man with the baseball bat and Ebbi in his hiking boots, feigning ignorance.

'He was literally stunned,' Sigurdur Óli said. 'Ebbi's a guide,' he added with a grin. 'He could do with some guidance right now.'

'Do people really get up to that sort of thing?' Bergthóra sighed.

'I wouldn't know.'

'I don't know anyone who goes in for that – wife-swapping, I mean. They must be mad. And to get into such a mess.'

'Well, this is a bit of a one-off.'

'It must be hard for Súsanna's sister, what with her being in politics. To have this come back to haunt them.'

'Yes, but what kind of idiot is she to put herself in that position in the first place? Especially when she's in politics. Don't start feeling sorry for them.'

'You're not big on sympathy, are you?' Bergthóra said.

'What do you mean?' Sigurdur Óli demanded.

They were interrupted by the friendly middle-aged waiter who brought over the bottle of red wine, and after showing Sigurdur Óli the label, poured some into his glass. Sigurdur Óli watched him.

'You've already uncorked the bottle?'

The waiter did not understand the question.

'You're supposed to do it in front of me,' Sigurdur Óli said. 'How do I know how long ago this bottle was opened or what you've been doing with it behind the scenes?'

The waiter looked at him in surprise.

'I've only just opened it,' he mumbled apologetically.

'Well, you're supposed to uncork it here at the table, not in some back room.'

'I'll fetch another bottle.' The waiter hurried away.

'He's doing his best,' Bergthóra objected.

'He's an amateur,' Sigurdur Óli said dismissively. 'We pay a lot to eat here and they're supposed to know what they're doing. Anyway, what did you mean when you said I'm not big on sympathy?'

Bergthóra looked at him. 'All that just now,' she said. 'It's typical.'

'The poor service, you mean?'

'You're just like your mother.'

'What do you mean?'

'You're both so . . . cold. Such snobs.'

'Oh, for goodness' sake . . .'

'I was never good enough for you,' Bergthóra went on, 'and she used to make sure I knew it. Whereas your father was always such a sweetheart. I don't understand how a woman like her could ever have stooped so low as to get involved with a plumber, or how on earth he put up with her for so long.'

'I've often wondered that myself,' Sigurdur Óli admitted. 'But Mum really likes you. She told me so. There's no need to bad-mouth her.'

'She never showed me any support when we lost . . . when we had our problems. Never. I got the impression she felt it had nothing to do with her. I felt as if she blamed it all on me – ruining things for you by not being able to have children.'

70

'Why do you say that?'

'Because it's true.'

'You've never mentioned this before.'

'Sure I have; you just didn't want to listen.'

The waiter returned with a new bottle, showed Sigurdur Óli the label and began to remove the cork under his nose. Then he poured some and Sigurdur Óli tasted and approved the wine. The waiter filled their glasses and left the bottle on the table.

'You've never wanted to listen to a word I say,' Bergthóra said.

'That's not true.'

She looked at him, her eyes filling with tears, then picked up a napkin.

'All right,' she said, changing tack. 'Let's not quarrel. It's over and done with and we can't change anything.'

Sigurdur Óli looked down at his plate; he found scenes hard to cope with. Happy as he was to subject criminal lowlifes to a tirade of abuse, he would do anything to keep the peace when it came to his home life. He had once asked himself if it stemmed from the role he played as a boy during his parents' divorce, when he had tried to keep everyone happy and discovered that it was impossible.

'I feel as if you often forget that it was hard for me too,' he said carefully. 'You never asked how I felt. It was all about you. And you insisted on adoption, you never really asked my opinion. You were just determined to go ahead. We've been over this so often, I really don't want to discuss it this evening.'

'No,' Bergthóra agreed, 'let's not talk about it. I didn't mean to either. Let's drop it.'

'I'm surprised to hear you say that about Mum,' Sigurdur Óli said after a pause. 'Though I know what she can be like. I seem to remember warning you about her when we first got together.'

'Yes, you told me not to let her get to me.'

'And I hope you didn't.'

There was a long silence. The wine was from Tuscany, smooth and mellow on the palate; the music over their heads was Italian too, and the food they were waiting for. Only the silence between them was Icelandic.

'I don't want to adopt,' Sigurdur Óli said.

'I know,' Bergthóra answered. 'You'll find another woman and have your own babies with her.'

'No,' Sigurdur Óli said, 'I don't think I'd make a good father.'

When he got home he turned on the television and started watching the baseball but the Red Sox put in an atrocious performance which did nothing to cheer him up after his dinner with Bergthóra. Then his phone started ringing on the kitchen table where he had left it. Sigurdur Óli did not recognise the number and was about to turn it off when curiosity got the better of him.

'Yes?' he answered with unnecessary brusqueness. It was a tactic he had developed long ago for dealing with unknown callers. After all, it might be a charity. His name was marked with a red cross in the telephone directory, indicating that he was not to receive any cold calls, but there was always the odd one that slipped through the net and the caller was immediately made to regret it.

'Sigurdur?' said a female voice.

'Who's that?'

'Is this Sigurdur Óli?'

'Yes.'

'It's Eva.'

'Eva?'

'Eva Lind. Erlendur's daughter.'

'Oh. Hi.'

There was no warmth in his voice. Sigurdur Óli was well aware of who she was; he and Erlendur had been colleagues for years, and he had encountered her professionally too. Eva Lind had led an unruly life that had brought her into contact with the police on more than one occasion. Indeed, her life as an addict had caused her father untold grief.

'Have you heard from him at all?' Eva Lind asked.

'Your father? No, nothing. All I know is that he took some leave and was intending to head to the East Fjords for a few days.'

'Oh. Didn't he take his phone with him? He's only got the one mobile number, hasn't he?'

'Yes, I think so.'

'He hasn't got any other phone? Because he's not picking up.'

'Not as far as I know.'

'If he gets in touch, could you tell him I was asking after him?'

'Sure, but . . .'

'What?'

'I'm not expecting to hear from him,' Sigurdur Óli said, 'so . . .'

'No, me neither,' Eva Lind said. 'We . . .'

'Yes?'

'We went for a drive the other day; he wanted to look at some lakes around Reykjavík. He was . . .'

'What?'

'He seemed so down.'

'Isn't he always? I wouldn't worry about it. I've never known your dad to be anything but down.'

'I know.'

Neither of them spoke.

'Will you say hi from me?' Eva Lind asked.

'Sure.'

'Bye then.'

Sigurdur Óli said goodbye and put down the phone. Then he turned off the television and went to bed.

11

It took him some time to find the old projector, tucked away in a low cubbyhole in the kitchen broom cupboard.

He had been sure the old man would not have destroyed it; a machine like that would never end up on the tip if that bastard had anything to do with it. Amazingly, after all these years the old lead-grey device still worked, but then the bastard was probably still using it. He felt its familiar weight as he lifted it out of its hiding place and set it up on the table in the sitting room, his eye falling on the manufacturer's logo: Bell & Howell. He remembered how puzzled he had been as a boy by this name, until a friend explained it as almost certainly the names of two men, one called Bell, the other Howell, who had manufactured the machine together, most likely in America. The projector itself was concealed in a deep compartment under the lid. He pulled the lid off, swung out the reel arms, plugged in the old electric cable and flicked the switch. The wall opposite lit up.

The projector was one of the few possessions the bastard had brought with him when he moved in with his mother, Sigurveig. He had been unaware of the new man in her life since he was in the countryside at the time. Then one day word had come that his mother wanted him back. She had moved into a council block in one of the newer suburbs, and claimed that she had quit the booze and met a new man. Next he received a phone call from the woman whom he never addressed as Mother, only Sigurveig, because after two years apart she was like a stranger to him. It was the first and only time she rang him at the farm and the conversation was brief: she wanted her youngest child to come and live with her. He replied that he was happy on the farm. 'I know, dear,' he heard her say down the phone, 'but now you're coming home to me. It's been approved. It's all sorted.'

Some days later he said goodbye to the farmer's wife and the couple's two daughters, and the farmer himself drove him down to the main road and waited with him until the bus arrived. It was the height of summer and he felt he was betraying the farmer because the hay harvest was under way and they needed his help. The couple had often praised him for his diligence and help-fulness. One day, they said, he would turn out all right, more than all right. In the distance they saw the bus approaching and eventually it drew up beside them in a cloud of dust.

'All the best, and maybe you'll drop by and see us when you get the chance,' the farmer said, making as if to shake his hand, then giving him a hug. He slipped a thousand-krona note into his hand. The bus set off with a jerk and the farmer disappeared as the dust rose again. He had never in his life owned any money before and on the journey to Reykjavík he kept taking the note out of his pocket and examining it in wonder, then folding it up and putting it back in his pocket, only to fish it out a minute or two later to study it again.

Sigurveig was supposed to be meeting him at the bus station but when he arrived she was nowhere to be seen. It was a cold evening and he stood for a long time beside his suitcase, waiting for her. Eventually he sat down on the case. He did not know how to get home, or what district the block of flats was in or even the name of the street, and he grew increasingly anxious as the evening wore on. There was no one he could turn to for help. He had been away for a long time; the farmer had told him ages ago that his father had gone to live abroad and he knew nothing about his two siblings, who were considerably older. There was nobody else.

He sat on his case, casting his mind back to his home or rather to the place that he had called home for the last two years. They would have finished in the cowshed by now and the girls would be mucking around. Then they would shoo the dogs out of the kitchen and dinner would be served up: boiled trout from the lake with melted butter, perhaps – his favourite.

'I assume you're the brat I'm supposed to be meeting.'

He looked up. A man he had never seen before was looming over him.

'You're little Andy, aren't you?' the man said.

No one had called him Andy since he had left town.

'My name's Andrés,' he replied.

The man looked him up and down.

'Then it must be you. Your mum says hello – or at least I think that's what she said. She hasn't been on particularly good form lately.'

He did not know how to answer, did not know what the man's words meant or what he meant by form.

'Let's get a move on then,' the man said. 'Don't forget your case.'

The man walked off in the direction of the car park in front of the bus station. After watching the stranger disappear round the corner, he stood up, picked up his case and followed. He did not know what else to do, but he was wary; from the first instant he had got the impression that this was a man who would not be easy to please. His tone of voice when he referred to his mother told him this, the scorn with which he had said 'little Andy'. The man had not even greeted him; all he had said was: 'I assume you're the brat I'm supposed to be meeting.' He noticed that the tip of one of the man's forefingers was missing but it did not cross his mind either then or later to ask how it had happened.

Sigurveig was asleep in the bedroom when they reached the flat. The man announced that he was going out and said he was not to make any noise or to wake his mother, so he sat waiting quietly on a chair in the kitchen. The flat had one bedroom, behind a closed door, a living room, a kitchen and a small bathroom. Apparently the sofa in the living room was to be his bed. He was worn out from the journey and his long wait at the bus station but did not dare to lie down on the sofa, so he laid his head on his arms on the kitchen table and before he knew it he was asleep.

Just before he had dropped off his eye had been caught

by an object in the living room. He had no idea what it was but there it stood on the table by the sofa, square and boxy, with a handle on top; an alien object from the outside world, with that incomprehensible logo on the side: Bell & Howell.

He was to discover later that the new man in his mother's life also owned a film camera with another name that he could make neither head nor tail of, which puzzled him no less than the name of the projector. The name, Eumig, was burnt into his memory.

He stared for a long time at the old Bell & Howell projector and at the light it cast on the facing wall; snatches of memory seemed to play themselves out in the glare of the machine. The old man whimpered something and he turned round.

'What do you want?' he asked.

The man in the chair was silent. There was a powerful stench of urine and the mask over his face was damp with sweat.

'Where's the camera?'

The man stared at him through the slits in the death mask.

'And the films? Where are the films? Tell me. I can kill you if I want to. Do you understand that? I'm the one in control now! Me! Not you, you old shit. Me! I'm in control.'

Nothing. Neither cough nor groan emerged from behind the mask.

'How do you like that, eh? How do you like that? Don't you find it strange, after all these years, that I should be stronger than you? Who's the wimp now, eh? Tell me that. Who's the wimp now?'

The man did not move.

'Look at me! Look at me if you dare. Do you see? Do you see what little Andy has turned into? Not so little now, is he? He's all grown up and strong. Maybe you didn't think that would ever happen. Maybe you thought Andy would always be the same little boy?'

He hit the old man.

'Where's the camera?' he snarled.

He was going to find that camera and destroy it, along with all the films and the images they had recorded. He was convinced that the bastard still had the lot stashed away somewhere and he was not going to give up until he had found them and burnt them.

Still no answer.

'Do you think I won't find it? I'm going to tear this dump apart until I find it. I'm going to rip up the floors and pull down the ceilings. How do you like that, eh? How do you like little Andy now?'

The eyes behind the mask closed.

'You took my thousand-krona note,' he whispered. 'I

know it was you. You lied that I'd lost it but I know you took it.'

He was sobbing as he spoke.

'You'll burn in hell for that. For that and everything else you did. You'll burn in hell!'

12

One of the measures taken by the police in connection with the attack on Lína was to note down the licence plates of every vehicle parked near her house, in the hope that her assailant might have arrived by car. The idea was not implausible; in fact, it was highly likely. He would hardly have travelled on public transport with the baseball bat hidden inside his jacket, and a simple check confirmed that he had not taken a taxi. Another possibility was that he had walked there, in which case he was unlikely to have come far and might well live within a few kilometres of the crime scene. It was also conceivable that someone had given him a lift and had been waiting outside when they saw Sigurdur Óli enter the house, but Sigurdur Óli had not noticed anyone. The most likely scenario was that the assailant had arrived by car but instead of parking outside had left it in a side street and been forced to abandon it when Sigurdur Óli had disturbed him.

Most of the licence plates collected by the police, and there were dozens of them, were traced to addresses nearby, decent people with families and jobs who would not hurt a soul and did not know Lína and Ebbi from Adam. However, several were registered to owners who lived further away, in other neighbourhoods or even other parts of the country, though none had a police record for violence.

Sigurdur Óli, who was at least familiar with the assailant's running style, volunteered to talk to the owners of any cars which required further investigation.

Lína's condition remained unchanged and Ebbi had hardly left her bedside. The doctors believed that it could still go either way.

Sigurdur Óli's evening with Bergthóra had ended badly, with accusations flying back and forth, until Bergthóra had finally stood up, said she could no longer cope with this and left.

Sigurdur Óli believed himself to be perfectly capable of working on the investigation despite his highly irregular personal involvement in the affair. After thinking it through, he decided that nothing he knew could be prejudicial to the interests of the inquiry, since he had absolutely no desire to protect Hermann and his wife, and Patrekur was not involved. He had done nothing that would require him to declare an interest and resign from the case. The only point that troubled him, and then only briefly, was the conversation about the photos he had had with Ebbi at the hospital. He was not acquainted with Lína or Ebbi; for all he knew they might be up to their necks in debt from drug use, a mortgage or a car loan, and might owe money to the kind of people who employed debt collectors. After all, drugs were not the only reason enforcers were set on defaulters. Sigurdur Óli thought it likely that Lína and Ebbi had gone too far in their clumsy attempts to black-mail fools like Hermann and his wife with their incrimi-nating photos. It was not improbable that somebody who felt pushed into a corner would want to shut them up by violence, or at least by the threat of violence. Whether Hermann was behind it or not was another matter. He denied it now but time would tell.

He felt a nagging guilt at not having come clean to Finnur, either about the photos or Lína and Ebbi's alleged blackmail attempt, since it was only a matter of time before the information would come out. And when that happened, and Hermann and his wife's names became mixed up in the inquiry, Sigurdur Óli would have some explaining to do.

Preoccupied by these thoughts, he walked into a small meat-processing factory in search of a man called Hafsteinn, who turned out to be the foreman and who professed himself astonished by Sigurdur Óli's visit, exclaiming that he had never spoken to a detective before in his life, as if this were a guarantee of a blameless existence. Hafsteinn invited him into his office and they both sat down. The foreman was wearing a white coat and a lightweight white hat bearing the firm's logo on his head. He had the figure of a German beer drinker at Oktoberfest, stout and cheery, with plump red cheeks; hardly the type to attack a defenceless woman with a baseball bat, let alone run further than ten metres. This fact did not deter Sigurdur Óli, however, and he stuck doggedly to his task. After a short preamble, he said he wanted to know what Hafsteinn had been doing in the area where Lína was attacked, and whether there was anyone who could provide an alibi for his explanation, whatever it was.

The foreman gave Sigurdur Óli a long look.

'Hang on a minute, what are you saying? Do I have to tell you what I was doing there?'

'Your car was parked one street down from the crime scene. You live in Hafnarfjördur. What were you doing in Reykjavík? Were you driving the car yourself?'

Sigurdur Óli reasoned that even if the man had not attacked Lína, he might conceivably know something about the attack; he might have driven the assailant to the scene and abandoned his car in a panic.

'Yes, I was driving. I was visiting someone. Do you need to know any more?'

'Yes.'

'May I ask what you're going to do with the information?'

'We're trying to find the assailant.'

'You don't think I attacked the poor woman?'

'Did you take part in the attack?'

'Are you out of your mind?'

Sigurdur Óli observed that the red cheeks had lost some of their colour.

'Can I speak to someone who can confirm your alibi?'

'Are you going to mention this to my wife?' Hafsteinn asked hesitantly.

'Do I need to?' Sigurdur Óli asked.

The man sighed heavily.

'There's no need,' he said after a long pause. 'I . . . I have a lady friend on that road. If you need to confirm my story you can talk to her. I can't believe I'm telling you this.'

'A lady friend?'

The man nodded.

'You mean a mistress?'

'Yes.'

'And you were visiting her?'

'Yes.'

'I see. Did you notice anyone in the area who could have been connected to the attack?'

'No. Is that it?'

'Yes, I believe that's all,' Sigurdur Óli said.

'Are you going to speak to my wife?'

'Can she confirm any of this?'

The man shook his head.

'Then I've no interest in talking to her,' Sigurdur Óli said. He took the lady friend's phone number just in case, then got up and left.

Later that day he met a man who was unaware that his car had been parked near Lína's house, as he had not been driving it himself but had lent it to his son. After the man had made some enquiries it turned out that his son had been round at a nearby house with a friend. They were visiting a classmate from their sixth-form college and had all gone together to a film in the Laugarás cinema which had started at around the time Lína was attacked.

The man gave Sigurdur Óli a considering look.

'You needn't bother about the boy,' he said.

'Really?'

'He wouldn't hurt a fly. Scared of his own shadow.'

Finally Sigurdur Óli sat down with a woman of about thirty who worked on the switchboard at a soft-drinks bottling plant. After Sigurdur Óli had introduced himself, she asked someone to cover for her and since he did not want to explain his business where they could be overheard, she went and sat with him in the staff cafeteria.

'What's going on exactly?' the woman asked. She had dark hair and a broad face, a small metal ring in one eyebrow and a tattoo on her forearm. Sigurdur Óli could not see what it was supposed to be; it looked like a cat but could equally have been a snake that wound around her arm. Her name was Sara.

'I'd like to know what you were doing in the east of town, near the Laugarás cinema, on the evening of the day before yesterday.'

'The day before yesterday?' she said. 'Why do you want to know that?'

'Your car was parked not far from the street where a brutal attack occurred.'

'I didn't attack anyone,' she said.

'No,' Sigurdur Óli agreed. 'But your car was in the area.'

He explained that the police were checking up on the owners of any vehicle that had been seen in the vicinity that evening. It was a serious case of assault and battery, and the police wanted to ask all those who had been in the area whether they had noticed anything that might assist the investigation. It was a long speech and Sigurdur Óli could tell that Sara was bored.

'I didn't see anything,' she said.

'What were you doing in the area?'

'Visiting a friend. What actually happened? I saw something on the news about a break-in.'

'We don't have any more information as yet,' Sigurdur Óli said. 'I'll need your friend's details.'

Sara gave them to him.

'Did you stay the night?'

'What? Are you spying on me?' she asked.

The cafeteria door opened and an employee of the bottling plant nodded to Sara.

'No. Is there any reason why I should?' Sigurdur Óli asked.

Sara smiled. 'I very much doubt it.'

Sigurdur Óli was getting into his car outside the plant when his phone rang. He recognised the number immediately. It was Finnur, who informed him brusquely that Sigurlína Thorgrímsdóttir had died a quarter of an hour earlier as a result of the blow to her head.

'What the hell were you doing at her place, Siggi?' Finnur whispered and hung up.

13

Sigurdur Óli's mother opened the door, her expression indicating that he was late. He did not have his own key because she said she would feel uncomfortable knowing that he could walk in on her whenever he liked. She had invited him for supper but had not waited for him before serving up, and now the food was growing cold on the table. Saemundur was nowhere to be seen.

His mother, known to all as Gagga, was on the wrong side of sixty and lived in a large detached house in the smart satellite town of Gardabaer, surrounded by fellow accountants, doctors, lawyers and other wealthy professionals, the kind of people who owned two to three cars apiece and hired professionals to look after their homes and gardens and put up their Christmas lights. Not that Gagga had always lived this well; she had been hard up when she met Sigurdur Óli's father and in the period immediately after the divorce, although 'the plumber', as she insisted on calling her ex-husband, had offered to assist in any way he could. She had rented at first but was forever falling out with her landlords. Then there was nothing for it but to move on. It made no difference when Sigurdur Óli complained that he found it hard to keep changing schools. His mother had a talent for putting people's backs up, including the teachers and principals of his schools, so in the end his father had to take over all communication about his education.

Gagga had studied business at college and was working as a bookkeeper when Sigurdur Óli was born, but subsequently improved her qualifications at university and gradually worked her way up to a good position in an accountancy firm that was eventually taken over by a large international corporation. She now occupied a managerial position at the company.

'Where's Saemundur?' Sigurdur Óli asked, slipping off the winter coat he had bought the year before; bloody expensive it had been too, from one of the most exclusive clothing stores in the country. Bergthóra had shaken her head when he brought the coat home and accused him of being the worst label snob she knew. He recalled the way she used to say 'you mean gaga', whenever his mother came up in conversation.

'He's in London,' Gagga said. 'One of those bright young entrepreneurs who's hit the big time abroad is opening an office there with the president in attendance and all that razzmatazz. Everything flown out by corporate jet; nothing less will do.'

'They've done bloody well for themselves.'

'It's all on credit, you know. All they really own is debts which somebody will have to pay off in the end.'

'Well, I think they're doing a fantastic job,' objected Sigurdur Óli, who had been taking a close interest in the success of Icelandic businessmen at home and abroad. He was impressed by their drive and enterprise, especially when it came to buying up household-name companies in Britain and Denmark.

They sat down at the table. His mother had made tuna lasagne, an old favourite of his.

'Would you like me to heat it up for you?' she asked, taking his plate and putting it in the microwave before he could reply. The oven pinged and Gagga passed the plate back to her son. He was still disturbed by his short conversation with Finnur about Lína's death. Finnur had sounded quite worked up, angry even, and that anger had been directed at him. 'What the hell were you doing at her place, Siggi?' Finnur had asked. He loathed being called Siggi.

'Have you heard from Bergthóra at all?' asked his mother.

'Saw her yesterday.'

'Oh? And what's she got to say for herself?'

'She said you never liked her.'

Gagga was silent. She had not taken any food, despite having laid a place for herself, but now she picked up a spoon, helped herself to some lasagne, then got up and put it in the microwave. Sigurdur Óli was still feeling resentful about all the time he had wasted watching postboxes for her, and by the fact that she had interrupted the American football with her phone call the night before, but most of all because of what Bergthóra had said.

'Why does she say that?' his mother asked as she stood by the oven, waiting for the bell.

'She's adamant that it's true.'

'So she blames me for everything, does she? For what happened to your relationship?'

'I don't seem to remember you being particularly sad about it.'

'Of course I was,' his mother said, but did not sound very convincing.

'Bergthóra's never mentioned this before. But when I started thinking back, it occurred to me that you never used to come round and see us, and you had very little contact with her. Were you trying to avoid her?'

'Of course not.'

'She talked a lot about you yesterday. She was very honest, but then we don't have anything to hide from each other any more. She said you didn't think she was good enough for me and that you blamed her for the fact we couldn't have children.'

'What nonsense!' Gagga exclaimed.

'Is it?'

'It's ridiculous,' his mother declared and sat down with her steaming plate, but did not touch her food. 'She can't say things like that, the silly girl. What utter nonsense.'

'Did you blame her for not being able to have children?'

'Oh, for goodness' sake, it *is* her fault! I didn't need to blame her.'

Sigurdur Óli put down his fork.

'And that was all the support she got from you,' he said.

'Support? I didn't get any support when your father and I divorced.'

'Oh, you generally manage to get your own way. And what do you mean by support? It was you who left him.'

'Well, anyway, what now? What's going to happen to you two now?'

Sigurdur Óli pushed away his plate and looked around him; at the spacious sitting room that opened off the kitchen, decorated in his mother's impersonal style: white walls, heated floors covered in large black tiles, expensive new blocky furniture, and art that was pricey without necessarily being in good taste.

'I don't know. I suppose it's over.'

Ebeneser had been weeping. He was still at the hospital when Sigurdur Óli went over later that evening to express his condolences. Ebeneser had been gone briefly that afternoon and by the time he returned Lína was dead. Now he was alone in the visitors' lounge in a state of bewilderment, as if he did not know whether to go or stay. He had watched as they took her body away for an urgent post-mortem to establish the precise cause of death.

'I wasn't there,' Ebeneser said after Sigurdur Óli had been sitting with him for a little while. 'When she died, I mean.'

'So I gather. I'm sorry,' Sigurdur Óli said. He had been itching to talk to Ebeneser but had thought it best to give him some space to recover, though no longer than the time it took for him to visit Gagga.

'She never woke up,' Ebeneser continued. 'Never opened her eyes. I didn't realise it was that serious. When

I came back she was gone. Dead. How . . . how the hell did this happen?'

'We mean to find out,' Sigurdur Óli said. 'But you have to help us.'

'Help you? How?'

'Why was she attacked?'

'I don't know. I don't know who did it.'

'Who knew she'd be alone at home?'

'Knew . . . ? I don't know.'

'Have you had any trouble before with violent types – debt collectors, for example?'

'No.'

'Are you sure?'

'Yes, of course I'm sure.'

'I don't believe the man who attacked Lína was necessarily a burglar. It seems much more likely, judging from what I saw, that he was a debt collector, but we can't be certain that he was acting on his own behalf. Do you follow me?'

'No.'

'It's just as likely that he was working for someone else who sent him round to your place with the express intention of using violence against you, or against Lína. That's why I'm asking: who knew that you would be out of town that day? And that Lína would be alone?'

'I really have no idea. Look, do we have to discuss this now?'

They were facing one another; the hospital was silent all around them and the hands of the large clock over the door crawled round. Sigurdur Óli leaned forward and whispered: 'Ebeneser, I know you and your wife were trying to blackmail people with photos.'

Ebeneser said nothing.

'That sort of thing can be risky,' Sigurdur Óli continued. 'I know you did it because I know the people involved. Are you aware of who I'm talking about?'

Ebeneser shook his head.

'All right,' Sigurdur Óli said. 'Have it your way. I don't believe the people I know would have set that animal on you. In fact, I find the idea highly unlikely because I know them and it would have required a lot more initiative than I credit them with. I'd gone round to see Lína myself when she was attacked.'

'You were there?'

'Yes. My acquaintances asked me to persuade her, to persuade both of you, to abandon your attempt at blackmail and give me the photos.'

'What . . . Can you . . . ?' Ebeneser did not know what to say.

'Do you know who I'm talking about?'

Ebeneser shook his head again.

'Please, can we talk about this another time?' he asked, his voice so low that it was barely audible. 'For Christ's sake, Lína just died.'

'I have reason to believe,' Sigurdur Óli ploughed on, 'that her attacker may have been at your house on the same errand as me. Do you follow?'

Ebeneser did not answer.

'He must have been there for exactly the same reason; to try and dissuade Lína from persisting with the stupid course of action that you were both set on. Could I be right?'

'I don't know what motive he could have had,' Ebeneser said.

'Have you tried to blackmail anyone?'

'No.'

'Who knew that Lína would be alone at home?'

'No one, everyone, I don't know. Anyone. I haven't a clue, I don't keep a list.'

'Don't you want to try to solve this?'

'Of course I do! What's the matter with you? Of course I want this solved.'

'Then who's been threatening you – threatening to attack you and beat the hell out of you?'

'No one. This is just some bullshit you've dreamt up.'

'I'm almost certain that Lína's death was an accident,' Sigurdur Óli said. 'A tragic accident. A mistake by someone who went too far. Don't you want to help us find him?'

'Of course, but could you please give me a break? I've got to go home. I've got to see Lína's parents. I've got to . . .'

He seemed on the verge of tears again.

'I want the photos, Ebeneser,' said Sigurdur Óli.

'I've got to go.'

'Where are they?'

'I just can't cope with this.'

'I only know about one couple. Were there others? Who's after you? What were you two up to?'

'Nothing, leave me alone,' said Ebeneser. 'Leave me alone!' He rushed out of the room.

As Sigurdur Óli was leaving the hospital, he passed a patient being pushed in a wheelchair. He had plaster casts on both arms, a bandage round his jaw, one of his eyes was closed by a large swelling and his nose was strapped up as if it had been broken. Sigurdur Óli failed to recognise him at first, then realised on closer inspection that it was the youth who had been sitting in the corridor at the police station; the one he had abused for being a pathetic loser and a waste of space. The boy, whose name he now remembered was Pétur, glanced up as they passed. Sigurdur Óli stopped him.

'What happened to you?' he asked.

The boy could not answer for himself but the woman pushing the wheelchair had no difficulty in doing so. Apparently he had been beaten senseless not far from the police station on Hverfisgata on Monday evening. She was taking him for yet another X-ray.

As far as she knew they had not yet caught the bastards who had given him such a vicious kicking. And he was not saying a word.

14

Shortly afterwards, as Sigurdur Óli was entering the police station on Hverfisgata by the back door, a rough-looking man who stank to high heaven stepped out of the shadows in front of him.

'It's impossible to get hold of you lot,' the man whispered in a strangely weak, hoarse voice, seizing hold of his arm.

Sigurdur Óli was momentarily startled but recovered quickly and reacted angrily. To him the man looked like any other tramp – and Sigurdur Óli had come across enough of those in his time – yet he felt a dim sense of recognition. But he could not place the man immediately, and had no interest in doing so.

'What do you mean by jumping out at me like that?' he snapped, snatching his arm away and causing the man to lose his grip and stumble backwards.

'I need to talk to Erlendur,' the tramp whimpered.

'Then you've got the wrong guy,' Sigurdur Óli said, and continued walking.

'I know that,' the tramp shrieked in his high, hoarse voice, following him. 'Where is he? I need to talk to Erlendur.'

'He's not here. I don't know where he is,' said Sigurdur Óli dismissively as he opened the door.

'What about you then?'

'What about me?'

'Don't you remember me?' the man asked.

Sigurdur Óli paused.

'Don't you remember Andy? You were with Erlendur. You were there when he came round to mine and I told you both about him.'

Sigurdur Óli stood holding the door open, and considered the man at length.

'Andy?' he repeated.

'Don't you remember Andy?' the tramp asked again, scratching his crotch and sniffing back his dripping nose.

Sigurdur Óli vaguely recalled meeting him but it took him a minute to remember the circumstances. The man had lost weight since then and his ragged clothes – the filthy anorak, Icelandic jumper at least two sizes too big for him and threadbare jeans – hung loosely from his frame. The old black waders on his feet were hardly any better. His face looked gaunt too, the eyes blank, the mouth sunken and the expression lifeless, the skin hanging from it like the clothes from his body. It was impossible to guess his age with any accuracy, though Sigurdur Óli seemed to recall that he was only about forty-five.

'Are you Andrés?'

'I have to tell him something, Erlendur that is. I have to talk to him.'

'I'm afraid that's not possible,' Sigurdur Óli said. 'Why do you need to see him?'

'I just need to talk to him.'

'That's no answer. Look, I can't be doing with this. Erlendur will be back soon and you can talk to him then.'

The door closed on Andrés and Sigurdur Óli strode towards his office. He now remembered the man clearly and the case with which he had been connected. It had been shortly after New Year, in the frozen depths of winter.

Catching sight of Finnur in the distance, he attempted to take evasive action but it was too late.

'Siggi!' he heard him call.

Sigurdur Óli accelerated, pretending not to have heard. Anyway, he was not in the habit of answering when his colleagues addressed him as Siggi.

'I need to talk to you,' he heard Finnur shout as he pursued him down the corridor and into his office.

'I haven't got time for this,' Sigurdur Óli protested.

'Then you'll just have to make time. What were you doing at Sigurlína's? Why did you jump straight to the conclusion that her attacker was a debt collector? And what are those dodgy photos you were talking about? Come on. What do you know that we don't? And why the hell are you trying to hide it from us?'

'I'm not –' began Sigurdur Óli.

'Do you want me to take this upstairs?' Finnur interrupted. 'It's easily done.'

Sigurdur Óli knew that Finnur would not hesitate and would maybe even report him for professional misconduct. He would have liked more time to work out a story, and was concerned too that Patrekur might get dragged into the investigation, though he couldn't give a toss about Hermann or his wife.

'Calm down, it's nothing serious,' he said. 'I just didn't want to complicate matters unnecessarily. At the time it was only GBH; now it's murder. I was going to talk to you –'

'How very decent of you. Out with it then.'

'The photos are of people my friend, Patrekur, knows,' Sigurdur Óli explained. 'He put me in touch with them. The man's name is Hermann. I went round to have a word with Sigurlína and Ebeneser because they were using the pictures against him and his wife. They're photos of them having sex – they showed me one in which this bloke Hermann was clearly identifiable. Lína and Ebbi were involved in blackmail. They invited couples round for swingers' parties – wife-swapping, in other words. Nothing out of the ordinary as these things go, except that Lína and Ebbi had the bright idea of trying to make some money out of it. There may be other victims but, if so, I'm not aware of them.'

'What? You're saying you were conducting a private investigation *for your friend*?'

'I always intended to report it. I'm telling you now, aren't I? There's no harm done. I was just going to talk to Lína and Ebbi before things got out of hand. Hermann's wife is particularly vulnerable because she's trying to get ahead in politics. When I arrived on the scene Lína was already lying on the floor. Next thing I know the guy jumps out at me. I rang for backup but we lost him.'

'So what does this Hermann say?'

'He denies having anything to do with the attack. I've no reason to believe he's lying, but no particular reason to believe he's telling the truth either. Then again, the assailant could have been acting alone.'

'And of course there may be others in the same boat as this Hermann,' Finnur said, 'people who are more likely to have underworld contacts. Is that what you're getting at?'

'Yes, though I don't think there's cause to rule out Hermann.'

'Did you get anything out of Sigurlína while you were there?'

'No, she was unconscious when I arrived.'

'And Ebeneser?'

'He's playing dumb. He denies having any photos and claims not to have a clue why Lína was attacked. We should put the screws on him first thing tomorrow morning, while he's still vulnerable.'

'What did you mean by keeping this hidden from us?'

'I . . . It was a mistake. I didn't mean to conceal anything.'

'No, right. That's why you've been conducting some kind of private investigation. Does that seem normal to you?'

'I haven't experienced a normal day since I joined the force.'

'You know I'll have to report this. But it would look better if you came clean yourself.'

'Do what you like. I haven't compromised the case. I consider myself perfectly fit to remain involved. But it's your inquiry.'

'Fit? So you're not just looking out for your friend?'

'It has nothing to do with him.'

'Wake up!' exploded Finnur. 'Why the hell did he come to you? Stop talking bullshit and stop making things worse for yourself. He came to you because he's mixed up in this and wants to avoid an official inquiry. He's using you, Siggi. Try to get your head round the fact!'

With that, Finnur swept out of the office, slamming the door behind him.

Instead of switching on the TV as usual when he got home that evening, Sigurdur Óli went into the kitchen, made a sandwich and poured himself a glass of orange juice, then sat down at the kitchen table to eat. It was after midnight and silence reigned in the building. There were five other flats but he had not got to know any of his neighbours since moving in. He greeted them from time to time, if it was unavoidable, but otherwise kept himself to himself. He had no interest in talking to strangers unless it was directly connected to work. The other residents consisted of three families with children, an old couple and a single man of about forty, whom he had once seen wearing a jacket branded with the logo of a tyre company. The man had tried to strike up a friendship, saying hello to Sigurdur Óli a couple of times on his way in or out of the building, and one Saturday afternoon had knocked on his door to ask if he could borrow some sugar. Sigurdur Óli replied guardedly that he did not have any and when the man tried to initiate a conversation about English football he had excused himself claiming that he was busy and closed the door.

As he ate his sandwich he thought about Patrekur and Hermann and what Finnur had said. And about the tramp who had asked after Erlendur. He thought Andrés had looked better, though still a wreck, the last time they met. The man was an alcoholic and lived in a block of flats, probably council-owned, not far from where a young boy of Thai descent had been found stabbed to death back in January. The little boy had been frozen to the ground by the time he was discovered. It had been a bitterly cold spell. The police had put all their resources into solving the case, interviewing Andrés among countless other people from the surrounding area. He was a repeat offender with a long police record for crimes ranging from breaking and entering to affray. After being taken in for questioning, however, they had concluded that although peculiar and an unreliable witness, he was unlikely to constitute any sort of threat.

Now, in the late autumn, Andrés had emerged again, like a ghost from the shadows behind the police station. Sigurdur Óli could not imagine what was bothering him or what he could possibly want with Erlendur, and experienced a momentary twinge of concern about having slammed the door on him. But only momentary.

15

The day after his return from the countryside he woke up on the living-room sofa. Someone had moved him there from the kitchen table where he had fallen asleep. It took him a long time to become fully awake and he briefly thought he was still on the farm, with the morning chores waiting to be attended to. Then he remembered the journey and the wait at the bus station and the stranger who had come to collect him.

He sat up on the sofa, unsure how long he had slept. It was a sunny morning outside and in the light that streamed into the flat he noticed some items of furniture that were familiar, others not, and some that were completely alien, like the television set that he had not noticed the night before, which sat on a table, with a curved screen, black plastic sides and a strange row of buttons. Getting up, he crossed the room to the television, seeing himself reflected oddly in the screen, head elongated, body grotesquely distorted, and smiled at the caricature. He ran a hand over the glass, fiddled with the buttons, and suddenly something happened; there was a low hissing sound and an incomprehensible symbol appeared, accompanied by a terrible piercing wail that he thought would drive him mad. He reeled back from the machine, looking round helplessly, then began to jab frantically at the buttons in an attempt to stop the noise. Suddenly the strange picture shrank into a small dot, before disappearing altogether, and the sound abated. He breathed a sigh of relief.

'What on earth's that racket?'

His mother came out of the bedroom.

'I think I must have turned on the machine,' he said awkwardly. 'I didn't mean to.'

'Is that you, love?' his mother said. 'Sorry – I meant to come and meet you yesterday evening but I couldn't make it; I've been a bit under the weather lately. Have you seen my fags anywhere?'

He looked around and shook his head.

'What have I done with the pack?' she asked with a sigh, scanning the room. 'Röggi met you, did he?'

He did not know how to answer this because the man who collected him had not told him his name. She found a packet of cigarettes and some matches, lit one and inhaled, exhaled, took another drag, then blew out smoke through her nose.

'What do you think of him, love?' she asked.

'Who?'

'Röggi, of course. Bit slow on the uptake, aren't you?'

'I don't know,' he answered. 'All right, I suppose.'

'Röggi's OK,' she said, sucking in smoke. 'He's a bit of a dark horse but I like him. Better than that sodding father of yours, I can tell you. Better than that bastard. Have you eaten, love? What did you used to have for breakfast on the farm?'

'Porridge,' he said.

'Horrible muck, isn't it?' his mother said. 'Wouldn't you rather have some of that breakfast cereal? It's what everyone eats in America. I bought a packet specially for you. Chocolate flavour.'

'Maybe,' he said, so as not to seem ungrateful. He liked starting the day with porridge and had always had it for breakfast, except when there was thick rhubarb stew, which he enjoyed with sugar.

He followed his mother into the kitchen where she took down two bowls and a brown packet. From this she shook out a shower of small brown balls. Then, fetching milk from the fridge, she poured it into the bowls and handed one to him. She chucked her cigarette in the sink without stubbing it out and began to munch on the cereal. Spooning up some of the balls, he put them in his mouth. They were hard and shattered between his teeth.

'Good, isn't it?' said his mother.

'All right,' he said.

'Better than porridge,' his mother added.

The milk turned brown and tasted nice when he drank it out of the bowl. He studied his mother covertly. She had changed since he last saw her, had grown fatter and somehow puffier about the face. One of the front teeth was missing from her lower jaw.

'Good to be home?' she asked.

He thought.

'Sure,' he said at last, not managing to sound very convincing.

'Eh? Aren't you pleased to see your mum? That's nice, after all the trouble I've taken to get you home. You should be grateful. You should thank your mum for everything she's done for you.'

She lit a new cigarette and eyed him.

'That's nice,' she said again, inhaling until the tip of the cigarette glowed.

*   *   *

When he needed to rest he would lie down on the floor of the basement flat in Grettisgata and doze for an hour or two at a time. He had not been home for days and could not afford a proper sleep, not while he needed to keep an eye on the old man, to make sure he did not escape. On no account must he get away.

So far he had failed to find the Eumig camera or any of the films, despite overturning tables, pulling out drawers and throwing the contents on the floor, breaking open cupboards and sweeping the bookshelves clear. Finally, after some hesitation, he had opened the door to the bedroom. Like the rest of the flat it was a pigsty: the bed unmade; the sheet missing, revealing a filthy mattress; no cover on the duvet. There was an old chest in one corner containing four drawers, the chair beside the bed was covered with a pile of clothing, and a large wardrobe stood against one wall. The floor was covered in brown vinyl. He tackled the wardrobe first, chucking out shirts and trousers, tearing out every garment and hacking into the lining of some with the knife he always carried. The rage boiled inside him. Climbing into the wardrobe he struck the back and sides until one of the panels broke. After that he dragged the drawers out of the old chest and flung them down, along with underwear, socks and some papers he could not be bothered to examine. He broke the bottom out of one of the drawers by stamping on it. Finally he overturned the chest and smashed it open at the back. Then he cut the mattress to shreds and scattered it all over the floor. Underneath was the bed frame which he propped up on its side, but found no trace of the camera or films there either.

Returning to the living room, he sat down beside the bound man. The only illumination in the basement was the beam from the Bell & Howell projector, still shining onto one wall. Its lamp was as good as new and he had not turned it off since he had found it. Now he adjusted the projector until the beam fell on the man slumped in his bonds on the chair, his face covered.

'Where do you keep the filth?' he asked, still breathless from his exertions.

The man raised his head, screwing up his eyes against the light.

'Let me go,' he heard him groan from behind the mask.

'Where's the camera?'

'Let me go.'

'Where are the films you made with it?'

'Let me go, Andy, so we can talk.'

'No.'

'Untie me.'

'Shut up!'

The man was racked by a rattling cough.

'Untie me and I'll tell you everything.'

'Shut up.'

He stood up and looked around for the hammer, unable to remember where he had put it. He had destroyed the flat in his search for the camera. As he surveyed the ruins, he saw tables and chairs littered about like matchwood, and suddenly he remembered that the last time he had used it was in the kitchen. He crossed the room, stepping over the rubbish he had strewn around the flat, and glimpsed the handle. It had fallen on the floor. He carried it back into the living room and took up position in front of the old man. Grasping the man's chin firmly, he forced his head back until the spike was poking up vertically.

'Tell me!' he snarled, raising the hammer aloft.

He let the hammer fall but just before it struck the spike he checked the momentum so that it merely tapped the end.

'Tell me!'

'Shut up, you bastard!'

'Next time I'll go all the way,' he whispered.

He raised the hammer and was on the point of striking when the man began to shout.

'Don't, don't, wait . . . don't do it, no more, let me go . . . let me go . . .'

'Let you go?' he echoed.

'Let me . . . go . . . untie me . . .' The man's words had dropped to a whisper. 'Stop . . . that's enough . . .'

'Enough? You've had enough? Isn't that what I used to cry at you? Remember? Remember? When I begged you to stop. Remember, you piece of shit?!'

The hammer had drooped in his hand but now he raised it high and brought it down with all his strength. It passed within a few millimetres of the man's head.

He bent down to him.

'Tell me where you hide the shit or the spike is going in your head!'

16

Patrekur was in his office and visibly busy when Sigurdur Óli barged in. He worked for an engineering firm, where he specialised in load-bearing capacity, concentrating mainly on the construction of bridges and dams for hydroelectric stations. The firm was one of the largest of its kind in Iceland and Patrekur, who was well regarded in his field, was in charge of a sizeable team as deputy director. The country's engineering firms had experienced an unprecedented expansion thanks to the current economic boom which manifested itself in high bank interest rates, the rampant acquisition of foreign assets by Icelandic business tycoons and companies, the huge proliferation of new buildings in the capital area and massive infrastructural projects connected to the hydro-electric dam and aluminium smelting factory in the East Fjords. Patrekur certainly could not complain of any shortage of work. It was still early in the morning and he was standing in rolled-up shirtsleeves, mobile phone in one hand, office phone in the other, reading out information from one of the two computer monitors on his desk. Closing the door behind him, Sigurdur Óli sat down on a black leather sofa facing the desk, crossed his legs and waited patiently.

Patrekur's face registered surprise when he saw him enter and take a seat. He hurriedly finished one of his phone calls but had more trouble concluding the other. At first Sigurdur Óli listened but his interest soon faded when the conversation turned to quantities of reinforced concrete and incremental design costs. Patrekur's desk was covered in piles of paper which had also colonised the windowsill; rolled-up engineering plans were propped against the wall, a safety helmet hung from a peg and there was a photo of his wife Súsanna and their children on the desk.

'They're giving me a hard time,' Sigurdur Óli said when Patrekur finally extricated himself.

The desk phone rang. Patrekur picked up the receiver and laid it on the desk, cutting off the call. He silenced his mobile as well.

'Who?' he asked. 'What for? What are you talking about?'

'My colleagues. I'm afraid I had to tell them about you – that we're friends.'

'About me? Why, for God's sake?'

'They think you're more involved than you're letting on. The whole thing got a lot more serious after Lína died yesterday. Strictly speaking, I shouldn't even be sitting here talking to you.'

'You've got to be kidding?'

Sigurdur Óli shook his head.

'Why did you have to tell them about me?'

'Why did you have to come to me?' Sigurdur Óli countered.

'I saw on the news yesterday that she'd died. They don't seriously believe I'm mixed up in all this, do they?'

'Are you?'

'Don't be ridiculous. I'd have told you if I was. Have you got into trouble?'

'Nothing I can't handle,' Sigurdur Óli assured him. 'What did Hermann say when he heard about Lína?'

'I haven't spoken to him. Will all the details be made public?'

Sigurdur Óli nodded.

'I just wanted to warn you about what's going to happen. You'll be called in for questioning, probably later this afternoon. So will Hermann and his wife. And of course Súsanna won't escape either, though I don't know that for sure. The man who'll do the first round of interviews is called Finnur. He's OK. For your own sake, I hope you tell him everything you know. Don't hold back and don't be difficult; just keep it short and sweet. Stick to answering their questions and don't volunteer any extra information. Don't say anything unless you're asked, and don't start talking about bringing in a lawyer – your situation is nowhere near serious enough and it'll just cause surprise and suspicion. Be yourself and try to stay calm.'

'Are you . . . Do they suspect us of having done this?' Patrekur asked miserably.

'Hermann's in a much worse position than you,' Sigurdur Óli pointed out. 'I don't know what they'll do about you but I told Finnur about us, about the photos and the blackmail and how you know Hermann and how it was you who brought us together.'

Patrekur had slumped in his chair in horrified amazement. He shot a glance at the photo of Súsanna and the children.

'So this is what I get for coming to you for advice,' he said.

'It would all have come out eventually.'

'Come out? What do you mean? Súsanna and I haven't done anything!'

'That's not what Finnur thinks,' Sigurdur Óli said. 'He says that you've been using me, that you're mixed up in this sordid little mess yourself and that I was supposed to intimidate the blackmailers into handing over the photos.'

'I don't believe this,' Patrekur gasped.

Sigurdur Óli watched his friend squirm in his chair.

'Nor do I,' he conceded. 'Finnur's OK, but if you ask me the whole thing's ridiculous. He's choosing to ignore the fact that you would hardly have sent me and the debt collector to see Lína at the same time. Look, is there anything you can tell me that we don't know yet? Anything that could help us find whoever did this? Do you know anyone at all that Lína and Ebbi had dealings with?'

He saw his friend's relief when he said he did not believe Finnur's version of events.

'I'm completely in the dark,' Patrekur assured him. 'I've told you what I know and that's next to nothing. Really, nothing. These people are complete strangers to us.'

'Good,' said Sigurdur Óli. 'Say that when you meet Finnur and everything should be all right. But, for God's sake, don't mention that I came here to warn you.'

Patrekur looked imploringly at Sigurdur Óli.

'Can't you do something?' he said. 'I've never been hauled in by the police before.'

'It's out of my hands, I'm afraid.'

'And the media, will they get wind of this?'

Sigurdur Óli had no words of comfort.

'That's a given,' he said.

'Why the hell did you have to drag me into this?'

'It was Hermann who did that for you,' Sigurdur Óli pointed out drily, 'not me.'

Sigurdur Óli arrived back at the station on Hverfisgata to find his father waiting for him. He was taken aback.

'Is everything all right?' was his first reaction.

'Yes, fine, Siggi,' his father replied. 'I wondered how you were. I'm working nearby and decided to drop in. I've never visited you at work.'

Sigurdur Óli showed him into his office, astonished and somewhat irritated by this intrusion. His father let out a quiet sigh as he sat down, as if he was tired. He was short but sturdily built, his strong hands worn from years of toiling with pipes and wrenches, and he limped a little from bad joints after spending so much of his working life on his knees. Where it was visible under his baseball cap, his hair was streaked with grey, though the thick brows over his kindly eyes still retained their reddish tint. The hairs of his brows stood up in tufts as he had not been to a barber for a while and he had several days' stubble on his chin as usual. Sigurdur Óli knew that he only shaved once a week, on Saturdays, and never touched his eyebrows if he could help it.

'Seen your mother at all?' his father asked, rubbing his painful knee.

'I was round at hers yesterday evening,' Sigurdur Óli answered. He was sure this was no courtesy call. His father had never been one to waste time on inessentials. 'Shall I get you a coffee?' he asked.

'No, thank you, don't go to any trouble,' his father said quickly. 'Was she on good form?'

'Yes, pretty good.'

'Still spending all her time with that man?'

'Saemundur, yes.'

It was more or less the same conversation they had had when his father rang him nearly three weeks ago. They had not spoken since. There had been no reason for his call then, apart from the questions he dropped in here and there about Gagga and her live-in partner.

'Perfectly decent bloke, I suppose,' his father said.

'I don't really know him,' Sigurdur Óli said truthfully. He did his best to avoid contact with Saemundur.

'She's done well for herself.'

'Are you planning anything for your birthday?' Sigurdur Óli asked, watching his father massage his knee.

'No, I don't suppose so. I . . .'

'What?'

'The thing is, I've got to go to hospital, Siggi.'

'Oh?'

'They found something in my prostate. Apparently it's not uncommon with men my age.'

'What . . . what is it? Cancer?'

'I'm hoping it's not very advanced – they don't think it's spread at all – but they need to operate as soon as possible and I just wanted to let you know.'

'Bloody hell,' Sigurdur Óli blurted out.

'Yes, these things happen,' his father said. 'No point dwelling on it. Now, how's Bergthóra getting on?'

'Bergthóra? Fine, I guess. But aren't you scared? What do the doctors say?'

'Well, they asked if I had any children and I told them about you and they mentioned wanting to see you too.'

'Me?'

'They talked about risk groups; that you were in a risk group. Men used not to have to worry about these things until they were in their fifties but apparently it's happening younger and younger these days. And since it can be hereditary they'd like to see you too, or at least for you to go for a check-up.'

'When are you going under the knife?'

'Next Monday. They say they can't hang around.'

His business finished, his father stood up and opened the door.

'That was all, Siggi. You look into getting yourself checked out. Don't put it off.'

Then he was gone, limping a little from his worn-out knee.

17

When Sigurdur Óli drove to Ebbi and Lína's house, towards evening, everything was quiet. Ebeneser's large jeep was parked in front of the house, jacked up on enormous tyres designed to cope with all manner of off-road conditions involving rock, ice and snow. As Sigurdur Óli parked behind it, he thought about adventure tours into the interior. Personally he had never seen the attraction, never had the slightest interest in sightseeing in his own country, let alone giving up his creature comforts to camp or rough it. Why on earth would he want to trek up an Icelandic glacier? Bergthóra had sometimes tried to encourage him to travel around Iceland with her, but found that he was as reluctant and unenthusiastic about the idea as he was about so much else. All he really wanted was to stay in Reykjavík, preferably near his own flat.

His summer holidays were generally spent abroad, in search of guaranteed sunshine rather than horizon-broadening experiences. It came as no surprise to Bergthóra that one of his favourite places was Florida. He was less keen to visit Spain or other southern European beach destinations, regarding them as dirty and poor, with suspect food. Historical sites, museums and architecture held absolutely no appeal for him, which made Orlando the ideal spot. His taste in films was similar: he could not stand pretentious European films, plotless arty flicks, in which nothing ever happened. Hollywood movies, with their thrills, laughs and glamorous stars, were more to his taste. In his opinion, cinema was made for the English-speaking world. If any programme came on TV that was neither British nor American he was quick to change channels. All other languages, especially Icelandic, sounded childish on-screen. Naturally, he avoided Icelandic films like the plague. Nor was he a reader, barely managing to plod through one book a year, and when he listened to music it was invariably classic American rock or country.

He sat for some time in his car behind Ebbi's monster jeep, thinking about his father and their meeting earlier that day, the cancer diagnosis and the recommendation that he too should go for screening. He grimaced. It would take a lot to let them check his prostate. The memory was still too fresh of all those disagreeable trips to the National Hospital, bearing those little plastic pots, when he and Bergthóra had been trying to conceive using IVF. He used to have to go into the bathroom early in the morning and ejaculate into a pot, then keep the contents warm and deliver them to the girls on reception, revealing intimate details about how things were going, feeling compelled to throw in little jokes for their benefit. In prospect now was a visit to a specialist who, while he snapped on his latex gloves, would ask him to lie on his side and draw up his knees, no doubt chatting about the weather, prior to probing him for lumps.

'Shit!' Sigurdur Óli swore and thumped the steering wheel.

Ebeneser opened the door and admitted him reluctantly, pointing out that he was working through the mourning process. It sounded as if he had been talking to a priest or a therapist. Sigurdur Óli said he quite understood and would not keep him long.

Ebeneser had tidied the house since Sigurdur Óli's last visit. Then the sitting room had been a bomb site; now it was almost cosy in the low light of a standard lamp, the chairs in their places, pictures straight on the walls;

a framed photograph of Lína on the table, with a candle burning in front of it.

Ebeneser had been in the kitchen, about to make coffee, when Sigurdur Óli disturbed him; the packet was on the table, the filter open in the coffee-maker. Sigurdur Óli waited to be offered a cup but the offer was not forthcoming. Ebeneser's movements were slow and he seemed distracted. No doubt Lína's death was beginning to become real, the shocking circumstances slowly sinking in as incontrovertible fact.

'Did she say anything?' Ebeneser asked as he measured out the coffee. 'When you found her?'

'No,' said Sigurdur Óli. 'She was unconscious. And her assailant went for me almost immediately.'

'You needn't have chased him.' Ebeneser turned to Sigurdur Óli. 'You could have tended to her instead, but you didn't. She might have got to hospital sooner. That's all that counts, all that counts in . . . circumstances like that.'

'Of course,' said Sigurdur Óli. 'That's why I rang for assistance straight away. I'd already done that when the man jumped me. I wanted to catch her attacker – it was a natural reaction. In fact I don't see how I could have behaved any differently.'

Ebeneser switched on the coffee-maker but remained standing.

'Anyway, what about you?' asked Sigurdur Óli.

'What about me?' Ebeneser responded, his eyes on the coffee machine.

'You're obviously looking for a scapegoat, but what about you? What part did you play in the attack on Lína? What were you two up to? Who did you cross? Was it all your idea? Did you drag Lína into some scam? Are you in debt? What about your responsibility, Ebeneser? Have you asked yourself that?'

The other man was silent.

'Why won't you tell us?' persisted Sigurdur Óli. 'I know you've tried to blackmail people with photographs, there's no use denying it. We're in the process of interviewing them now, hearing how you and Lína held swingers' parties and took photos of people having sex with you, then used the pictures to extort money from them. You're going down, Ebeneser. On top of everything else, you'll be charged with blackmail.'

Ebeneser did not look up. The coffee-maker belched and black liquid began to rise inside the glass jug.

'You've destroyed these people's lives,' Sigurdur Óli said. 'You've destroyed your own life, Ebeneser. And for what? For who? How much was it worth to you? What price did you put on Lína? Half a million? Was that what she was worth to you?'

'Shut the fuck up,' hissed Ebeneser through clenched teeth, his eyes still glued to the coffee. 'And get out.'

'You'll be called in for questioning, probably later this evening, and treated as a suspect in a sordid case of blackmail. You may even be remanded in custody, for all I know. Maybe you'll find yourself having to apply for parole to attend Lína's funeral.'

Ebeneser stared at the coffee jug as if it were the only fixed point in his life.

'Think about it, Ebbi.'

The man did not answer.

'Are you acquainted with a man by the name of Hermann? You sent him a photo. He showed it to me.'

Ebeneser did not flinch. Sigurdur Óli took a deep breath: he was not sure if he wanted to ask the next question.

'What about a man called Patrekur?' he asked after a moment. 'With a wife called Súsanna. Are they involved as well?'

Rising to his feet, he walked over to Ebeneser and took a photo from his coat pocket. He had fetched it from his flat before coming there; it showed Patrekur and Súsanna at home with him and Bergthóra back in the days when life was still good. The picture had been taken in summer, their faces were tanned and they were holding glasses of white wine. Sigurdur Óli placed the photo on the table beside the percolator.

'Do you know these people?' he asked.

Ebeneser glanced at the picture.

'You have no right to be here,' he said, so quietly that Sigurdur Óli could barely hear him. 'Get out. Get out and take that bloody thing with you!' He swept the photograph to the floor. 'Get out!' he yelled again, raising his arms as if to shove Sigurdur Óli away. Having rescued the picture, Sigurdur Óli backed off. They eyed each other until Sigurdur Óli turned on his heel and walked out of the kitchen, out of the house and back to his car. As he was getting in he looked up at the kitchen window which faced onto the street and saw Ebeneser grab the coffee jug and hurl it at the wall with all his strength. The jug shattered and black liquid spattered all over the kitchen like bloodstained vomit.

On his way home Sigurdur Óli stopped at the gym, where he ran several kilometres, lifted weights as if his life depended on it and burnt off his energy on a variety of machines. He generally bumped into the same people during these morning and evening sessions. Sometimes he would share a little light banter, at other times he would shut himself off, wanting to be left in peace. Like now, for instance. He spoke to nobody and if anyone addressed him he answered tersely and moved away. After finishing his exercises, he made straight for home.

Once there he prepared himself a thick hamburger on

ciabatta, with sweet onion and fried egg, which he consumed with an American beer, while watching an American comedy on TV. He was too restless to watch television for long, however, and switched it off when a Swedish crime series came on. He sat in his TV chair, still preoccupied with thoughts of his father's visit, wondering if he should make an appointment with a specialist or leave it and hope for the best. He hated the idea of suddenly becoming a statistic, a member of some risk group. As someone who had always taken great care of his health and never needed to visit a doctor, he regarded himself as the robust type and was proud of never having been in hospital. Admittedly, he came down with heavy colds or flu from time to time, like the bout he was recovering from now, but that was about it.

His notebook lay on the floor where it had fallen out of his pocket when he folded his coat over the back of the chair. Sigurdur Óli stood up, retrieved it and turned the pages before putting it on the desk in the sitting room. He had never been a hypochondriac, never worried about contracting a serious, incurable illness; since he was the picture of health the possibility had simply never crossed his mind. Eventually, however, after mulling it over, he decided to talk to a specialist, knowing it would be impossible to live with the uncertainty.

He picked up the notebook again. There was a detail

he needed to check, one he had forgotten to pin down. He reread his jottings from the past few days and saw that his oversight was minor: he had not yet checked a phone number that really ought to be verified. He looked at the clock; it was not that late, so he picked up the phone.

'Hello,' a voice said. It was a weary and indifferent woman's voice.

'Please excuse my ringing so late,' Sigurdur Óli said. 'But do you know a woman called Sara? Is she a friend of yours?'

There was a silence on the other end.

'What can I do for you?' the woman asked eventually.

'Ah,' said Sigurdur Óli. 'Did she visit you last Monday evening? Could you confirm the fact?'

'Who?'

'Sara.'

'Sara who?'

'Your friend.'

'Who is this, please?'

'The police.'

'What do you want with me?'

'Was Sara at your address last Monday evening?'

'Is this a joke?'

'A joke?'

'You must have the wrong number.'

Sigurdur Óli read out the number he had been given.

'Yes, that's right,' the woman said, 'but there's no Sara working here. I don't know any Sara. This is the box office at the University Cinema.'

'So you're not Dóra?'

'No, and there's no Dóra here either. I've been working here for years and I've never known anyone called Dóra.'

Sigurdur Óli stared at the number in his notebook, seeing in his mind's eye the pierced eyebrow and tattooed arm of yet another liar, and a convincing one at that.

18

Sigurdur Óli was debating if he should call Sara in for questioning, send a car to fetch her from her workplace and see how she liked being escorted from the bottling plant between uniformed officers. That was one method he could envisage. Another would be to pay her a visit at work and intimidate her with all sorts of dire threats, such as leading her out in handcuffs, speaking to her boss, making her lies public. Since he did not know her at all, he was not sure how tough Sara was, but assumed she would be an unreliable witness and quick to lie. She had reeled off the telephone number of the cinema without hesitation, gambling that he would never check up on it.

He decided to adopt the latter approach, for although Sara had lied to him about her movements, this was no guarantee that the truth would have any bearing on Lína's attack. She could have a hundred other reasons for lying to him.

There she sat at the bottling-plant switchboard with the ring through her eyebrow and the snake around her arm, each indicative of a small rebellion against bourgeois conservatism. Tasteless and tacky, thought Sigurdur Óli as he approached her. Sara was on the phone dealing with a customer, so he waited at first but when it appeared that the conversation would never end he lost patience and, seizing the receiver, cut the connection.

'You and I need another chat,' he announced.

Sara looked startled. 'Hey, what's the matter?' she asked.

'Either here or down at the station, it's up to you.'

A somewhat older woman was standing behind the desk, observing their conversation with surprise. Sara glanced at her and Sigurdur Óli saw that she was keen to avoid any trouble at work.

'Is it OK with you if I take a short break?' she asked the woman, who nodded calmly but asked her not to be long.

Sara led Sigurdur Óli towards the cafeteria, opened a door beside it, which turned out to lead to a staircase, and stopped just inside.

'What on earth are you on about?' she asked as the door closed behind them. 'Why can't you leave me alone?'

'You weren't visiting a friend on the evening of the attack – incidentally, it's murder now, not assault and battery. The number you gave me for your friend was false.'

'I don't know what you're talking about,' Sara said, scratching her tattoo.

'Why was your car parked in the area?'

'I was visiting a friend.'

'Dóra?'

'Yes.'

'Either you must be stupid or you think I am,' Sigurdur Óli said. 'Whatever, you'll have plenty of time to mull it over while you're in custody. From now on you'll be treated as a suspect: the police will be coming to take you in later today. I'm going to go and print out a warrant for your arrest right now. It shouldn't take long. By the way, don't forget your toothbrush.'

Sigurdur Óli opened the door to the corridor.

'I lent it to my brother,' said Sara in a low voice.

'What did you say?'

'My brother borrowed the car,' the girl said, louder this time. The look of defiance was gradually fading from her face.

'Who's he? What does he do?'

'He doesn't do anything. I sometimes lend him the car. He was driving it that evening, but I don't know where he went or what he was up to.'

'So why did you lie to me?'

'He's always getting into trouble. When you started asking about the car and where I'd been, I figured he might have done something stupid. But there's no way I'm going to prison for his sake. He had the car.'

Sigurdur Óli fixed Sara with a penetrating glare, but she kept her gaze lowered. He wondered if she was lying again.

'Why should I believe you?'

'I don't care what you believe. He had the car. That's all I know. It's not my problem. Ask him.'

'What was he doing? What did he tell you?'

'Nothing. We don't talk much. He's . . .' Sara trailed off.

'You just lend him your car,' Sigurdur Óli finished for her.

Sara met Sigurdur Óli's gaze. 'No . . . I lied about that too,' she said.

'What?'

'He didn't borrow the car, he stole it. I was late for work the next day thanks to him. Had to take a taxi. My car was just missing from its parking space. He may be my brother but he's a total dickhead.'

* * *

Sigurdur Óli learned that Sara's brother was called Kristján and that she had stopped lending him her car a long time ago. He never kept his word; he had already lost his licence twice and often could not be bothered to bring the car back or else was incapable of doing so. On those occasions, rather than take the risk that her battered Micra might be sitting in the town centre, accumulating parking tickets, she would have to fetch it herself. As a result she would not lend him the car any more – or indeed money or any of her other possessions. He had stolen cash from her too, even taken her credit card once, as well as belongings from her flat that he would sell to buy drugs. He was forever in trouble, why she had no idea, since he had had no worse an upbringing than she had. Their parents were both teachers. There were five kids in all, four of them living respectable lives, but he had always been at odds with everyone and everything. The evening he took the car he had dropped in to see her, but as so often he had been restless and twitchy and only stayed briefly.

When she woke up the next day to go to work, she had been unable to find her car keys, then discovered that the car itself was missing.

Later, Sigurdur Óli checked whether Kristján was known to the police but there was nothing in the files. Following Sara's directions, he drove over to where she believed her brother was living, in a basement flat owned by a friend. Officially he was still domiciled with his parents but had not in reality lived there in the last two years. Nor did he have a regular job. He had lasted precisely a week in his most recent employment at a twenty-four-hour grocery store, before being sacked for pilfering from the till on an almost daily basis.

Sigurdur Óli knocked on the door. The flat was located in a block in the Fell neighbourhood but had its own entrance. He knocked again and, getting no response, tried the bell, but there was no sound from within. Next he tried peering through the window that faced onto a dreary communal back garden but could see nothing of interest, only beer cans and rubbish littering all the surfaces, and other signs of squalor. Returning to the front door, he banged on it again, finally giving it a resounding kick.

At last a scrawny figure in underpants answered the door. He had a corpse-like pallor, unkempt shoulder-length hair and a grungy, hung-over air.

'What's going on?' he mumbled, squinting blearily at Sigurdur Óli.

'I'm looking for Kristján. Is that you?'

'Me, nah . . .'

'Then do you know where he is?'

'What about him? Why –'

'Is he in the flat?'

'No.'

'Are you expecting him?'

'No. Anyway, who are you?'

'I'm from the police and I need to get hold of him. Do you know where he might be?'

'Well, he won't be showing his face round here – he owes me big time for rent and that. If you see him you can tell him to pay up. Why are you from the police?'

'Do you know where he might be?' repeated Sigurdur Óli, trying to see past him into the flat. He did not believe a word the little runt said. Uncertain what the question 'Why are you from the police?' meant, he did not even attempt to answer it.

'You can try the Hard Hat, he often hangs out there,' the boy answered. 'He's a real basket case, man. A real basket case,' he repeated, as if to emphasise that this did not apply to him.

The bartender at the Hard Hat knew Kristján all right, though he had not seen him recently and reckoned that the bar tab he had run up might be something of a deterrent. He smiled as he said this, as if it was no skin off his nose if someone owed the owner money. It was shortly after midday and the few customers were huddled over their beer glasses either by the bar or round a table. They regarded Sigurdur Óli with curiosity. He was not one of the regulars at this time of day, and they eavesdropped on every word that passed between him and the bartender. Sigurdur Óli had not yet revealed that he was from the police when a man of about thirty unexpectedly came to his assistance.

'I saw Kiddi at Bíkó yesterday; I think he's started working there,' he volunteered.

'Which branch of Bíkó?'

'The one on Hringbraut.'

Sigurdur Óli recognised Kristján immediately from his sister's description. It was true: he had just been taken on by the west Reykjavík branch of the DIY chain. Sigurdur Óli watched him before making his move, and observed that Kristján did his utmost to avoid any contact with customers, pretending to busy himself by the racks of screws but moving over to the light bulbs as soon as a customer approached, only to retreat from there slap bang into a man who said he needed help choosing a paintbrush. Kristján claimed to be busy and told the man to ask another member of staff. He had clocked Sigurdur Óli and was evidently nervous that he was going to ask for help when Sigurdur Óli finally managed to corner him.

'Are you Kristján?' he asked directly.

Kristján admitted that he was. The moment he set eyes on him, Sigurdur Óli realised that this could not be the man who had sprinted with such a terrific turn of speed towards the Kleppur mental hospital before vanishing into the night. He was not even convinced that such a feeble specimen would be able to lift a baseball bat, let alone wield it. Kristján cut an unimpressive figure: about twenty years old, his Bíkó uniform hanging from his skinny body like dirty laundry. Sheepish was the word that sprang to mind.

'I'm from the police,' Sigurdur Óli said, taking in their surroundings as he spoke. They were standing in the shelter of shelves displaying gardening tools, where Kristján was pretending to arrange the pruning shears. 'I've just been talking to your sister,' Sigurdur Óli continued, 'and she told me you stole her car.'

'That's a lie, I didn't steal it,' Kristján said. 'She lent it to me. And she got it back too.'

'Where did you go in it?'

'You what?'

'What did you need the car for?'

Kristján hesitated. Avoiding Sigurdur Óli's eye, he put down the shears and picked up a plastic bottle of weedkiller.

'That's my business,' he said, with an unconvincing show of bravado.

'The car was parked in a street not far from the Laugarás cinema, near where a woman was attacked and murdered on the same evening that you had use of the car. We know you were in the vicinity when the crime was committed.'

Kristján gaped at Sigurdur Óli, who pressed on before the boy could collect his wits.

'What were you doing with the car? Why did you leave it behind overnight?'

'It's just that there's been some kind of, some kind of misunderstanding,' Kristján stammered.

'Who were you with?' Sigurdur Óli demanded. He spoke in a brusque, impatient voice, taking a step closer. 'We know there were two of you. Who was with you? And why did you attack the woman?'

However Kristján may have prepared himself for this eventuality, his mind went blank when it came to the crunch. Sigurdur Óli had often seen boys like Kristján lose their nerve. They would stand in front of him, full of lies and defiance, answering back, denying everything and telling him to fuck off, then quite suddenly they would crumple, abandoning their insolence and becoming pathetically cooperative. Looking even more sheepish, Kristján replaced the weedkiller so clumsily that he knocked over three other bottles in the process, then stooped to pick them up and return them to the shelf.

Sigurdur Óli watched his efforts dispassionately, offering no help.

'I can't believe Sara blabbed to you,' Kristján said.

You contemptible little creep, thought Sigurdur Óli.

19

Sigurdur Óli had no interest whatsoever in learning how Kristján had gone off the rails. He had heard countless similar sob stories, used either as an excuse for a career of criminality, or as proof of the mess the welfare state was in. It was enough for him to know that Kristján had messed up to the point where he was up to his neck in debts, mostly drugs-related, and owed money all over town, even, in two instances, to individuals based in other parts of the country. Kristján was not much of an earner either; he managed to score casual jobs here and there, as there were more than enough to go round these days, but for the most part he loafed about, idle and shiftless. He scrounged loans for as long as he could get away with it, particularly from banks and savings institutions, managing to amass an array of debit and credit cards, which had now been passed on as bad debts to official debt-collection agencies. But it was the thought of another kind of debt collector that made Kristján nervous.

He had broken the law and got away with it, though he was not prepared to go into details for Sigurdur Óli, and had a history of using girls, sucking them dry financially before they eventually got wise to him. One prospective father-in-law, a former championship-winning footballer, had beaten him to a pulp when he discovered that Kristján had stolen valuables from his house and pawned them.

Some of this information had been supplied by his sister Sara; the rest Kristján explained to Sigurdur Óli down at the station on Hverfisgata.

For it seemed that Kristján was not averse to talking, now that he was in the hands of the police. Of course, it helped that he was suspected of being party to a murder and was therefore anxious to clear his name, but Sigurdur Óli thought that this was not the only reason. It was as if Kristján had never spoken to anyone about his life and after some initial vacillation and awkwardness, the floodgates opened and out poured episodes from his past and encounters with people who had led him astray. To begin with, his account was incoherent but gradually he managed to impose some order on the tale and one name began to crop up repeatedly, that of a certain Thórarinn who drove a delivery van for a living.

If Kristján's word was anything to go by, Thórarinn was both a dealer and a debt collector, a common arrangement, which made for efficiency. Kristján did not think he imported drugs on any large scale but he was a hard man with little tolerance for people who owed him money, which was how Kristján had ended up in his hands. Since Kristján was seldom able to pay for his habit, and no amount of threats or beatings did any good, Thórarinn had started to use him instead for small jobs in part payment for the drugs. These ranged from being sent out to buy alcohol or groceries to picking up new consignments from smugglers or cannabis farmers, since Thórarinn avoided undertaking such errands personally. Nor did Thórarinn touch drugs himself, though he could drink anyone under the table, according to Kristján. A former athlete and now a family man with a wife and three children, he was careful to stay under the radar and often claimed that the drugs money was his pension and that he would quit the business once he had raised enough. Kristján frequently had to do jobs for him in the van and his wages went towards paying off his debts.

Sigurdur Óli studied Kristján as he sat facing him in the interview room, a miserable, hunched figure. He was inclined to take his statement with a pinch of salt, though he was prepared to believe that this feckless boy was effectively a slave to his dealer. His request to smoke had been met with a flat refusal, and he had received short shrift from Sigurdur Óli when he asked if he had anything for him to eat. Finally, he asked if he could go to the Gents but that was refused as well.

'You can't ban me from that,' Kristján objected.

'Oh, shut up,' Sigurdur Óli said. 'So, what happened on Monday evening?'

'He didn't want to use the van,' Kristján said. 'So he asked me to get hold of a car. Ordered me, more like. I told him I didn't own one and he said to talk to my sister. I'd mentioned her to him, you see, and he knew she had a car.'

'Did he tell you what he was going to do with it?'

'No, he was just going to return it to me later that evening.'

'You didn't go with him?'

'No.'

'Did he go alone?'

'Yes, I think so. I don't know. I don't know anything about it.'

'Is he always that careful? Taking the precaution of obtaining a car specially?'

'He's very careful,' Kristján confirmed.

'Have you met him since he borrowed the car?'

'I . . . he dropped into Bíkó the next day,' Kristján said after a pause. 'Only for a minute. He told me where he'd left the car and that I wasn't to mention to anyone that he'd borrowed it and that we mustn't be in touch for the next few weeks or months or whatever. Then he just walked out. I spoke to Sara and told her where the car was. She went ballistic.'

'Did this Thórarinn tell you what business he had with the woman in the house?'

'No.'

'Did he go to see her for reasons of his own or was he acting for someone else?'

Kristján stared at him, and Sigurdur Óli realised that he had lost concentration. This had happened several times during their conversation, especially when Sigurdur Óli's questions were too convoluted. Kristján would gawp at him with incomprehension and Sigurdur Óli would have to rephrase his question more concisely. He did so again, trying not to speak too quickly.

'Did Thórarinn know the woman?'

'The one he attacked?' Kristján asked knowledgeably. 'No, I don't think so. I don't know. He didn't mention it.'

'Was he calling in a drugs debt?'

'I don't know.'

'Have you any idea what he wanted with her?'

'No.'

'Does Thórarinn know the woman's partner? His name's Ebeneser.'

'I've never heard him mention anyone called Ebeneser. Is he a foreigner?'

'Would you say that Thórarinn was a violent man?'

Kristján thought. He wondered if he should tell them about the time Thórarinn had battered him for being behind on his debts, or the time he had broken his middle finger. He had held his finger and bent it slowly but inexorably backwards until something inside it snapped. The pain had been unbearable. But Thórarinn could be OK; that is, once he had come to terms with the fact that he would never get any money out of Kristján except by making him work. After that they had become mates of sorts, though he did not think that Thórarinn could have many friends, at least not that he knew of. He had heard how he spoke to his wife as well and it was not pretty; he had once seen her with a bump on her forehead and a split lip. The way Thórarinn talked about her was not pretty either, though he was good to his kids. But he was no barrel of laughs; indeed he had never really seen Thórarinn in a good mood, and he had warned Kristján on numerous occasions that if he squealed to the police he would kill him. Without hesitation. Just take him out.

'What did you say?' asked Kristján, having forgotten the question.

Sigurdur Óli sighed in exasperation and repeated himself.

'He certainly can be,' Kristján replied. 'I don't think his wife has a very good time.'

'And you claim that Thórarinn is a debt collector?'

'Yes.'

'Do you know that for sure? Have you witnessed it?'

'He came after me for money,' Kristján said. 'And there are others I know about. He's not a guy to mess with when he's calling in his own debts. And he works for other people too.'

'What people?'

'Other dealers. Anyone, really.'

'Does he use a baseball bat?'

'No question,' said Kristján without hesitation. But then he had never heard of a debt collector who did not use a baseball bat.

'When were you last in contact with him?'

'When he came to see me, the day after it happened.'

'Do you know where he is now?'

'I expect he's at home. Or at work.'

'You don't think he's gone into hiding?'

Kristján shrugged. 'Maybe.'

'Where would he go in that case?'

'I don't know.'

'Are you sure?'

'Yes.'

Sigurdur Óli continued to grill Kristján with some success. In spite of the countless death threats he had received, the boy held nothing back. It turned out that like so many other members of Reykjavík's benighted underworld, Thórarinn had a nickname that explained a lot to Sigurdur Óli. Toggi 'Sprint'.

20

To begin with, he hardly got to know his mother's new boyfriend, as the man, who she never called anything but Röggi, was rarely home. Röggi was either at sea or working out of town and had little contact with mother and son.

After moving home from the farm he mostly looked after himself. He met other kids in the neighbourhood and would go to the three o'clock cinema showings with them. When school began in the autumn he ended up in the same class as some of these new friends. He was entirely responsible for getting himself to school; waking himself up in the morning, finding his clothes and, if there was any food to be had in the kitchen, making a packed lunch. His mother never surfaced that early, since she would invariably stay up late at night, sometimes receiving visitors that he did not know and tried to avoid meeting. Unable to sleep in the living room, he would flee into his mother's room. Sometimes he heard the sounds of drinking and once a fight broke out and someone called the police. He watched from the bedroom window as a staggering drunk was hustled into a police car, hurling abuse at the officers. They were not gentle with him either, ramming him into the car door and knocking his feet from under him. He saw his mother standing in the doorway, yelling obscenities. Then she slammed the door and the noise of partying continued unabated till morning.

He was ashamed of himself for losing the thousand-krona note that the farmer had given him in parting. He had had it in the bus on the way to town, stuffed for safe keeping into his trouser pocket which he patted from time to time. But he had forgotten all about the money during the long wait at the bus station, such was his fear that no one would come to fetch him. When he got home he had fallen asleep at the kitchen table and by the time he woke up on the sofa the next day he had forgotten all about the money, unused as he was to owning anything, least of all a treasure like that. It was not until late in the evening that he remembered the gift. As he was still wearing the same trousers, he shoved his hand in his pocket, then in the other, then in the back pockets, then in increasing desperation he found the jacket he had been wearing and searched all its pockets, followed by his suitcase, the kitchen, the sofa, the living room, even behind the television. He told his mother that he had lost the money and asked if they could go down to the bus station to see if anyone had returned it.

'A thousand kronur!' his mother exclaimed. 'Who do you think would give you a thousand kronur?'

It took him a while to convince her that he was telling the truth.

'It must have fallen out of your pocket,' said Sigurveig. 'You can forget it. Nobody will hand in a thousand kronur. Nobody. You're such an idiot – it's a lot of money. Are you sure you weren't just dreaming?' She lit a cigarette.

Eventually, after persistent pleading on his part, she agreed to ring the bus station. He listened to the extremely brief conversation.

'No, of course not, I didn't think so,' she said when she was satisfied that no thousand-krona note had been handed in.

And that was that. His mother cut short any further mention of the money and the next time the subject came up when Röggi was at home, he claimed he had no idea what the boy was on about: he had never seen any thousand-krona note.

He felt unable to establish any real connection with his mother, and was at a loss to understand why she had insisted on summoning him home from the countryside. He knew precious little about her; she behaved like a stranger and showed virtually no interest in him. She seemed to live in a world of her own in which there was no place for him, nor did she have any contact with her other children or relatives. Since she was unemployed, the only people she mixed with seemed to be night owls like herself. She rarely asked how he was, if he had made any friends, if he liked school, if he was bullied.

If she had ever shown any curiosity he would have told her that he was happy at school and getting on fine with his lessons. He could have done with some help with arithmetic, but he did not know where to look for that. Spelling was difficult too; the rules were a mystery and he got poor marks in his tests, although his teacher was understanding and patient. He was also slow at writing, which did not help when they played the spelling test unnecessarily fast on the tape player, making it hard for him to get it all down. He could have told her too that he found it uncomfortable when people noticed that he had no packed lunch or that he had been wearing the same clothes for so long that they had begun to smell.

He did his homework conscientiously every day and spent the evenings glued to the television; it was like having a cinema in your living room. He watched the entire schedule with equal enthusiasm: news, chat shows, cop dramas and Icelandic light-entertainment programmes with musical interludes. At weekends they showed the odd film and he never missed any. Along with the cartoons, the films were probably his favourite.

Röggi was taciturn when he was at home and gave away little about what he did. He did not appear to have any friends or acquaintances. Nobody came round and no one ever rang for him. The man slept a lot on his days off and was up all night. Once he woke up in the middle of the night to see Röggi in the kitchen, smoking a cigarette with a bottle in front of him. Another time he woke up to find Röggi standing over him, watching him expressionlessly, before returning to the bedroom without saying a word. If anything, he felt that Röggi showed more interest in him than his mother did. He would ask him about school and about his teachers, and watch TV with him. He gave him little presents too: sweets, fizzy drinks, chewing gum.

Then, one autumn evening while his mother was out and Röggi was at home sitting in front of the TV with him, Röggi asked if he would like to see some proper films, cartoons. Yes, he said. Röggi went into the bedroom and came out carrying the strange box that he had noticed on the living-room table on his first evening home from the country. Röggi prised off the cover to reveal the projector, then went back into the bedroom to fetch a cardboard box full of films, and finally a small screen on a tripod that he pulled down out of a long cylinder.

'I'm going to show you some cartoons I've got,' Röggi said, taking some reels from the box and starting to thread one into the machine.

He flicked a switch and the machine started up. A white glare lit up the screen. The projector emitted a pleasant whirring sound as the film ran in front of the bulb and the glare developed lines, dots and numbers until finally images appeared.

They watched it through to the end. Then Röggi rewound the film, put it away and took out another, just as lively and entertaining as the first. Both were Donald Duck cartoons.

When it was over, Röggi threaded a third reel into the projector without saying a word. The film was in colour, foreign, and began with a grown-up man stroking the hair of a girl who could not have been more than seven years old. Then he started to undress her.

*   *   *

'I never wanted it!' he shouted, as he stood over the old man. He had toppled backwards on to the floor, still tied to the chair. 'I never wanted to watch that filthy shit. You made me do it, you forced me and forced me . . . you forced me . . .'

He kicked the man, kicked him like a dog, kicked him and sobbed and yelled at him, kept on kicking and sobbing.

'I never wanted it!'

21

Thórarinn had gone into hiding.

Sigurdur Óli had headed over to the modest terraced house on Sogavegur where Thórarinn lived, taking a small team after deciding that there was no need to call in the special squad. As he knocked on the door it was getting on for evening and a cold pall of drizzle hung low over the city. The street lights had come on some time ago and cast a misty glow over the surroundings. Sigurdur Óli stood waiting for the door to open, Finnur at his side and a couple of policemen a little way behind them. Two officers had gone round behind the house in case Thórarinn made a break for it out of the back exit.

Suddenly, the front door opened and a little girl of about six years old stood gazing up at them.

Sigurdur Óli bent down. 'Is your daddy home?' he asked, trying to smile.

'No,' said the little girl.

Another girl appeared behind her. She must have been around ten and gazed at Sigurdur Óli, Finnur and the other officers.

'Is your mummy home?' asked Sigurdur Óli, addressing his question to the elder girl this time.

'She's asleep,' said the girl.

'Could you wake her up for us, please?' asked Sigurdur Óli, attempting to sound friendly. It did not seem to work.

'We're not to wake her,' said the girl.

Sigurdur Óli glanced at Finnur.

'You'll need to wake her up for us, dear,' said Finnur firmly. 'We're from the police and we need to talk to your father. Do you know where he is?'

'He's at work,' answered the girl. 'I'll wake Mum,' she added, vanishing into the house.

They waited on the steps for some time, the other officers shuffling their feet in the drizzle. The younger girl was still standing in the doorway, her eyes full of doubt. They had a warrant to enter and search the house but, ignoring Sigurdur Óli's advice, Finnur had announced that he did not want to cause unnecessary alarm if there were children involved. They knew that there were three, the youngest of whom was only four years old. They also knew that Thórarinn was not at work. On enquiry they had discovered that he had not done any jobs since Monday. The police had already issued an alert for his van.

At last the elder girl returned to stare at them in silence from the doorway, and shortly afterwards their mother appeared. She had clearly been having a nap and was not yet fully awake. Her plump face was creased from the pillow, her hair a tousled mess.

'We have a warrant to search these premises,' Sigurdur Óli announced, 'though we would rather you let us in voluntarily. And we need to speak to your husband, Thórarinn. Do you know where he might be?'

The woman did not answer.

'We would rather do this with the minimum of unpleasantness,' Finnur said.

The woman seemed to be taking a long time to wake up.

'What . . . what do you want with him?' she asked, her voice drugged with sleep.

Sigurdur Óli was not prepared to enter into any further discussion at this point. Ordering his men to follow, he ushered the girls carefully aside and entered the house, the woman retreating before him. The search was soon in full swing, with the officers on the lookout for bloodstained or torn clothing, drugs, cash, a list of clients, anything that could be linked to the attack on Lína or give a clue as to its motive. The youngest girl was discovered asleep in her parents' bed. Her mother woke her and took her into another room. The woman did not seem unduly surprised by this invasion nor did she raise any objections; merely stood in silence with her daughters, watching a group of policemen turning her home upside down. The house was exceptionally neat and tidy, with clean laundry folded in all the drawers, everything in the kitchen put away, all the surfaces dusted. There were no signs of affluence: the ornaments on the tables in the sitting room were cheap, the three-piece suite shabby. If Thórarinn made any money from his drug-dealing it was certainly not evident in his home, and the only vehicle registered in his name was the delivery van.

'Do you remember what your husband was wearing last Monday?' asked Sigurdur Óli.

'Wearing?' echoed the woman. 'He always wears the same things.'

'Can you tell us what?'

The woman gave a detailed description that tallied with what Sigurdur Óli had seen. She wanted to know what Thórarinn had done.

'Where was he on Monday evening?' asked Sigurdur Óli, ignoring her question.

'He was here at home all evening,' the woman said without hesitation. 'He didn't go out on Monday evening,' she added, in case Sigurdur Óli had missed the fact.

'We have information that suggests otherwise,' he said. 'In fact he was spotted, so he can't have been here all evening. I saw him myself. If you want to carry on lying to us, you're welcome to, but you'll have to do so at the station. The girls can go to a babysitter in the meantime. If you can't find anyone yourself, we'll provide a childminder.'

The woman gaped at him.

'Or you can tell us what we need to know and then you can go back to bed,' he added.

When she looked at her three daughters the woman knew she had no alternative. The eldest had been having problems at school, not only with her lessons but in the playground, and was refusing to go swimming or do games.

'He never tells me anything,' she said. 'I don't know anything.'

'So he wasn't at home on Monday evening?'

She shook her head.

'Did he tell you to say that?'

After a second's hesitation, she nodded.

'Where is he now?'

'I don't know. What's he done? I haven't seen him since

he came home on Monday evening and I could hardly understand a word he was saying. He said he needed to get out of town for a while but would be back soon.'

'What did he mean, get out of town? Where was he going?'

'I don't know – we don't have a holiday cottage or anything like that.'

'Does he have any family outside Reykjavík?'

'No, I don't think so. Please, what's he done?'

The three girls had been listening open-mouthed to the conversation, their eyes darting from their mother to the detective. Sigurdur Óli indicated to the woman that it would be inappropriate for them to over-hear the rest and she reacted quickly, herding her daughters into the kitchen and telling the eldest to make them a chocolate-milk drink.

'We believe he attacked a woman here in the east of town,' Sigurdur Óli said when the woman returned from the kitchen. 'He was identified at the scene.'

'You mean he was seeing another woman?'

'No, I don't think so,' said Sigurdur Óli. 'We don't believe the attack was of that nature. Can you tell me who he was in contact with in the days before he disappeared?'

They had asked the telephone company for a log of all calls made to and from Thórarinn's home phone, and this might conceivably shed light on the events leading up to the attack on Lína, though Sigurdur Óli doubted it. From Kristján's description, he judged that Thórarinn would be too careful for that. It was telling that there was no mobile phone registered in his name, although Kristján confirmed that he used one.

'I know very little about what Toggi gets up to,' said his wife. 'He never says a word to me. All I know is that he drives a van and works very long hours, sometimes evenings and nights as well. And now he's vanished.'

'Has he been in touch since he disappeared?'

'No,' his wife answered firmly. 'Why did he attack the woman?'

'We don't know.'

'Was it the one in the news, the one who died?' she asked.

Sigurdur Óli nodded.

'And you think Thórarinn did it?'

'Were you aware that your husband is a debt collector?' asked Sigurdur Óli.

'A debt collector?' repeated his wife. 'No. What makes you think that? Why . . . I don't believe this!'

Although Thórarinn had a criminal record, it dated from before his eldest daughter was born, possibly from before he met his wife. He had twice been charged with assault and battery. For the first offence he had received a four-month suspended sentence for attacking a man outside a Reykjavík nightclub and inflicting a severe beating on him; for the second he had received a six-month sentence, of which he served only three, for assaulting someone at a restaurant in the neighbouring town of Hafnarfjördur. When the police had issued a wanted notice for Thórarinn that afternoon, they had stressed that he could be violent and dangerous.

If Kristján's account was anything to go by, Thórarinn could also be physically abusive towards his wife, though Sigurdur Óli could see no sign of it. He wondered if he should pursue it but decided not to.

'We're investigating his connection to the crime,' he said. 'You had better believe it. Is it you who keeps the house clean?'

'He likes to have everything just so,' the woman said automatically.

Finnur emerged from the kitchen and asked Sigurdur Óli to come with him. They went outside.

'We can't find a thing to link him to Lína,' Finnur said. 'Have you got anything out of her?'

'She's just learned that her husband may be a murderer. Perhaps she'll be able to tell us more once it's sunk in.'

'And your friends, what do they say?' asked Finnur.

'My friends? You're not going to start on that again?'

'Don't you want to know how the interviews went?'

'I really couldn't give a toss.'

Sigurdur Óli knew that Patrekur, Hermann and their respective wives had been brought in for questioning. Finnur had been in charge of the interviews and Sigurdur Óli would have obtained a transcript had he not been so busy trying to track down Thórarinn.

'Hermann showed me a picture of himself and claimed that Lína and Ebeneser had been blackmailing him. Of course, he didn't admit to having attacked Lína or to sending someone to find the photos. He was pretty pathetic in fact, and his wife was in tears throughout the interview. Patrekur was tougher, though. He denied everything.'

'What are you going to do with them?'

'I've put them under a travel ban. Patrekur admitted to having gone to see you, so it's on record – that you knew about the case but failed to report it. I'll be writing a report later and intend to send it to Internal Affairs. You can expect to hear from them.'

'Why are you doing this, Finnur?' asked Sigurdur Óli.

'I'm surprised you've got the nerve to continue with this case,' Finnur replied. 'You're far too closely involved, and if you don't see sense, I'll have to deal with the situation myself. I'm in charge of this inquiry; it's not your little game.'

'Are you sure you can afford to threaten me?' said Sigurdur Óli.

'Your position is not looking good, Siggi. You're compromising this inquiry by turning it into a private vendetta. I call the shots and you should do as I say.'

'Do you really think I can't be trusted? Is that what you're implying? You, of all people?'

'Yes, that's what I'm implying.'

Sigurdur Óli gave Finnur a steady look. He knew that Finnur was a good policeman but his manner had begun to smack of bullying and that would have to stop. There was no way Sigurdur Óli was going to put up with it, not from Finnur. From someone else maybe, but not Finnur.

'If you keep up this bullshit,' he murmured, leaning towards Finnur, 'I'll talk. Think about it. For your own sake, you'd better leave me alone.'

'What are you talking about?'

'You know a boy called Pétur, don't you?'

Finnur stared at him without answering, his expression grave.

'You know him – one of those lowlifes, never out of trouble,' Sigurdur Óli said. 'A brain-dead thug. Well, he was nearly killed the other day, just down the road from the station. Ring any bells?'

Finnur continued to watch Sigurdur Óli in silence.

'If you think you're the only straight cop around here,

you're deluding yourself. So you'd better drop your preaching and your threats, and just let us both get on with our jobs.'

Finnur's eyes were riveted on him, as if he was trying to grasp what Sigurdur Óli was insinuating. Whether he understood or not, he swore violently at Sigurdur Óli before disappearing inside the house.

When Sigurdur Óli went into the station late that afternoon he found a package waiting for him. The man who had brought it in had refused to leave his name but his description matched that of Andrés, the drunk who had accosted him behind the station. The package was wrapped in a large crumpled plastic bag from a supermarket, but the object it contained was so small that at first he thought there was nothing in the bag, that it was just some stupid prank. Finally, after he had turned it inside out and shaken it vigorously, the contents fell out on the floor.

It was a rolled-up strip of eight-millimetre film. Sigurdur Óli placed the film on his desk and searched the bag again for a message or any more rolls of film, but there was nothing.

He picked up the film and, unrolling it, held it up to his desk lamp and tried unsuccessfully to make out what was on it. Then he sat, deep in thought, picturing Andrés as he had stood behind the station, trying to work out what it could be that he wanted.

He stared at the strip of film, unsure how he was supposed to react to this meagre offering in a dirty carrier bag. There could hardly be much to be gained from such a short piece of footage, and he had no idea why the film had been sent to his office.

It transpired later that the film was twelve seconds long.

22

Lína's colleagues at the accountancy firm where she had worked as a secretary expressed themselves shocked and horrified by her fate when Sigurdur Óli went to visit them at lunchtime on Saturday. He had intended to leave it until Monday but was told that most of the staff would be working through the weekend because the company could hardly cope with all the business flooding through its doors. No one he spoke to could begin to imagine why Lína had been attacked or who could have wished her harm. He had a chat with one of her fellow secretaries and some of the accountants she worked for, as well as sitting down in a small meeting room with the deputy director, Ísleifur, with whom Lína had worked most closely. He was in his early fifties, overweight and prosperous-looking in an expensive bespoke suit. The company's fortunes had been transformed by the economic boom and he put two mobile phones on the table in front of him, switched to silent mode, which took it in turn to vibrate during their conversation. Ísleifur glanced at the screens and dismissed the calls, answering only one, which presumably, to judge from the exchange that ensued, was from his wife. He told her gently that he was in a meeting and would call her back later; a line she seemed to have heard before.

He described Lína as an outstanding employee, a verdict that everyone would endorse. It was true: no one Sigurdur Óli spoke to had a bad word to say about her.

'I believe she was interested in becoming an accountant herself,' Ísleifur said. 'She had a good grasp of what the job entails, which is more than can be said of most,' he added smugly.

'Isn't it just a question of adding and subtracting?' Sigurdur Óli said.

Ísleifur laughed drily. 'That's what many people assume, but I assure you there's much more to it.'

'Did Lína do a lot of work for you?'

'I suppose you could say that. And she was a hard

worker too. We often have to work late and at weekends, as you can see, but she never failed to pull her weight.'

'What sort of business do you do here?' asked Sigurdur Óli. 'What kind of clients do you deal with?'

'The whole spectrum,' Ísleifur answered, picking up a vibrating phone, examining the screen and killing the call. 'Individuals and corporate, big business. We do the whole caboodle, from the simplest bookkeeping to the most complicated contracts.'

'Did Lína have a relationship with any of your clients?'

'How do you mean?'

'Can you name any clients that Lína dealt with directly?'

'Well, I don't know . . .'

One of the phones began to vibrate.

'. . . do you mean involved with personally or . . . ?'

He checked the number and cut the call again.

'Any sort of involvement – was she personally involved with any of the firm's clients?'

'Not that I'm aware of,' answered Ísleifur. 'Naturally you form more of a relationship with some clients than others, but as a rule it's the accountants who get to know the clients rather than the secretaries.'

'Do you know her husband, Ebeneser?'

'Yes, but not well. He's a guide or something, isn't he? I know he's organised corporate entertainment events for us in the highlands – barbecues on the Vatnajökull glacier, that sort of thing.'

'How was his relationship with Lína? Good? Bad? Do you know anything about that?'

Both phones started vibrating and Ísleifur picked one up, apologising.

'I should probably take this,' he said. 'The person Lína had most to do with was Kolfinna. She's a secretary as well. Perhaps you should talk to her.'

Kolfinna was as frantically busy as her boss. She sat at her computer, fielding phone calls and entering data into an Excel file. Sigurdur Óli asked if she had a few minutes to spare as he was investigating Sigurlína's death.

'God, yes,' Kolfinna said, 'I heard the police were here. Just a sec. Do you smoke?'

Sigurdur Óli shook his head.

'We'll take a cigarette break anyway,' she said, closing the file. Pulling open a drawer, she took out a packet of cigarettes and a lighter, then asked him to follow her. Then they were outside the back of the building, standing beside a tub half full of cigarette butts floating in dirty water. Kolfinna lit up and drew the smoke deep into her lungs.

'God, it's so terrible,' she said with a sigh. 'Those burglars must be complete psychos to attack someone like that.'

'You think it was a burglar?' said Sigurdur Óli, trying to find a place to stand where the smoke did not blow in his face.

'Sure, wasn't it? That's what I heard. Wasn't it something like that?'

'It's under investigation,' Sigurdur Óli answered curtly. He could not bear smokers and was delighted that there were plans to ban smoking in public spaces, even restaurants and pubs. They were welcome to kill themselves in private for all he cared.

'How was her relationship with Ebeneser?' he asked, coughing politely, but Kolfinna failed to take the hint.

'Her relationship? Fine, I think. It was a bit of a struggle though. They had massive debts – some sort of foreign currency loan, as well as loans on their car and the holiday cottage they're building. They didn't earn a huge amount but they wanted a share of the pie, you know? Didn't want to deny themselves anything, so they just took out more loans. Isn't that what everyone does nowadays?'

'You mentioned a holiday cottage?'

'Yes, in the south-west, at Grímsnes.'

'I gather Ebeneser organised tours for your company,' Sigurdur Óli said. 'Corporate entertainments.'

'Yes, he did two trips, I think. I didn't go along but Lína did, of course. It's supposed to be amazing – they're two- to three-day tours, as far as I can remember. You know, jeep tours of the glacier. All these guys own off-roaders: the smaller their dicks, the bigger their cars.' She flicked her cigarette into the mess of stubs. 'Or at least that's what Lína used to say.'

'Was she speaking from personal experience?' asked Sigurdur Óli.

Kolfinna fished another cigarette from the packet, determined to make the most of her break.

'Well, naturally, she had Ebbi.'

She emitted an abrupt, husky laugh and Sigurdur Óli smiled.

'Do you mean, had she been with any of those guys?' Kolfinna asked, returning to his question. 'She may well have done. Lína was the type, you know? She saw nothing wrong in sleeping around. Do the police know something? Was she involved with any of them?'

Her interest was genuine and her disappointment obvious when Sigurdur Óli claimed to have no information on that score. He asked if she could provide him with the names of clients who had participated in the glacier tours run by Ebeneser, and she said nothing could be easier, she had the lists on her computer. Although she was not aware that the couple had been in the sort of difficulties that might result in a visit from a debt collector, she reiterated that they owed a lot of money and pointed out that Lína had never been one to talk much about herself. They had got on well and worked together for several years but the truth was that Kolfinna knew very little about Lína's life.

'She was brilliant to work with,' she said, 'but she always kept you at a certain distance, you know? That's just how she was. It never bothered me though.'

'Did she ever give any indication of being frightened, or in danger, or mixed up in something she couldn't handle?' asked Sigurdur Óli.

'No,' replied Kolfinna. 'Everything was fine with Lína, as far as I know.'

She could only locate the list for one of the jeep trips on her computer, but printed it out, saying she would email him the other as soon as she found it. Sigurdur Óli glanced down the list but did not recognise any of the names.

Later that afternoon Elínborg rang to ask if he could help her out in the evening. Despite feeling that he had better things to do on a Saturday night, he let himself be persuaded. Elínborg was engaged in a tough case, working almost day and night on the Thingholt murder. She picked him up and they drove to meet a man called Valur, a uniquely irritating character who immediately succeeded in annoying Sigurdur Óli further.

'Have you heard anything from Erlendur?' asked

Sigurdur Óli once the visit was over and they were getting back into the car. He remembered the phone call from Eva Lind who had been asking after her father.

'Nothing at all,' Elínborg answered wearily. 'Didn't he say he was heading east for a few days?'

'How long ago was that?'

'A week, probably.'

'How long a holiday was he planning to take?'

'I don't know.'

'What was he doing out east anyway?'

'Visiting where he grew up.'

'Any word from that woman he's seeing?'

'Valgerdur? No. Perhaps I should ring her, find out if he's been in touch with her.'

23

Sigurdur Óli was lurking in his car outside the block of flats for the second Sunday in a row, keeping an eye on the newspaper that protruded from one of the postboxes in the lobby. He had taken up position early that morning, shortly after the paper was delivered, and watched the comings and goings, keeping himself warm with the car heater. He had brought a Thermos of coffee and something to read – the papers and a handful of new holiday brochures for Florida. If anything, there were even fewer people about than the previous Sunday. No sign of the girl who had staggered up the stairs, or that waster who called himself a composer. Time crawled by. Sigurdur Óli read every word of the papers and pored avidly over the sunny images in the Florida brochures. He had switched on the radio but could find nothing to his taste, despite flicking from talk shows to music stations and back again. Finally he found a station playing classic rock and settled on that.

An elderly man walked into the block carrying a bag from a nearby bakery. He did not give the paper so much as a glance, but at the sight of the man's bag Sigurdur Óli was assailed by hunger pangs. The bakery was only just round the corner; he would be able to see the sign if he reversed a few metres. He considered his situation. He could almost smell the aroma of fresh baking, so strong was his desire, if only for a scone, but on the other hand he might miss the thief. I wonder if there's a queue? he thought, craning his neck in the direction of the bakery.

Little of interest happened until just before midday when an elderly woman came down into the lobby and, after peering out through the glass door, turned to the postboxes, seized the newspaper without hesitation and pushed open the door to the stairwell again. Sigurdur Óli, who had been struggling with the crossword while trying to stave off his hunger, threw it down, leapt out of the car and charged inside, jamming his foot between the inner door and the frame, and caught the woman red-handed as she began to climb the stairs.

'What are you doing with that?' he demanded sharply, taking hold of the woman's arm.

She stared at him in terror.

'Leave me alone,' she said. 'You can't have my paper!' She began to cry 'Thief!' in a weak voice.

'I'm no thief,' said Sigurdur Óli, 'I'm from the police. Why are you stealing Gudmunda's paper?'

The woman's expression relaxed.

'Are you Gagga's son?' she asked.

'Yes,' Sigurdur Óli replied, taken aback.

'I'm Gudmunda, dear.'

Sigurdur Óli released her arm.

'Didn't Gagga talk to you?' he said. 'I was going to keep an eye on the paper for you.'

'Oh, heavens, yes, but I did so want to read it.'

'But you can't read the paper if I'm supposed to be watching it.'

'No,' said Gudmunda, continuing on her way up the stairs, unperturbed, 'that's the snag. Do give my regards to your mother, dear.'

Shortly afterwards, as he prepared to tuck into the lunch she had cooked for him, Sigurdur Óli reported this exchange to Gagga, adding that he had no intention of lying in wait for the paper thief again. There would be no more of that nonsense.

Gagga seemed to derive some amusement from her

son's displeasure. She stood behind him, struggling to suppress her laughter, then offered him a second helping and expressed surprise at his appetite.

When she had poured the coffee, she asked if his father had spoken to him. Sigurdur Óli described how he had turned up at the station with the news about his prostate.

'I expect the poor man was a bit anxious?' said his mother, sitting down with him at the kitchen table. 'He sounded pretty subdued when he rang to tell me.'

'Not that I noticed,' said Sigurdur Óli. 'I'm going to look in on him later as the operation's tomorrow. He said I should get myself checked out – that I was in a risk group.'

'Then you should do it,' Gagga said. 'He mentioned it to me too. Don't put it off.'

Sigurdur Óli sipped his coffee, thinking about his father and mother and their relationship back in the days when they were still together. He remembered overhearing a conversation about himself; that for his sake they could not get divorced. That had been his father. Whereas Gagga had said she could look after him perfectly well on her own. His father had done what he could to avoid a divorce but it was no good. It had felt inevitable when he moved out, taking a couple of suitcases stuffed full of clothes, an old trunk that had been in his family a long time, a table that was his, pictures, books and various other bits and pieces, all of which disappeared into a small van parked outside the block of flats. Gagga had been out that day. Sigurdur Óli and his father had said their goodbyes in the car park, though his father had pointed out that it was not really goodbye as they would still see a lot of each other.

'Perhaps it's for the best,' he had said. 'Not that I really understand what's going on.' The words had stuck in Sigurdur Óli's mind.

When he had asked his mother why, he had received no satisfactory answer. 'It's been over between us for a long time,' she had said, then told him not to pester her any more with such questions.

As long as he could remember, his father had bent over backwards to please her, until by the end he was completely under her thumb. She used to humiliate him in front of Sigurdur Óli who would wait in vain for his father to react, to do something, say something, lose his temper, shout at her, tell her in no uncertain terms what an unjust, domineering bitch she was. But he never said a word, never showed any backbone, just let her walk all over him. Sigurdur Óli knew that his mother was not blameless – she was born demanding and inflexible – but he also started to see his father in a new light and began to blame him, mentally accusing him of spinelessness and of failing to keep their family together. He trained himself to be indifferent to him.

He would never allow himself to be pushed about in a relationship like that; he would do his damnedest to avoid turning out like his father.

'What did you see in him when you first met?' he asked his mother, finishing his coffee.

'Your dad?' Gagga said, offering him more. He refused it and rose. He needed to head over to the hospital and wanted to call at the station afterwards.

'What was it?' he asked again.

Gagga regarded him thoughtfully.

'I thought he had more guts, but your dad never had any guts.'

'He was always trying to please you,' Sigurdur Óli pointed out. 'I remember it distinctly. And I remember how often you were nasty to him.'

'What's this about? Why are you raking this up now? Is it because of what's happened between you and Bergthóra? Are you having regrets?'

'Perhaps I sided with you too much. Perhaps I should have stuck up for him more.'

'You shouldn't have had to make the choice. The marriage was over. It had nothing to do with you.'

'No,' said Sigurdur Óli. 'It had nothing to do with me.

That's what you've always said. Do you think that was fair?'

'Well, what do you want me to say? Anyway, why are you brooding over this now? It was all such a long time ago.'

'Yeah, right,' said Sigurdur Óli. 'Whatever, I've got to go.'

'I had nothing against Bergthóra.'

'That's not what she says.'

'Never mind what she says; it doesn't make her right.'

'I've got to go.'

'Give my regards to your father,' said Gagga, clearing away the cups.

His father was asleep when Sigurdur Óli went to visit him in the urology ward at the National Hospital on Hringbraut, near the old town centre. Unwilling to wake him, he sat down to wait. His father had a room to himself and lay there, wrapped in silence under the white bedclothes.

As Sigurdur Óli waited for him to stir, he thought about Bergthóra, wondering if he had been too inflexible and whether it was too late to rescue the situation.

24

By Monday afternoon the search for Thórarinn had still not yielded any result. The police had interviewed a large number of people who either knew him or had some connection to him, including other van drivers, relatives and regular customers, but no one had heard from him or knew where he was hiding, though various theories were put forward. The police followed up some, though others were deemed too far-fetched to be worth investigating. Wanted notices had been put out for him in the media using a recent photo supplied by his wife. The police announcement warned that he was wanted in connection with the murder of Sigurlína Thorgrímsdóttir and might be dangerous. They did not have to wait long before news of sightings started to flood in, not only from Reykjavík but from other parts of the country, even from as far away as the East Fjords.

While this was going on, Sigurdur Óli spent the best part of the day dealing with another, more puzzling matter that required him, among other things, to find a lip-reader. He finally managed to arrange a meeting with one towards evening. At Elínborg's suggestion, he had called the Society for the Deaf and the woman in the office there had proved very helpful, providing further contacts until he was eventually put in touch with a woman reputed to be one of the top lip-readers in the country. He emailed her and they arranged to meet at Hverfisgata at six.

Sigurdur Óli wanted her to watch the film clip that had been sent to him wrapped in a dirty carrier bag.

He had handed the film over to the experts who examined it, transferred it to DVD and did their best to clean it up and sharpen the images in the limited time available. The film turned out to be an eight-millimetre Kodak type, which the firm had stopped making in 1990. From the contents, it appeared to be an amateur effort intended for home viewing, though it was very hard to be certain, or indeed to guess, what country it had been filmed in. It might be Icelandic but could equally well be foreign, as one of the technicians put it bluntly when he rang Sigurdur Óli with the results of his analysis.

For a variety of reasons it was difficult to guess where or when the film had been recorded. For one thing, it had a very narrow field of view, as the technician explained, referring to the fact that not much of the surroundings were visible, apart from a glimpse of a piece of furniture that might have been a bed or a couch. In this respect the material offered very little to go on. It could have been recent, meaning shortly before 1990, but then again it could date from the period when this type of Kodak film was most commonly used, around half a century ago. There was no way of telling. Moreover, the clip was extremely short – sixteen frames a second, 192 frames in all – and the view was the same in all of them, same angle, same movement. It was clearly shot indoors, in a house or flat where people were living at the time, and the presence of a bed or couch would suggest a bedroom. But in the absence of any view from a window there was no way to locate the house: the lens was pointed downwards throughout the clip.

The clip was also silent and yet words were clearly being spoken. The technicians could not distinguish them, however, nor could Sigurdur Óli work out what was being said, and it was then that the idea of a lip-reader came to him.

He would not have been interested in the film at all, but for what those twelve brief seconds failed to show. What caught Sigurdur Óli's attention was what was hinted at. For the clip, however uninformative, told a very specific story; it was a silent witness to the misfortune and suffering endured by some of the most helpless members of society, giving a depressing promise of more and worse events than those it revealed. There was no reason to discount these fears, bearing in mind the manner in which the film clip had come into police hands. Experience suggested otherwise. Sigurdur Óli could not shake off the feeling that something much more harrowing would be revealed if the rest of the film could be found.

It was nearly six when he was called down to the lobby with the news that two women had arrived to see him. One, the lip-reader, was called Elísabet; the other, Hildur, was a sign-language interpreter. They exchanged introductions, then went up to Sigurdur Óli's office where he had positioned a trolley carrying a DVD player and flat-screen TV. They took their seats on three chairs that he had arranged in front of the TV and he explained the situation in more detail for the lip-reader. The police had been sent a clip from a film but did not know exactly who it belonged to. It showed a possible crime, which seemed to have taken place at some indeterminate time in the past, and she might be able to help them by providing the missing soundtrack to the images. The sign-language interpreter conveyed his words as he was speaking. The two women could not have been more different: the lip-reader was around thirty, slender and petite, almost bird-like – she looked to Sigurdur Óli as fragile as a china doll – whereas the interpreter was a tall, immensely fat woman in her late fifties, with a booming voice. She had perfect hearing and it was fairly evident that she had never been mute, but what mattered was the unusual speed at which she was able to sign; nothing threw her, and she interpreted the lip-reader's words clearly and concisely.

They watched the film. Then watched it again. Then a third time. What they saw was a boy of not much older than ten, who was trying to get away from the unseen person holding the camera. The boy was naked and fell off what appeared to be a couch or bed, lay on the floor for a moment, then crawled away from the camera, spider-like, looking directly either at the camera or at the person holding it, his lips moving. His grotesque efforts to escape were reminiscent of an animal in a trap. It was obvious that he was terrified of the cameraman and he appeared to be begging for mercy. The clip broke off as suddenly as it had begun, during a scene of help-lessness and degradation. The suffering in the boy's face

distressed the two women as much as it had Sigurdur
Óli when he first watched it. They both turned to him.

'Who is it?' Hildur asked. 'Who's the boy?'

'We don't know,' Sigurdur Óli answered, and Hildur
interpreted his words. 'We're trying to find out.'

'What happened to him?' asked Elísabet.

'We don't know that either,' Sigurdur Óli said. 'This is
all we were sent. Can you tell us what the boy's saying?'

'It's very hard to tell,' Elísabet said via the interpreter.
'I'll need to see it again.'

'You can watch it as many times as you like,' said
Sigurdur Óli.

'Do you know who filmed this?'

'No.'

'It's only short. Do you have any idea if there's more?'

'No. This is all we have.'

'What year was it filmed?'

'We don't know but it's probably old. We don't have
much to go on because there's nothing in the frame that
can be dated with any accuracy, and although we know
that this type of film was in use up until 1990, there's
nothing to say that it wasn't used more recently. The
only thing we could conceivably go by is the boy's
haircut.'

Sigurdur Óli told the women that he had had three
stills made and taken them to several barbershops with

long-serving staff. When he showed them the pictures, all had made the same comment: the boy had the sort of cut that had been in fashion until about 1970, a short back and sides, with a long fringe.

'So the film was made in the 1960s?' Elísabet asked.

'Possibly,' replied Sigurdur Óli.

'Weren't lots of boys given a short back and sides in those days before being sent to work on farms over the summer?' said Hildur. 'I have two younger brothers who were born around 1960 and they were always trimmed like that before going to the country.'

'You mean this might have been filmed somewhere in the countryside?' said Sigurdur Óli.

Hildur shrugged.

'It's very difficult to see what he's saying,' she interpreted Elísabet's comment, 'but I think it could be Icelandic.'

They watched the clip again and Elísabet concentrated hard on the boy's lip movements. The clip passed before their eyes again and again, ten times, twenty times, while Elísabet focused wholly on the boy's mouth. Sigurdur Óli had tried himself to guess what the boy was saying, without success. He would have liked it to be a name, for it to transpire that he was addressing the cameraman by name, but knew it was unlikely to be that simple.

'. . . *stop it* . . .'

The words were uttered by Elísabet, her eyes still fixed on the screen.

They emerged without emphasis, monotonous, robotic and a little distorted, her voice as high and clear as a child's.

Hildur glanced from her to Sigurdur Óli.

'I've never heard her speak before,' she whispered in amazement.

'. . . *stop it* . . .' said Elísabet again. Then repeated: '*Stop it.*'

It was late in the evening before Elísabet finally felt fairly confident that she had made out the boy's pleading words.

Stop it.

Stop it.

No more, please . . .

Please, stop it.

25

Earlier that day, while driving between barbershops with the film stills, Sigurdur Óli had made an effort to track down Andrés. He discovered that Andrés was registered at the same block of flats as the previous winter, so he drove there and banged on his door till the stairwell echoed. No one answered. He was considering forcing an entry when the door of the neighbouring flat opened and a woman of about seventy came out.

'Are you the one making all this noise?' She glared at Sigurdur Óli.

'Do you know anything about Andrés's whereabouts?

Have you seen him recently?' asked Sigurdur Óli, ignoring the woman's angry expression.

'Andrés? What do you want with him?'

'Nothing. I just need to talk to him,' said Sigurdur Óli, suppressing the impulse to tell the woman that it was none of her business.

'Andrés hasn't been around for ages,' the woman said, giving Sigurdur Óli an appraising look.

'He's a bit of a tramp, isn't he? An alcoholic?' said Sigurdur Óli.

'So what if he is?' the woman replied, affronted. 'He's never bothered me. He'd do anything for you, he's never noisy, never makes demands on other people. What does it matter if he has the odd drink?'

'When did you last see him?'

'And who are you, might I ask?'

'I'm from the police,' Sigurdur Óli answered, 'and I need to talk to him. It's nothing serious. I just need to see him. Can you tell me where he is?'

'I haven't a clue,' the woman said, regarding Sigurdur Óli suspiciously.

'Is it possible that he's in his flat? In some sort of state which means he can't hear me?'

Her eyes flitted to Andrés's door.

'You haven't seen him for a long time,' Sigurdur Óli

said. 'Has it occurred to you that he might be lying helpless in his flat?'

'He gave me a key,' the woman said.

'You have a key to his flat?'

'He said he was always losing his, so he asked me to keep a spare. He's needed it sometimes too. Last time I saw Andrés was when he came to fetch the spare key.'

'What sort of state was he in?'

'Pretty rough, poor thing,' admitted the woman. 'He seemed very worked up, I don't know why, but he told me not to worry about him.'

'When was this?'

'Late in the summer.'

'Late summer!'

'It's perfectly normal for me not to see him for a while.' The woman became defensive, as if she were somehow responsible for her neighbour.

'Shouldn't we open the door and check on him?' suggested Sigurdur Óli.

The woman dithered. According to the smart copper plaque on her door, her name was Margrét Eymunds.

'I can't imagine that he would be in there,' she said.

'Wouldn't it be better to make sure?'

'I suppose it wouldn't do any harm,' she said. 'Of course

there's a danger the poor man could have hurt himself. But you're not to touch anything. I doubt he'd want the police snooping around his flat.'

She went and fetched the spare key, then unlocked Andrés's door. As they stepped inside they were met by a shocking stench of filth and rotting food. Sigurdur Óli had been in this flat before and knew what to expect: the squalid evidence of an alcoholic existence. The flat was not large, so it did not take them long to assure themselves that Andrés was not lying there at death's door or worse; in fact he was not there at all. Sigurdur Óli switched on the lights, revealing a scene of slovenly disorder.

He cast his mind back to the last time he had been there and what had passed between Andrés and Erlendur and himself. Andrés's behaviour had been bizarre and he seemed to have been on a long bender. He had dropped hints that a dangerous man was living in the neighbourhood, a man he knew of old, who, from what they could gather, was a paedophile. But Andrés had obstinately refused to give them any more information about the man in question. They had found out by other means that he had been Andrés's stepfather, a man called Rögnvaldur, who had used a number of aliases, including Gestur. After an initial sighting, he had given them the slip, however, and it did not help that all they had was Andrés's limited and incoherent testimony, which they considered far from reliable. Andrés claimed that the man had ruined his life, that Rögnvaldur was a nightmare he could never wake from, and implied that he had committed a murder, but would not say a word more. Erlendur had taken this to mean that Andrés himself had been the victim of this 'murder', strange as it might seem; that he was referring obliquely to the suffering that Rögnvaldur had inflicted on him, which had blighted the rest of his life.

Sigurdur Óli could find no indications in the flat as to Andrés's current whereabouts.

But there was one detail that took him by surprise amid the rubbish and neglect: Andrés had apparently been engaged in cutting up pieces of leather in the kitchen. Scraps of it littered the kitchen table and the floor around it, and a strong needle and thick thread lay on the table. Sigurdur Óli spent some time poring over the offcuts of leather, trying to deduce what Andrés had been up to. The woman tried to insist on his leaving, since Andrés was not at home, but he ignored her, stubbornly continuing to inspect the bits of leather, trying to assemble them mentally. There was some logic to them that escaped him at first, so he began to piece them together on the table in an attempt to work out what the man had been cutting out. Soon he stood back to find himself confronted by a square, with sides about forty centimetres long, out of which had been cut an oval piece that tapered towards the bottom.

Sigurdur Óli stared down at the table; at the needle and thread. There were a few small scraps of leather remaining, which he tried to fit into the picture. It was not very difficult and once they were in place he was met by the image of a face, with eyes and a mouth. It seemed, to Sigurdur Óli's puzzlement, that Andrés had been making a mask of some kind.

Back at the station, Sigurdur Óli dug out Andrés's police file. He had done time for theft and violence, though only for short stints. He was never a career criminal. Essentially, he was an alcoholic and drug addict who financed his habit largely by burglary and theft, and was sometimes forced to act in self-defence, or so he claimed in his statements to the police. People had often attacked Andrés unprovoked, in an attempt to take what was lawfully his, but he was quoted as saying that he wasn't going to let any bloody bastard walk all over him.

Sigurdur Óli asked around among the experienced officers in an attempt to find out the latest news of Andrés. It turned out that he was pretty much out of sight, out of mind. Most people had forgotten all about Andrés, though one officer, at Sigurdur Óli's insistence, rang a retired colleague and managed to obtain some further information. The man remembered Andrés clearly and mentioned that his chief friend and companion in the old days when both were living as down-and-outs in Reykjavík was a man called Hólmgeir, known as Geiri. Although straight nowadays and sober, with a regular job, he had spent many years in the gutter, well known to the police as a drunk and minor offender.

These days, Geiri was employed as a security guard on night shifts at a large furniture warehouse, part of an international chain, and was at work when Sigurdur Óli wanted to talk to him, so he decided to drop by and see him on his way home that evening. He had rung ahead and Hólmgeir, forewarned, let him in the back entrance. He was dressed in uniform, with a walkie-talkie fixed to one shoulder in a leather holster, a torch and other gear. There's nothing like a convert, thought Sigurdur Óli, remembering that a mere decade earlier, Geiri had been on the streets.

Sigurdur Óli had already explained his business and asked him to think about it, so he weighed straight in, asking if Hólmgeir had any idea where Andrés might be living.

'I've been racking my brains but I'm afraid I can't be much help,' said Hólmgeir, a fat man nearing fifty, who appeared to take pleasure in his uniform. His face bore evidence of past hardship and his voice was hoarse, as if from chronic catarrh.

'When did you last see him?'

'A lifetime ago,' said Hólmgeir. 'Maybe you haven't heard but I was in a hell of a state back then, pretty down on my luck, living rough, sleeping in dumps. I'd been a drunk for years and that's how I met Andrés. He was in an even worse state than me.'

'What kind of man was he?' asked Sigurdur Óli.

'Wouldn't hurt a fly,' Hólmgeir answered promptly. 'Always a bit of a loner; just wanted to be left in peace. I don't know how to describe it: he was very touchy about what people said or did to him. He could be totally impossible. I often had to help him out when he was being hassled. Why are the police looking for him? Can you say?'

'We need to talk to him about an old case,' Sigurdur Óli replied, avoiding going into any detail. 'Nothing particularly urgent but we do need to track him down.'

He had been convinced from the outset that the boy in the film was Andrés himself and that by sending him the clip Andrés wanted to draw the attention of the police, or more precisely of Sigurdur Óli whom he had met before, to a crime or crimes that had been committed against him in his youth. The time frame fitted. The boy in the film was about ten years old. Andrés was forty-five, born in 1960, according to his police file. His statement about Rögnvaldur, his stepfather, had alleged that he was a paedophile, and Rögnvaldur had lived with Andrés's mother during the period when it seemed likely that the film had been made.

'Did he ever talk about how he ended up on the streets?' asked Sigurdur Óli.

'He never opened up about himself,' Hólmgeir replied. 'I sometimes used to ask him but he never answered. Some of the others were forever whining and moaning and blaming everyone but themselves. Pointing the finger, making accusations, that sort of crap. Including me, I might add. But I never heard him complain about anything. He just accepted his lot. But . . .'

'Yes?'

'But you got the feeling that he was angry; I never knew what about exactly. Although we hung around together, I never really got to know him. Andrés was very secretive. He was filled with loathing and rage, a seething rage he bottled up, which could boil over when you least expected it. But a lot of this is very hazy, you understand; I'm afraid there are long gaps in my memory.'

'Do you know what he did before – what job, if he had one?'

'Yes, he once tried to train as an upholsterer,' Hólmgeir said. 'He'd meant to learn the trade once, when he was young.'

'Upholsterer?' repeated Sigurdur Óli, picturing the scraps of leather at Andrés's flat.

'But it all came to nothing, of course.'

'You don't know if he's been doing that sort of work recently?'

'I don't.'

'And you have no idea where he might be living?'

'No.'

'Did he have any friends he could turn to?' asked Sigurdur Óli. 'Can you suggest anyone he might still be in touch with?'

'No, he never went anywhere and no one ever visited him. There was a time he used to hang about the bus station at Hlemmur. It was warm and we were left in peace as long as we didn't make any trouble. But he didn't have any friends. Anyway, those friendships didn't usually last long because people often wouldn't survive the winter.'

'No family?'

Hólmgeir thought.

'He sometimes talked about his mother but I gathered that she had died long ago.'

'What did he say about her?'

'He didn't have a good word to say about her.'

'Why was that?'

'I don't remember exactly. I have a feeling it was to do with some people he'd been staying with in the country-side.'

'Do you remember who they were?'

'No, but Andrés spoke well of them. I think he'd wanted to stay there instead of coming to live in town. He said it was the only time in his life he'd been happy.'

26

Sigurdur Óli got home around midnight and collapsed on the sofa in front of the TV. He turned on an American comedy but soon lost interest and channel-surfed until he found a live broadcast of an American football game. But he could not concentrate on that either. His mind kept drifting to his mother and father and to Bergthóra and their relationship, and how it had all come off the rails without his making any real effort to save it. He had just let things run their course until they had gone irretrievably wrong and there was no turning back. Perhaps it was his obstinacy and indifference that had caused everything to break down.

His thoughts moved on to Patrekur, from whom he had heard nothing since he was called in for questioning, and to Finnur, who had threatened to throw the book at him. This was unlike Finnur. He was good at what he did and it was out of character for him to act precipitately, but then of course Patrekur and Súsanna were not friends of his. Sigurdur Óli had nothing against Finnur. He was a family man, meticulous in his private and professional lives. His three daughters had been born at two-year intervals and all had birthdays in the same month. His wife was a part-time sixth-form teacher. He was conscientious almost to the point of pedantry, concerned that all his dealings should be above board, both with his colleagues and in his capacity generally as a police officer. So it was no surprise that he should take exception when Sigurdur Óli failed to take himself off the case, citing a conflict of interest. But Finnur had his foibles too, as Sigurdur Óli had reminded him. He had managed to pacify him for now but how long that would last he could not say. Sigurdur Óli could see nothing improper in continuing to work on the investigation despite his friend's connection to the case. He had full confidence in his own judgement, and anyway Iceland was a small country; links to friends, acquaintances or family were inevitable. All that mattered was that they were handled in an honest, professional manner.

The game ended and as Sigurdur Óli changed channels he thought about the film clip and the boy's distressing pleas for mercy. He recalled the time he and Erlendur had visited Andrés shortly after New Year. Andrés, stinking and repulsive, had clearly been drinking for a long time. He had suddenly started referring to himself as *little Andy*, which Erlendur took to be a childhood nickname. So could it be little Andy on the clip? And where was the rest of the film? Were there others? Just what had little Andy been forced to endure at the hands of his stepfather? And where was this stepfather today? Rögnvaldur. Sigurdur Óli had checked the police records but found nobody by that name who could have been Andrés's stepfather.

If Andrés had looked terrible back in January when they had confronted him in his lair, he seemed in an even worse condition now, in the autumn. The wraith-like figure who had accosted Sigurdur Óli behind the police station had been a shadow of his former self: his haggard, grey face unshaven, a disgusting stench rising from his filthy clothes, his back hunched. A bundle of nerves. What had happened? Where had Andrés been hiding?

Surely the boy in the film must be Andrés?

Sigurdur Óli remembered how he had been at that age. His parents had recently divorced and he had been living with his mother but would spend some weekends with his father, accompanying him to work at times, as he seemed to work late seven days a week. Sigurdur Óli had learned a little about plumbing and discovered that his father had a nickname among his fellow tradesmen that puzzled him at first. He had gone with his father to a cafeteria one lunchtime; it was midweek but he had a day off school because it was Ash Wednesday, so he went with his father, who always ate lunch at the same place. The cafeteria was on Ármúli, somewhere tradesmen and labourers gathered to enjoy cheap, unpretentious platefuls of meatballs or roast lamb, shovelling down their food, smoking and swapping gossip before returning to work. It took no more than twenty minutes, half an hour at most, and then they were gone.

He was standing by a table, waiting while his father queued for food, when a man hurrying out bumped into him, almost knocking Sigurdur Óli over.

'Sorry, son,' the man said, catching him before he could fall. 'But what the hell are you doing getting in the way like that?'

He spoke roughly, as if the boy had no right to get under the feet of his elders and betters. Perhaps he was curious about what a youngster like him was doing in a workers' canteen.

'I'm with him,' explained Sigurdur Óli timidly, pointing

to his father who had just turned round and smiled at him.

'Oh, Permaflush, eh?' said the man, nodding to his father and patting the boy on the head before going on his way.

It was the smirk, the tone of mockery, the lack of respect that winded Sigurdur Óli. He had never before had any cause to assess his father's position in society and it took him some time to grasp that the man had been referring to his father with this peculiar name, and that it was intended to belittle him.

He never mentioned the incident to his father. Later he discovered what Permaflush meant but could not work out why he had acquired this nickname. He had assumed that his father was like any other tradesman and it upset him to find out that he bore such a humiliating moniker. In some way that Sigurdur Óli could not fully understand it diminished him. Did his father cut a ridiculous figure in the eyes of others? Was he seen as a failure? Was it because his father preferred to work alone, had no interest in joining a firm, had few friends and tended to be unsociable and eccentric? He was the first to admit that he did not particularly enjoy company.

Earlier that day Sigurdur Óli had gone to the hospital and sat by his father's bed, waiting for him to come round from his operation. He had been dwelling on the time he heard the nickname. Years later he understood more clearly what had happened, the emotions he had felt. It was that he had suddenly been put in the uncomfortable position of feeling sorry for his father, of pitying him, defending him even.

His father stirred and opened his eyes. They had informed Sigurdur Óli that the operation had gone well, the prostate had been removed and they had found no sign that the cancer had spread; it appeared to have been restricted to the gland itself, and his father was expected to make a quick recovery.

'How do you feel?' he asked, once his father had woken up.

'All right,' he answered. 'A bit groggy.'

'You look fine,' said Sigurdur Óli. 'You just need a proper rest.'

'Thank you for looking in on me, Siggi,' his father said. 'There was no need. You shouldn't be wasting your time on an old codger like me.'

'I was thinking about you and Mum.'

'Were you?'

'Wondering why you two ever got together when you're so different.'

'You're right, we are, we're poles apart.' The words emerged with an effort. 'That was obvious from the off but it wasn't a problem until later. She changed when she started working – when she got the accountancy job, I mean. So you find the whole thing a mystery do you? That she got together with a plumber like me?'

'I don't know,' said Sigurdur Óli. 'I suppose it seems a bit unlike her. When you say later, do you mean after I arrived on the scene?'

'It had nothing to do with you, Siggi. Your mother's just a piece of work.'

They were both silent and eventually his father drifted off to sleep again. Sigurdur Óli remained sitting beside him for a while.

Sigurdur Óli stood up and switched off the TV. He glanced at his watch; it was probably too late to call but he wanted to hear the sound of her voice. He had been thinking about it all day. He picked up the receiver and weighed it in his hand, hesitating, then dialled her number. She answered on the third ring.

'Am I calling too late?' he asked.

'No . . . it's OK,' said Bergthóra. 'I wasn't asleep. Is everything all right? Why are you ringing so late?' She sounded concerned but excited too, almost breathless.

'I just wanted a chat, to tell you about the old man. He's in hospital.'

He told Bergthóra about his father's illness, how the

216

operation had gone well and that he would be discharged in a few days. And how he had visited him twice and intended to look in on him regularly while he was recuperating.

'Not that he'll let anyone do anything for him.'

'You've never been very close,' said Bergthóra, who had not known her former father-in-law well.

'No,' admitted Sigurdur Óli. 'Things just turned out that way, I don't really know why. Look, I was wondering if we could see each other again? Maybe at your place. Do something fun.'

Bergthóra was silent. He heard a noise, a muffled voice.

'Is there somebody with you?' he asked.

She did not answer.

'Bergthóra?'

'Sorry,' she said. 'I dropped the phone.'

'Who's that with you?'

'Maybe we should talk another time,' she said. 'This isn't really a good moment.'

'Bergthóra . . . ?'

'Let's talk another time,' she said. 'I'll call you.'

She hung up. Sigurdur Óli stared at the phone. Inexplicably, it had never occurred to him that Bergthóra would go in search of pastures new. He had been open to the idea himself but was completely thrown by the fact that Bergthóra had beaten him to it.

'Fuck!' he heard himself whisper furiously.

He should never have rung.

What was she doing with someone else?

'Fuck,' he whispered again, putting down the phone.

27

They did not think it necessary to take Kristján into custody, as the accomplice, if accomplice was the right word, of Thórarinn, the debt collector and drug dealer. All the evidence suggested that Thórarinn was the man who had attacked and killed Lína. Kristján was no longer employed by the DIY store; he had gone back to his old work-shy ways and was easily tracked down at the pub where Sigurdur Óli had gone in search of him before. He had downed a few pints by the time Sigurdur Óli arrived and waved from his seat in the corner, looking for all the world as if they were old friends.

'They told me at Bíkó that you'd quit,' Sigurdur Óli said, joining him.

It was shortly after midday and Kristján was alone at the table, a half-empty beer glass, a packet of cigarettes and a disposable lighter in front of him. He was in no better or worse shape than the last time they had met and claimed, with obvious relief, not to have heard from Thórarinn. He was evidently hoping that the police would arrest Thórarinn as quickly as possible and put him away for life.

'He's no friend of mine,' Kristján declared, 'if that's what you think.'

He was almost the only customer in the pub and was enjoying life, at peace with the world after receiving his wages for the few days he had worked. There had been occasions in the past few years when he had been so hard up that he had gone hungry.

'No, I can imagine,' said Sigurdur Óli. 'I doubt he's pleasant company. I saw his wife but she didn't know where he could be hiding.'

'What? Are you telling me that you lot haven't managed to find Toggi yet?'

'No, he's vanished into thin air. It's just a question now of how long he'll be able to hold out. People usually admit defeat after a few days. Have you got any idea where he could be?'

'Not a clue. Why don't you relax and have a beer. Cigarette?'

Kristján pushed the packet towards him, much cockier now that he was on his home turf, the beer providing Dutch courage. Sigurdur Óli studied him in silence, hardly recognising him as the same person. Could he stomach any more of this sort of humiliation? If there was one thing that deeply pissed him off about his job it was having to be matey with little jerks like Kristján, having to suck up to people he despised and stoop to their level, even pretend to be one of them, try to put himself in their shoes. His colleague Erlendur found it easy because he understood these losers, and Elínborg could call on some sort of feminine intuition when forced to consort with criminal lowlifes. But the way Sigurdur Óli saw it, there was an unbridgeable gulf between him and a delinquent like Kristján. They had nothing in common, never would have, and would never exist on any sort of level playing field; one a law-abiding member of society, the other a repeat offender. From Sigurdur Óli's point of view, the little shit had forfeited the right to stand up and be counted, to be listened to or treated as a member of society. But there were times, like now, when Sigurdur Óli had to put on a show of caring about what one of these deadbeats thought, about his opinions, about how his tiny mind worked. He had decided to ingratiate himself with Kristján in the hope of gleaning some more information.

'No, thanks, I don't smoke,' he said, forcing a smile. 'It's absolutely vital that we find him as soon as possible. If you have the faintest idea where Toggi could be or who he might be in touch with, we'd be extremely grateful.'

Kristján was instantly wary. The detective's manner was nothing like before and he was unsure how to react.

'I don't know a thing,' he objected.

'Who are his mates? Who does he hang out with? We've got nothing on him. He's not had any brush with the law recently, so we have to put our trust in people like you, you see?'

'Yes, but like I said –'

'One name, that's all. Someone he's mentioned in your hearing. It might only have been once.'

Kristján studied him, then drained his glass and held it out.

'You can get me a refill, mate,' said the little runt. 'Then come and park yourself here for a nice cosy chat. Who knows, something might come back to me.'

Three pints and a period of interminable boredom later, Sigurdur Óli was driving east along the Miklabraut dual carriageway, searching for a mechanic's specialising in motorbikes and snowmobiles, where, according to

Kristján, he would find a man called Höddi who belonged to Thórarinn's tiny circle of friends. Kristján had forgotten how their paths had crossed originally but they used to help each other out with debt collecting and other jobs that might crop up. That was how Höddi had once come to set fire to a white Range Rover with leather fittings and all the extras, worth a cool twelve million kronur, at the request of the owner. He needed to pay off a loan that was causing him grief and also wanted to squeeze some cash out of his insurance company. The request had come via Toggi, who was in contact with the owner – Kristján did not know how – but it so happened that Toggi was in Spain at the time and the job needed doing quickly. Höddi had sorted out the matter easily; Kristján said he was considered a dab hand at arson jobs. Apart from that, he claimed he did not know who Toggi 'Sprint' was friendly with.

Höddi turned out to be a tall, powerfully built figure, with the beginnings of a paunch, a totally bald head and a thick goatee. He was wearing jeans and a black T-shirt bearing the Confederate flag, like a caricature of an American redneck. When Sigurdur Óli arrived he was inside the workshop, stooped over a motorbike with chrome fittings. The workshop was small and he was the owner and sole member of staff, as far as Kristján knew.

'Good afternoon,' said Sigurdur Óli. 'I'm looking for Höddi. Is that you, by any chance?'

The man straightened up. 'Who wants to know?' he asked, as if he could smell trouble at a hundred paces.

'I need to find Toggi – Thórarinn – and I gather you know him,' Sigurdur Óli said. 'It's a police matter. You may have heard about it. I'm with the police.'

'What police matter?'

'An attack on a woman in the eastern suburbs.'

'Why are you asking me?'

'Well, I –'

'Who sent you here?' asked Höddi. 'Are you alone?'

Sigurdur Óli was unsure how to take this last question. A policeman was by his nature never alone, but he had no intention of engaging in philosophical debate with Höddi. So what did the question mean? If he was alone was the man intending to attack him? Nor was there any way Sigurdur Óli could answer his first question, as he did not intend to divulge Kristján's identity, despite the niggling desire to do so in revenge for the mind-numbing tedium of their lunchtime chat. So he merely stood there in silence, gazing round the workshop at the snowmobiles which were in the process of being converted to make them even faster and noisier, and the motorbikes being souped up in order to break the speed limit with even greater ease.

Höddi advanced towards him. 'Why do you think I've got anything to say about this guy Toggi?' he demanded.

'I'm asking you,' said Sigurdur Óli. 'Do you know where he could be?'

Höddi glowered at him. 'No, is the answer. I don't know the bloke.'

'Then do you know a man called Ebeneser, known as Ebbi?'

'I thought you were asking about Toggi.'

'Ebbi too.'

'Never heard of him.'

'He has a wife called Lína. Do you know her?'

'Nope.'

The man's phone started ringing in his pocket. He looked at Sigurdur Óli as the phone rang, four, five, six times, and when he finally deigned to answer, he continued to eyeball Sigurdur Óli.

'Yup,' he said, then listened for a while.

'I don't give a shit,' he said. 'Yup . . . yup . . . yup, doesn't matter to me.'

He listened again.

'I don't care if he's related to you,' he snarled. 'I'm going to kneecap the fucker.'

His eyes were fixed provocatively on Sigurdur Óli as he said this. In what sounded like either an act of revenge or the calling in of a debt Höddi was threatening to take a baseball bat to somebody. Whichever it was, Höddi clearly felt no compulsion to conceal it. He was deliberately provoking Sigurdur Óli, as if to demonstrate that they had nothing on him and could not touch him.

'Shut the fuck up!' said Höddi into the phone. 'Yeah . . . yeah . . . right, yeah, and up yours. You can shut the fuck up, mate.'

He ended the call and stuffed the phone back in his pocket.

'Has Toggi been in touch with you recently?' asked Sigurdur Óli, as if he had not heard the exchange.

'I don't know any Toggi.'

'He's known as Toggi "Sprint".'

'I don't know him either.'

'I assume you travel in the highlands on those things,' commented Sigurdur Óli, gesturing towards the powerful snowmobiles.

'Why don't you just cut the crap and get the hell out of here?' said Höddi.

'Or maybe on glacier trips,' Sigurdur Óli continued, unperturbed by the man's rising anger. 'Am I right? I'm talking about organised tours for businesses or institutions, not just mucking about by yourself.'

'What's this bullshit?'

'Do you organise tours like that? Are you involved with them at all? Glacier tours for corporate clients: snowmobiles, barbecues, the works?'

'I often go on glacier trips. What's it to you?'

'This bloke I mentioned – Ebbi – he runs highland tours. Ever worked with him?'

'I don't know any Ebbi, mate.'

'All right,' said Sigurdur Óli. 'Have it your way.'

'Yeah, right. Now get the fuck out and leave me alone,' he said, turning back to his motorbike.

When Sigurdur Óli returned to Hverfisgata he found an email waiting for him from Kolfinna, the secretary at Lína's accountancy firm. She had promised to send him the list of employees and clients who had gone on the company's second glacier tour with Ebbi and Lína. Sigurdur Óli printed it and glanced down the list. To his surprise and consternation, he encountered Hermann's name. Then, further down, he was brought up short by another name so familiar he could hardly believe his eyes.

It was the name of his friend, Patrekur.

28

They had watched him suspiciously when he went into the state off-licence to buy two bottles of Icelandic *brennivín*. He had made an effort to smarten himself up by hitching up his trousers, pulling on an anorak and donning a woolly hat to hide his dirty, unkempt hair and keep out the cold. Then he had walked the long distance to the off-licence on Eidistorg Square, on the Seltjarnarnes Peninsula at the westernmost end of the city. He had taken the decision to avoid visiting the same shop too often after noticing the glances of the staff when he went to the town centre off-licence, near Grettisgata. The branch in the Kringlan shopping centre was also out.

He had been there recently too. He had had to pay using cash because he did not own a credit card, never had, which meant he sometimes had to go to the bank to withdraw money. His disability benefit was paid directly into his account and in addition to this he had some savings left over from his last job. Not that he needed much these days, because he hardly ate; the *brennivín* served as both food and drink.

The staff at the off-licence watched him as if he had committed a crime. Perhaps it was his appearance? He hoped so. What could they know, anyway? They knew nothing. Nor did they refuse to serve him; after all, his money was good, even if he didn't exactly look like a banker. They avoided engaging with him, though; did not address a single word to him. Well, what did he care what they thought? They meant nothing to him. And anyway, what did he have to do with them? Not a thing. He was just there to buy a couple of bottles of spirits and that was all. He was causing no trouble; he was a customer, just like anyone else.

So why the hell were they gawping at him like that?

Was there a dress code for drinking *brennivín*?

He walked out of the off-licence, his mind churning, casting frequent glances behind him, as if he expected to be followed. Could they have called the cops? His pace quickened. The young man who had served him sat on his chair by the till, watching him through the glass frontage until he was out of sight.

He did not see any police officers but took the precaution of turning down a side street as soon as he could. From there he made his slow way back towards the centre of Reykjavík, heading for the old graveyard, instinctively picking the quietest back streets and alleyways. From time to time, when no one was looking, he stopped, removed one of the bottles from the bag and took a swig. When he finally reached the graveyard the bottle was nearly empty. He would have to go easy if the other one was to last.

The old cemetery on Sudurgata was a favourite refuge when he needed peace and quiet. He sat down now for a rest on a low stone wall that fenced in a large tomb, taking frequent sips from the second bottle, and although it was cold he did not feel it, protected as he was by the drink and his thick, padded jacket.

The alcohol had a restorative effect and he felt livelier, somewhat lighter of heart. A snatch of verse kept repeating itself in his head, as it often did when he was drinking: *Brennivín is the best of friends / It never lets you down.* In future he would avoid the town centre; you never knew when you might bump into some acquaintance, or even a cop, and that was the last thing he needed. More than once he had been picked up for the sole crime of showing his face in town. He had not been pestering anybody, merely sitting on a bench in Austurvöllur Square, minding his own business, when two policemen had approached him. He had told them to get lost – maybe adding a few obscenities, not that he could remember – and before he knew it he was in the cells. 'You spoil the view for the tourists,' they had told him.

He gazed across the graveyard at the mossy headstones and the trees that grew amid the tumbled graves, then raised his eyes heavenwards. The sky was gloomy and overcast; to him it seemed almost black, but then the clouds over the mountains parted for an instant, showing a gleam of sunlight and a pale strip of blue sky before it was obscured again by a dark bank of cloud.

He had not attended his mother's funeral. Sometime, somewhere – probably when she was admitted to hospital, he did not know – she had given his name as next of kin, to be contacted in the event of her death. One day he had received a phone call that he still heard occasionally, as if from afar, from beyond the rim of sky over the mountains, telling him that his mother Sigurveig was dead.

'Why are you telling me?' he had asked.

He had felt neither gladness nor sorrow, neither surprise nor anger. Just numbness, but then he had been numb for a long time.

The woman had wanted to discuss arrangements about the body and the undertaker, and something else he did not catch.

He took a slug from the bottle and looked up at the clouds, checking to see if they had parted again but he could see no sunlight. He knew the graveyard well, often coming here in search of respite. No one bothered him here.

As he sat there among the old graves he was filled with a strange sense of tranquillity, and so he remained, uncertain, as sometimes happened, which side of the grave he was really on.

He had almost forgotten why he had come when he noticed a policeman approaching. The name escaped him at first. Sigur-something.

Sigurdur.

29

Sigurdur Óli was standing reading the printout when the phone on his desk rang. He answered testily and could hear nothing but breathing at first, the faint snuffling sounds of rapid breathing.

'Who's that?' he asked.

'I need to see you,' said a voice which he immediately identified as belonging to Andrés.

'Is that Andrés?'

'I . . . can you meet me now?'

'Where are you?'

'In a call box. I'm . . . I'll be in the graveyard.'

'Which graveyard?'

'On Sudurgata.'

'All right,' said Sigurdur Óli. 'Where are you now?'

'. . . about two hours.'

'OK. In two hours. In the graveyard. Whereabouts in the graveyard?'

There was no answer. Andrés had hung up.

Nearly two hours later Sigurdur Óli parked his car and entered the old Reykjavík cemetery from the western end. He had no idea where to find Andrés but decided to try going left first. He walked some way down the hill past tombs and headstones, along narrow footpaths that wound between grey slabs, and had almost reached Sudurgata, the road at the bottom, when he caught sight of Andrés sitting on a low, mossy wall that had long ago been erected around a double tomb. Andrés watched as Sigurdur Óli approached. His hands, glimpsed beneath the long sleeves of his jacket, were black with dirt; he wore a woollen hat on his head and looked as dishevelled as he had when he last spoke to Sigurdur Óli behind the police station.

Andrés made to stand up but abandoned the idea. The stench he gave off was beyond belief; a reek of excrement combined with alcohol and urine. Apparently he had not changed his clothes for weeks.

'You came then?' he said.

'I've been looking for you,' Sigurdur Óli replied.

'Well, here I am.'

He had a plastic bag from the state off-licence that looked to Sigurdur Óli as if it contained two bottles. He sat down on the wall beside Andrés, watching him take one bottle out of the bag, loosen the cork and swig from the neck. Noticing that he had almost finished it, Sigurdur Óli reflected that there was probably more to be gained from him drunk than sober.

'What's going on, Andrés?' he asked. 'Why do you keep contacting me? What do you want from us?'

Andrés looked around him, his eyes straying from one gravestone to the next, then took another gulp of alcohol.

'And what are you doing here in the graveyard? I've been asking after you at your block of flats.'

'There's no peace anywhere. Except here.'

'Yes, it's a quiet spot,' said Sigurdur Óli, remembering how the body of a young girl had once been found on the grave of Jón Sigurdsson, Iceland's national hero. Bergthóra had been a witness on the case, which was how they had met. The occasional car drove past along Sudurgata and on the other side of the wall the pleasant houses of Kirkjugardsstígur slumbered in the quiet afternoon.

'Did you get my package?' asked Andrés.

'You mean the film clip?'

'Yes, the bit of film. I found it in the end. Not much,

235

but enough. He only kept two short films. He'd thrown all the rest away.'

'Is it you we can see in the film?'

'We? Who's *we*? I sent it to *you*. Have you shown it to somebody? Nobody else was supposed to see it! Nobody else can see it! You mustn't show it!'

Andrés became so agitated that Sigurdur Óli tried to calm him down by reassuring him that he had only allowed a lip-reader to watch it to find out what the boy in the film was saying. No one else had seen it, he added, which was not far from the truth. He had not put the inquiry on an official footing yet because he wanted to conduct his own investigation first, to see if there were sufficient grounds to call in the vice squad and devote time and manpower to pursuing the case.

'Is it you in the film?'

'Yes, it's me,' said Andrés faintly. 'Who else . . . who else would it be?'

He fell silent and drank from the bottle.

'It took you a long time to find the film, did it? So where did you find it in the end?'

'You see, my mother . . . wasn't . . . she wasn't strong, she couldn't control him, you know?' Andrés said, ignoring the question and following some thread of his own. He was unshaven, his tufty beard sparse, his face grimy. A bloody bruise stood out under one eye as if he had been in a fight or an accident. His eyes were small, grey, watery, almost colourless, his nose swollen and crooked as if it had once been broken and never properly set, perhaps during the years that he had spent loitering around the bus station at Hlemmur for warmth.

'Who are you talking about? Who couldn't she control?'

'He just used her, you know? She gave him a home and he kept her in drink and drugs, and no one bothered about me, eh? He could do what he liked with me.'

His voice was hoarse and slurred, fuelled with ancient anger and loathing.

'Are there any other films?'

'He got a kick out of making them,' Andrés said. 'He had a projector that he stole from some school when he was working in the countryside. Had a stash of porn that they used to smuggle in on the boats.'

He was quiet again.

'Are you talking about a man called Rögnvaldur?' asked Sigurdur Óli.

Andrés was staring into space. 'Do you know who he is?'

'We spoke to you in January, on another matter,' said Sigurdur Óli. 'Do you remember? You remembered the other day. We spoke to you about this Rögnvaldur back then. He was your stepfather, wasn't he?'

Andrés did not answer.

'Was it him who made the film you sent us?'

'He was missing a finger. He never told me why. But I sometimes comforted myself by hoping that it hurt, hoping that he had suffered and screamed from the pain. Because he bloody well deserved to.'

'Is he the man you're describing?'

Andrés hung his head, nodding reluctantly.

'When did this happen?'

'A long time ago, years ago.'

'How old were you?'

'Ten. When it started.'

'So, around 1970? We tried to work it out.'

'You can never be free of it,' Andrés said, so quietly that Sigurdur Óli could barely hear him. 'However hard you try, you can never be free of it. Mostly I've tried to drown it in drink, but that doesn't work either.'

He raised his head, straightened his back and cast a glance at the sky, as if seeking something in the heavens. His voice dropped to a whisper.

'I was in hell for two years. Almost constantly. Then he left.'

30

A bus drove past noisily, down Sudurgata in the direction of the city centre, and the sound of laughter rose from Kirkjugardsstígur: life in the city carried on as usual but in the graveyard where Andrés sat it might as well have stopped altogether. He did not say another word. Sigurdur Óli waited for him to continue, unwilling to press him. The minutes passed. Andrés had picked up one of the bottles, taken a long draught, then shoved it back in the bag with the other one. He had retreated into a private world. When all hope of his resuming the story seemed lost, Sigurdur Óli coughed.

'Why now?' he asked.

He was not sure if Andrés had heard him.

'Why now, Andrés?'

The other man turned his head and regarded Sigurdur Óli as if he were a complete stranger.

'What?' he asked.

'Why are you telling us this now?' Sigurdur Óli asked again. 'Even if we caught this Rögnvaldur, the case is long dead, long over. There's nothing we can do. There are no laws that can touch him now.'

'No,' Andrés said slowly. 'You lot can't do anything. You never could have . . .' He trailed off.

'What happened to Rögnvaldur?'

'He moved out and never showed his face again,' said Andrés. 'I didn't know any more about him. He just disappeared. For all these years.'

'But then?'

'Then I saw him again. I told you about that.'

'We couldn't find him, and we lost interest once we had closed the case that he was thought to be involved in, because it turned out he hadn't been anywhere near it. There was no way we could use your statement; it was so vague and you refused to give us any more specific information. So why do you want to talk about it now?'

Sigurdur Óli waited for an answer but Andrés merely gazed down at his feet.

'If I remember right,' Sigurdur Óli went on, 'you hinted that he had killed someone of your age. Were you talking about yourself? Is that how you experienced what he did to you? That he killed some part of you?'

'Maybe he should have finished me off,' said Andrés. 'Maybe it would have been better. I don't remember what I told you. I haven't been . . . I haven't been in a good way for a long time.'

'There's support available, you know,' said Sigurdur Óli. 'For people like you, people who've gone through this sort of thing. Have you tried any help like that?'

Andrés shook his head. 'I wanted to see you to tell you . . . to tell you that whatever happens, however things turn out, it wasn't all my fault. Do you understand? It wasn't all my fault. I want you – the police – to know that.'

'How what turns out?' asked Sigurdur Óli. 'What do you mean?'

'You'll find out.'

'Have you found Rögnvaldur?'

Andrés did not answer.

'I can't let you leave without answering. You can't just drop hints like that.'

'I'm not trying to make excuses. What's done is done and it's too late to undo it. After he left I tried to . . . I tried to pull myself together but I couldn't deaden the

241

feelings. Then I found that I could keep them away with booze and dope, so I turned to them, to the people who could supply them, and that way I managed to keep the feelings under control. The minute he was gone. I got drunk for the first time when I was twelve years old. Sniffed glue. Took anything I could lay my hands on. I've hardly been sober since. That's the way it is – I'm not making excuses.'

He paused, coughed, and delved into the bag for the bottle.

'You'll find out,' he added.

'What?'

'You'll find out.'

'I gather you wanted to train as an upholsterer,' said Sigurdur Óli, keen to keep him talking, to encourage him to open up, in the hope that more would emerge about Rögnvaldur. It did not take an expert to see that Andrés was on the verge of mental and physical collapse.

'I've tried to clean up my act over the years,' he said. 'But it never lasted.'

'Have you tried making anything out of leather recently?' Sigurdur Óli asked carefully.

'What do you mean?' Andrés said, immediately on his guard.

'Your neighbour, the woman next door, was worried about you,' Sigurdur Óli explained. 'She thought something might have happened to you, so she let me into your flat. I found bits of leather in the kitchen and when I put them together they made a round shape, a bit like a face.'

Andrés did not respond.

'What were you cutting out?'

'Nothing,' Andrés said, beginning to scan his surroundings as if in search of an escape route. 'I don't understand why you had to go into my flat. I don't understand.'

'Your neighbour was concerned,' Sigurdur Óli repeated.

'You talked her into it.'

'No, I didn't.'

'You shouldn't have gone into my place.'

'What are you doing with the leather?'

'It's private.'

'Do you remember we found child pornography at your flat in January?' said Sigurdur Óli, changing tack.

'I . . .' Andrés faltered.

'What were you doing with that?'

'You don't understand.'

'You're right, I don't.'

'I . . . I despise myself more than anyone else . . . I . . .' He started mumbling again.

'Where is Rögnvaldur?' asked Sigurdur Óli.

'I don't know.'

'I can't let you leave until you've told me.'

'I didn't know what to do. Then I remembered. How the farmer used the spike. Then I knew how to do it.'

'The spike?'

'It's no thicker than a krona piece at the end.'

Andrés was no longer making sense.

'Where is Rögnvaldur?' asked Sigurdur Óli again. 'Do you know where he is?'

Andrés sat there dumbly, his eyes on the ground.

'I always wanted to go back there,' he said at last. 'But I never got round to it.'

He drifted off again.

'Röggi was a fucking bastard. I despise him, he disgusts me. He's repulsive!'

He was staring into the distance, at what infinitely remote scenes no one could say, whispering words inaudible to Sigurdur Óli.

'But I disgust myself most of all.'

At that moment Sigurdur Óli's phone rang, shattering the peace in the graveyard. Hastily, he fumbled for it in his coat pocket and saw that it was Patrekur calling. He dithered, glancing from Andrés to the phone, then decided to answer.

'I need to see you,' he said before Patrekur could utter a word.

'Sure.'

'You lied to me,' said Sigurdur Óli.

'What?'

'You think it's OK to lie to me, do you? You think it's OK to get me into trouble and lie to me?'

'What do you mean?' asked Patrekur. 'Calm down.'

'You said you'd never met Lína in your life.'

'That's right.'

'And you're sticking to that story, are you?'

'Sticking to what? What are you getting at?'

'I'm talking about you, Patrekur. And me.'

'Don't get all worked up. Just explain what you're on about.'

'You went on a glacier trip with her, you jerk!' said Sigurdur Óli. 'With a bunch of other pricks. Remember now? A glacier trip, last year. Does that refresh your memory?'

There was a lengthy silence at the other end.

'We need to meet,' Patrekur said at last.

'You bet we do,' snapped Sigurdur Óli.

He had turned away from Andrés during the conversation to gain a modicum of privacy, but when he turned back Andrés had vanished.

He reacted instantly, breaking off the call and sprinting up the hill through the graveyard, scanning the surroundings for Andrés, but he was nowhere to be seen. Reaching the gate, he ran out into the street, which was deserted, so he raced back into the graveyard and across it, looking all around him in vain. He had allowed Andrés to slip through his fingers again.

'Shit, shit, shit!' he shouted, coming to a halt. Andrés had been quick to make himself scarce and could have left by any gate while Sigurdur Óli was occupied.

He walked back to where he had parked, got into his car and wasted some considerable time combing the nearby streets in the hope of catching sight of Andrés, but to no avail.

The man had vanished into thin air and Sigurdur Óli did not have the first idea where he might be hiding or whether he had found Rögnvaldur and, if so, what might have become of him.

He tried to recall their conversation but did not get very far. Andrés had talked about his mother, and towards the end had begun rambling about a spike that had looked like a krona piece, and the revulsion he felt for Rögnvaldur, and that Sigurdur Óli must know that whatever happened, it was not all his fault.

For some reason it mattered to him that the police should understand this.

31

Patrekur looked up, shamefaced, as Sigurdur Óli entered the cafe and sat down opposite him. It was the same place as they had met before but now it was busier and the hubbub of conversation and other noise made it hard for them to talk without raising their voices. Realising how unsuitable the venue was, they agreed to go elsewhere and, since they were in the town centre, they started to drift slowly in the direction of the docks, past the old Icelandic Steam Ship Company headquarters, across the coast road and over towards the eastern harbour, the intended site for a giant concert hall and conference centre. They had been walking in silence but now started to talk in a desultory way about the plans.

'We're doing the groundwork,' Patrekur offered, stopping to survey the site. 'I'm not sure people realise the scale of this thing – just how massive it's going to be.'

'All this, when there are barely a thousand music lovers bothered enough to turn up to concerts in Reykjavík?' exclaimed Sigurdur Óli disapprovingly, though he could hardly even spell the word 'symphony'.

'Search me.'

They had not yet touched on the subject of Patrekur's lie. Sigurdur Óli wanted to wait and see what Patrekur said, but guessed that he was almost certainly thinking the same thing.

Work had started on demolishing the old buildings to make way for the new concert hall. Sigurdur Óli remembered reading a critical newspaper article by an economist who expressed dismay at the project's vulgarity and said the building was the dream child of a nouveau-riche country desperate to raise a monument to Icelandic greed. Across the road, fortress-like, loomed the Central Bank headquarters, clad with heavy, pitch-black gabbro from the East Fjords.

Patrekur agreed with the economist, dismissing the concert hall as a typical white elephant, born of small-country syndrome. The man who had abandoned neoconservatism for radicalism during his school years still lurked not far beneath the surface.

'I think our financiers are losing the plot,' he added.

'That's rich coming from you,' said Sigurdur Óli. 'Haven't you lost the plot yourself?'

The silence stretched out between them.

'Have you heard from Hermann at all?' asked Sigurdur Óli eventually.

'No,' replied Patrekur.

Sigurdur Óli had glanced over the transcripts of their interviews and noted that both had adhered to the story they had first told him. There was every chance that Finnur would call them back for further questioning. Patrekur had categorically denied knowing Lína or having any sort of relationship with her. Both had disclaimed all knowledge of a van driver called Thórarinn and denied any responsibility for the attack on Lína.

'How did you come to know Lína?' asked Sigurdur Óli.

'I thought you could just make this disappear,' said Patrekur. 'I was going to tell you the truth when it was all over. You may not believe me, but that was my intention.'

'Just answer the question,' said Sigurdur Óli. 'Didn't I go over all this with you? Don't avoid the issue.'

'I feel bad about lying to you.'

'Get to the point.'

'I went on that glacier trip a year ago,' Patrekur explained. 'With some foreign clients. There were several groups: one from our firm, another from Lína's firm and some bankers. Ebbi took care of all the preparations and organisation. It was your typical boozy excursion to entertain the foreigners by showing them the scenery, the glaciers. We drove up on to the Vatnajökull ice cap and held a barbecue there. Then – it was a weekend trip – we spent the second night out east in Höfn.'

'Did Hermann go along?'

'I invited him but in the end he could only make it for one of the days. He introduced me to Lína. She came over and he seemed oddly flustered. Now I know why he couldn't stay for the whole trip – he already knew her, of course.'

Patrekur hesitated.

'And?' prompted Sigurdur Óli.

'And I slept with Lína.'

Patrekur looked mortified as he met Sigurdur Óli's eye.

'You slept with Lína?'

Patrekur nodded. 'Ebbi wasn't there. He stayed somewhere else and she . . . we . . . anyway, we ended up in bed together.'

'Jesus.' Sigurdur Óli was completely thrown.

'I should have told you at once.'

'Do you make a habit of cheating on Súsanna?'

'I've done it once before,' said Patrekur. 'Two years ago. Similar circumstances, different woman. When I was out east on the big dam project. I wasn't exactly sober but of course that's no excuse. Lína was a lot of fun and very forward, and naturally I was up for it in the end.'

'Naturally?' said Sigurdur Óli.

'What can I say? It happened. I have no excuse, it just happened.'

'Did she tell you how she knew Hermann? That she was planning to blackmail him?'

'No, of course not.'

'So she didn't want to take pictures of you?'

'Give me a break.'

Sigurdur Óli shrugged.

'You can't imagine how shocked I was when Hermann and my sister-in-law came round the other day and started asking about my mate in the police,' said Patrekur. 'When he explained what it was all about and who was involved, I nearly lost it. My biggest fear was that he would let the cat out of the bag about me and Lína – that she might have told him. I couldn't think about anything but myself.'

'You haven't got the nerve for it,' said Sigurdur Óli, who was having difficulty feeling any sympathy for his friend, though Patrekur did sound genuinely repentant.

'Do you think I don't know that?'

'What about all Hermann's talk of swingers' parties? His claim that they met purely by chance?'

'I believe all that,' replied Patrekur. 'I don't think Hermann's lying. We didn't have a clue that they went in for wife-swapping. Súsanna was speechless – she can't understand that game, but then she doesn't understand about lies and infidelity and all that stuff either. We wanted to help them. After all, it's Súsanna's sister, as I keep telling you. To react any other way would have been out of the question. So I agreed to talk to you and ask you to put pressure on Lína and Ebbi, to put an end to it all before it got out of hand. Of course, I should have told you the whole story. It was cowardly and selfish of me not to. To deceive you. I do realise that. I was involving you. But the whole mess was just so embarrassing. Then she was attacked and suddenly it was deadly serious and I just clammed up even more, and – I'm being completely honest – I'm so shit-scared I can hardly breathe.'

'It didn't occur to you to have a word with Lína yourself, seeing as you knew her?'

'I hadn't had any contact with her since that night in Höfn and there was no way I was going to talk to her.'

'Do you think she might have got the idea from you? About blackmail?'

'Christ, no, I don't think so.'

'Did you tell her Hermann's wife was an up-and-coming politician?'

'No, I don't think so, I really can't remember.'

'So why on earth did you have to drag me into this?'

'It was never meant to become official,' Patrekur said. 'You were supposed to deal with it, to make the problem disappear. They were threatening God knows what: the tabloids, the Internet. Hermann had clearly got mixed up with a couple of nutters. I didn't want to get embroiled; it didn't occur to me to approach them myself. I just assumed that you were the right person to cut them down to size and make them see sense, threaten them with the law, like we discussed. I know you would have pulled it off. They were unbelievably brazen but I was convinced that it wouldn't take much to talk them out of such a crazy plan.'

'Were they heavily in debt? Do you know anything about that?'

'Hermann reckons they must have been, and that's why they went so far. And I'm not necessarily talking about bank loans. They'll be blacklisted for those. They were both into drugs. Hermann's convinced they're in debt to a bunch of dealers and that that's why she was attacked.'

'Are you sure? About the drugs?'

'Hermann told me they offered him something, Es or speed, probably. He didn't even know what it was called, but they had plenty of it.'

'Did he know where they got it?'

'No, he didn't ask,' Patrekur said.

'So you didn't meet Lína again after what happened?'

'No. Well, yes, she did call me once. Rang me at work and asked how things were. We chatted for a bit, then I asked her not to contact me any more; it had been a mistake and I didn't want to see her again.'

'Did she want to see you?'

'Yes.'

'And you said no?'

'That's right.'

'Does Ebbi know you slept together?'

'I don't think so,' said Patrekur. 'At least I assume not, though given the sort of life they lived, I suppose she could have told him. But if so I'm not aware of it.'

The conversation lapsed. Eventually, Patrekur sighed and added, 'I should have told you immediately. About me and Lína, I mean. I was shit-scared all along that you'd find out somehow. But I didn't want to destroy our friendship. And I really hope I haven't.'

Sigurdur Óli did not reply and they stood watching what was happening on the dockside. Sigurdur Óli's thoughts ranged from Ebbi and Lína, to threats, blackmail, debt collectors, glacier trips and accountants; his colleague Finnur and the wretched youth Pétur who had been beaten up behind the police station; Súsanna who was ignorant of her husband's infidelity; Hermann and his wife who wanted to make it in politics; Bergthóra and their last conversation, and his father in hospital.

'Are you going to tell Súsanna?' he asked at last.

'I already have,' said Patrekur. 'I couldn't stand it any longer, so I told her everything.'

'And?'

'I don't know. She's thinking it over. She was angry, of course. Completely lost it, more like. She reckons everyone's gone crazy, at it like rabbits all over the place.'

'Perhaps it's all this money,' said Sigurdur Óli.

He studied his friend.

'You didn't do anything to her, Patrekur? To Lína?'

'No way.'

'You didn't want to shut her up?'

'No. By killing her, you mean? Are you mad? I haven't been within a million miles of this. For Christ's sake, it wasn't like that.'

'What about Hermann?'

'No, I don't think so – definitely not. But you'd have to ask him. I've told you what I know.'

'All right. Who else was on this trip with you? I didn't recognise any of the names.'

'Foreigners,' Patrekur replied, 'engineers like me, bankers. I don't know them very well. They were Americans, here to learn about geothermal energy, renewable energy. I was sent with them because I did my postgrad degree in the States and we've been doing a lot of research into alternative energy sources. Then . . .'

'What?'

'Oh, one of them died in an accident not long afterwards, one of the Icelandic bankers; I don't remember his name. He was on a trip with some of the others and went missing. He wasn't found until last spring. What was left of him, that is.'

32

Höddi lived in an old, rather run-down terraced house in the unsmart Breidholt district. There were two snow-mobiles under covers parked on a small paved area in front of the garage, and a large, new-looking SUV and trailer in the street outside the house, in addition to a motorbike. Höddi's repair shop must be doing well if he could afford toys like these. Sigurdur Óli had watched him finish work, go to the gym, then return home. But he had not seen anyone else around the house and had no idea if Höddi was a family man. Apart from one arrest three years ago for assault, for which the charges were dropped, he had no police record.

Sigurdur Óli was cold. He was sitting in his car a short distance from the house, trying to look inconspicuous and unsure how long he intended to stay or why exactly he was keeping tabs on Höddi. Other officers were keeping Thórarinn's house under surveillance in case he came back, and his home phone was being monitored in case he made contact with his wife, since there was no mobile phone registered to her either.

Sigurdur Óli had not heard any more from Andrés and hardly knew where to begin when it came to tracking him down, or even if there was any value in doing so. As he sat in his chilly car he wondered why Andrés kept seeking him out. It was evident that he had something on his mind that was linked to the events of his childhood, events which were clearly unresolved from his point of view, however long ago they had happened. He was filled with bitterness, rage and unmitigated hatred towards those responsible. His silence about his mother was symptomatic. Everything he had said about Rögnvaldur had dripped with loathing. Sigurdur Óli wondered if Andrés had gone to see him and, if so, how the encounter had ended. How could anyone face a monster like that, who had inflicted such suffering over so long a period? Andrés had not given the impression that there would be any question of forgiveness.

Sigurdur Óli had wanted to bring Andrés back to the station with him, so Andrés could receive the help he needed and they could establish what exactly he wanted. It was impossible to guess from what he said, some of which had been incomprehensible. He was far gone with drink and neglect, had clearly not been looking after himself and was being tortured by his memories. Drink was his way of anaesthetising the pain. Sigurdur Óli had issued a notice to the state off-licences in the capital, asking them to alert the police if Andrés showed his face.

He had been touched by the boy in the film clip. It was a new experience, as he rarely felt any sympathy for the luckless individuals he came across in the line of duty, but there was something about the boy's wretchedness, his anguish and defencelessness, that had moved him. His usual attitude was that these people were responsible for their own plight. He did his job and once he had left the office for the day it was over – he had done his duty and there was no need to think about work again until he returned to the station. Some of the other officers who worked on difficult cases let it get to them, especially new recruits and old-timers, but he regarded emotional involvement as an obstacle to performing one's role. He had often been criticised for his cynicism and detachment but this meant nothing to him.

Apart from the obvious fact that a child had been abused, Andrés's plight was having an inexplicably strong impact on him. The police were forever having to deal with cases like this but it was not often that Sigurdur Óli was presented with such clear evidence of the consequences of chronic abuse. Andrés straightforwardly blamed his past for what had become of him today. He had certainly experienced little joy in his life and was still consumed by grief and anger.

The car windows were misting up so he cracked one open to let in some fresh air. He did not know how long he should stay watching Höddi's house. It was already past 10 p.m. and he had not seen any movement.

His phone rang. It was his mother.

'Have you been to see your father?' asked Gagga the moment he answered.

He said yes and told her that the operation had gone well; the old man was on good form and would be discharged soon.

'Have you had yourself checked out?' she shot back.

'No,' he said. 'There's plenty of time for that.'

'You should get a move on,' said Gagga. 'There's no point delaying.'

'I'm going to,' said Sigurdur Óli reluctantly, though he was unsure if he would ever actually get round to it. Not only because he dreaded this particular examination but because he had a long-standing phobia about doctors and could not face medical appointments. He could not bear the smell of the waiting rooms and surgeries, the waiting, and, worst of all, meeting the doctors – though dentists were top of the list. He could think of nothing worse than lying in a chair, gaping up at one of those millionaires, while he or she grumbled about the cost of living. Ear, nose and throat specialists came a close second. When he was a boy his mother had insisted that they take his tonsils out, blaming them for his constant ailments, the colds, runny noses, sore throats and earache, and he could still hardly bear to think about the anaesthetic, the foul taste in his mouth. And A&E was a chapter all to itself. Sigurdur Óli had once been involved in a fight while on a case and had to go to A&E: the endless wait had been the stuff of nightmares, on top of his horror of the reek of antiseptic and the old, thumbed magazines. He felt a special revulsion for those magazines. He had read somewhere that they did not actually carry any diseases, despite being fingered all day by sick people, but he found it hard to believe.

Having said all she wanted to, his mother ended the call. Five minutes later his phone rang again. This time it was Bergthóra.

'How's your father?' she asked.

'Fine,' answered Sigurdur Óli, rather curtly.

'Is everything OK?'

'Yes. I'm working.'

'Then I won't bother you,' said Bergthóra.

Höddi stepped out of his house as she spoke. He closed the door carefully behind him, testing the handle twice to make sure it was locked, then went over to the SUV and began detaching the trailer.

'No, it's OK,' said Sigurdur Óli, trying not to sound too resentful, though he found it hard, recalling their last conversation. 'Did I interrupt something last night?'

Höddi wheeled the trailer over to the snowmobiles and set it down, then climbed into his car and drove off. Sigurdur Óli allowed a few seconds to pass before starting his own engine and shadowing him at a distance.

'Look,' said Bergthóra. 'I've been meaning to say that I met someone about three weeks ago and we've started seeing each other.'

'Really?'

'I was going to tell you the evening we met but somehow I couldn't bring myself to.'

'Who is he?'

'No one you know,' said Bergthóra. 'At least, he's not in the police. He works for a bank. And he's very nice.'

'I'm glad he's nice,' said Sigurdur Óli, finding it a challenge to follow Höddi's SUV inconspicuously, while simultaneously talking to Bergthóra about things he really did not want to hear and not giving the fact away.

'I can tell you're busy,' said Bergthóra. 'Perhaps we should talk later.'

'No, it's all right,' said Sigurdur Óli, turning on to the Breidholt dual carriageway behind Höddi, who was driving very fast. The temperature had dropped below freezing, the roads were as slippery as glass, and Sigurdur Óli still had summer tyres on his car. He struggled to maintain control. Höddi had opened up a lead and was storming north.

'Did you call for any particular reason?' asked Bergthóra.

'Reason?'

'When you called last night. You rang so late that I thought maybe something was wrong.'

'No, I . . .'

Another turning, taken far too fast, through an amber light onto Bústadavegur. His tyres lost their grip momentarily. Höddi had disappeared over the hill by Bústadir Church. He was losing him, and sensed that he was losing Bergthóra too.

'. . . just wanted to talk to you. I . . . I don't know, I didn't feel right about the way our meal ended. I just wanted to discuss it.'

'Are you driving?'

'Yes.'

'Is that a good idea? Talking on the phone?'

'No, not really.'

Höddi turned up another road while Sigurdur Óli was faced with a red light. There was not much traffic, so after taking a quick glance around he shot the lights.

'I know it's none of your business really but I thought . . .'

'What?'

'I thought you seemed a bit . . . when you rang last night, you seemed so odd,' said Bergthóra, as Sigurdur Óli watched Höddi cross the bridge over the Miklabraut dual carriageway. 'Do you mind my seeing someone? Do you object?'

'I . . .' stammered Sigurdur Óli, wishing he could focus, '. . . I don't have any right to object. You must do as you like.'

Bergthóra was silent, as if waiting for him to carry on. His tone of voice belied the words he had spoken. The silence became oppressive as he struggled mutely. He had rung her to find out if she was willing to see him again. It would be different from last time. He had meant to get a grip on himself, to listen to her point of view, to try not to be rigid and difficult. Not like his mother. But as he hurtled over the city's icy roads, on summer tyres ill-equipped for the job, the right words eluded him.

'I won't take up any more of your time,' said Bergthóra

at last. 'We'll be in touch. Be careful – you shouldn't use your phone while driving.'

All he wanted was to keep her talking, but his mind was blank.

'OK,' he said.

This could not have gone worse, thought Sigurdur Óli, as he watched Höddi disappear into the Vogar district and heard Bergthóra disconnect.

33

He had lost Höddi's car but dared not drive any faster in these treacherous conditions. Turning into the street he thought Höddi had taken, he drove to the end, only to discover that it was a cul-de-sac, so he turned round, looking out for the SUV, and drove into the next street where he came to a junction. With no idea where to go, he decided to try left – home lay in that direction anyway and he was ready to give up. Then he caught sight of Höddi's SUV parked outside a takeaway.

He cruised past, noting the sizeable queue and that Höddi was halfway along it, staring up at the illuminated pictures of the dishes. Sigurdur Óli parked at a safe distance and waited. The decision to follow Höddi had been entirely his own, the result of a sudden hunch. Usually he would not have been shadowing a suspect alone like this; there would have been other officers involved and the operation would have been carefully planned. But with nothing to go on but Höddi's objectionable attitude, he had acted single-handedly, as he could not be certain of receiving the go-ahead. Yes, the man had undeniably set Sigurdur Óli's teeth on edge, but that did not necessarily mean that he deserved to be put under twenty-four-hour surveillance.

Meanwhile, the takeaway queue inched forward. Sigurdur Óli assumed that Höddi was probably taking himself and the SUV for a drive, picking up a burger from his favourite place on the way. He certainly looked capable of putting away any number of cheeseburgers.

Hungry now himself, Sigurdur Óli imagined all the sizzling hamburgers in the joint, and this did nothing to strengthen his resolve. He had just decided to give up and go home, stopping on the way at some other greasy burger bar, when Höddi reappeared carrying a takeaway bag and climbed into his car.

He drove out of the neighbourhood and came to a junction where he crossed the coast road, heading east, down towards the Ellidavogur inlet. There he took a right, drove past a row of workshops and small business premises, and stopped outside one of them. Stepping out of his car, he went over to a workshop and opened the door with a key. No lights came on. Sigurdur Óli could not immediately see what the place was called but remembered how Thórarinn had escaped in the direction of the Kleppur mental hospital, then south towards the Ellidavogur inlet. Could he have ended up here? Was this where he had been hiding since he attacked Lína?

Knocking at the door did not seem a very sensible option, given that he was not sure how he would shape up against two debt collectors. But nor did he want to call for backup, since he had no proof that Toggi 'Sprint' was hiding inside. It was perfectly possible that Höddi had some legitimate business here; given his vehicle collection, he must have plenty of repair jobs on. Sigurdur Óli opted to wait in his car at a discreet distance, keeping an eye on the door.

Half an hour later, without any lights being switched on in the workshop, the door opened and Höddi emerged, no longer carrying the takeaway bag. Looking neither left nor right, he got into his car and drove away.

Sigurdur Óli allowed a decent interval to pass before easing himself out of his car and walking over to the building. He laid his ear to the door and listened. Nothing. When he looked up, he saw a sign: Birgir's Auto Repair Shop. Next he went round behind the building, having to walk the length of the row before he could get round the back, then had to calculate how far along the repair shop was before he could establish that there was no exit on that side.

He walked softly back to the front of the workshop, gently tried the handle and discovered that the door was locked. He aimed three blows at it, and the large, sliding door of the adjoining garage entrance boomed loudly each time. Pressing his ear close again, he listened, but there was no sound. He banged the door with even greater force, but there was no reaction, apart from what sounded like a low rumble that stopped as suddenly as it had begun.

Sigurdur Óli could see only two alternatives: either to break in somehow, or to wait for the staff to come to work the following morning. He looked at his watch: it would be a long night. He peered round for some sort of implement – even a rock would do. There were four small panes of glass in the door and he could see no sign that the building was alarmed. It probably did not contain anything worth stealing.

After hunting around he found a length of discarded piping nearby, weighed it in his hand, then used it to smash one of the panes. Then, having cleared the shards, he inserted his arm carefully, located the lock and opened the door. If questioned he would mention an anonymous tip-off and claim that the workshop had been like this when he arrived.

He closed the door behind him and tiptoed into the repair shop, groping for a light switch near the entrance and finding three in a row. A dim light came on somewhere up in the rafters at the back of the room where car tyres were piled. He remained motionless while getting his bearings. The place looked like any other garage in town and Sigurdur Óli wondered who this Birgir was and whether he was either a relative of Höddi's or otherwise connected to Thórarinn – if indeed he was hiding here.

'Hello!' Sigurdur Óli called out but received no response. 'Thórarinn!' he shouted. 'Are you in here?'

He walked past a small glass booth containing a reception desk, two chairs and a pile of grubby magazines on a table. The office presumably. Behind it he detected a faint smell of coffee and opened a door to a staffroom, which contained a table and seats for three people, a grimy coffee machine and any number of dirty mugs. In the bin he noticed the bag that Höddi had brought and a box containing a half-eaten burger and chips. Sigurdur Óli's gaze lingered on the bin: could Höddi have been so desperate to eat his burger in peace that he had taken it to an empty garage on Ellidavogur, late at night?

'Thórarinn! This is the police. We know you're in here. We need to talk to you.'

There was no answer.

Sigurdur Óli walked back into the workshop.

'Stop wasting my time!' he called.

He was keen not to linger, feeling idiotic enough as it was, shouting like this in the hope that Toggi was hiding among the spare parts or heaps of tyres. If it turned out that he was not, Sigurdur Óli would feel a complete fool.

As he crossed the workshop, it occurred to him that something was missing. Over the years he had had a variety of cars, some good, others not so good, and he had often had occasion to go to repair shops and if the job was small hang around, or else hitch a lift home, or in the worst case call a taxi, though he tried to avoid that unless he had no other option. Generally he tried to get the mechanics to finish the job while he waited in the office or went for a stroll, so he reckoned he knew a thing or two about auto repair shops and in his estimation Birgir's equipment was not exactly state-of-the-art.

He was standing in the middle of the floor when it dawned on him what was missing. The car lift.

Just at that instant he thought he heard a faint scraping sound beneath his feet.

Sigurdur Óli looked down. He was standing on a large, rectangular metal hatch, and the sound seemed to have come from underneath it. He stamped his foot.

'Thórarinn!' he called again.

There was no answer. But Sigurdur Óli understood now why there was no car lift in the garage: instead of raising the cars to get at their undersides, the mechanic would climb down into a pit which the vehicle was parked over. Birgir probably could not afford a hoist, but then perhaps he did not have any use for such equipment, nor for the pit, given that it was covered.

Sigurdur Óli soon discovered how to slide the metal hatch off the pit, and when he looked down there was Thórarinn sitting against the wall, staring up at him.

'How the hell did you find me?' he asked, unable to conceal his astonishment. He rose to his feet, still staring at Sigurdur Óli, then clambered out and dusted himself down.

'Are you going to make trouble?' asked Sigurdur Óli, who had rung for backup as Thórarinn was climbing out.

'How the hell did you manage it?'

He did not put up any resistance.

'Maybe I'll tell you some time,' said Sigurdur Óli. 'Have you been here long?'

'Only just arrived.'

'So where have you been hiding?'

'Jesus, I got a shock,' Thórarinn said, ignoring the question. 'I was eating a burger when I heard you banging on the door. All I could think of was the pit. Was it Höddi?

Did you follow him?' He had started to inch his way unobtrusively towards the door.

'Stand still,' ordered Sigurdur Óli. 'There are cars on their way. You're not going anywhere.'

'You're alone?' exclaimed Thórarinn.

It was the second time that day Sigurdur Óli had been asked this question.

'There are two men outside,' he said. 'They're waiting for us.'

He hoped his lie sounded plausible enough to give Thórarinn pause, as he had no desire to be involved in another chase. They heard sirens in the distance.

'And the street is filling with other units, as you can hear.'

'Who grassed on Höddi?'

'Just take it easy,' said Sigurdur Óli, inserting himself between Thórarinn and the door. 'We'd have found you eventually. Or you'd have given yourself up: you lot always do in the end.'

34

Thórarinn was taken to the police station on Hverfisgata. By then it was past midnight and they decided his interview could wait until morning, so Sigurdur Óli saw him safely installed in a cell. He had intended to lie about how he had tracked Thórarinn down in order to keep Kristján's name out of it, but was not sure he would get away with this. It would be better to claim he had received one of those anonymous phone calls saying that Höddi was somehow linked to Thórarinn. The tip-off, he would say, had not seemed particularly credible but he had decided to follow it up anyway, by shadowing Höddi, who he had seen buying a hamburger before heading towards the Ellidavogur inlet area. At that point he had remembered the direction Toggi had taken after Lína's attack, and thought the matter deserved closer investigation. After Höddi had entered the garage and emerged minus the takeaway, Sigurdur Óli had decided to take immediate action and broke into the workshop, finding Thórarinn inside.

By telling the story this way, he hoped to deflect attention from Kristján and did not feel remotely ashamed of his lie. Kristján may have been a bloody fool but there was no need to set two debt collectors on him. In the event, no one questioned his account: what mattered was that Thórarinn had been caught; how it had happened was less important. The police often found themselves having to improvise.

Later that night Höddi and the garage owner, Birgir, together with an employee, were arrested and escorted to Hverfisgata. The baseball bat that Thórarinn had used to batter Lína was found in a skip about two hundred metres from the garage, stained with blood at one end.

As he was leaving the office, Sigurdur Óli bumped into Finnur.

'You should have called for backup,' said Finnur, who was still in charge of the investigation. 'It's not your own show, even if your friends are mixed up in it.'

'I'll remember that next time,' said Sigurdur Óli.

Early next morning he took part in the interrogation of the three suspects. Birgir claimed complete ignorance that his workshop was being used as a safe house for criminals and flatly denied any complicity. It transpired that Höddi owned a share in the business and had his own key. Neither Birgir nor his employee had been aware of Toggi's presence during opening hours, so he must have hidden himself unbelievably well if he had been there during the day. The workshop was small and in the course of a normal day's work they were in and out of every corner, so it was more likely that he had hidden there at night. Since neither Birgir nor the man who worked for him had a police record, their statements were taken on trust and there was deemed to be no reason to keep them in custody.

'Who's going to pay for the broken glass?' asked Birgir despondently when he heard about the damage to the garage door. He had mentioned that business was slack and that they could not afford any setbacks.

'You can send us the bill,' Sigurdur Óli said, not sounding particularly encouraging.

Höddi proved a tougher nut to crack. He was in a sullen, obstructive mood after a night in the cells and took exception to everything he was asked.

'How do you know Thórarinn?' asked Sigurdur Óli for the third time.

'Shut your face,' said Höddi. 'You'd better watch your back when I get out of here.'

'Why, are you going to kneecap me?'

'Fuck you.'

'Are you threatening me, you prick?'

Höddi stared at Sigurdur Óli, who smiled back.

'Shut your face,' he said again.

'How do you know Thórarinn?'

'We both fucked your mother.'

Höddi was escorted back to the cells.

Thórarinn did not appear remotely intimidated when he was brought up for questioning. In the interview room he took a seat next to his lawyer, facing Sigurdur Óli, and lounged with his legs spread, drumming one foot rhythmically on the floor. Finnur joined in the questioning. They asked Thórarinn first where he had been hiding for the last few days and the answer came promptly: when he shook off the police that evening, he had run to Birgir's repair shop and hidden outside, before later fleeing to Höddi's place. Höddi had initially hidden him in his own house but after receiving a visit from the police he had told him to go down to the garage and wait for him there. They had met after closing time and Höddi had let him in, then come back later with food. Next, Thórarinn had been planning to move to Höddi's summer cottage in Borgarfjördur, in the west of the country, where he would hide out for a few days while considering his options.

'Didn't it occur to you to give yourself up?' asked Finnur.

'I didn't kill her,' said Thórarinn. 'She was alive when this bloke turned up.' He pointed at Sigurdur Óli. 'He must have finished her off. I knew you'd try to frame me for what he did; that's why I legged it.'

Sigurdur Óli turned to Thórarinn's lawyer in astonishment.

'And you believe this?' he asked. 'Haven't you done any homework at all?'

The lawyer shrugged. 'That's his statement,' he said.

'Sure, she was alive when I found you both,' said Sigurdur Óli, 'and she was still alive when the ambulance men took her to hospital, where she died the next day. But the post-mortem revealed that she died from a blow to the head – a blow administered using the implement we found two hundred metres from your hiding place. I didn't run there carrying it. You must have hired the worst lawyer in Iceland, Toggi. A four-year-old could have told you that. Then you wouldn't have been left looking like an idiot right from the off.'

Thórarinn glanced at his lawyer.

'We want to know what you were doing at the scene,'

retorted the lawyer, in an attempt to save face. 'What was your business with Sigurlína? I think my client has a right to know that.'

'On the contrary, it's none of your business,' corrected Sigurdur Óli. 'Thórarinn is a drug dealer and a debt collector. I found him at Lína's house where she was lying on the floor, more dead than alive, and bleeding from a head wound. My visit was connected with the investigation of a completely unrelated matter. Thórarinn attacked me, then fled from a large number of police officers – made off in a hell of a hurry. Not exactly the behaviour of an innocent man, was it?'

'What were you doing at Sigurlína's place, Thórarinn?' asked Finnur, who had been silent.

Sigurdur Óli had been trying to calculate what was on Finnur's mind and how he would react to the ludicrous defence put forward by Thórarinn and his lawyer. There was no possible way they could know Sigurdur Óli's business with Lína; they were merely trying to complicate the matter and cast doubt on him. He was not sure whether the reason for his presence at Lína's would ever need to come out officially, since so much about the sequence of events still remained obscure. But there was little he could do to influence the course of the investigation, so he could only hope for the best. In fact, what happened next was pretty much up to Finnur.

Thórarinn caught the eye of his lawyer, who nodded.

'A drugs debt,' he said. 'You're right. I sometimes sell a little dope and she owed me money. There was some aggro; I acted in self-defence and hit her. Never intended to do any damage, mind. It was accidental. Then I panicked when that prick appeared.' Thórarinn gestured at Sigurdur Óli again.

'Is that your defence?' asked Sigurdur Óli.

'It was an accident. It all happened by mistake,' said Thórarinn. 'She went for me. I defended myself. End of.'

'She went for you?'

'Yes.'

'You forced your way into her home with a baseball bat, smashed the place up and she went for you?'

'Yes.'

'That will be all for now,' announced Finnur.

'Can I go then?' said Thórarinn with a grin. 'I haven't got time for this, you know. I have a family. Us van drivers don't get paid like bank managers.'

'I reckon it'll be a while before you go anywhere except on the odd little prison outing,' replied Finnur.

'What car were you driving when you went to her house?' asked Sigurdur Óli.

Thórarinn paused.

'Car?'

'Yes.'

'What's that got to do with anything?'

'If you didn't mean to do her any harm and the whole thing was an accident, why did you need to borrow a car to go to her place?'

'How is that relevant?' asked the lawyer.

'It shows premeditation – *mens rea* is probably the phrase you'd use. He didn't want to be spotted near the house.'

'Was it Kiddi?' said Thórarinn, leaning forward in his chair. 'Of course, you've spoken to Kiddi. The stupid twat! I'll fucking –'

'Kiddi who?' asked Finnur, looking at Sigurdur Óli.

'Just answer the question,' said Sigurdur Óli, aware that he had said too much, too soon.

'Was it Kristján who squealed? Was it him who told you about Höddi? The stupid little fucker.'

'Kristján who?' asked Finnur again.

'Search me,' said Sigurdur Óli.

35

It took him forever to wake up and when he did, he had no idea whether it was day or night. He lay motionless while he was getting his bearings and gradually it came back to him: the conversation in the graveyard, the greyness, the cold, the twisted trees and tumbledown gravestones. The peace.

His memory of what had passed between him and the policeman was hazy, though he recalled meeting him, recalled sitting and talking to him for a while. But then something had happened and he could remember no more. Exactly what had happened, how they had left each other or how much he had revealed, he did not know.

He had meant to tell him everything. When he rang the policeman, he had been determined to tell him the lot, about Grettisgata and Röggi and his mother, about what had happened to him when he was a boy, how he had been mistreated. He had meant to take the policeman back to Grettisgata, show him the old man and tell him the whole story. But for some reason he had not done so. Had he run away? All he remembered was waking up just now on the floor of the basement flat.

Sitting up with difficulty, he groped for the plastic bag. He had finished one of the bottles but the other was still half full, so he took a deep draught, thinking that he would have to go straight back to the off-licence. A sudden memory returned, of climbing over the graveyard wall into the road where a car had almost knocked him down. Yes, it came back to him now; the policeman had been on the phone.

He could not make up his mind whether he should ring the man again and try to arrange another meeting. He was almost certain that he had sent him a short strip of one of the films he had found in the old man's flat. As far as he could remember, there had been two reels, but he had not found any more, despite turning the flat upside down, smashing holes in the walls and tearing up the floorboards.

Hours after discovering the films he had attempted to watch them but the experience proved too overwhelming.

Having threaded one into the projector, he turned it on, the film began to roll and an image suddenly appeared on the white wall of a boy – himself. Then all the circumstances of the shoot flooded back. Ironically, although he had trouble remembering the last twenty-four hours, he had absolutely no difficulty recalling the events of more than thirty years ago. In frantic haste he switched off the projector, pulled out the film, and finding a pair of scissors in the chaos, snipped off a short section and put it in a plastic bag lying on the floor.

He did not want anyone to watch the films; they were his secret, so he put them in the kitchen sink and set fire to them. The burning reels emitted a great cloud of foul-smelling smoke, as was only to be expected of such filth, so he opened the window in the kitchen and another in the living room to air the flat. Once he had made sure that every last frame had been reduced to ashes, he washed the remains down the sink.

It was over, finished.

He took another swig from the bottle, almost draining it. He would have to get more.

He wanted to talk to the policeman again, to unburden himself. Not to run away. This time he would try not to run away.

36

There was no answer from Ebeneser when Sigurdur Óli rang the bell, then rapped on his door. He tried calling his name, to no avail, though Ebeneser's jeep was parked in front of the house and Sigurdur Óli felt instinctively that he was at home. Next he tried the windows, peering first into the kitchen, which needed tidying, then going round the back of the house to the sitting-room window and squinting inside. Only after straining his eyes could he make out a man's leg, then a head under a blanket. He banged on the windowpane till it rattled and saw Ebeneser stir, only to turn onto his side. The coffee table was littered with bottles and beer cans: Ebbi had been drowning his sorrows.

Sigurdur Óli banged on the glass again and shouted at Ebeneser, who regained consciousness by slow degrees. He struggled to work out where the noise was coming from but eventually he caught sight of the obnoxious policeman outside the window and sat up on the sofa. Sigurdur Óli went round to wait at the door of the house. Nothing happened. He lost patience, assuming that Ebeneser must have fallen asleep again, and started ringing the bell and thumping on the door.

After a considerable delay Ebeneser appeared, looking extremely rough.

'What's all this noise in aid of?' he asked huskily.

'Do you mind if I come in for a minute?' said Sigurdur Óli. 'It won't take long.'

Ebeneser screwed up his eyes against the sunlight which was still bright, though it was getting late. He glanced at his watch, then back at Sigurdur Óli before inviting him in. Sigurdur Óli followed him into the sitting room where they both sat down.

'Just look at this mess,' Ebeneser remarked. 'I haven't . . .' He searched for something to say that would justify the disorder and his own dishevelled state, but finding nothing satisfactory, he gave up the attempt. 'I saw on the news that you've caught him,' he said instead.

'Yes, we've arrested the assailant,' said Sigurdur Óli. 'He gave us a motive but we can't be certain what's true and what's not at this stage. That's why I'm after additional information.'

'What motive?'

'The motive for his attack on Lína,' Sigurdur Óli explained.

'Oh. Who is he?' Ebeneser was still half asleep.

'His name's Thórarinn. We know it was him who attacked her.'

'She didn't know anyone called Thórarinn,' said Ebbi, picking up a can and giving it a hopeful shake. It was empty.

'No, they didn't know each other.'

Sigurdur Óli did not want to disclose too much about the investigation at this stage, so he gave him a brief summary of the latest developments, describing the circumstances in which Toggi had been located and stressing that, now that questioning was under way, it would be a good time to go over a few details. Ebeneser did not appear to be listening.

'Perhaps you need more time to wake up,' prompted Sigurdur Óli.

'No,' Ebbi replied. 'It's all right.'

'It won't take a moment,' said Sigurdur Óli, hoping this was not too wide of the mark.

Ebeneser looked tired and haggard; his air of heavy numbness went beyond a simple hangover. It occurred to Sigurdur Óli that he might have been mistaken; that Lína's death might in fact have had a much more serious impact on Ebbi than he had imagined, so he resolved to be polite and tactful, though neither was his forte. And it did not help that he had taken a dislike to the man, being unable to forget what Patrekur had said about Ebbi and Lína's demented threats of exposure in the gutter press and on the Internet.

'So what was his motive?' asked Ebeneser. 'The man you're holding, I mean.'

'A drugs debt,' answered Sigurdur Óli. 'I've been informed by other sources that you do drugs – that you and Lína were regular users – so, in our view, a drugs debt doesn't seem implausible.'

Ebeneser eyed Sigurdur Óli.

'We didn't owe anyone,' he said at last.

'Thórarinn both deals and collects debts, though he's managed to avoid any trouble with the law. He's careful to keep a low profile and works as a van driver. What motive could a guy like that have for attacking Lína unless you owed him money? You tell me.'

Ebeneser sat in silence, mulling over the question.

'I don't know,' he said. 'I . . . Lína and I were recreational users, if I'm being honest, but we both worked hard and had the money for it. I don't know this Thórarinn at all and I don't believe Lína did either. I couldn't say why he attacked her.'

'All right,' said Sigurdur Óli. 'Say it's not drugs, say it's something else. What could it be? What else were you and Lína up to apart from taking drugs and blackmailing people?'

Ebeneser did not answer.

'It's obvious that you got on the wrong side of somebody. Who could it have been?'

Still nothing.

'What are you scared of? Or should I say who are you scared of? Were you trying to blackmail someone else?'

'Those pictures,' said Ebeneser, after long reflection. 'We hadn't done anything like that before. Lína wanted to try it, to see what would happen. If it worked, we'd make a bit of money; if it didn't, there'd be no harm done. I'm not trying to shift the blame on to her but the fact is that it was her idea and she was much more gung-ho than me. In the end, though, we didn't make any use of the photos until the other day, when Lína saw her on TV.'

'Hermann's wife?'

'Yes.'

'So you sent them the photo?' prompted Sigurdur Óli.

This was the first time Ebeneser had admitted their involvement in blackmail.

'Yes. Lína said she was going to be a big deal in politics, so she wanted to try it – just for a laugh.'

'For a laugh? You've ruined the lives of two families! Lína got killed!'

Sigurdur Óli had spoken harshly, in anger, and realised too late that it was not his place to lose his temper. Finnur had warned him that there was no way he could remain detached.

'I'm sorry,' he said more gently. 'But aren't you just trying to pass the buck?'

'Not at all,' replied Ebeneser. 'Lína was always coming up with wild ideas.'

'What kind of ideas? Blackmail?'

'No, just all kinds of insane ideas. But she never followed them through, except this one time.'

'You'd know, would you?'

'Yes, I'd know.'

'You didn't mind her sleeping with other men?'

'It's the way we wanted it,' said Ebeneser. 'She wasn't bothered if I slept with other women. That's just the way it was.'

'And the wife-swapping?'

'We've been doing that since we were at college. That's when it started – when we got together. Somehow we just carried on.'

'Did she tell you about the men she slept with?'

'Sometimes, yes. Usually, I think.'

'Did she sleep with anyone at work?'

'Not as far as I know.'

'Did you go with her on those corporate trips to the highlands?'

'Usually. Lína persuaded her company to hire me to organise them. They knew I was a guide and arranged that sort of excursion, so when Lína said I could take care of the whole thing for them, they jumped at the chance. They were very satisfied with the results – the tours were a big success.'

'Did you know the people who went?'

'No, never.'

'Were they bankers? Engineers? Foreign investors?'

'Yes, that sort of type. Quite a few foreigners.'

'I gather there was an accident,' Sigurdur Óli said. 'Someone went missing and wasn't found for months. Do you recall anything about that?'

'Lína mentioned it – I don't remember exactly what she said. But it didn't happen on one of my trips.'

'Did she know the people involved?'

'I don't think so.'

'So she didn't sleep with them?'

Ebeneser did not answer, offended by the tenor of the question. In Sigurdur Óli's opinion it was a perfectly valid point: Lína had had no qualms about jumping into bed with Patrekur, and she and Ebbi did not exactly have a normal marriage. At least not his idea of a normal marriage.

'I want the photos,' he said.

'What photos?'

'Of you two with Hermann and his wife. Do you have them here?'

Ebeneser considered this, then got up and went into the kitchen, off which a small utility room opened. Sigurdur Óli sat and waited. After a short interval Ebeneser returned with an envelope which he handed over.

'Is that all of them?' asked Sigurdur Óli.

'Yes.'

'You haven't got them on your computer?'

'No. We printed these four out in order to send one to them, to show them we meant business. We were never going to circulate them. It was just a joke.'

Ebeneser seemed to have run out of explanations. His discomfort was obvious. He glanced round the room.

'God, it's such a bloody mess in here,' he said with a sigh.

'Are you still going to deny that you're broke?' asked Sigurdur Óli.

Ebeneser shook his head, his face a picture of

defeat. Sigurdur Óli thought he was going to burst into tears.

'We're up shit creek,' he confessed. 'This house, the car. Everything's on a hundred per cent loan; we're mortgaged to the hilt. We owe money everywhere. For the drugs too.'

'Who supplies your drugs?'

'I'd rather not say.'

'You may have to.'

'Well, I'm not going to.'

'Has he been threatening you?'

'We've got several dealers who supply us but none of them has threatened us. That's bullshit. And I don't know anyone called Thórarinn. I've never bought from him. I don't know what he means by talking about a debt. We don't owe him anything.'

'He's known as Toggi.'

'Never heard of him.'

'No idea why he might have attacked Lína?'

'No, none.'

'You must excuse these questions,' said Sigurdur Óli, 'but somehow we have to get to the bottom of this. Do you know if Lína ever slept with anyone for money?'

The question had no effect on Ebeneser. He had taken offence before when asked about the couple's sex lives but now he was utterly indifferent. Sigurdur Óli wondered what sort of relationship they had had, what it was based on.

'If she did, she never told me. That's all I can say.'

'Would you have minded?'

'Lína was a very unusual woman,' replied Ebeneser.

'Who might it have been, if she had done? Someone from her office?'

Ebeneser shrugged. 'Actually, she did mention one thing, in connection with the business of that bloke – the one who'd been on a trip with us.'

'You mean the banker? The one who went missing?'

Ebeneser picked up another beer can, shook it and heard the sloshing of liquid inside. He drained it, then crushed the can in his hand. It crackled loudly.

'Apparently they were operating some kind of money-making scheme.'

'Scheme?'

'Those blokes were on the make,' Ebeneser said. 'The ones on the trip with him. Lína said something about it.'

'When?'

'Just the other day.'

'What did she say?'

'You know, that they had an incredible nerve to attempt something like that.'

'What?'

'I don't know. A banking deal. Lína didn't get it

completely but it was some kind of scheme and she thought they were unbelievable.'

'In what way?'

'Just how cool they were. That was the gist of it. What an incredible nerve they had.'

37

Sigurdur Óli did not open the envelope. Unsure what to do with it when he got back to Hverfisgata, he put it away in a drawer. For all he knew, Ebeneser might have been lying when he claimed not to have any copies. Anyway, in view of the way it had developed Sigurdur Óli no longer felt that the pictures were of any relevance to the case. Ebbi had done his best to play down the matter, to give the impression that the blackmail was just a game of bluff which Lína had indulged in on the off chance that it might pay. If not, they would have abandoned the attempt; or so Ebbi would have him believe.

He was preoccupied with these thoughts when the phone on his desk began to ring.

'Yup?' he answered.

'I didn't . . .'

'Hello?'

There was a rustling, followed by a bump at the other end of the line.

'What?' said Sigurdur Óli. 'Who is this?'

There was no answer. 'Andrés?' Sigurdur Óli had thought he recognised the voice.

'I said . . . didn't . . .' The voice was slurred and thick; the words almost incomprehensible. 'I didn't tell you . . .'

He did not finish the sentence. Sigurdur Óli could hear him breathing.

'Andrés? Is that you? Tell me what?'

'. . . know . . . know all about . . . about the old bastard . . .'

'What do you mean? What are you trying to say?'

'Was it you? That I talked to in . . . in the graveyard?'

'Yes. Why did you run away? In fact, where are you? Can I come and get you?'

'Where am I? Who cares? Who gives a toss? No one. No one gave a toss. And now . . . got him . . . got the bastard . . .'

'Who?' asked Sigurdur Óli. 'Got who?'

Sigurdur Óli waited. There was just static for a long

time, then Andrés carried on speaking abruptly, as if he had pulled himself together.

'. . . and . . . got him! I was going to tell you when we met. I was going to tell you that I've got him. And he won't get away. You needn't worry about him getting away. I made . . . made a mask . . . and he didn't like that at all . . . wasn't pleased to see me at all. He wasn't pleased to see me again after all these years, I can tell you. He wasn't pleased to see little Andy. Oh no. No, he wasn't.'

'Where are you, Andrés?' asked Sigurdur Óli firmly, taking note of the number that flashed up on-screen as he did so and typing it into the online telephone directory. Andrés's name and address appeared. 'I can help you,' said Sigurdur Óli. 'Let me help you, Andrés. Are you at home?'

'But I could take him,' Andrés continued, oblivious. 'I . . . I thought it might be difficult but he's just an old man. A feeble old bastard . . .'

'Are you talking about Rögnvaldur? Is it Rögnvaldur you've got? Andrés!'

The line went dead. Sigurdur Óli leapt from his chair, grabbing his mobile as he went and dialling directory enquiries to get the number of Andrés's neighbour. He knew her address but could not immediately recall her name. He racked his brains.

Margrét Eymunds, that was it.

They put him straight through and Margrét answered at the third ring. By now, Sigurdur Óli was in his car and on the move. He introduced himself and when he was sure she remembered who he was and that he had come round before in search of Andrés, he asked her to go to her neighbour's flat and check if he was at home.

'Do you mean Andrés?' the woman asked.

'Yes. If you see him, could you try to keep him there until I arrive, please? He just rang me and I think he needs help. Are you outside his door yet?'

'What, you want me to spy on him?'

'Are you on a cordless phone?'

'Cordless? Yes.'

'I'm trying to help him. I'm afraid he might do something stupid. Could you hand him the phone? Please?'

'Just a minute.'

He heard a door opening, then the sound of knocking and Margrét's voice calling Andrés's name. Sigurdur Óli braked and swore. There had been an accident ahead that had caused a tailback.

'What have you been doing to yourself, Andrés dear?' he heard her ask in a shocked tone.

Sigurdur Óli leaned on the horn and tried to change lanes. He could not hear Andrés at all but could vaguely make out Margrét saying something about a policeman wanting to speak to him, then 'Where are you going?', followed by an oddly maternal phrase like, 'You can't go out looking like that, dear.' He tried to attract her attention but she obviously did not have the phone held to her ear.

He passed the scene of the accident and was dodging between other cars at twice the speed limit when Margrét came back on the line.

'Hello?' she said, sounding uncertain.

'Yes, I'm still here,' answered Sigurdur Óli.

'The poor man,' said Margrét. 'He looked absolutely dreadful.'

'Has he gone?'

'Yes, I couldn't stop him. He wouldn't have anything to do with me, just went down the stairs, almost at a run. He seemed very drunk.'

'Which way did he go when he left the building?'

'I didn't see. I didn't see where he went.'

Sigurdur Óli pulled up at the block of flats and scanned the surroundings for Andrés but could see no trace of him. He started combing the nearby roads but it was evident that he had lost his man, so he parked outside the flats again and rang Margrét's bell. She buzzed him in and was waiting for him on the landing, looking extremely worried.

'Didn't you find him?' she asked as soon as she saw Sigurdur Óli.

'He's vanished. Did he say much to you?'

'Not a word. The poor man. He clearly hasn't washed in ages and stinks to high heaven. And he looks like a tramp. I've never seen him in such a state before. Never.'

'Have you any idea where he might be going?'

'No. I asked him but he wouldn't answer, just rushed downstairs and disappeared.'

'Was he carrying anything when he left the flat?'

'No, nothing.'

'Have you ever heard him talk about a man by the name of Rögnvaldur?'

'Rögnvaldur? No, I don't think so. Is that a friend of his?'

'No,' said Sigurdur Óli. 'Hardly.'

Margrét let him into Andrés's flat as she had done before. Sigurdur Óli took a quick glance round while Margrét stood in the doorway. Nothing seemed to have changed. From what he could tell, Andrés had gone there for the sole purpose of calling Sigurdur Óli to inform him that he had got Rögnvaldur, whatever that meant.

Sigurdur Óli's phone rang. It was a colleague from the drug squad.

'I just heard that you're holding Hördur Vagnsson.'

'Höddi? Yeah. What about him?'

'We've been keeping tabs on him for a while but no joy yet. But we've been recording his phone calls and it occurred to me that you might like to take a look.'

'Have you got a transcript?'

'Yup, I put it on your desk.'

'Have you got anything on him?'

'We will eventually. Unless you've done it for us. There's one thing you should know about Höddi – the poor bastard's a complete moron.'

He heard chuckling at the other end of the line.

'You haven't by any chance tapped his friend Thórarinn's phone or been monitoring him at all?'

'Toggi?'

'Yes.'

'No, we only know him by name. If he's dealing, he must be a very cagey operator, to say the least, especially if he's been doing it for a while. All I can say is that he must be a lot brighter than Höddi.'

It was the first time Sigurdur Óli had entered the head-quarters of the bank and he was instantly impressed with the opulence of it all. He might have stepped from the centre of Reykjavík into a whole other world. The design was all glass and steel and dark wood, with pure, classical lines amid the tropical foliage. No luxury had been spared. Eventually he found what appeared to be a reception desk, where an elderly man was attempting to pay a bill by bank giro.

'Yes, but I'm afraid that's just the way it is – you can't pay that here,' said the woman behind the desk, which formed a small island in the midst of all the grandeur.

'But this is a bank, isn't it?' asked the old man.

'Yes, we are, but you'll have to go to one of our branches if you want to pay that.'

'But I only wanted to settle a bill,' the man persisted.

'What can I do for you?' asked the woman, turning to Sigurdur Óli, too impatient to waste any more time on him.

'Sverrir in Corporate Finance. Is he in?'

The woman typed in the name. 'Unfortunately he's just gone out and won't be back for a couple of hours.'

'What about Knútur then?' asked Sigurdur Óli. 'Knútur Jónsson?'

'Is he expecting you?' asked the receptionist in the sing-song tone of one who has asked the question a thousand times.

'I very much doubt it.'

'Where's the nearest branch then?' asked the old man, who had still not given up trying to pay his bill.

'Laugavegur,' the receptionist said, without bothering to look up.

'Knútur Jónsson's in a meeting. Would you mind waiting? And who shall I say is asking for him? Are you looking for advice on currency accounts?'

Deciding to answer only the second question, Sigurdur Óli agreed that he was as he watched the old man depart through the massive glass doors, still clutching his bill.

'Second floor,' said the receptionist, 'the lifts are over there.'

Sigurdur Óli had been waiting for around a quarter of an hour when a man emerged from a meeting room, accompanied by a young couple. He had an oddly child-like face, blond hair, and a stocky body encased in a designer suit. Having taken his leave of the couple with a smile and a promise to send them more detailed information about foreign currency accounts, he turned to Sigurdur Óli.

'Are you waiting for me?' he asked, still smiling.

'If you're Knútur,' said Sigurdur Óli.

'I am. Are you interested in a currency account?'

'Not exactly. I'm from the police and I'd like to know more about the circumstances in which your colleague, Thorfinnur, lost his life. It won't take long.'

'Why? Have there been any new developments?'

'Perhaps we shouldn't be discussing this in the middle of the corridor.'

Knútur stared at Sigurdur Óli, then glanced down at his watch. Sigurdur Óli stood there in silence until Knútur eventually invited him to come and take a seat in his office. He was very busy but could fit him in quickly, he explained, though he did not quite understand what he wanted.

38

Knútur's account of how his colleague had died the year before on the Snaefellsnes Peninsula in west Iceland coincided in almost every detail with the police report. Four men, all of whom worked for the bank, had embarked on a trip together to Hótel Búdir on Snaefellsnes. They had driven up on the Friday in two four-wheel drives, intending to stay at the hotel for two nights, do some work, explore the peninsula, and return to town on the Sunday. When they arrived on the Friday evening the weather was calm and several degrees below zero. On the Saturday morning they split up, two of them, Knútur and Arnar, deciding to join a group of tourists who were going to climb the Snaefellsjökull glacier, while the other two, Sverrir and Thorfinnur, drove out to Svörtuloft, the cliffs at the westernmost point of the peninsula, between Skálasnagi to the south and Öndvardarnes to the north. The plan was to meet at the hotel later that afternoon, but as the day went on the weather had deteriorated, with strengthening winds and an unexpected snowstorm. The two men who had gone out to climb the glacier returned at the appointed time but there was no sign of their colleagues who had left for Svörtuloft. They had not made any detailed contingency plans but it was known more or less where they were intending to hike.

The two men's mobile phones had lost their signal when they left the main road.

Only one of the pair ever came back from Svörtuloft. The moment Sverrir had phone reception he called his colleagues to alert them to the fact that he and Thorfinnur had become separated. They had been walking south along the cliffs, heading for the lighthouse at Skálasnagi, when Sverrir decided to turn back. It was getting late. But Thorfinnur was keen to press on, so they had agreed that Sverrir would fetch the car and meet Thorfinnur on the road near Beruvík. When Sverrir arrived, however, Thorfinnur was nowhere to be seen. After waiting for some time, he had looked high and low for him for at least an hour until the weather took a turn for the worse.

Sverrir wanted to know if his colleagues had heard from Thorfinnur but they had not and by now three hours had passed since they had split up. Knútur and Arnar drove out to the lava field and the three of them continued the search before finally deciding to contact the police and rescue services.

It was pitch dark and the storm had grown increasingly severe by the time the rescue team began to assemble at Gufuskálar prior to setting out for Svörtuloft. The three companions joined in the search and Sverrir was able to show them where Thorfinnur and he had parted company, though he could give them little help beyond that. This area of the lava field was difficult to traverse and after several hours' battling with darkness and extreme weather conditions, the rescue team were forced to abandon their task. As soon as it was light the next day, however, the hunt was resumed, with rescue workers combing the rim of the lava field where it fell into the sea, but the precipitous cliffs were so battered by waves and gale-force gusts that it was almost impossible to stay on one's feet.

The rescue team told the three Reykjavík men that the cliffs were known locally as the 'Black Fort', the pitch-black precipice being the last thing fishermen would see looming over them as their ship went down, as so many had in those parts. The cliff edge was scored with deep clefts, gullies and dangerous fissures which were continually being worn away by the action of the surf. One theory was that Thorfinnur might have stepped too close to the edge and that it had crumbled, plunging him into the sea.

'They didn't find him,' Knútur told Sigurdur Óli. 'You know the phrase – it was as if the earth had swallowed him up. Well, I never thought I'd experience it literally.'

'Until the following spring,' said Sigurdur Óli.

'Exactly. I can't begin to describe how horrible it was. Horrific. Of course, he wasn't a family man – he was single – but that doesn't really make it any the less tragic.'

'You think that matters, do you?'

'No, no, of course not.'

'And this happened a year ago.'

'Yes.'

'I gather that none of you were particularly familiar with the area.'

'Sverrir is. He took us there. His family comes from round there and he knows it . . . so . . . no, I don't know the area. It was my first time on the glacier. I don't know if I'll ever go back.'

'The post-mortem revealed nothing except death by misadventure. Some Swedish tourists found his body where it had washed up on a small sandy beach in Skardsvík cove. He was unrecognisable after being in the sea so long but an identification was made later. The verdict was accidental death; that he had simply failed to take sufficient care and fell over the cliff.'

'Yes, something like that.'

'You all worked together here at the bank?'

'Yes.'

'And Sverrir was the last person to see Thorfinnur alive?'

'Yes. Naturally he regrets not having taken better care of him. He rather blames himself for what happened, but of course it wasn't his fault. Thorfinnur could be really stubborn.'

'He insisted on carrying on alone?'

'Yes, according to Sverrir. Thorfinnur was really into the scenery.'

Knútur's BlackBerry began to buzz and, after glancing at the screen, he asked Sigurdur Óli to excuse him. He sat down at his desk, turning his chair away for a semblance of privacy, but Sigurdur Óli overheard the whole conversation.

'Where did you get hold of that orchestra you had the other day, the chamber group?' Knútur asked. 'No, I'm having a little dinner party,' he continued, in reply to a question. 'Yes, I know it's short notice but it was a classy outfit and I've got one of the senior execs coming to dinner. I just thought it was kind of smart when you had the chamber orchestra.'

After jotting something down, he said a brisk goodbye and turned back to Sigurdur Óli.

'Was that all?' he asked, checking the time on his computer screen as if to underline that he was too busy to pursue their conversation.

'Did you all work in the same area?'

'No, though our projects overlapped of course. We worked on a lot of the same deals.'

'Any you'd care to mention?'

'Not without breaking confidentiality. There's a reason for banking confidentiality, you know.' Knútur smiled.

Sigurdur Óli had the feeling he was being patronised. Knútur was several years younger than him but probably fifty times richer; a baby-face like that, booking chamber groups for dinner parties. As a rule Sigurdur Óli admired people who succeeded in life on their own merits and initiative, rather than envying them for their achievements, but Knútur's manner irritated him and for some reason the business with the musicians had annoyed him.

'I understand,' he said. 'So you four didn't know each other particularly well?'

'Sure, we were pretty close through work. Why are you asking about this now? Have you reopened the case?'

'To tell the truth, I don't really know. Are you acquainted with a woman called Sigurlína Thorgrímsdóttir?'

'Sigurlína?' said Knútur pensively, rising to his feet as

if the meeting was, as far as he was concerned, over. He walked across to the door and opened it but Sigurdur Óli remained glued to his seat.

'Not off the top of my head. Should I be?'

He nodded to someone in the corridor. His next meeting was due; there were deals to be done.

'She was a secretary at an accountancy firm,' replied Sigurdur Óli, 'who was the victim of a brutal attack in her own home. You'll have seen it on the news. She died in hospital.'

'I've seen the news but I can't place her.'

'You and your colleagues all went on an excursion in the highlands organised by her firm, shortly before the tragic accident on Snaefellsnes. Her husband was your guide. She was known as Lína.'

'Oh, her. Was it really her who was attacked?' asked Knútur, finally appearing to understand. 'Do the police know what happened?'

'The case is under investigation. So you do remember her then?'

'Yes, now that you mention the trip. It was awesome – the trip, I mean.'

'Did you have any further contact with her? Afterwards?'

'No, none at all.'

'What about one of your colleagues, one of the group from your bank?'

'No, I don't think so. Not as far as I know.'

'Are you sure?'

Sigurdur Óli stood up and walked over to the door that Knútur was still holding open, late now for his next meeting. Money would wait for no man.

'Yes,' Knútur replied. 'I'm quite sure. But you'll have to ask the others. I for one didn't know the woman at all. Did she mention us or something?'

Sigurdur Óli could not resist tormenting him a little.

'Yes,' he said. 'To her husband. She thought you people were incredible, quite incredible.'

'Really?'

'She talked about some "scheme". Any idea what she meant?'

'Scheme?'

'Some plan you lot had, some scheme you were mixed up in. The words she used were that you had "an incredible nerve". She didn't know what the scheme involved but it won't take me long to find out. Thanks for your cooperation.'

They shook hands and he left Knútur standing in the doorway, his baby face twisted with anxiety.

39

The police had made little headway with Höddi and Thórarinn, and Sigurdur Óli and Finnur were confronted by the same show of rudeness and arrogance when they resumed their questioning later that day.

'What bitch is that then?' retorted Höddi, when asked whether he knew Lína.

'Taking that tone won't help you,' Finnur informed him.

'Taking that tone,' Höddi mimicked him. 'Are you telling me how to talk now? Try talking less like a twat yourself.'

'How do you know Thórarinn?' asked Sigurdur Óli.

'I don't know him. Thórarinn who? Who's he when he's at home?'

Höddi was escorted back to his cell and Thórarinn brought to the interview room instead. He made himself comfortable, his gaze swinging from Finnur to Sigurdur Óli in turn, as if he were enjoying the whole performance.

'You claim you were calling in a drugs debt when you attacked Sigurlína Thorgrímsdóttir, but her husband knows nothing about any such debt. He says they never bought anything from you.'

'Why should he know about it?' countered Thórarinn.

'Are you implying that Lína did business with you without her husband's knowledge?'

'Wow, were you born yesterday or what? She owed me money for drugs. And the whole thing was self-defence.'

'You're prepared to spend sixteen years inside for the sake of a minor debt?'

'What do you mean?'

'Don't you think it's rather a feeble motive for a life sentence? A bit of dope?'

'I don't get it.'

'A minor drugs deal.'

'What? You mean, what if it was something else? Would that make a difference?'

The question sounded sincere. Thórarinn's lawyer, who was also present, sat up in his chair.

'There could be all sorts of mitigating circumstances,' said Finnur.

'Like, for example, let's say you were acting on someone else's behalf, just being used by them,' suggested Sigurdur Óli. 'While you yourself were unconnected to the case; had no direct link and therefore no personal interest in it.'

Sigurdur Óli did his best to put it tactfully, though he was far from confident that there was any truth in what he was suggesting.

'And we would be able to inform the court that you'd been cooperative,' he added, 'which could be to your advantage.'

'Cooperative?'

'All we want is to solve this case. The question is, what do you want? How do you want us to solve it? And don't waste our time making up crap about self-defence. You were at the scene. You were the cause of Lína's death. We know that. Everyone knows that. All we need is the motive, the real reason you went to see her. Or we can solve it on your terms and you can do sixteen years – ten with time off for good behaviour – all for the sake of something that can hardly have been worth more than, what, a hundred thousand, two hundred thousand kronur?'

Sigurdur Óli had Thórarinn's full attention now.

'It might be possible to understand how you could

have lost control and hit Lína too hard, when all you meant to do was hurt her, not kill her. Get it? It wouldn't make sense to get rid of her, after all, since she wouldn't be able pay you back if you killed her. Then not only would you never recover your money but you'd be in a worse predicament than before; forced to hide out under Birgir's floor. But maybe there's another side to the story. Maybe someone sent you to see Lína and asked you to knock her around a bit and you accidentally overdid it. Then whoever sent you would be liable too. On the other hand, perhaps he did send you to kill her. We have to consider that possibility too. In which case he'll walk free for all the years that you're going to spend inside. Does that sound fair to you?'

Thórarinn was still listening intently.

'Then of course there's the most straightforward explanation,' continued Sigurdur Óli. 'That you went there with the intention of killing her and that it had nothing to do with any debt or job for anyone else, but was prompted by some other motive that you don't want us to know about. It's perfectly conceivable, you know, that you went to see her with the sole purpose of killing her and were just taking a final swing at her head when you were interrupted. I'm inclined to that explanation because of the stupid way you fled the scene. And because you tried to cover your tracks when you went round to her house in the first place. That tells us that the whole thing was premeditated; that you always intended to kill Lína.'

It had been a long speech and Sigurdur Óli was not sure whether Thórarinn had taken in everything he had spelled out or insinuated, all the aspects he had played down or exaggerated; the way he had tried to close one avenue while opening another, all depending on how Thórarinn read the situation. Sigurdur Óli knew he had nothing to go on except vague suspicions but he had decided to lay them on the table and examine the reaction. Some of what he said must have sounded far-fetched to Thórarinn, but other parts – or so Sigurdur Óli hoped – might open up the way for a conversation.

'Do you make a lot of ridiculous speeches?' asked Thórarinn's fat, sleepy-eyed lawyer.

'I'm not aware that anyone was talking to you,' snapped Sigurdur Óli.

Thórarinn giggled. Finnur, meanwhile, sat silently at Sigurdur Óli's side, his expression unchanging.

'What kind of manners do you call that?' asked the lawyer.

'That was the biggest load of shit I've ever heard,' said Thórarinn.

'Fine, Toggi,' replied Sigurdur Óli. 'Then the case is closed. We couldn't be happier.'

'Yeah, right, I can tell.'

'Then it's just a question of how you want the murder to go on the record and whether someone else is clever enough to get off scot-free and enjoy the high life while you're serving a sixteen-year jail sentence. You'll look like a prize idiot.'

'Hey, wait a minute,' protested the lawyer.

'I just thought you ought to mull it over.'

'Thank you,' said Thórarinn. 'You're a real gent.'

When they met that evening at a quiet Thai restaurant near the Hlemmur bus station, Sigurdur Óli sensed immediately that Bergthóra was in a better mood. She had arrived before him and got up and kissed him on the cheek when he came in, fresh from interrogating Thórarinn.

'Are you getting anywhere with the case?' she asked.

'I don't know. There's a chance it's more complicated than we thought. What about you? How are things?'

'Bearable.'

'So, you've got a new boyfriend?'

His attempt to sound indifferent was only partially successful and she picked up the signals.

'I don't know – it's all so recent.'

'It's what, three weeks since you got together?'

'Yes, or a month, something like that. He works for a bank.'

'Who doesn't these days?'

'Is everything OK?'

'Yes, fine, I just thought that we, that we were going to try every avenue . . .'

'I thought so too,' Bergthóra answered, 'but you never made any concessions . . .'

'. . . and then this happens.'

'. . . and you never showed any interest.'

The waiter came over and they asked him to choose their dishes for them. Sigurdur Óli decided to have a beer, Bergthóra a glass of white wine. They tried to conduct their conversation in low murmurs as the room was small and all the tables were occupied. The aroma of Thai cooking, the quiet oriental music and chatter of the other customers had a soothing effect and they sat in silence for some minutes after the waiter had gone.

'Anyone would think I was cheating on you,' Bergthóra said at last.

'No,' said Sigurdur Óli, 'of course not. So you'd already started seeing him last time we met? You didn't tell me.'

'No, maybe I should have done. I was going to, but then it's not as if we're in a relationship any longer. I don't know what we are. We're nothing – it's over. I thought perhaps there was still something there, but when we met the other day I realised it was over.'

'I got a shock when I rang you late at night and heard someone there with you.'

'You didn't give our relationship a chance.'

Bergthóra spoke matter-of-factly, with no hint of accusation or resentment. The waiter brought their drinks. The beer, a Thai brew, was deliciously chilled and refreshing.

'I'm not sure that's quite fair,' Sigurdur Óli said, but his words held no real conviction.

'I was prepared to try,' Bergthóra said, 'and I believe I did what I could, but I never got anything back from you except negativity and resistance. Well, now it's finished and we can get on with our lives. It came as quite a relief to realise that I didn't need to go on living like that, all knotted up and on the defensive. Now I'm carrying on with my life and you are with yours.'

'So it's over then,' said Sigurdur Óli.

'It was over a long time ago,' Berthóra replied. 'It just took us time to realise. And now that I have, I've accepted the fact.'

'This is obviously no ordinary banker you've met,' said Sigurdur Óli.

Bergthóra smiled. 'He's great. He plays the piano.'

'Have you told him . . . ?'

He blurted it out without thinking, then realised in mid-sentence that he had no right to ask. But the words hung in the air and Bergthóra guessed what he had been going to say. She knew how his mind worked, knew that his resentment would have to find an outlet.

'That's so typical of you. Is that how you want it to end?' she asked.

'No, of course not. I didn't mean . . . I rang you to see if we could try to patch things up, but it was too late. It's my fault – I have only myself to blame. You're right about that.'

'I've told him I can't have children.'

'It only really came home to me that we were finished when I rang you,' said Sigurdur Óli.

'You can be so like your mother sometimes,' said Bergthóra, irritated.

'And how much I regretted it. How stupid it was.'

'I regret it too,' said Bergthóra, 'but it's done now.'

'Anyway, I don't see what it has to do with her,' said Sigurdur Óli.

'More than you think,' replied Bergthóra, finishing her wine.

40

The teacher asked again why he was so down in the mouth. It was during a biology lesson, one in which he dreaded being asked a question he could not answer. The teacher had asked him the same thing several days earlier but he had not known what to say then either. He enjoyed biology but he had not managed to do any of his homework, not for this subject nor his maths nor any other. Aware that he was falling behind, he tried his best to shape up but could not find the energy. These days he felt too apathetic to do anything and had drifted apart from the friends he had made when he started at the school. He had not realised that he looked miserable and, unable to answer the teacher's question, simply stared back at him, saying nothing.

'Is everything all right, Andrés?' the teacher asked.

The class were watching. Why did the teacher have to ask such questions? Why couldn't he just leave him alone?

'Sure,' he answered.

But it was not all right.

He was living in a state of perpetual fear. Rögnvaldur had said he would kill him if he told anyone what they did together. But he did not need to threaten him: Andrés would not have told anyone to save his life. What was he supposed to say anyway? He did not have the words to describe what they did, and tried to avoid even thinking about it.

He locked the ugliness away where no one could reach it. Locked it away in a place where the blood and tears ran down the walls and no one could hear his screams.

Realising that the boy was uncomfortable with the attention he had drawn to him, the teacher hastened to change the subject, asking Andrés instead to name two perennial plants, which after a brief hesitation he did. The teacher turned to the next pupil and the class's attention was deflected from Andrés.

He could breathe easily again. Down in the mouth. He had not experienced a moment's happiness since coming to live with his mother. Instead his life was an un-relieved nightmare. He dreaded going to school and having to answer questions such as why he was so unhappy, why he did not have any clean clothes to wear, why he had not brought a packed lunch. He dreaded attracting attention, dreaded waking up because the moment he did so the memories flooded back. He dreaded going to sleep because he never knew when Rögnvaldur would come for him in the night. And he dreaded the coming of day because then he was alone in the world.

His mother knew what was going on, although she was never home when it happened. He knew she knew, because he had once heard her beg Rögnvaldur to leave the boy alone. She had been drunk as usual.

'Mind your own business,' Rögnvaldur had snapped.

'It's gone far enough,' his mother had said. 'And why do you have to film the whole thing?'

'Shut your mouth,' had come the reply.

He used to threaten her too and hit her sometimes.

Then one day Rögnvaldur was gone – the projector, the films, the camera, his clothes, shoes, boots, and shaving things from the bathroom, his hats, coats – all gone one day when he woke up. Rögnvaldur had some-times disappeared before for short periods but he had always left his belongings behind. Now, however, it seemed that he did not intend to come back; he had vanished, taking everything he owned.

The day passed. Two days. Three days. There was no sign of Rögnvaldur. Five days. Ten days. Two weeks. Still no sign. He woke up in the night, thinking Rögnvaldur was prodding him, but it was not him, he was not there. Three weeks. Andrés kept pestering his mother.

'Is he coming back?'

The answer was always the same.

'How the hell should I know?'

A month.

A year.

By then he had learned to deaden the pain; it was strange how good sniffing glue could make him feel.

As far as he could, he avoided opening the door to the room where the blood still ran down the walls.

And Rögnvaldur did not come back.

He gazed up at the gloomy grey sky.

Strange, how contented he felt in the graveyard. He was sitting with his back against a lichened old stone, oblivious to the cold. He must have dozed off. Twilight was falling over the city and the rumble of traffic carried to him from beyond the wall, beyond the tall trees that overshadowed the long-forgotten graves. He was surrounded on every side by tranquil death.

Time had ceased to pass.

It had no business here.

41

Sigurdur Óli was unsure how far to trust Andrés and what had emerged during their last conversation. Despite its confused, rambling nature, Andrés had seemed to be claiming that he had somehow got his hands on Rögnvaldur, and his allusion to a mask tallied with the scraps of leather that Sigurdur Óli had seen in his kitchen. Andrés had called with the express intention of giving him this information but had been unwilling to go any further and his hesitation implied that he was not sure what he wanted to achieve. From the state of his flat it was clear that he was not living at home, indeed had not for a long time. Sigurdur Óli had tried to establish the identity and address of the Rögnvaldur that Andrés had mentioned but there were only a handful of men in the capital area whose name and age fitted and none of these had been reported missing. But Andrés's stepfather had used an alias before – more than one in fact – and could still be doing so, which would make it even harder to find him. Was it possible that Andrés had attacked him? Or was this simply the confused fantasy of a man far gone in alcoholism? Should he take him at his word? Should any claims from such a troublesome man with a long record of vagrancy and substance abuse be taken seriously?

These and many more questions preoccupied Sigurdur Óli as he drove to his mother's house after his meeting with Bergthóra. In spite of everything, he thought that Andrés ought to be believed, at least to a degree. He had in no way come to terms with the demons of his youth, which still oppressed his soul nightmarishly. He needed help, and he was making a plea, though he had gone about it in a strange manner. The film footage and their meeting in the graveyard were enough to convince Sigurdur Óli to give him the benefit of the doubt.

Andrés haunted Sigurdur Óli; his thoughts kept returning to him, triggered by random sights or sounds. What had Andrés said about his mother? 'Don't ask me about her. I don't want to talk about her.' What had

Bergthóra said about Sigurdur Óli? 'You can be so like your mother sometimes.' After all their problems Bergthóra had been the one to end their relationship. It was over, they were going their separate ways and now he did not know what to think. He regretted losing Bergthóra. At last it had come home to him that he wanted to try again, to do his best, but it had been too late. He had lost his temper and she had talked of emotional coldness, of his and his mother's snobbery. Yet he could not remember uttering a single critical word about Bergthóra at any point in their years together.

Tired and depressed, Sigurdur Óli would have preferred to go home to bed but there were questions he wanted to ask his mother on two unrelated topics; one as his mother, the other as an accountant unimpressed by the so-called 'New Vikings' and sky-high rates of return.

Gagga was somewhat surprised to receive a visit from her son so late at night. As Sigurdur Óli took a seat in her kitchen he heard the sound of the television from the sitting room and asked if Saemundur was home. Yes, Gagga said, he was watching some programme. Was he going to say hello? Sigurdur Óli shook his head.

'You were talking about the banks the other day. Do you know much about how they operate?' he asked.

'What do you need to know?'

'Why have they got so much money all of a sudden?

Where does it all come from? And what might bankers be doing that wouldn't stand up to scrutiny? Any ideas?'

'I don't know,' Gagga replied. 'You hear so many stories. Some people say we're heading for a crash if we go on like this. The incredible expansion we've been witnessing is based almost entirely on foreign credit and there are various signs that these sources are either going to be blocked soon, or just dry up. If this global recession they talk about does happen, the banks will be in big trouble. The risk is that instead of trimming their sails and being more cautious they'll simply up the ante. Only yesterday I heard that they're planning to get their hands on more foreign currency by launching deposit accounts in other European countries. At least I gather that there are plans afoot. Are you investigating the banks now?'

'I'm not sure,' said Sigurdur Óli. 'Maybe some people connected to them.'

'Icelandic tycoons who have acquired large holdings in the banks via their companies are taking loans from them, which is unethical, of course, quite apart from being risky if practised to excess. They're using the banks, which are public limited companies, for their own profit. And having carved up all the biggest companies in the country between them, they're now busy buying anything they can lay their hands on abroad, all funded by cheap borrowing. Not to mention all the games they play to boost the value of their companies, which is often based on nothing more than an illusion. On top of that they make inroads into public companies by selling their own assets to them at inflated prices. Meanwhile the bank executives award themselves options worth hundreds of millions if not billions of kronur, and then gamble by taking out loans to buy shares in the banks themselves.'

'We're always hearing about that sort of thing.'

'That's how they're paid for cooperating with the owners,' Gagga explained. 'Then there are the cross-holdings. It's always the same handful of people doing these deals, giving and taking loans. The danger is of course that if one link is broken, the whole edifice will come tumbling down like a house of cards.'

Sigurdur Óli stared thoughtfully at his mother. 'Is this all legal?'

'Why don't you talk to your colleagues in the fraud squad? Or have you already?'

'I may need to soon,' he said, his thoughts going to Finnur.

'I don't think Icelandic law has adequate provisions to cover half of what these people are up to. Parliament is a joke – they're thirty years behind what's happening here. All they ever talk about is the price of agricultural products – they're completely powerless. Meanwhile the government controls everything and they're encouraging this madness, making a fuss of the New Vikings and bankers being flown all over the shop in their corporate jets. Bank debt is approaching twelve times GDP but no one's doing a thing about it. But what exactly are you investigating?'

'I haven't a clue,' said Sigurdur Óli, 'I don't even know if there's much in it, but it involves four bankers who went on a trip to Snaefellsnes from which only three returned. The fourth fell over a cliff. Nothing suspicious about that. His body was found months later and it's impossible to tell if anything untoward happened. But a year on, a secretary from a major accountancy firm, who had invited the four men on a glacier tour organised by herself and her husband, was attacked. As it happens, the secretary, Lína, was in a mess – both financially and in her private life. The kind of hopeless case who's forever coming unstuck.'

'In other words, you need to know what four bankers might have been up to that cost one of them his life, then led to this woman's death a year later?'

Sigurdur Óli frowned. 'Or maybe just two. They weren't all necessarily involved in fraud.'

'What kind of fraud?'

'Look, I've said too much. You mustn't breathe a word about this to anyone, OK? If you do, I'm dead meat. I'm in big enough trouble as it is. Anyway, I expect I'm blowing the whole thing out of proportion; it's probably nothing but a straightforward drugs debt. And we've got two brainless thugs in custody who are almost certainly responsible for the woman's death.'

'Well, it's hard to exaggerate when it comes to banking,' Gagga said. 'One of the things they say is that the financiers are shifting hundreds of millions, even billions of kronur, to tax havens to avoid paying their share of tax here in Iceland. They set up holding companies which they then use to do business that involves all kinds of secret accounts. It's almost impossible to find out what's going on because of the confidentiality laws in the tax havens.'

'What about money laundering?'

'I wouldn't know about that.'

'Maybe they were embezzling from the bank – the four men, that is.'

'It's not unheard of.'

'That would be the most obvious assumption, if I was going to suspect them of illegal conduct. All I've heard is that they had an incredible nerve and were operating some sort of scheme.'

'A scheme?'

'Yes, something illegal. Two or more of them were in on it.'

'So it needn't necessarily be connected to their bank?'

'No. I've spoken to one of them.'

'And?'

'Nothing doing. He could hardly find the time to talk to me. Too busy booking a chamber orchestra to play at his dinner party.'

Sigurdur Óli heard Saemundur cough from the other room and hoped he was not going to come through.

'I saw Bergthóra,' he said. 'We've sorted matters out, once and for all.'

'Really? What do you mean, once and for all?'

'It's over.'

'Hasn't it been over for ages? And you're taking it badly?'

'I am, actually.'

'You'll find someone else. Was it her who broke it off in the end?'

'Yes, she's started a new relationship.'

'Typical,' said Gagga.

'What do you mean?'

'She doesn't hang about.'

'You never could stand her.'

'No,' his mother replied. 'You're probably right. And don't start having regrets about losing her. It's a waste of time.'

'How can you say that? Just admit it, as if it were nothing?'

'Would you rather I lied to you? You were far too good for Bergthóra. That's my opinion and I'm not going to hide it.'

A question that had long been nagging at him rose to Sigurdur Óli's lips.

'What did you see in Dad?'

His mother looked as if she did not understand the question.

'Why did you ever get together?'

'What are you raking up now?' asked Gagga.

'You're so different,' said Sigurdur Óli. 'You must have realised. But . . . what was it?'

'Oh, for goodness' sake, don't start harping on about that again.'

'You had more to gain from it, didn't you?'

'What do you mean?'

'He paid your way through university.'

'Look, dear: people get together and break up for no particular reason and the same applies to me and your father. The mistake was probably mine, I admit. Now stop going on about it.'

He was worried that it was too late when he rang the doorbell, as he did not want to drag him out of bed. There was an interminable wait and he was about to steal away when someone took hold of the handle and the door opened.

'Is that you, Siggi?' asked his father.

'Were you asleep?'

'No, no. Come in, son. Is Bergthóra with you?'

'No, I'm alone,' said Sigurdur Óli.

His father was wearing an old blue dressing gown with a narrow plastic tube dangling below the hem. He noticed Sigurdur Óli's eyes fasten on the tube.

'I've got a catheter,' his father explained. 'For the urine. They're taking it out tomorrow.'

'Ah, right. So, how are you?'

'Fine. I'm sorry I haven't got any food to offer you, Siggi. Are you hungry?'

'No. I just wanted to look in on my way home, to see if there was anything you needed.'

'I'm all right. Do you mind if I lie down?'

Sigurdur Óli took a seat. His father lay down on the sofa in the sitting room and closed his eyes: he looked very tired and could probably have done with a longer stay in hospital but thanks to the never-ending cuts, they were sending patients home at the earliest opportunity. Sigurdur Óli looked around at the bookcase and chest of drawers, the old TV set and the framed 'Master Plumber' certificate. There were two photos of himself on the table, and a thirty-year-old picture of Gagga and his father. Sigurdur Óli remembered the occasion well; it had been his birthday, the last one at which they had all been together.

He told his father about him and Bergthóra. His father listened in silence to the brief, edited account and Sigurdur Óli waited for his reaction, but it did not come.

There was a long pause during which he thought his father had dozed off, and he was just about to tiptoe out when his father half opened his eyes.

'At least you didn't have any children,' he said.

'Perhaps it would have been different if we'd had children,' said Sigurdur Óli.

A lengthy silence followed. He was convinced that his father had fallen asleep again and did not dare disturb him, but then he opened his eyes and focused on Sigurdur Óli.

'They always come out of it worst. You should know that yourself. The children always come out of it worst.'

42

The next day, Sigurdur Óli came across the name of one of the banker Thorfinnur's closest friends, a man called Ragnar who, according to the police file, had joined the hunt for his body. He taught Icelandic at the teacher training college and was busy taking a class when Sigurdur Óli dropped by shortly after lunch to speak to him. It was Ragnar's last class that day, he was told, so Sigurdur Óli waited patiently in the corridor outside the college office for the door to open and the students to stream out.

He did not have to wait long. Soon the corridor was full of chattering people armed with bags, laptops and phones, and a raucous cacophony of ringtones. When Sigurdur Óli felt it was safe to enter the classroom, he found Ragnar still in conversation with two students, so he loitered while the teacher finished dealing with the students' questions. They had obviously failed to acquit themselves adequately, as Ragnar was telling them to pull their socks up.

The students left the room looking chastened and Sigurdur Óli greeted Ragnar. He explained that he was from the police and wanted to ask him about his friend Thorfinnur who had died on Snaefellsnes. Ragnar paused in the act of putting away his laptop in his briefcase. He was fairly short with a shock of red hair and large sideburns, which were back in fashion – not that Sigurdur Óli was aware of the fact – a wide mouth and guileless eyes that blinked continually.

'At last,' he said. 'I thought you lot were never going to get round to it.'

'Get round to what?' asked Sigurdur Óli.

'To investigating it properly, of course,' said Ragnar. 'It wasn't natural what happened to him.'

'Why do you say that?' Sigurdur Óli asked.

'Well, I mean, there was something very odd about it. They go to Snaefellsnes, the four of them, intending to stick together, then suddenly he's not with them, there are just the two of them, and then he gets lost.'

'It happens, you know. People are always getting into difficulties, what with the weather and all the natural hazards.'

'I pointed out all sorts of problems that no one listened to. They let a long time pass before raising the alert. And not everything they said was consistent; they gave different accounts, then corrected themselves about what time they had set off and when they meant to come back. That Sverrir is a complete idiot.'

'In what way?'

'He said Thorfinnur shouldn't have been wandering around there on his own. The two of them were meant to go together, but Sverrir claimed that Thorfinnur asked him to head back and get the car while he carried on. Why? He didn't explain, just said that Thorfinnur had wanted to plough on alone through the lava field while he fetched the car.'

'Doesn't that seem a reasonable explanation of what happened?'

'I suppose so. But it's the sort of place where you have to be careful. The weather can turn without warning, and there are dangers everywhere – like cliffs and fissures that you have to watch out for. Especially out west at Svörtuloft. So it seems crazy to leave someone alone out there.'

'Was Thorfinnur an experienced hiker?'

'Yes, he was actually. He was quite a keen walker.'

'Did he ever mention a woman called Lína or Sigurlína? She went on a glacier tour with him and a bunch of other people that same autumn.'

'No, I don't think so.' Ragnar looked at him enquiringly. 'Is that the woman who was killed, the woman in the news? That was her name, wasn't it?'

'Yes.'

'Is there some link? Is that why you're here? Are the two cases connected?'

'I couldn't say,' said Sigurdur Óli. 'We're investigating her activities in order to try and work out what happened, and one of those activities was an expedition to the highlands with a group of bankers and foreign businessmen. You don't happen to have any idea what your friend was doing with his colleagues – what they were working on?'

'I never understood, to be honest,' said Ragnar. 'I knew Thorfinnur had something to do with foreign currency accounts and pensions, but we never discussed it in any detail. Financial stuff bores me.'

'Would you say he was honest?'

'He was the soul of integrity, in everything he did.'

'Did he ever mention any problems at work?'

'No.'

'Or his friends or colleagues at the bank, the ones who were on the trip with him?'

'No. Anyway, I don't think they were friends. Thorfinnur got to know them when he started working there, four or five years ago.'

'So they weren't close mates?'

'He certainly never described them like that and I don't think he particularly wanted to go on that trip to Snaefellsnes. He wasn't looking forward to it and would have preferred to get out of it.'

'But he went anyway.'

'Yes, and didn't come back.'

Sverrir kept him waiting outside his office for forty-five minutes, during which time bank employees came and went along the corridor without giving him so much as a glance.

Finally the door opened and Sverrir stuck his head out.

'Are you Sigurdur?' he asked.

'Sigurdur Óli, yes.'

'What do you want?'

'To talk to you about Thorfinnur.'

'Are you from the police?'

'Yes.'

'What do the police want with the case?'

Sverrir had pointedly not invited him in, so Sigurdur Óli remained seated on the chair in the corridor, which was fixed to another chair and a table with a pile of old magazines from which he had carefully averted his eyes.

'Are you happy to discuss this in the corridor?' asked Sigurdur Óli.

'No, of course not, sorry, come in.'

Sverrir's office was bright and airy, furnished with a new leather suite and two wall-mounted flat screens displaying exchange rates and graphs.

'Did you and Thorfinnur fall out? Is that why you parted ways?' Sigurdur Óli asked, sitting down to face Sverrir across his desk.

'Fall out? Why are you looking into this now? Has there been a new development? Where did you get the idea that we fell out? Was it you who talked to Knútur downstairs?'

Sverrir's questions came so thick and fast that Sigurdur Óli wondered whether to bother answering all of them.

'So he must – Knútur, I mean – must have told you that I was asking questions about Lína. She said you boys had an incredible nerve and were running some kind of scheme. That's why I'm looking into this now, since you ask; that's the new development. What scheme was she talking about and why would she say you had an incredible nerve?'

Sverrir studied Sigurdur Óli impassively.

'I don't know what you're implying,' he said finally. 'Knútur came in here telling me that you'd been talking to him about Thorfinnur and making all kinds of insinuations that sounded pretty tasteless to me.'

'Did you know Lína?'

'I only remembered her when Knútur started talking about the tour we went on. I had no idea she was the same woman who was attacked the other day.'

'What about you and Thorfinnur? Why did you go back to fetch the car alone? Did you quarrel? What happened?'

'I presume you've read the files. I have nothing to add. I was going to pick him up at Beruvík but he never turned up.'

'I gather he could be really stubborn. That's how one witness put it.'

'He could be, yes. He wanted to go on further than I thought advisable, given how late it was. I wanted to go back but he didn't, so eventually we agreed that I would fetch the car, then come and pick him up. There are tracks where you can drive through the lava field.'

'So he just charged on regardless and you couldn't stop him, and then he went missing?'

'It's all in the files. And he didn't charge on. He'd never been there before and was very taken with the scenery.'

'But you've been there often?

'Naturally. My family comes from Snaefellsnes.'

'And you know this particular area well?'

'Yes.'

'Was it your idea to go there in the first place?'

Sverrir cast his mind back. 'Yes, you can probably blame me.'

'And you've often walked through the lava field?'

'Not often, no.'

'But you know how dangerous it is. Yet you left him behind on his own.'

'It's no more dangerous than a hundred other places in Iceland. You just have to be sensible.'

'What was this scheme that Lína overheard you plotting?' asked Sigurdur Óli.

'There was no scheme, no plot,' Sverrir replied. 'I don't know what she was on about, what the context was. Could it have been some sort of joke?'

'Not according to her husband.'

'Well, I don't know him. And I didn't know her either, and I can't imagine what kind of rubbish she could have been saying about us.'

'Yet not long afterwards, one of your group was killed. That very same autumn.'

'Look, I'm sorry, but I don't think I can help you any further,' said Sverrir. 'I'm extremely busy, so we'd better call it a day.'

He stood up.

'His body was found washed up in Skardsvík cove,' persevered Sigurdur Óli. 'Have you been there?'

'Yes. He had an accident. The case was closed. I don't need to tell you that.'

'His body was so badly decomposed after so long in the sea that even if there had been injuries, they wouldn't have been visible,' observed Sigurdur Óli, standing up as well. 'So you didn't get better acquainted with Lína?'

'No!'

'She was promiscuous. Maybe she just liked men; got a kick out of wrapping them round her little finger. Even the most careful of men.'

'Yes, well, I didn't know her at all,' Sverrir repeated, opening the door.

'Then how about a couple of individuals called Thórarinn and Hördur, alias Toggi and Höddi? One's a van driver, the other owns a garage. Animals, the pair of them.'

'No, I don't know them. Is there any reason I should?'

'They're debt collectors. One of them killed Lína – Toggi, that is, or Toggi "Sprint" as he's known. He certainly runs like a motherfucker. I believe he's about to start talking. Maybe we'll have another little chat after that.'

'Are you threatening me?'

'I wouldn't dream of it,' said Sigurdur Óli. 'Did any of you sleep with her? Lína, I mean.'

'Not me,' answered Sverrir. 'And let me repeat that I find these questions deeply offensive. I don't know what you're trying to achieve but I'm sure there must be other ways of going about it.'

43

Arnar, the fourth member of that fateful trip, worked on the floor above Sverrir. Sigurdur Óli went straight upstairs, asked where he could find him and located a door marked 'Arnar Jósefsson'. After tapping several times, he pushed it open. Arnar, who was on his feet, phone pressed to his ear, gave Sigurdur Óli a look of puzzled enquiry.

'I'd like to talk to you about your late colleague Thorfinnur,' announced Sigurdur Óli.

Arnar apologised to the person on the phone, saying he would call back later, and hung up.

'I don't believe you have an appointment,' he said, turning the pages of his desk diary.

'No, I don't believe I do,' said Sigurdur Óli and explained briefly who he was and why he was there. 'Am I right that you were with your colleagues when Thorfinnur was killed?'

Arnar stopped flicking through his diary, gestured to Sigurdur Óli to sit down and took a seat himself.

'Yes. Have the police reopened the investigation?'

'Could you tell me roughly what happened?' asked Sigurdur Óli, ignoring his question.

Arnar resigned himself to answering and started to recount the events surrounding his colleague's death. His account was consistent with the statements given by Sverrir and Knútur. Arnar confirmed that Sverrir had been the last to see Thorfinnur alive.

'Were you good friends?' asked Sigurdur Óli. 'What sort of relationship did you have?'

'I have to ask why you're questioning me about this now.'

'So the others haven't talked to you?'

'Knútur has; he's completely in the dark about what's going on.'

'Yes, well, maybe things will become clearer in due course. Were the four of you good friends?'

'Friends? I wouldn't really say that. More like associates.'

'Colleagues?'

'Colleagues, of course, as we all work here. What exactly are you driving at?'

Sigurdur Óli took a folded piece of paper from his coat pocket.

'Can you tell me who these people are?' he asked, handing Arnar the list of those who had accompanied Lína and Ebbi on the glacier tour.

Arnar took the list and scanned it briefly before passing it back.

'No, except for the people who invited us, the people from the accountancy firm.'

'You don't know any of the foreigners, the foreign names?'

'No,' said Arnar.

'Did you know Lína, or Sigurlína Thorgrímsdóttir, from the accountant's? Apart from meeting her on the tour?'

'No. Was she the one who organised it?'

'That's right. Did any of you know her?'

'I don't think so.'

'None of you?'

'No, unless Thorfinnur did,' said Arnar, apparently feeling compelled to add: 'He was single.'

'I don't suppose that would have mattered to her,' said Sigurdur Óli. 'How did he know Lína?'

'All I mean is, if I've got the right woman, I have a vague memory of her flirting with him a bit, teasing him and that sort of thing. Thorfinnur was very shy around women, a bit awkward in their company, if you know what I mean. Was there anything else? I don't want to be rude but I'm afraid I'm really pushed for time.'

'So, did anything happen between them?'

'No,' said Arnar, 'not that I know of.'

'What about between her and Sverrir or Knútur?'

'I don't know what you're implying.'

'Lína was the type,' Sigurdur Óli said. 'If you get my drift.'

'Well, you'll have to ask them.'

On his way out of the bank, Sigurdur Óli looked in on both Sverrir and Knútur to show them the list and ask them the same questions that he had put to Arnar, including whether they recognised any of the names. He had delayed showing it to them in the hope of catching them off guard and leaving them unsure of exactly how much he knew. Sverrir hardly read the list, merely handed it back saying he had known nobody on the trip. Knútur took more time to assess the names. He was less self-assured in Sigurdur Óli's presence than the others but gave the same answer, that he had not been acquainted with anyone except his colleagues.

'Are you sure?' asked Sigurdur Óli.

'Yes,' replied Knútur. 'Absolutely positive.'

Sigurdur Óli was walking out of the building when he heard someone call his name and, turning, saw his old school friend Steinunn coming towards him with a smile on her face. He had not seen her since the reunion, when she had mentioned her new job at the bank and advised him that he was not her type.

'What are you doing here – after a loan?' she asked, looking hotter than ever with her blonde hair, dark eyebrows and tight black trousers.

'No, I . . .'

'Did you come to see Guffi?' Steinunn asked. 'He's on holiday; he's gone to Florida.'

'No, I had a meeting on the first floor,' Sigurdur Óli explained. 'How are you doing?'

'Fine, thanks. I enjoy working here, not like the tax office. You lot must have more than enough on your plate with two murders. It's a bit excessive, isn't it?'

'Yes, I'm investigating the woman who was battered to death.'

'It sounded horrific. Was it debt collectors? You hear rumours.'

'We'll get to the bottom of it,' Sigurdur Óli replied non-committally, relieved that Steinunn did not appear to have heard about Patrekur being called in for interview.

'It's unbelievable what those debt collectors get away with,' Steinunn said.

'Yeah.'

'Now, who was it who was talking about guys like that?' she added, as if to herself.

'About debt collectors?'

'Yes, something about bullying at school. God, my mind's a blank. Anyway, he soon put a stop to it.'

'Who was it?'

'The debt collector? No idea.'

'No, the person who told you.'

'Oh, I can't remember where I heard it. I'll let you know when it comes back to me. I have a feeling it was someone we both know, unless I'm getting confused. Or maybe I heard it at the tax office.'

'Call me,' said Sigurdur Óli.

'It was good to see you. Say hi to Bergthóra, or is it all over?'

'See you,' said Sigurdur Óli and hurried out.

44

Kolfinna, Lína's friend who had given Sigurdur Óli the guest lists for the company's glacier tours, recognised him immediately when he went back to see her. She was dashing about in preparation for some meeting and he had to follow her down the corridors before he could persuade her to slow down enough to hand her back the lists of names.

'Could you run through who these people are for me?' he asked.

'I'm sorry but I'm in a terrible hurry.'

'Is there any more you can tell me about Lína?'

'Are these people connected to her in some way?' asked

Kolfinna, running an eye down the list. 'Christ, I've missed the meeting!' she exclaimed, looking at her watch.

'I don't know,' Sigurdur Óli said. 'But I know this man,' he added, pointing at Patrekur's name. 'This one too,' indicating Hermann. 'And I know who these four are.' He pointed to the four bankers. 'And of course I know Lína and Ebeneser, but there are lots of others left. Three foreigners, for example. They are foreigners, aren't they? These ones here.'

'It looks like it from the names. Are you wondering whether they might be resident in Iceland?'

'Can you fill in any of the gaps?'

'These two, Snorri and Einar, work here with us. I think this guy, Gudmundur, is a VIP client of theirs, and this one here, Ísak, is a big client too. I don't know the foreigners. Maybe you should talk to Snorri; he might know more.'

'Snorri?'

'He deals with our parent company overseas. Maybe he knows who these foreigners are. Sorry, got to dash. Nice to see you again.'

Snorri was no less pressed than Kolfinna and Sigurdur Óli had to resign himself to waiting outside his office for twenty minutes before the door finally opened and he was ushered in. During their conversation the phone rang incessantly and Snorri answered some of the calls while ignoring the rest.

Sigurdur Óli explained the situation and the reason he needed information about the foreigners who had been on the corporate excursion. He did not mention the attack on Lína or Thorfinnur's death, only that the police were investigating links between individuals in the corporate world. Snorri, a lean, agile man who obviously spent a good deal of time at the gym, answered quickly and concisely. He studied the list.

'These two came to Iceland as our guests,' he said, pointing to two of the foreign names. 'We're only a subsidiary of an international accountancy firm, as our name suggests. These men look after relations between us and their other subsidiaries in Scandinavia. They visit Iceland regularly, so we decided to send them on this tour. I gather they had a great time too.'

'What about this one?' asked Sigurdur Óli, pointing to the third foreign name.

'No, I don't know about him,' said Snorri. 'I think he must have been with the bankers.'

'Do you know them at all?'

'No. But we were doing a lot of business with the bank at the time, so I assume that's how they came to be invited. Shall we check out this guy?'

'If you wouldn't mind.'

'No problem.'

Snorri opened a search engine on his computer and

typed in the man's name. A number of results appeared and he clicked on the top one, then closed it and tried the next. In under a minute he had the facts.

'He's some executive at a bank in Luxembourg, not right at the top but in a good position. A middle manager, you might say. Alain Sörensen. Swedish on his father's side, French on his mother's, brought up in Sweden. Born 1969. Specialises in derivatives. Wife, two kids. Educated in France. Hobbies: cycling and travelling. Is that him?' Snorri asked, looking up from the screen.

'It's the right name,' Sigurdur Óli said.

'He has nothing to do with our company; I think I can say that with confidence.'

'Isn't it likely then that he was with the bankers?'

'Very likely. They're the only people in the group who would have dealings with foreign banks.'

Sigurdur Óli thought back to the three men who had studied the list and claimed not to know anyone on it.

'What's it all about?' asked Snorri. 'Surely a bankers' get-together isn't a police matter?'

'You wouldn't have thought so,' said Sigurdur Óli. 'What do you make of it? What's going on with all these banks and new billionaires?'

'It's not complicated,' said Snorri.

'Are they all financial rocket scientists?'

'If only. The problem is that very few of the people

involved in this new big-bucks business have much expertise in finance, and quite frankly some of them aren't all that bright.'

'Personally I've been quite impressed by what they've achieved,' said Sigurdur Óli.

'Yeah, sure, they're buying up big-name companies in Denmark and the UK and putting Iceland on the map, as they say. Some of them are cleverer than others. And the boost to the banking sector has created a huge amount of work, not least for people in my line of business, as well as bringing plenty of revenue into the country. But they're no wizards. They've simply discovered that there's a vast supply of cheap credit in the world, short-term borrowing, just there for the taking. They have complex ownership arrangements and scoop up all the credit they can lay their hands on before lending it back to themselves, their companies and each other in order to buy companies, banks and airlines, paying enormous sums for them.'

'So what's wrong with that?' asked Sigurdur Óli.

'On the surface it looks as if they're making money and accumulating businesses,' explained Snorri, 'but all that's happening is that the shares in their companies are rising, so it looks as if they're making a profit and that their loans are increasing simultaneously in value. There are indications that they're pushing the share prices way beyond their economic value. Then when the public and so-called professional investors like pension funds see the share price going through the roof, they jump on the bandwagon, and the New Vikings take out even bigger loans against the rise, which is driven by a vastly inflated asset valuation. And so on.'

'Is there no regulation?'

'The valuation of assets is governed entirely by them. Look how they're permitted to record goodwill, which is just some kind of expectation of future revenue. They decide how it's calculated themselves. It's a completely fictional number that can be blown up to tens of billions without having any basis in reality, but it helps them ramp up their market price still further. There's next to no regulation of this sort of trick.'

'Goodwill?' echoed Sigurdur Óli.

'They do whatever they can to make the numbers look good,' said Snorri. 'When the economy's being run on this sort of model, it only needs one thing to go wrong for it to have catastrophic results. Hardly a single credit repayment can be made without the whole system coming crashing down. You may not have heard much about goodwill yet, but just you wait until you start hearing talk of credit lines.'

'But isn't it up to auditors like you to make sure that everything's above board?'

'That's my point. We're gradually easing ourselves out of a relationship with these individuals,' said Snorri. 'I've been fighting for this in our company and people are starting to listen to me. We're not going to connive in these practices any more.'

'What about Alain Sörensen?'

'I don't know him,' said Snorri. 'There are all sorts of banking scams that involve shifting money into tax havens and so on. But I don't know this man.'

'Tax havens?'

'I only say that because he's based in Luxembourg. A lot of that stuff passes through Luxembourg.'

45

When the interrogation of Thórarinn and Hördur resumed that afternoon at the Litla-Hraun prison, where the two men had been remanded in custody, Sigurdur Óli joined Finnur to interview Thórarinn. He had given Finnur an update on his investigation into Lína's links with the three bankers and a summary of his conversations with them, which had not proved particularly informative. They had agreed on a strategy for dealing with Thórarinn, who until now had been singularly uncooperative. It was time, they resolved, that he woke up to the predicament he was in.

'A tiresome character,' commented Finnur.

'Insufferable,' agreed Sigurdur Óli.

But Thórarinn appeared undaunted when he was led into the interview room, smirking at them, accompanied by his lawyer.

'What's with the porridge in this place, day in, day out?' he asked.

'You'd better get used to it,' Finnur said.

Sigurdur Óli switched on the tape recorder and they began by repeating the same questions about Lína and the reason Thórarinn had turned up at her house, armed with a weapon, and hit her, thereby causing her death. Thórarinn stuck to his story about a debt and to his claim that he had not meant to go so far. He remained adamant that he had acted in self-defence.

'All right,' said Sigurdur Óli. 'Let's change the subject. Do you know a banker called Sverrir?'

'Who's he?'

'Can't you tell me?'

'I don't know a Sverrir. What's he saying? Is he telling lies about me? I don't know him.'

'What about a man called Arnar, also a banker? He works at the same firm.'

'No idea.'

'The third banker I'm going to ask you about is called Knútur. Ring any bells?'

'Nope.'

'What about a man called Thorfinnur?'

'No. Who are these guys?'

'Have you had any business dealings with the men I've just named?'

'No.'

'Have you had any other sort of dealings with them?'

'No.'

'Did one of them approach you about Lína?'

'I'm telling you, I don't know them.'

'So you deny having any dealings with them?'

'Yes, I do. I don't bloody know them.'

'Have you heard the name Alain Sörensen?'

'Who the hell is he?'

'All right,' said Sigurdur Óli. 'That's all. Thank you.'

He reached over to the tape recorder and turned it off.

'You're admitting sole liability for Lína's death so you're looking at a life sentence,' said Sigurdur Óli. 'You've got what you wanted. You should be pleased. Congratulations.'

'What? Is that it?' asked Thórarinn in surprise. 'Who are these characters you were asking about?'

'I think we're finished here,' said Finnur to Thórarinn's lawyer. Neither he nor Sigurdur Óli looked at the prisoner. They explained that as far as they were concerned the case was solved and no longer a matter for the police but would now be passed to the public prosecutor's office. Toggi listened intently. Gradually it dawned on him that he no longer had any power over the assembled company.

'We expect he'll remain in custody here at Litla-Hraun until the trial, and ultimately he'll probably get a reduced sentence. That's par for the course,' Sigurdur Óli told the lawyer.

'Run that bit about liability by me again,' said Thórarinn, glancing from one of the police officers to the other.

'What about liability?' asked Sigurdur Óli. 'What are you talking about?'

'If someone . . . how did you put it? That thing you said last time. If someone's just . . . if someone's just an instrument or whatever the hell you said.'

'Are you referring to what I explained about complicity?'

'Yeah, what was that all about?'

'Are you suggesting that you want to alter your statement?'

Thórarinn was silent.

'Do you want to change your statement?' repeated Finnur.

'Let's just say that I'm not necessarily the only one to blame,' Thórarinn replied, still addressing Sigurdur Óli. 'Let's just say that. You said yourself that it wasn't necessarily all my fault. You said that last time.'

'What are you getting at?' asked Sigurdur Óli. 'Could you try to be clearer?'

'I'm just saying that maybe it wasn't all my fault.'

'Oh?'

'Yeah.'

'You'll have to be more precise,' said Finnur. 'How exactly?'

Thórarinn's lawyer leaned over and whispered in his ear. Thórarinn nodded. The lawyer whispered something more and Thórarinn shook his head.

'My client has expressed an interest in cooperating with the police,' announced the lawyer, once their conference was over. 'He wishes to know if he can come to an accommodation that would grant him leniency in return for information.'

'There will be no leniency on our part,' said Finnur. 'But the prosecution is another matter.'

'He's wasted too much of our time,' added Sigurdur Óli.

'He's offering to cooperate,' the lawyer pointed out.

'Lighten up, man,' said Thórarinn. 'What's the problem?'

'Right,' said Sigurdur Óli, sitting down by the tape recorder again. 'Out with it then.'

An hour or so later Höddi was led into the interview room with his lawyer. Sigurdur Óli and Finnur were there to receive him. Soon the barely audible hissing of the tape recorder started up again and Sigurdur Óli conscientiously announced the time and place and those present. Höddi seemed to sense that something had changed, that the game might be turning against him. His eyes flickered from them to his lawyer, who shrugged.

Finnur cleared his throat. 'Your friend and associate, Thórarinn, has volunteered under questioning that he was acting as a favour to you when he forced entry to Sigurlína Thorgrímsdóttir's home.'

'He's lying,' said Höddi.

Finnur continued unperturbed. 'He claims that you asked him to go to the home of Sigurlína Thorgrímsdóttir, or Lína, in order to intimidate her by inflicting injuries on her that would cause her considerable pain, and to deliver the message that if she didn't stop she would be killed. He was also told to find and bring away certain photographs.'

'That's a pack of lies!'

'He alleges moreover that you told him you had received this request from a party who was known to you and that you had found it amusing that this person should have contacted you about this favour.'

'Fucking bullshit.'

'Thórarinn asserts furthermore that he did not receive payment for his attack on Sigurlína because you were calling in a favour that he owed you, dating back to when you set fire to a four-wheel drive that was parked in front of a car sales office in Selfoss, as part of a tax avoidance and insurance scam perpetrated by one of Toggi's acquaintances.'

'Is that what he's claiming? The man's a nutter!'

'He also pleaded that it had not been his intention to kill Sigurlína but that the two blows had struck her unfortunately, as he put it. It was not his intention, nor the intention of you or the person who commissioned you, to kill the woman. That was merely an accident on Thórarinn's part.'

Finnur paused. Neither he nor Sigurdur Óli knew whether Thórarinn had told them the truth but his statement had sounded plausible, in spite of the holes it still contained. He had shown a willingness to help them bring the case to a conclusion. But Höddi might conceivably be right: Thórarinn might be trying to frame him, unlikely though it seemed.

Finnur and Sigurdur Óli gave him time to digest this new development. Eventually he leaned over to his lawyer and they began conferring. The lawyer requested a break so that he could take further instruction from his client. They agreed, and he and Höddi went out into the corridor.

'It's all bullshit,' they heard Höddi saying as the door swung closed behind them. Sigurdur Óli and Finnur waited patiently. It was many minutes before the two men reappeared.

'I want to go back to my cell,' announced Höddi on re-entering the room.

'Who told you to attack Lína?' asked Sigurdur Óli.

'No one,' replied Höddi.

'What was the purpose behind it?' asked Finnur.

'Nothing. There was no purpose.'

'What was it that Lína was supposed to stop doing?' asked Sigurdur Óli.

Höddi did not answer.

'Do you know any of the following bankers: Sverrir, Arnar or Knútur?' asked Finnur.

Höddi remained mute.

'Was it one of them who encouraged you to prevent Lína from talking?'

Still no answer.

'What about men called Patrekur and Hermann?' asked Finnur, with an eye on Sigurdur Óli, as if he should have put the question himself.

'I want to go back to my cell,' repeated Höddi. 'You won't get me to back up Toggi's lies. He's just trying to stitch me up. You must see that! Don't you get it? It was him who killed that woman. Him and no one else. There's no way he's going to pin it on me. No fucking way!'

'Are you acquainted with any of the men we named?'

'No! I don't know them.'

'What was Lína supposed to stop doing?' asked Sigurdur Óli again.

Thórarinn had been extremely evasive on this point. He had claimed that Höddi had said something along these lines, though he had forgotten the precise words, so he had simply told her to stop. According to Thórarinn's statement, he had driven up to the house, seen Lína arrive home and assumed she was alone. After parking some distance away he had launched his attack, not giving her a chance to defend herself or to demand an explanation, and he had not really taken in whatever she was saying. He had struck her on the shoulder as he passed on the message but she had not seemed to understand. He had intended to hit her again, a harder blow to her shoulder or upper body, but the baseball bat had struck her head instead and she had fallen to the floor. Just then he had heard someone outside the house and hastily sought a hiding place.

'Don't tell me you're so thick that you can't remember,' said Sigurdur Óli.

'Shut your face!' said Höddi.

'Stop what?' repeated Finnur. 'What was Lína doing that you were supposed to stop?'

'Nothing.'

'Who sent you?'

'No one.'

Sigurdur Óli switched off the tape recorder.

'We'll resume this interview tomorrow morning,' he said. 'I hope you'll give it some thought tonight.'

'Dream on,' retorted Höddi.

46

It was evening by the time Sigurdur Óli pulled up to a smart detached house in one of the new suburbs up by Lake Ellidavatn. It was a white, modernist building with a flat roof and large, aluminium-framed picture windows designed to make the most of the superb views. There were two black SUVs parked in the drive outside the double garage, and the garden, which had obviously been land-scaped, boasted a sun deck, jacuzzi and large stone slabs on a bed of smooth, sea-washed pebbles. Three mature trees, including a laburnum, had been planted to pleasing effect.

Sigurdur Óli rang the bell. A child's bicycle had been abandoned by the front door, colourful ribbons decorating the handlebars and a stabiliser on one side. Someone was clearly making progress with their cycling.

He was perfectly aware that he was attacking the weakest link in the chain and had no qualms about doing what was required. It struck him as worth applying a little pressure to see what would come of it.

The door opened and he was greeted by a smiling woman in her late twenties or early thirties. She was wearing a white, short-sleeved shirt and brand-new jeans, and looked cheerful and busy.

'Come in,' she said with a charming smile. 'He's packing and I'm in the middle of baking, so I'm afraid you'll have to excuse me.'

'Thank you,' said Sigurdur Óli. 'Is he going far?'

'No, London first, then Luxembourg.'

'Always working,' commented Sigurdur Óli.

'I know, and all this travelling,' she said, as if it were utterly exhausting. 'It's a nightmare.'

She did not ask who he was or what he wanted with her husband: so open and easy-going, so entirely free of suspicion. Perhaps she had fallen for his baby face, Sigurdur Óli thought, or the name, Knútur – 'cute', it sounded like.

'Anyway, we're going to meet up in Greece afterwards for a little break,' she said as she disappeared back into the kitchen. 'We decided yesterday. He says he's earned it.'

A boy of no more than five appeared in the kitchen doorway, completely covered in flour. He gazed at Sigurdur Óli, shy and sceptical, then ran back to his mother's side.

The woman had gone through the kitchen to find her husband. When Knútur emerged from the depths of the house and saw Sigurdur Óli standing in the hall, he was instantly wary.

'What are you doing here?' he asked in a low voice, almost a whisper.

'We need to ask your opinion on a couple of matters,' said Sigurdur Óli. 'It's rather urgent. The investigation is moving ahead quickly and we need to clear up a few points.'

He used the plural deliberately as if he were not acting alone. In his view he was not. And he left the nature of the urgent investigation deliberately vague.

'What about?' asked Knútur, glancing in the direction of the kitchen. He could not disguise his trepidation.

'It might be better if we sat down,' suggested Sigurdur Óli.

'Is it important?'

'Could be.'

'Right, come with me, we'll go to my office.'

Sigurdur Óli followed him through the house. Everywhere Sigurdur Óli looked projected wealth: the graphic designs on the walls, the pristine white sofa suite, the gleaming walnut floors.

'How did you get on with the chamber orchestra?' asked Sigurdur Óli.

'What? I'm sorry?'

'You were trying to book one when I met you the other day.'

'Oh, fine, thanks. It went well.'

'Did they perform here?'

'Yes.'

'Are you off somewhere?'

'No. Well, yes, actually. Did Maja tell you? I've got to go abroad, on business.'

'Followed by a holiday, I understand?'

Knútur showed him into his study.

'We're going to spend a few days in Greece,' he said, closing the door behind them.

'I hope I'm not the reason for that,' Sigurdur Óli said, looking round the room. It was just to his taste: no books, white shelves graced only by ornaments, parquet flooring of some light-coloured wood, a flat screen and a sound system that would have cost him more than a month's salary. There were two computer screens on the white-varnished desk. He had not seen a radiator anywhere in the house, so they presumably had underfloor heating. He would have liked that himself, if he had money to burn.

'No,' replied Knútur with a weak smile.

'Have you just moved in?' asked Sigurdur Óli.

'Six months ago.'

'It must have cost you an arm and a leg. Two cars as well. Unless it's all on credit? Everything's on credit these days.'

Knútur forced himself to smile again. He was not about to divulge his financial arrangements.

'What are you worth?' asked Sigurdur Óli. 'Isn't that the party game with you boys? When the chamber orchestra's gone home and you're trying not to pass out over the brandy? What are you worth?'

'No, I don't know.'

'How much do you reckon you're worth? Do you know? Exactly?'

Knútur pulled himself together. 'I don't see what that has to do with you.'

'It may be relevant. To the police.'

'I can't imagine why it should –'

'We know about Alain Sörensen,' interrupted Sigurdur Óli.

Knútur did not flinch.

'We know about Luxembourg.'

Still no reaction. Knútur merely watched Sigurdur Óli take the list of participants on the glacier tour from his pocket and hold it out.

'It wasn't all that difficult to trace the connection.'

Knútur took the list.

'Why didn't you admit you knew Sörensen?'

'I don't know him,' said Knútur, not looking at the piece of paper.

'We've received confirmation that you went on the glacier tour with him.'

'That's not true.'

'I have a witness,' said Sigurdur Óli. He had rung Patrekur who had told him that the Swede – as he called Sörensen – and the bankers had been travelling together; he had a clear memory of them as a group. Sigurdur Óli had felt this was sufficient evidence for the moment. He cleared his throat. 'The witness confirms that Alain Sörensen was travelling with you and your colleagues from the bank.'

Knútur had turned pale.

'Yet you didn't recognise his name on the list. Nor did your colleagues. And now you're claiming not to know him at all.'

Knútur still did not say a word.

'Why would you all be lying? Can you tell me that? Why lie about such a trivial fact as knowing Sörensen when it's so easy to catch you out?'

Knútur sat motionless.

'It leads me to conclude that you must be hiding something.'

Sigurdur Óli stepped up the pressure.

'We know all about him,' he said, though really he knew next to nothing, certainly nothing connected to any conceivable misconduct. 'Father of two. Of Swedish-French parents, brought up in Sweden but educated in France. Hobbies include cycling and travelling, which is presumably why he took the risk of joining you on the glacier trip.'

Knútur now lifted the list and stared at the names.

'We've arranged to go and pay him a visit in Luxembourg,' Sigurdur Óli added.

Knútur appeared to be on the verge of breaking. He had no answers to Sigurdur Óli's questions.

'Getting involved in fraud on this scale can be highly stressful,' Sigurdur Óli continued. 'And of course we don't know the half of it yet, such as . . .'

Apparently Knútur did not trust himself to look up from the list.

'. . . such as what Lína was up to.'

Knútur's wife opened the door, interrupting the conversation.

'Would you two like some coffee?'

She noticed immediately that the atmosphere in the room was tense.

'What is it?' she asked anxiously.

Knútur's eyes filled.

'What's happened?' she asked. 'What's the matter?'

She went over to her husband who, struggling to hold back his tears, clasped her to him as if she were the last refuge in a storm.

'What?' she asked again. 'What is it, darling? Has somebody died?'

Knútur buried his face in his wife's chest and she stared at Sigurdur Óli, her eyes suddenly wide with surprise and concern.

'What's happening, Knútur? Who is this man?' She tore herself from his embrace. 'What's going on, Knútur?'

'Oh God!' he gasped. 'I can't do this any more.'

The woman turned to Sigurdur Óli.

'Who are you?'

Sigurdur Óli looked at Knútur. He had come intending to apply the thumbscrews but had not anticipated a reaction like this. Knútur was at the end of his tether.

'I'm from the police,' he replied. 'I'm afraid he'll have to come with me, though you can accompany him to the station if you like. I imagine he'll be staying in overnight.'

She seemed unable to grasp what he was saying. She could understand the words but could not connect them. Observing her incomprehension, Sigurdur Óli hoped that Knútur would come to his aid, but he did not react.

'What does he mean, Knútur?' asked the woman. 'Answer me. Answer me, Knútur! Say something!'

Their little boy had come to the door of the office and

was regarding Sigurdur Óli, his eyes still full of mistrust. His parents had not noticed him.

'Say something!' shouted the woman. 'Don't just sit there like a lemon! Is it true? Is it true what he's saying?'

'Mummy,' said the little boy.

The woman did not hear him.

'What for? What have you done?'

Knútur eyed his wife dumbly.

'What have you done?'

'He's trying to talk to you,' interrupted Sigurdur Óli. 'Your little boy.'

'Mummy,' repeated the boy. 'Mummy!'

At last she noticed him.

'What? What is it, darling?' she asked, trying to sound calm.

The little boy glared accusingly at Sigurdur Óli who had destroyed his evening.

'The cake's ready, Mummy.'

47

They had stayed, courtesy of the bank, at an expensive hotel near Piccadilly where the rooms were so large that they were almost suites, with their own office areas and two bathrooms apiece. Everything they ordered, everything they did, was charged to their expense accounts, even their trip to *The Mousetrap* which Sverrir had always wanted to see, and another West End play starring a famous Hollywood actress. He had enjoyed the theatre. Since both Sverrir and Arnar were of the opinion that British food was inedible, they ate at expensive oriental restaurants, including their particular favourite, Mr Chow, a Chinese place near Harrods, where they were accustomed to eating whenever they came to London on bank business, letting the waiter select their dishes for them.

The two conferences they attended, along with several dozen other middle managers and senior executives of international finance firms, were devoted to the risks and potential profit of trading derivatives in minor currencies, though two of the lectures were on tax havens. Sverrir and Arnar were especially interested as they had been involved in providing information about these to the bank's wealthier clients. The process was perfectly straightforward and had many benefits. By registering a holding company in the British Virgin Islands, for example, and paying income into the account, it was possible to avoid paying tax, such as capital gains tax, in the country of origin. Many of the bank's clients had taken advantage of this service.

At the end of the second lecture, Alain Sörensen had approached them and greeted them with handshakes. Sverrir knew him well, partly from other conferences of this kind but mostly because they had been in regular communication about the administration of Icelandic holding companies in tax havens. Sörensen had been employed by the bank as an expert in the field. Sverrir had caught up with him the day before at the conference and now introduced him to Arnar, telling him that

Sörensen worked for an old, established bank in Luxembourg and took a keen interest in Iceland and its business sector.

Alain Sörensen asked if he could invite them out for some sushi.

Sverrir and Arnar exchanged glances. They had intended to eat at Mr Chow but sushi would be great.

'OK,' said Sverrir. 'Sure.'

He took them first to a popular watering hole nearby where they drank gin and tonic and discussed everything except banking. Later in the evening they took a table at a Japanese restaurant recommended by Sörensen, although the Icelanders were suspicious of anything advertising itself as fresh fish in the centre of London. The waiters greeted Sörensen as if he were an old friend. After a pleasant chat about Iceland, during which Sörensen claimed he had always wanted to go there, he got down to business, specifically Iceland's nominal interest rate.

He was extraordinarily well informed on the subject, so much so that they were rather taken aback by the depth of his knowledge of the Icelandic market, particularly the fact that Icelandic savers could achieve much higher interest rates than savers elsewhere in Europe. Interest on deposit accounts could rise to well over 10 per cent and the accounts moreover were pegged to the Icelandic inflation rate.

'Absolutely,' said Sverrir. 'If inflation rises, the interest rate rises accordingly, and if the economy continues to expand, as it seems set to carry on doing, interest rates will rocket.'

'I don't understand why the Icelandic banks don't take advantage of this wide margin by launching deposit accounts in Europe. They could offer much higher interest rates than anyone else.'

'Actually, I think they're already looking into it,' said Arnar with a smile.

Then they came to the purpose of the meeting, which turned out to be a seriously tempting proposition. Alain Sörensen had his hands on forty-five million euros. Where the money came from was immaterial, he said, but it was deposited in an account on Tortola, the largest of the British Virgin Islands, one of the world's most popular tax havens. He could lend them the money at very low interest via his bank in Luxembourg, opening an account that only they would know about. They could use this forty-five million to buy index-linked securities, such as government bonds, in Iceland, which would pay a high rate of interest. The interest would be paid to Sörensen, who would subsequently divide it up between them. Given the high yield in Iceland, the profit from such a sum would be substantial. And their share would be paid to a shell company registered by them in Tortola.

His speech was greeted by silence.

'Where does this money come from?' asked Sverrir eventually.

Sörensen smiled.

'Are you talking about black money?' asked Arnar.

'I'm saying that you needn't have any worries on that score,' replied Sörensen. 'I, or rather the bank I work for, will lend you this money as if it's just an ordinary transaction, which it is, of course. The best return would be to convert it into Japanese yen and increase the interest margin still further.'

They had finished their meal and downed glasses of saki, before moving on to the sports bar next door. It was a Wednesday evening and there was live coverage of the Champions League. Alain Sörensen took a table by a screen showing the Arsenal game.

'It's a lot of money,' remarked Sverrir.

'I imagine you'll find a way to transfer it to special accounts in your own names,' said Sörensen.

'Why us?' asked Sverrir.

'Iceland is an intriguing prospect,' said Alain Sörensen. 'We predict that Icelandic interest rates will continue to rise and net us a good return. All those construction projects in the interior coupled with the expansion in the banking sector and the high-risk investment using cheap borrowing will result in inflation to a level over and above the present high interest rates. I've done the sums for you, based on the present situation, and the figures aren't bad, in Icelandic kronur. My bank will take care of setting up a holding company for you and could take care of its administration too, if you like.'

He removed a sheet of paper from his pocket and passed it across the table. Sverrir took it, read the figures, and handed it to Arnar.

'You won't be breaking any laws,' continued Sörensen. 'You'll simply be taking a loan from my bank, investing the money in Iceland and then transferring the profit to Tortola. None of this is illegal.'

'Basically you're looking to invest in Iceland, using money that you want to put into circulation, and we get to keep the profit?' said Sverrir.

'That's right, a simple carry trade,' agreed Sörensen.

'Are we talking about money laundering here?' asked Arnar, who was prepared to be blunt as he did not know Sörensen.

The Luxembourg banker looked at them in turn.

'If you want to think about it, that's fine,' he said. 'If you need to discuss it with other colleagues, spread the loan further so as not to arouse suspicion, then that's OK too – it's a lot of money, even for bank employees.'

'Why do you need a middleman?' asked Sverrir. 'Why

don't you plough this money into Iceland yourself? Take advantage of the interest rates?'

'Of course I could do if I wanted,' said Sörensen. 'But my borrowing has – how shall I put it? – peaked for the moment. I'm not a major player, just an ordinary bank employee like you guys – though hopefully that will change. I'm interested in investing in Iceland further down the road, possibly in renewable energy. I gather there are opportunities in that area, in hydroelectric and geothermal power. That's where the investors will be looking in future. And I hope you'll be there to help me when the time comes.' His lips stretched in a smile.

'So, what you're saying is that you're interested in profiting from Iceland's interest-rate policy?' said Sverrir.

'Not just me,' replied Sörensen. 'Your economic miracle is attracting interest from investors everywhere with their eyes on the interest margin. Your glacier bonds have been selling well.'

'The glacier bonds are selling like crazy,' agreed Arnar, nodding.

At this point Sörensen glanced at his watch and said that regrettably he would have to be leaving.

'Let me know what you decide,' he said. 'If you find you need more than forty-five million, it can be arranged.'

'It's a lot of money,' said Sverrir.

'Carve it up into three or four parts, if there's anyone

you trust to get in on the act with you. Like I said, it would probably make sense to spread the money. I can ensure a low interest rate and no repayments for the first year; after that we can split the profit between us.'

Sverrir and Arnar took a taxi back to the hotel and sat up half the night in the bar, discussing Sörensen's proposition. Based on his predictions, the trade should deliver them a handsome profit. Neither was instinctively opposed to the idea; both thought it worth taking a closer look. The loan they would be taking from Sörensen's bank would be like any other; it was not their concern where the money came from, though Sörensen had been decent enough to give them a hint. They knew from their own experience that Icelandic entrepreneurs and banking clients used tax havens and shell companies as a matter of course.

'It's a hell of a gamble,' said Arnar.

'I reckon it could work,' countered Sverrir.

'You know him, do you?'

'Yes, I've got to know him pretty well. He's been pumping me about the situation in Iceland. And as you can see, he knows what he's on about.'

'Sure does,' said Arnar with a smile.

They discussed every angle of the proposition, all the pros and cons. Alain Sörensen's bank was a venerable, highly trustworthy institution, but the question of the money's provenance was more troublesome. They went over these two aspects again and again.

'Shall we look into it?' said Sverrir at last, when the night was half over and they were the only souls left in the bar.

'I was thinking about Thorfinnur,' said Arnar. 'He started at the same time as me and I know he's interested in making money.'

'Yeah, it would probably be sensible to spread it out a bit. Not too much, though; we don't want word getting out.'

'No, we'll keep it to ourselves,' said Arnar. 'If we decide to go for it, of course. No one, absolutely no one, must know.'

'Not because there's anything irregular about it,' interjected Sverrir.

'No, it would just be simpler to keep it under the radar,' said Arnar.

'Not a bad return,' said Sverrir, studying the breakdown Sörensen had given them.

'Unbelievable interest rates,' said Arnar, smiling again. 'For those with the means to exploit them.'

Knútur was sitting in Sigurdur Óli's office, telling him and Finnur the story of how their dealings with Alain Sörensen had begun. He had allowed Sigurdur Óli to escort him to the station and had declined the services of a lawyer.

'Maybe later,' he had said, hanging his head. 'I just want to tell it like it happened.'

Sigurdur Óli had given Finnur the salient facts over the phone. The matter would be handed over to the fraud squad the following morning.

Knútur had been visibly crushed as he tried to explain to his wife why, out of the blue, on an ordinary autumn evening, they had received a visit from the police. Sigurdur Óli had left the room while this was going on, asking them to leave the door open. About ten minutes later they came out, along with the little boy. The woman immediately accosted Sigurdur Óli, a grim expression on her face.

'Couldn't you have found another way?' she snapped at him accusingly. Gone was the gentle wife.

'Perhaps you should ask Knútur the same thing,' he replied, unmoved.

Now Knútur was sitting before them, explaining how they had originally got involved with the Luxembourg banker and how Sverrir and Arnar had decided to accept Sörensen's offer almost the very same night. Both took home decent salaries but no more than that. Like the rest of the staff, they had a few shares in the bank but were not otherwise active players of the market. They had no share option like the senior executives, who also borrowed from the bank to buy call options in the bank's shares. They were just employees, there to serve clients.

'So you jumped at it?' said Finnur.

'Without thinking twice, to be honest,' answered Knútur. 'Everybody's making money, so why shouldn't we?'

'What about Thorfinnur? Did he jump at the chance too?'

Knútur nodded. 'There were four of us,' he said.

'No one else?'

'No.'

'What happened to Thorfinnur?'

'You'll have to ask Sverrir.'

'You must know,' said Finnur.

'All I know is that he regretted the whole thing. He told us he didn't want to be involved any more.'

'So you got rid of him.'

'You'll have to talk to Sverrir.'

'Was this the scheme that Lína was talking about?'

'Who's Lína?'

'Sigurlína Thorgrímsdóttir. She was murdered in her home last week.'

'Well, I don't know who she is. I've already told you that. Her name means nothing to me.'

'She was on the glacier tour with you, the same tour

as Alain Sörensen. Arnar remembers her, yet you claimed not to know her.'

Knútur was silent.

'She knew what you were up to,' said Sigurdur Óli.

'Speak to Sverrir. He knows everything. I just put my name to the loans and opened some accounts. He knows all about Thorfinnur. I could never have laid a finger on him. Not in a million years.'

'What about Sverrir then?' asked Sigurdur Óli. 'Could he have silenced Thorfinnur?'

'You'll have to ask him about that.'

'Have you ever heard mention of Thórarinn or Hördur? One's a van driver, the other runs a car repair shop.'

'No.'

'How about Toggi and Höddi?'

'No. I wasn't in the know. Sverrir and Arnar took care of all the finer points. I don't know who these men are.'

'Where were you going?'

'How do you mean?'

'You were packing.'

'They wanted to send me away,' said Knútur, 'when you started poking around. They thought I'd crack, so they told me to get the hell out of the country.'

'And you did crack.'

'If telling the truth counts as cracking.'

There was a silence which lasted until Knútur cleared

his throat. Sigurdur Óli saw that he was struggling to remain composed.

'Thorfinnur wanted to pull out when he heard where Sörensen's money came from,' Knútur said.

'Oh?'

'Yes. Alain blurted it out. He was showing off. He should never have told us.'

'Where did it come from?'

'Thorfinnur went mental.'

'Where did the money come from?'

Knútur hesitated. 'Ask Sverrir. He was in charge.'

48

In the interests of the investigation it was thought inadvisable to postpone the arrests of Sverrir and Arnar until the morning. So towards midnight the police went to their homes with warrants for their arrest, and they were taken down to Hverfisgata on suspicion of large-scale money laundering. Sigurdur Óli assumed that it would not be long before additional charges were brought against them for the murders of Sigurlína and Thorfinnur.

He was not present at the arrests, not out of any particular sympathy for the suspects but because after witnessing Knútur's life come crashing down around his ears he did not have the stomach for any further scenes. The formal interrogation of Sverrir and Arnar would begin the following day. They had both requested lawyers and, according to the officers who brought them in, appeared unflustered, almost as if they were expecting the police. Sigurdur Óli guessed that Knútur's wife must have called them with the news and they had foreseen the inevitable. They would be detained at Hverfisgata overnight before being transferred into custody at the Litla-Hraun prison in the morning.

He decided to wait for them to be brought in and in the meantime started reading the drug squad's transcripts of Höddi's phone calls over the last few weeks. It was mind-numbing stuff and his attention wandered.

On his way to his office he had noticed a young offender in the corridor, the kind of waster he would sometimes go out of his way to abuse. He remembered having a go at Pétur and encountering him later in hospital. The boy had certainly got a taste of his own medicine when he was beaten to a pulp not far from the police station. As far as Sigurdur Óli was aware, no one had yet been picked up for the incident, but then it was Finnur's case and he did not know much about it.

He wondered if Finnur was also in charge of the case of the kid sitting out there now. After trying in vain to focus on the transcripts of Höddi's inanities, he gave up and went out into the corridor.

'What is it this time, Kristófer?' he asked, sitting down next to him.

'None of your business,' said Kristófer, who was known to all as Krissi. He was twenty-two years old, with a mess of scar tissue on his forehead, and in many ways resembled Pétur, though he was chubbier and covered in tattoos, one of which extended from his throat to the nape of his neck. He was notorious for starting fights, either alone or with his mates, and it made little difference whether he was on drugs or sober. These incidents generally occurred in the city centre, and the victims tended to be out alone in the early hours of the morning. Like anyone who preys on easy, unsuspecting targets, Krissi was at heart a coward.

'Been kicking the shit out of someone again?' asked Sigurdur Óli.

'Fuck you.'

'Don't tell me, you've been in for questioning and now you're just waiting to be released?'

'Fuck you.'

'You should be happy, shouldn't you? We've got a dream system for losers like you.'

'Oh yeah, right.'

'What happened?'

Krissi ignored him.

'Who did you beat up this time?'

'He went for me.'

'Same old story,' said Sigurdur Óli.

Krissi was silent.

'People are always picking on you. Don't you find that odd?'

'I can't help that.'

'Oh, no, I know. It's not your fault that you're like you are.'

Krissi did not react.

'Is Finnur handling the case?'

Still no answer.

'I shouldn't be interfering,' said Sigurdur Óli, standing up.

'Don't then,' retorted Krissi.

Instead of returning to his office, Sigurdur Óli went and examined the report of Kristófer's arrest earlier that evening. He had attacked a nineteen-year-old sixth-former outside a nightclub where a school disco was being held. The victim had to be taken to hospital by ambulance, having been kicked unconscious by Kristófer and sustained serious injuries. The witness statements disagreed about the course of events, though one said that Kristófer had simply approached the boy and headbutted him unprovoked.

'Why do I concern myself with these tossers?' Sigurdur Óli asked himself with a sigh, putting down the report.

Having tried and failed to track down Finnur, who he assumed must be busy with the arrest of the two bankers, he returned to reading Höddi's transcripts. Many of the calls were short – his wife wanting him to go to the shops for her or to check on her mother or drive their children to school events. Höddi's wife was no cook; she was forever dispatching him to takeaways to buy fried chicken or burgers or pizzas to bring home. Other conversations were with friends, about body-building, how much he had lifted, what weights other people had done, about football, snowmobile trips, snowmobile repairs, which spare parts were required, and so on. Then there were the calls to or from customers of the garage. Sigurdur Óli glanced through the lot and could not see a single conversation with Thórarinn, about Lína or anything else, so he assumed they deliberately avoided using the phone and met in person to discuss anything serious.

Hearing a noise outside, he got up. The officers had returned with Arnar, and Sigurdur Óli looked on as he was booked.

'Was Finnur with you?' he asked one of the officers.

'No, I didn't see him,' the man said. 'Hasn't he gone home?'

'I expect so. He's not answering his phone.'

Arnar looked at him. He appeared to want to say

something, then hesitated, lowering his eyes, before eventually getting up the nerve.

'Did you bring Sverrir in too?' he asked.

Sigurdur Óli nodded.

'Has Knútur been helping you?'

'We'll talk tomorrow,' said Sigurdur Óli. 'Goodnight.'

Walking away, he noticed that Kristófer was no longer in the corridor. Finnur was just disappearing into his office and Sigurdur Óli called to him but the other man pretended not to hear and shut the door behind him. Sigurdur Óli barged in.

'Where's Kristófer?' he demanded. 'Have they let him go?'

'What's it to you?' asked Finnur.

'Where is he?'

'I don't know; I expect he's been released. It's not my case. Why are you asking me?'

'Where did he go?'

'Where did he go? Do you think I know or care where these dickheads go after they're released?'

Sigurdur Óli dashed back out into the corridor and rushed down to the yard behind the station and into the adjoining alleyway. As he left the building he caught sight of Sverrir being helped out of a police car, but he ran on down the side alley, calling Kristófer by name. After glancing up Snorrabraut, he decided to head down towards the coast road instead. He ran to the Freemasons' House, but seeing no sign of Krissi, turned and jogged back in the direction of the sea, then into Borgartún where he forlornly shouted Kristófer's name several times. Slowing his pace, he walked up the street, and was just about to turn back at the junction to a small side street when he spotted a man lying on the ground and three figures taking to their heels.

Sigurdur Óli ran to the spot just in time to see the men jump into a car, driven by a fourth, and vanish round the corner. The man on the ground was groaning in agony, his face a mask of blood. It was Kristófer. He was lying on his back, his front teeth smashed in, his eyes swollen shut. Sigurdur Óli gingerly turned him onto his side and rang for an ambulance.

'Who were they?'

'I . . . don't know,' whispered Kristófer.

'What happened?'

'They . . . they were waiting. Behind the station . . .'

Sigurdur Óli burst into the station and strode along the corridor to Finnur's office. Finnur was just leaving as Sigurdur Óli bore down on him, shoved him back into his office and slammed the door behind them.

'What the hell?' shouted Finnur, squaring up to him.

'I've just put Kristófer in an ambulance,' announced Sigurdur Óli.

'Kristófer? What's that got to do with me?'

'Shouldn't you ask what happened?'

'Why the hell would I do that?'

'I thought I'd warned you. If you don't stop this, I'll have to take it higher.'

'I don't know what the fuck you're talking about. Get out of here!'

'I'm talking about the fact that you tip people off when you know these fuckers are leaving the station. Do you think you're exacting some kind of justice? Is that the idea?'

Finnur backed away. 'You're out of your mind,' he said, though less convincingly this time.

'I know they don't get the sentences they deserve, that they usually get off scot-free after being questioned. But this isn't the solution.'

Finnur did not answer.

'You've done this before – three years ago. That girl on Pósthússtraeti. I wasn't the only one who knew. And now you're at it again. Well, there are people here who won't stand for it.'

'People want justice,' protested Finnur.

'You want justice,' corrected Sigurdur Óli.

'A boy ended up unconscious in hospital after what your friend Kristófer did to him,' said Finnur. 'Completely unprovoked, just for kicks. For all we know, the boy may be a vegetable when he comes round, but we can be sure that your friend Kristófer will be having a laugh with his mates when that happens. So I told the boy's father that if he had something he wanted to say to Kristófer, we'd be letting him go this evening, through the side alley.'

'So he gathers his mates together and beats him to a pulp.'

'People have had enough. They want justice. Kristófer didn't show any mercy.'

'You know the family's blood is up immediately after an incident like this,' said Sigurdur Óli. 'They want revenge. Do you really think you should encourage them? Is it your job to use their anger just so that you can feel some kind of price has been paid?'

'The girl on Pósthússtraeti didn't do anything wrong either,' said Finnur.

'I know she's family. That just makes it worse.'

'They kicked her in the head. Two cretins having a laugh on a Saturday night. She'll never recover. They got a few months, mostly suspended. They hadn't been in much trouble before and their age and all that counted in their favour.'

'So you had the shit kicked out of them,' said Sigurdur Óli. 'You had them followed from the station, attacked and knocked senseless.'

'It would do more good than a few months inside and a suspended sentence, though I don't know exactly what you're talking about.'

'You've got to stop,' warned Sigurdur Óli.

'It's all a misunderstanding, Siggi, I'm not doing anything.'

'You can't carry on like this.'

'Have you met my cousin's daughter? Since she came out of hospital?'

'No, but you're not going to do it again. If you do, I'll go to the top and I know you don't want that to happen.'

'These guys don't get any sort of punishment. You see them again and again, involved in the same old shit. What are we supposed to do?'

'Finnur, you've got to stop.'

'Personally,' said Finnur, opening the door for Sigurdur Óli, 'I think they should shoot the bloody scum the moment they lay hands on them.'

49

Sverrir was sitting on the bed in his cell but jumped to his feet as the bolt was shot back and Sigurdur Óli came in. The door closed behind him. He was still in a black mood after the scene with Finnur.

'Where did the money come from?' he demanded, taking up position just inside the heavy steel door.

'The money?'

'Where did it come from?'

'I don't under –'

'Knútur has told us everything that matters,' interrupted Sigurdur Óli.

Sverrir stared at him. 'I'm not supposed to talk to you without my lawyer present.'

'All that formal shit will start tomorrow,' said Sigurdur Óli. 'I just wanted to hear what you had to say; ask you about a few minor points that we can go over in more detail later. Like where the money that you laundered for Alain Sörensen came from. I gather he couldn't help telling you. Who is Sörensen involved with? Who's he acting for?'

'Sörensen?' asked Sverrir innocently.

'Yes, Sörensen.'

'What has Knútur been telling you?'

'All about Alain Sörensen and how you knew him; how you and Arnar met him in London and agreed to exploit the interest margin by taking a loan from him and using it to make a killing on the high rates here, before dividing up the profits. We'll start straight away tomorrow morning by examining your assets, bank accounts, share holdings, and all that crap. I imagine a lot of interesting things are going to come to light. About shell companies and tax havens, for example.'

Sverrir sat down again.

'As I said, he's being very cooperative,' continued Sigurdur Óli. 'He said you and Arnar were going to send him out of the country. You regard him as a total pussy, don't you? So why did you bring him in on the deal?'

Sverrir did not answer.

'Thorfinnur knew, didn't he?' said Sigurdur Óli. 'He knew where the money came from. And he wasn't happy. Oh no, far from it: Knútur says he hit the roof.'

The blue plastic mattress on which Sverrir would sleep that night squeaked slightly whenever he moved.

'Why did Thorfinnur go crazy?'

'I want my lawyer present,' said Sverrir. 'Surely it's my right?'

'But why did you have to have Sigurlína attacked? Why did she matter?'

'I don't know any Sigurlína.'

'What did she do to you? Don't you remember her? She was with you on the glacier trip a year ago. When Alain Sörensen visited Iceland. She found out about your scheme. Who told her?'

'I don't know what you're talking about.'

'Which of you did she sleep with?' persisted Sigurdur Óli.

'I want a lawyer,' said Sverrir. 'I think it would be best if a lawyer were present for all of this.'

Arnar was sitting in another cell on an identical bed, which was cemented to the floor. He did not bother to rise from the blue plastic mattress when Sigurdur Óli asked the guard to let him in, barely lifting his head before continuing to stare at the wall. It was getting on for one in the morning and Arnar looked weary and dejected.

In an attempt to elicit a reaction, Sigurdur Óli asked him the same questions he had just put to Sverrir. He mentioned that Knútur was cooperating and asked about the money laundering and where Alain Sörensen's funds had come from, about Lína and the scheme and why they had found it necessary to set a debt collector on her.

At the final question Arnar, who had been sitting in silence throughout, suddenly pulled himself together.

'Who's this Lína you keep banging on about?' he asked, his eyes on Sigurdur Óli, then rose.

'Her name was Sigurlína Thorgrímsdóttir. She was murdered at her home last week. A debt collector, commissioned by you and your colleagues, sent his friend round to see her and this friend accidentally killed her. Only one of them struck the blow but they're equally liable.'

'It's the first I've heard about it. Sverrir must have totally lost his mind.'

'She found out what you lot were up to. Maybe she threatened to go to the press. She was a bit inept like that, didn't know how to blackmail people into doing what she wanted. And what she wanted was money. Why didn't you just pay her off? Wouldn't it have been easier? After all, you'd made enough money.'

Arnar came a step closer to Sigurdur Óli, who was leaning against the steel door.

'Or maybe she knew where the money came from,' continued Sigurdur Óli.

'Her name doesn't ring any bells,' Arnar said. 'I just saw on the news that some woman had been killed.'

'She knew about the four of you. And she lost her life. And what about Thorfinnur? What happened to him? How did he die?'

'I don't know about this woman.'

'What about Thorfinnur then? I expect you know all about him.'

Arnar turned back towards the bed and sat down. Sigurdur Óli waited while the seconds ticked away.

'Did you plot to get rid of him?'

'No,' said Arnar.

'To push him over the cliff at Svörtuloft? Was that why you went to Snaefellsnes in the first place?'

'I wasn't with Sverrir and Thorfinnur. As far as I know, Sverrir told the truth.'

'Let's change the subject then,' said Sigurdur Óli. 'Where did the money come from?'

'The money?' repeated Arnar.

'The money that you put into circulation for Alain Sörensen. Where did it come from? Why did Thorfinnur go ballistic about it? Sverrir refuses to talk and Knútur's keeping shtum too. He told us to ask Sverrir. Where did the money come from?'

Again Arnar did not answer.

'It'll come out sooner or later,' Sigurdur Óli said.

Arnar straightened his back, trying to sit upright on the mattress. Unlike Sverrir, he had not said a word about a lawyer.

'Thorfinnur went mad when he found out and threatened to go straight to the police,' he said suddenly. 'Sverrir managed to pacify him, but not for long.'

He sighed heavily.

'Sörensen just kept saying that we didn't need to know where the money came from. Sverrir and I were perfectly happy with that, but after a while Thorfinnur started asking questions. He felt guilty. I think he just wanted out and was looking for an excuse. He was worried that we were profiting from drugs. But when we found out what was really behind it, he said it was ten times worse than drugs.'

'So he threatened to talk?'

'He wanted out and Sverrir said he'd started blabbing. I didn't ask any questions. Sverrir said we had to do something – I must stress that he only said it to me, not to Knútur. We'd got him and Thorfinnur involved at the outset because we needed to spread the loans, the sums were too big. Thorfinnur was like Knútur, a bit of a kid really, but he wanted the money, he wanted to get rich; everyone wanted to get rich.'

'So that's the explanation, is it? Greed?'

'Look, we seized the chance when it was offered to us. We could see what was going on around us and maybe we wanted a slice of the cake.'

Arnar looked up.

'Sverrir hasn't told me exactly what happened on the trip. You'll have to ask him about it, though I have my suspicions. And so will you, of course, now that the whole thing has blown up in our faces.'

'Why did they go to Svörtuloft? Because Sverrir knows it like the back of his hand?'

'It was sort of a joke to him. Everything Sörensen said was spot on: the economy just keeps on expanding; the Central Bank has doubled interest rates since last year.'

'Hang on a minute, what kind of joke?'

'You know, it's what people call the Central Bank – Svörtuloft, "the Black Fort". Sverrir found it funny. He said he would show us the real Svörtuloft. I didn't even know it existed.'

'And you know nothing about Lína?'

'No.'

'So she didn't pretend to have information on you? Didn't threaten you?'

'No. I don't know her.'

'But you recollect her from the glacier tour, don't you? When Alain Sörensen came over and you took him on a trip into the interior? You remembered her the last time we spoke.'

Arnar thought about this. 'She was the woman who organised the tour, right?'

'Correct.'

'I do vaguely remember her. Now I come to think of it, I have a feeling Knútur was interested in her.'

'Knútur?'

'Maybe I'm getting this wrong.'

'Did Knútur sleep with Lína?'

Arnar did not answer. It was evident he wanted to get something off his chest and Sigurdur Óli waited patiently.

'It was child porn,' he said finally.

'What?'

'The money we laundered for Alain Sörensen. The dirty money. Some of it was from drugs, some from normal porn, but some from child porn.'

'Child pornography?'

Arnar nodded. 'We were involved in laundering money for a porn ring, including paedophiles who produced child porn. Thorfinnur – he just couldn't live with that.'

50

Sigurdur Óli had Knútur brought up to his office. He meant to ask him about Lína, before heading home to get some sleep. It had been a long day but his curiosity would not allow him to give up quite yet. Finnur had already left. Sigurdur Óli did not know if he would take any notice of what he had said.

The door opened and Knútur was escorted into his office. He sat down, his youthful features betraying fear and anxiety. No doubt he would get little sleep that night, kept awake by thoughts of his wife and child, or Thorfinnur's fate, or the origin of the money from which he had made a profit.

'You knew where Alain Sörensen's money came from, didn't you?' said Sigurdur Óli.

'I'm not saying anything until I've spoken to a lawyer,' Knútur replied. 'I've changed my mind. I want a lawyer. I gather it's my right. I'd like to go back to my cell now, please.'

'Sure, and I want to go home,' said Sigurdur Óli. 'So let's not waste any more time. There's one matter I want to go over with you; it won't take long. I understand you knew Lína rather better than you want to admit – the woman who was attacked in her home.'

While waiting for Knútur to be brought up, Sigurdur Óli had continued leafing through the transcripts of Höddi's phone calls. The printout was still lying on the desk in front of him.

'You were flirting with her during the tour that you lot went on with your friend Sörensen.'

'Says who?'

'That doesn't matter. What matters is that you claimed not to know her. Until now I believe you've been telling the truth this evening, so why lie about her? Enlighten me.'

Sigurdur Óli fiddled with the papers on his desk, picking some up as if he were distracted and his question of incidental importance. He glanced over the printout, read a few words and turned the pages while Knútur looked on.

'Was it because of your wife?' Sigurdur Óli asked. 'Was that the reason? If so, I can well understand that.'

'I want a lawyer,' Knútur said again.

'There's one thing you should know about Lína, though,' Sigurdur Óli continued. 'Sure, she was friendly and great fun, a sassy woman, but she had a special interest in married men. I haven't been able to investigate it fully yet but it seems she found men more attractive if they were married. She had a rather unusual arrangement with her partner; an open relationship where they were both free to sleep around. It's not for everyone but it suited them. I don't know if she told you about that.'

Knútur listened.

'This is what I think, and you'll have to correct me if I'm wide of the mark. You slept with her, maybe after you got back to town. You may have slept together several times or only the once. Either way, it's quite possible that she threatened you, that she had pictures of you together and threatened to send them to your wife. She was deceitful like that, unscrupulous. And you'd told her once when you were in bed together that –'

'That's not true,' protested Knútur.

'– that you and your mates were involved in a clever scam that was going to make you stupidly rich. You didn't tell her everything, but enough for her to go away and tell her partner about some scheme and that you lot had an incredible nerve.'

'That's just not true.'

'You wanted to show off to her.'

'No.'

'Did she take pictures of you together?'

'No.'

'But you did sleep together?'

'She didn't take any pictures,' said Knútur angrily. It was the first time Sigurdur Óli had seen him lose his temper. 'And she didn't threaten to tell my wife anything. I met her twice, both times in Reykjavík and –' Knútur broke off. 'Does this have to come out?'

'Just tell me what happened.'

'I don't want my wife to find out.'

'Nor would I.'

'It was the only time,' Knútur said. 'I've never done it before – cheated, I mean – but I . . . she was very determined.'

'And you blurted it out to her?'

'She wanted to know all about my job. I think she was more intrigued that I worked for a bank than that I was married. We never discussed that.'

'But you talked a lot about the bank? And you tried to make yourself sound important.'

'I told her . . .' Knútur hesitated. 'I don't know if I was trying to show off. She was very interested and kept asking about all the ways people found to dodge paying tax and so on. She wanted to know about tax havens and I may have told her about some guys I knew who were working on a fail-safe plan to make a killing. But I didn't say who. And I mentioned all sorts of different scenarios. But . . . I may have hinted that I was involved.'

'So you weren't trying to big yourself up?'

Knútur did not answer.

'And your colleagues, Arnar, Sverrir and Thorfinnur; did you tell them about this liaison?'

'No.'

'Are you sure?'

'I didn't tell anyone anything.'

'Did she want money?'

'No.'

'Did you send the boys round to shut her up?'

'No. To shut her up? I didn't have any reason to. I don't know any "boys".'

'It was vital that your wife didn't find out.'

'Yes, but I'd never have harmed Lína.'

'So you don't know Thórarinn or Hördur?'

'No.'

'And you didn't send them round to persuade Lína to keep her mouth shut?'

'No.'

'Did she try to blackmail you when she found out what you and your friends were up to?'

'No. She didn't know because I didn't tell her.'

'I think you're lying,' said Sigurdur Óli, rising to his feet. 'But we'll go over it all in more detail tomorrow.'

'I'm not lying,' protested Knútur.

'We'll see about that.'

Knútur stood up as well. 'I said I'm not lying.'

'Did you know where Alain Sörensen's money came from?'

'No, not at first.'

'But later?'

Knútur said nothing.

'Was that why Thorfinnur died?' Sigurdur Óli asked.

'Get me a lawyer,' said Knútur.

'Is it not the case that you went up to Snaefellsnes with the intention of getting Thorfinnur back on side?'

'I want a lawyer present.'

'I suppose that might be best,' said Sigurdur Óli and escorted him back to his cell.

He returned to his office to fetch his car keys and sat down briefly to go over his conversations with the three men. It looked as if they were going to play ball. But Sverrir was a tricky customer – unsurprisingly, as he probably bore the most responsibility. And he would have time to get his defence straight overnight.

Sigurdur Óli leafed through the printout of Höddi's phone calls. He had not had a chance to read them properly and was not sure there was any point now. He noticed that Höddi was talking to someone who had been in contact before, someone who had come to his garage. The date of the call was recent.

SE: Will you do this for me?

HV: No problem, love.

SE: I can give you the fifty I mentioned.

HV: Consider it done.

SE: Thanks. Bye.

HV: Yeah, bye.

Sigurdur Óli stared at the printout. *SE: Will you do this for me?* The police knew the identities of Höddi's callers; a list of their full names was appended to the printout. He looked up the initials and when he saw that his suspicion was correct a strange numbness spread through his body. One veil after another was stripped from before his eyes. He would have to apologise to Knútur for all manner of accusations he had just made. And he would have to apologise to Finnur, who had been right all along, whereas he had made a catastrophic blunder.

'What were you thinking of?' Sigurdur Óli whispered, carefully replacing the printout on his desk.

That same night he drove east, over the mountains, to the prison at Litla-Hraun to put a single question to Höddi. He knew he would not be able to sleep and dreaded what tomorrow would bring, but as much as he dreaded the inevitable, he would rather deal with it himself than leave it to someone else. After that he would resign from the case. Sigurdur Óli knew that he had been blind and was painfully aware why: he had believed himself to be sufficiently tough, sufficiently impartial and a sufficiently good policeman to resist being influenced, regardless of who was involved. But it had turned out that he was none of these.

Finding a guard he knew on duty, he talked him into waking up Höddi and bringing him to the interview room. The guard was very reluctant at first but let himself be persuaded by Sigurdur Óli's repeated pleas that it was essential for the investigation.

As this was no formal interrogation they were alone in the interview room.

'Have you lost the plot?' asked Höddi, in a vile temper after being roused from a deep sleep.

'Just one question,' said Sigurdur Óli.

'What the fuck? Why the hell do you have to wake me up in the middle of the night?'

'How do you know Súsanna Einarsdóttir?'

51

They had a date at the cinema and he had asked to take his mother's car to give her a lift.

'Where are you going?' Gagga had demanded, as she always did when he borrowed the car. He had only had his licence for a year and, although he had never had an accident, she did not entirely trust him.

'The cinema,' he answered.

'Alone?'

'With Patrekur,' he lied, unwilling to admit the truth. That would come later, maybe, all being well.

'Have you done your homework?'

'Yes!'

He had scanned the listings and found that the American film she had mentioned was on at the Laugarás cinema. It was advertised as a romantic comedy, which should do. Something light, to make the experience less stressful, though hopefully not total dross.

He had met her at a school disco, the sort of gathering he usually made an effort to attend, especially if Patrekur was going too. In this case Patrekur had known about a party that was being held beforehand and had rustled up a litre of vodka, smuggled into the country by his cousin on the cargo ships.

Having drunk too much at the pre-party, Sigurdur Óli arrived to be met by a wall of heat, noise and people, and the alcohol immediately went to his head, making him dizzy. Sweat broke out on his brow and he flopped onto a chair, feeling queasy. Then suddenly she was there, trying to help, asking him if he was OK. He muttered something in reply. He knew she was at his school but had never talked to her, and did not know her name.

She helped him out into the lobby and propelled him into the Gents where he threw up until he thought he would never stop. In the end, the attendants whose job it was to make sure everyone behaved came across him there and chucked him out of the disco, so he crept home to his mother who greeted him with an uncharacteristic show of sympathy.

'You shouldn't drink, dear,' he heard Gagga saying through the haze of alcohol. 'You don't have the head for it.'

Several days later he was standing in the school corridor when the girl who had helped him came up. The memory of her kindness was still clearly etched in his mind.

'Feeling better?' she asked.

'Yes, actually,' he said diffidently. 'I don't normally get so . . .'

He was going to say 'pissed' but felt it was hardly his style. The whole incident was an embarrassment to him.

'I'm sure you don't,' she said and vanished into the nearest classroom.

Over the next few days he watched her from afar, and the following week he plucked up the courage to sit down next to her in the canteen where she was eating a sandwich and reading a discarded newspaper. He watched her before making his move, telling himself: 'I've got nothing to lose.'

'Anything in the news?' he asked.

'It's ancient,' she said, looking up.

'Oh,' he said. 'Have you got a free period?'

'No, I'm skiving. I can't stand my teacher – and he can't stand me, so we're quits.'

'Is he . . . ?'

'Oh, he's always showing off to us girls. Aren't you the guy who runs the neocon magazine?'

'*Milton*, yeah.'

'You're not exactly popular.'

'Well, what do you expect? The school's full of commies,' said Sigurdur Óli with a shrug.

After that, whenever they bumped into each other they would stop for a chat. One day she came across him in the cloakroom where he was hunting for his anorak.

'Are you doing anything tomorrow night?' she asked directly. 'Do you feel like coming to the cinema?'

'What? Yes . . . sure, of course.'

'Have you got a car or . . . ?'

He thought quickly: it would mean having to bargain with Gagga but it was worth it.

'I could pick you up,' he said.

He drove up to her house and waited, feeling far too self-conscious to go and knock on the door and risk having to ask for her. Nor did he want to use the horn, which might easily be misinterpreted as rudeness. So he just sat and waited in patient silence. The minutes ticked by, one by one, until abruptly the front door opened and she hurried out.

'Have you been waiting long?' she asked, climbing into the passenger seat.

'No.'

'I was waiting for you to honk your horn.'

'You didn't keep me,' he assured her.

The film was a disappointment and they could find little to say when they got back into the car afterwards. He headed towards the town centre, with the vague notion of doing a couple of circuits and maybe buying an ice cream. The late-night kiosks would still be open. They exchanged a few remarks about the female lead who she had found irritating, and he commented that the film had been seriously lacking in laughs. They bought ice creams and he paid, as he had paid for the cinema tickets and popcorn, then he drove slowly home. It was midweek and the streets were empty. Almost before he knew it they were outside her house again.

'Thanks for a nice evening,' she said, finishing her ice cream.

'Thank *you*,' he replied.

She moved closer and realising that she was going to kiss him, he leaned in towards her. Her lips were still cold from the ice cream, her tongue cool, with a lingering taste of sugar.

He was unable to get her out of his head and longed to meet her but could not see her anywhere in the school corridors. He had not been paying proper attention but vaguely remembered talk of a trip with her parents, which probably explained her absence. He tried to ring her but nobody answered, and twice he drove to her house in the evening and saw that all the lights were off. He had never before felt so peculiar, so tense, so tingling with anticipation, had never experienced such yearning.

A few days later he and Patrekur arranged to meet at a club in the city centre. When he arrived he found the place heaving and the noise level almost unbearable. Patrekur shouted in his ear that he had met an amazing girl who went to their school, and called her over to meet his friend. She appeared out of the throng.

It was Súsanna, the girl who had dominated his every thought since that evening.

'Hi,' she shouted over the din, adding in surprise: 'Do you two know each other?'

'Yes,' shouted Patrekur. 'Do you know Siggi?'

Sigurdur Óli looked uncomprehendingly at the pair of them.

'We went to the cinema the other day,' she shouted. 'To a really crap film.' She laughed. 'Didn't you think so?'

'Are you . . . are you two . . . ?'

Sigurdur Óli stumbled over the words, the deafening noise drowning out his whisper and before he knew it the two of them had disappeared into the crowd.

52

He thought it safe to assume that just before midday their children would be at school and she would be alone at home. Rather than ringing ahead, he had taken the precaution of calling her workplace, where he learned that Súsanna had reported in sick and had not been seen for several days. He considered calling Patrekur and including him in the plan but abandoned the idea in the end. This was her affair and there was no need to mix Patrekur up in it until after he had spoken to her. The possibility of sending someone else to bring her in had occurred to him, but he resolved to do it himself. Other people would take over the case once they reached Hverfisgata.

When the time came, he drove to his friend's house. Patrekur and Súsanna lived in an attractive detached house in the new suburb of Grafarholt. They had taken out a large mortgage, part of it as a foreign-currency loan, but Patrekur had assured him that they were perfectly able to afford it, though the monthly payments were well over a hundred thousand kronur. They had purchased their two cars on credit as well.

She answered the door herself, wearing jeans and a pretty, pale blue shirt, and did not seem surprised to see him, though her attempt at a smile was perfunctory and awkward. In spite of everything, he had always liked Súsanna: she was fun, sensible, clear-headed, and a good match for Patrekur. To his eyes, she had not aged at all, with her thick, fair hair and dark eyes, her determined expression and straightforward manner. As far as he knew, she and Patrekur had always had a good life together; at least he had never heard otherwise from his friend until Patrekur admitted to sleeping with Lína.

'You probably know why I'm here,' he said as she invited him in, and kissed her on the cheek. They always greeted each other this way.

'Have you spoken to Patrekur?' she asked.

'No.'

'I thought he might be with you,' said Súsanna.

'Would you have preferred that?' asked Sigurdur Óli.

'No, probably not.'

'Could we sit down?'

'Of course, come in.'

They sat down in the living room. It faced west and offered a fine view of the city. Sigurdur Óli had not slept all night.

'I've just been talking to a man called Hördur or Höddi, who says he's known you since primary school,' he began. 'Right now he's in custody at Litla-Hraun, charged as an accessory to the unlawful killing of a woman called Lína.'

'I know him,' replied Súsanna.

'He told me you'd always got on well. He didn't go into details about your relationship at school but said you two always had a laugh when you met up at reunions.'

'That's right.'

'He said you'd once come to him for a favour in connection with a friend of yours, or with her daughter, rather.'

'Perhaps it would be better if Patrekur was here,' she said.

'Of course,' said Sigurdur Óli. 'We can call him. I'm in no hurry. There's no need to rush this.'

'You must think I . . .'

'I don't think anything, Súsanna.'

She looked out of the window.

'It was three years ago,' she said at last. 'My friend was in trouble. She had a daughter at sixth-form college, who kept being threatened by a gang and forced to give them money that she didn't owe them. The girl was so afraid of them that she wanted to drop out of school, so I asked Höddi if there was anything he could do. I knew he took on various, well, jobs like that – I knew he sometimes called in debts. He stepped in and after that the girl was left alone. My friend was extremely grateful. But I never asked Höddi what he did.'

'So he helped you out,' Sigurdur Óli said.

'Yes, or rather my friend.'

'Have you met him since? Or heard from him at all?'

Súsanna hesitated.

'Have you asked him for another favour?'

She did not answer.

'I've just come from him,' Sigurdur Óli said. 'He said to say hello and that I was to tell you he had kept his mouth shut for as long as he could. He claimed that you got in touch with him.'

'You must think I'm insane,' said Súsanna after a long pause.

'I think you've made a mistake,' said Sigurdur Óli. 'Did you get in touch with him?'

'Yes,' said Súsanna. 'When those people started threatening my sister it occurred to me that Höddi could have a word with them.'

'And attack Lína?'

'No, just talk to her.'

'Did you know he would beat her up?'

'No.'

'So you didn't ask him to?'

Súsanna could sit still no longer. Getting up, she walked over to the picture window and stared blankly out over the city, then wiped her eyes on her shirtsleeve.

'Did you ask him to hit Lína?'

'I asked him to get them off our backs. I didn't go into any specifics. She was blackmailing my sister. She slept with Patrekur – I thought she was going to take him away from me. I just wanted to get them off our backs.'

'Súsanna, your sister is involved in the sort of sex that carries the risk of running into people like Lína. And it was Patrekur who fell for her. You can hardly blame her for that.'

'She wasn't supposed to die,' said Súsanna. Tears were pricking at her eyes.

He saw that she was fighting a losing battle to stop herself breaking down.

'I didn't ask them to do that. I was, I was so angry. With Patrekur of course, but with her too. She was destroying us – she was going to put the photos on the Internet.'

'Was it your sister's idea?' asked Sigurdur Óli.

Súsanna took a deep breath. She was holding back the sobs now.

'Are you trying to protect her?' asked Sigurdur Óli.

'She knew about Höddi too – about what he did for my friend. She asked if I could talk to him, persuade him to retrieve the photos since she couldn't do it herself. Höddi has always been very kind and sweet and nice to me and the rest of my class, so I've tried to ignore what he does, or what people say he does. I didn't want to know.'

'So she's involved too?'

'Yes.'

'The man Höddi sent to do the job claimed that he'd received veiled instructions to give Lína a beating; to retrieve the pictures and give her something to remember him by. In the event, he hit her too hard. Do you think Höddi got the message wrong?'

'I don't know. I should never have talked to him. You can't imagine how terrible I've been feeling.'

'No, I don't suppose I can.'

'What am I to do? What can I do? My life is over. And my sister's too. You have to help us. And all because of those shits!'

Sigurdur Óli said nothing. He had been devastated about losing Súsanna, though he had never admitted it, either to her or to his friend. Only once had the subject of their cinema date come up in conversation after she and Patrekur had started going out. This was several weeks afterwards, during a party at Patrekur's house, when Súsanna had told him that she had not been aware that he and Patrekur were friends. 'It doesn't matter,' he replied. 'Is everything OK between us, then?' she asked. He nodded. 'Forget it,' he said.

'I can't give you any advice, Súsanna,' he said now. 'Except for the obvious: don't try to kid yourself that the situation is better than it is, either for you or for Patrekur or Höddi or Lína. That's the way it was and is and always will be. The sooner you face up to that, the better.'

'It was an accident. She wasn't supposed to die. She was never supposed to go and die.'

Neither of them spoke. Súsanna looked out of the window at the city stretching out to the sea.

'You had your reasons,' said Sigurdur Óli finally.

'Which don't impress you.'

'Some are easier to understand than others. The other day I was sent some old film footage of a boy of maybe ten or twelve who's suffered all his life. The footage only lasts around twelve seconds but it says it all, his whole life in a nutshell: how he suffered neglect and violent abuse, and maybe it provides all the explanations necessary for why he ended up the way he did and what he has turned into, thirty years later.'

Sigurdur Óli stood up.

'I've always avoided joining in with the chorus of hand-wringers, but the fact is that you can't help being affected by horror stories like that. I would understand if *he* wanted revenge . . .'

'But not me?' said Súsanna.

At that moment the door opened and Patrekur walked in. He had recognised Sigurdur Óli's car in the drive and could not hide his anxiety.

'What's going on?' he asked. Immediately detecting that something was wrong, he tried to put his arms round Súsanna but she would not let him and backed away, holding up her hands as if to prevent him from touching her.

'What?' asked Patrekur.

'Súsanna?' said Sigurdur Óli.

She started to cry.

'Súsanna knows –'

'I'll do it, let me do it,' she interrupted.

'All right,' he said. 'I'll wait outside.'

A little over an hour later he accompanied them both to the police station on Hverfisgata. Patrekur was allowed no further than the entrance, where they said their good-byes. He had not fully grasped the sequence of events yet and it seemed as if he would never be able to tear himself away from his wife.

Sigurdur Óli tracked down Finnur and, after informing him of the latest developments, formally resigned from the investigation. He appreciated the fact that Finnur spared him any reprimand. He learned that Alain Sörensen had been arrested in Luxembourg on suspicion of money laundering and that the three Icelandic bankers would be critical witnesses in the case against him.

Given the way the two cases were linked, Sigurdur Óli could have no further involvement with the investigation into Thorfinnur's death, but before going home he decided to have one more conversation with Sverrir, who was waiting to be transferred from his cell at Hverfisgata into custody at Litla-Hraun.

'Why did you go to Snaefellsnes?' he asked once the steel door had closed behind him.

Sverrir was sitting on the blue mattress. After a sleepless night, he had spent the morning with his lawyer. The formal interview process would begin that afternoon, at Litla-Hraun.

'Was it for the sole purpose of getting rid of Thorfinnur?'

Sverrir did not answer. He was sitting with his back to the wall, head sunk on his chest.

'Or was it to get him back on side?'

Sverrir still did not speak.

'Thorfinnur had found out the source of the money you were laundering for Sörensen. He was angry because he didn't want any part in porn, least of all child porn. Though you were OK with it. Arnar and Knútur don't seem to have had any opinion, but Thorfinnur wanted to quit. And that wasn't all; he wanted to report what was going on, and your part in it, to the authorities. He wanted to come clean, to absolve himself of what you'd got him mixed up in and try to make a new start.'

Sverrir was as silent as the grave.

'Then you had an idea about how to get rid of him. You'd take a short trip out of town – after all, everyone knows that things can go wrong in the wilderness, what with the landscape and climate being so fraught with danger. You wanted Arnar and Knútur to come along to allay any suspicion. It was supposed to look like a working holiday. I don't know what part they played in Thorfinnur's death but perhaps you could enlighten me? Then at the last minute they decided to climb the glacier, or was that planned as well?

'No doubt you and Thorfinnur quarrelled,' continued Sigurdur Óli. 'You had all tried to talk him round but Thorfinnur wouldn't budge. He'd made millions, tens of millions, but he wanted to give it all back. You told him he'd bring the rest of you down with him. You told him you could sort things out, take over his share of the loan and cover his tracks. It would have been possible, but Thorfinnur didn't want that, he wanted to atone for the crime; he just couldn't ignore where the money came from.'

Sverrir straightened up and sat forward on the bed.

'I had no part in Thorfinnur's death,' he said at last. 'What you say about the money is true. I don't know what Arnar and Knútur have told you but I can hardly deny having taken part in money laundering with them and Alain Sörensen. I'm prepared to take responsibility for that. But I had no part in Thorfinnur's death. We had an argument, you're right. We quarrelled about money, about our secret accounts and the origin of the funds. He couldn't ignore how the money was made. I told him it didn't matter but that if he wanted to quit, we'd all quit. But it wasn't enough; he wanted to give the money back, open the accounts and tell the police the whole story. The rest of us had agreed to cut our ties to Sörensen; we were even prepared to give back the money; we were ready to do almost everything Thorfinnur asked but we couldn't agree to make the matter public the way he wanted.'

Sverrir stood up and took a deep breath.

'That's what we quarrelled about,' he said. 'That was the only thing we wouldn't do. We'd agreed to the rest.'

'So you pushed him over a cliff?'

'I left him behind,' said Sverrir. 'We had a row about the accounts and about Sörensen. He wouldn't give an inch, so I told him he could go to hell and left him on his own while I went to fetch the car. I was angry.'

'Before, you only said you'd gone to fetch the car. You said nothing about a row.'

'Well, I admit it now,' said Sverrir. 'You seem to know all about the accounts anyway. I lost my temper and left him. It's up to you whether you believe me or not but that's the truth. I blame myself for what happened to him – I haven't had a moment's peace since then. I was indirectly responsible for his death – I admit that – by leaving him, but it wasn't murder. I deny that; I deny that categorically. I always meant to go back for him, but then he went and got himself killed.'

Sigurdur Óli studied Sverrir and Sverrir avoided his gaze, standing there awkwardly, staring at the four walls that hemmed him in and now seemed to be pressing in from all sides.

'Did he have any suspicion of what you intended to do?' asked Sigurdur Óli. 'Towards the end?'

'Didn't you hear what I said? I wasn't there.'

'Did he die the moment he hit the rocks? Or did he live a little while longer?' Sigurdur Óli continued mercilessly.

'I didn't touch him,' protested Sverrir.

'Did you hear his screams as he fell?'

'I'm not answering that. It's not worthy of an answer.'

'It may not be easy to prove it but the fact is that you organised the trip, you took Thorfinnur with you, you came back alone, and you had a huge amount to lose. I doubt you'll get away with this.'

Sigurdur Óli turned and knocked on the steel door for someone to open it.

'I didn't kill him,' said Sverrir.

'I think you're still in denial,' said Sigurdur Óli. 'I think the judges will take Thorfinnur's side. I believe you pushed him; I believe you saw an opportunity to get rid of him. It's conceivable that you planned it before you went to Snaefellsnes – you and the others. Or possibly it was just a moment of madness. It makes no difference. But you pushed him over the edge.'

There was a slight squeak as the door opened and Sigurdur Óli stepped out into the corridor, thanked the guard, then locked the door painstakingly behind him. Sverrir hammered on the inside and started to shout.

'Speak to me! Speak to me!'

There was a hatch in the door. Sigurdur Óli opened it and they eyed each other through the hole. Sverrir was scarlet in the face.

'It was an accident,' he said.

Sigurdur Óli merely looked at him.

'It was an accident!' Sverrir repeated, more emphatically. 'An accident!'

Sigurdur Óli closed the hatch again and walked away, affecting not to hear when Sverrir started banging and kicking the door and yelling from the depths of his cell that it had been an accident, that he had had nothing to do with Thorfinnur's death.

53

Late that evening the phone rang in Sigurdur Óli's flat. It was Patrekur, asking if he could drop by. Not long afterwards there was a knock at his door and he opened it to find his friend standing there, looking lost.

'It was my fault,' he said. 'I'm the one who should go to prison.'

'Come in, I was just going to have some tea.' Sigurdur Óli showed him into the kitchen.

'I don't want anything,' said Patrekur. 'I just want to talk to you. What do you think will happen?'

'I gather Súsanna has confessed to her part in the attack on Lína,' said Sigurdur Óli, who had phoned the station earlier. 'That she got Höddi to go and fetch the photos – she and her sister. While you and Hermann were talking to me, they were talking to Höddi.'

'I had no idea.'

'You told Súsanna that you'd slept with Lína.'

'She completely lost it. She thought Lína was trying to destroy our marriage.'

'And Höddi put Thórarinn on the case.'

'Súsanna never told me what Höddi did for a living. He was just some friend from the old days. And Lína was no angel – far from it. I tried to explain that to Súsanna but she just screamed at me, said she never wanted to see me again. She blames me for the whole mess and I can understand that. She has to come to terms with having caused the death of another human being.'

'Indirectly,' said Sigurdur Óli.

'That's not the way she sees it.'

'Her sister and Hermann must take some of the blame. You have to look at the bigger picture.'

'She's angriest of all with me.'

'Look, the blame lies mainly with that lunatic Thórarinn who got carried away,' said Sigurdur Óli. 'Although I'm not excusing Súsanna's foolishness. Or any of yours. Next time you feel tempted to cheat on your wife, either forget it or keep your mouth shut.'

'What now?' asked Patrekur eventually.

'She'll have to serve a prison sentence.'

'She's been in a very bad way lately. I just didn't notice because I was so caught up in my own stupid affairs. I can see now that she was hardly in her right mind some days.'

'You should try to support her.'

'If she'll have me any more.'

'Well, you'll both just have to live with it. Maybe it'll bring you closer.'

'I wouldn't want to lose her.'

'Nor would I,' said Sigurdur Óli.

'What about you? Are you in trouble because of us?'

'I'll survive,' said Sigurdur Óli.

54

He sat outside the block of flats on Kleppsvegur, keeping an eye on the newspaper in the postbox. As usual, the radio was tuned to a station playing mostly classic rock. He was sleepy, as he had sat up late the night before watching the American football. Just briefly he had toyed with the idea of going to bed with a book. He had been given an Icelandic novel for Christmas nearly a year ago which was still in its wrapping, so he took it out of the drawer, tore off the plastic and started reading, only to return it to the drawer shortly afterwards.

He had been sleeping badly recently, still worked up about the events of the last few days. So when he woke at the crack of dawn, he had decided to go for a drive and, without realising it, found himself outside Gudmunda's block of flats, although he had told his mother he was done with guarding her postbox. Gagga had rung him, curious about the arrests of the bankers, which she had heard about on the news, and kept asking questions about Súsanna and Patrekur, whom she knew. He had fobbed her off. 'I'll tell you later,' he said.

His thoughts turned to the conversation he had had with Elínborg. She had rung him, worried about Erlendur, who was still travelling somewhere out east – in his birthplace – and had not been in contact for over a fortnight.

'What's he doing out there?' asked Elínborg.

'No idea,' replied Sigurdur Óli. 'He never tells me anything.'

'Do you know how long he intended to be away?'

'No. Just that he wanted to be left alone.'

'Yes, that's exactly it,' said Elínborg.

Sigurdur Óli yawned. As on the previous Sunday mornings, there was hardly anyone about and the few people who did appear, either on their way home after a night out or popping out to the bakery, did not so much as glance at the newspaper. He began to nod, his eyelids grew heavy, his breathing slowed and, without warning, he fell asleep.

While he was slumbering peacefully, a scruffy-looking individual of about fifty, hair sticking up on end and clad in a threadbare dressing gown, tiptoed down the staircase, opened the door to the lobby, peered out into the car park, then grabbed the paper and hurried back inside, vanishing up the stairs.

Sigurdur Óli slept for at least three-quarters of an hour and it took him several minutes to surface. The radio was emitting a familiar beat as he rubbed the sleep from his eyes. He looked around the car park, stretched his arms and yawned, then caught sight of a man who looked much like Andrés walking along the pavement, heading west on Kleppsvegur.

Sigurdur Óli sat up in his seat to get a better view.

There was no mistaking: it was Andrés.

He had already opened the door to jump out and run after him when he changed his mind. Shutting the door again he started the engine, drove out of the car park and began to shadow Andrés. He had to make a U-turn at the next junction and was afraid of losing him but quickly located him again, a stooped figure, apparently in another world, trudging along the coast road, past Kirkjusandur and the bus depot, across Kringlumýrarbraut and into Borgartún. He was carrying a plastic bag and wearing the same ragged clothes as before. Sigurdur Óli considered hailing him for a word but curiosity stopped him.

If Andrés was not living at home, where was he hiding?

Andrés walked up Nóatún, into the Laugavegur shopping street, past the bus station at Hlemmur, then turned south along Snorrabraut, before heading down Grettisgata in the direction of the old city centre. Sigurdur Óli had no difficulty following him but was careful to maintain his distance. He turned slowly into Grettisgata and crawled along the street until he found a parking space, then parked as quickly as he could, before trotting after Andrés, still keeping a little way behind him. Ahead, he saw Andrés turn abruptly and descend the steps to the basement of an old wooden house that had seen better days, where he opened the door with a key, then closed it behind him.

Sigurdur Óli halted and examined the house. It looked tumbledown, neglected, the corrugated-iron cladding covered in rust and large patches of worn paint, leaving it vulnerable to the wind and weather. The house consisted of one storey and a basement, but the ground floor looked unoccupied.

After waiting for about twenty minutes, he decided to knock at the door and climbed carefully down the steps which were crumbling dangerously. The door was unmarked and there was no bell. Sigurdur Óli knocked vigorously several times, then waited. He noticed a foul odour, like the stench of rotten fish.

No reply. He knocked on the door again, calling Andrés's name, then waited.

Pressing his ear to the door, he heard a faint noise inside. He called out to Andrés again, and after knocking loudly for the third time without receiving any answer, he decided to try to force his way in. The lock was old and rattled when Sigurdur Óli took hold of the handle, and gave way easily beneath the weight of his shoulder. He stopped in the open doorway and called Andrés's name again before moving further into the flat.

The stench hit him like a wall, causing him to gasp and stagger back outside onto the steps.

'Jesus Christ!' he exclaimed.

He was wearing a scarf round his neck and, using this to cover his nose and mouth, he made a second attempt. He found himself in a small hall and located a light switch which did not work, so he assumed the electricity supply had been cut off. He called Andrés's name again but to no avail. From what he could see, the flat had been completely trashed. Holes had been smashed in the walls and here and there the floorboards had been torn up, forcing him to clamber over broken planks and furniture, aware all the time, in spite of his scarf, that the smell was intensifying the further he went. He stood still while adjusting to the gloom, repeatedly calling Andrés. Either he was hiding somewhere in the flat or he had escaped through a back door or window. Once Sigurdur Óli's eyes grew accustomed to the darkness he saw that he was standing in what was probably a living room, with thick curtains drawn across the window. He ripped them apart to let the light flood in.

The daylight revealed a scene of devastation: tables, chairs and cupboards lay strewn all over the place like matchwood, as if someone had driven a bulldozer right through the flat. Sigurdur Óli picked his way gingerly through the wreckage, and seeing in one corner a blanket, leftovers of food and empty *brennivín* bottles, assumed that this was where Andrés had been holed up. Returning to the hallway, he cautiously opened a door which turned out to lead to the kitchen. The scene was no less chaotic here and he observed that Andrés had probably made his escape by crawling out of the large window into the back garden.

He had lost him.

Sigurdur Óli threaded his way back into the living room, hardly able to endure the suffocating stench any longer, and was about to back out when he trod on something he thought was alive. He nearly jumped out of his skin.

Looking down, he saw that he had bumped into a foot belonging to a man who was lying on the floor covered by a dirty blanket, with only his legs protruding. Bending down, Sigurdur Óli slowly drew the blanket off the man and at last understood where the horrific smell was emanating from.

He pressed the scarf tight over his nose. The man was lying on his back, tied to a chair, as if he had fallen over backwards. His dead eyes, half open, stared up at him. In the middle of his forehead was an object that looked like a coin. A dirty piece of leather with straps hanging from it lay on the floor beside the body.

Sigurdur Óli remembered Andrés muttering about a krona piece and, curiosity overcoming all his professional instincts, he reached down to the coin, intending to pick it up, only to discover that it was fixed.

Moving closer, he realised that it was not a coin: the surface was smooth. Slowly it dawned on him that the metallic disc on the man's forehead was the end of a spike that had been driven deep into his head.

The body was badly decomposed.

He reckoned the man had been dead for at least three months.

55

On Monday morning a groundsman for the Reykjavík cemeteries turned up to work in the old graveyard on Hólavallagata and unlocked one of the tool sheds. It was cold. There had been a heavy frost overnight and a northerly wind was blowing in off the highlands, but the man was well wrapped up in a woolly hat and thick mittens. He had a job to finish that he had been putting off, and now gathered the tools he thought he would need. He went about his business without hurrying, anticipating that the task would take him most of the morning. Once he had everything, he set off across the cemetery towards Sudurgata and the tomb of the independence hero, Jón

Sigurdsson. Someone had used a spray can to write *Jonny rules* on the stone monument. He did not really object, taking it as a sign of the younger generation's increased independence of mind. At least some idiot knew who Jón Sigurdsson was. Happening to glance to his left, the groundsman stopped short and peered across the graveyard: it looked as if a man was sitting against one of the tombstones. After watching him for some time without detecting any movement, he started walking slowly towards him and as he drew near he saw that the man was dead.

He was dressed in rags, covered with a shabby anorak, his knees clasped tight to his chest as if to ward off the cold. His deathly white face was turned, eyes half open, to the heavens, as if at the moment he died he had been looking up at the clouds, waiting for them to part for an instant to reveal a patch of clear blue sky.

Jar City

Winner of the Glass Key Award for Best Nordic Crime Novel

'Highly recommended . . . thoroughly gripping'
Time Out

A man is found murdered in his Reykjavík flat. The only
clues are a cryptic note left on the body and a photograph
of a young girl's grave. Delving into the dead man's life
Detective Erlendur discovers that forty years ago the victim
was accused of an appalling crime, but never convicted.
Had his past come back to haunt him?

As Erlendur struggles to build a relationship with his
unhappy daughter, his investigation takes him to Iceland's
Genetic Research Centre, where he uncovers disturbing
secrets that are even darker than the murder of an old man.

'A fascinating window on an unfamiliar world as well as
an original and puzzling mystery'
Val McDermid

'A chilling read'
The Times

'Plausible, well-constructed . . . poignant and clever'
Times Literary Supplement

VINTAGE BOOKS
London

Silence of the Grave

Winner of the CWA Gold Dagger

Winner of the Glass Key Award for Best Nordic Crime Novel

'Here is a new voice that demands to be listened to'
Reginald Hill

Building work in an expanding Reykjavík uncovers a
shallow grave. Years before, this part of the city was all
open hills, and Erlendur and his team hope this is a typical
Icelandic missing person scenario; perhaps someone once
lost in the snow, who has lain peacefully buried for decades.
Things are never that simple.

Whilst Erlendur struggles to hold together the crumbling
fragments of his own family, his case unearths many other
tales of family pain, anger, domestic violence and fear; of
family loyalty and family shame. Few people are still alive
who can tell the story, but even secrets taken to the grave
cannot remain hidden forever . . .

'A fascinating mystery . . . Indridason is a writer worth
seeking out'
Daily Telegraph

'A writer of astonishing gravitas and talent'
John Lescroart

VINTAGE BOOKS
London

Voices

'A slow-burner that draws you more and more deeply into the investigation and into the dark dilemmas of the principal characters'
Spectator

It is a few days before Christmas and Reykjavík doorman and occasional Santa Claus, Gudlauger, has been found stabbed to death. It soon becomes apparent that both staff and guests have something to hide, but it is the dead man who has the most shocking secret.

Detective Erlendur quickly discovers that the placidly affluent appearance of the hotel covers a multitude of sins.

'Indridason reaches extraordinary psychological depths'
Mail on Sunday

'Once again Indridason demonstrates that the best Scandinavian crime writers can hold their own against their British and American rivals'
Andrew Taylor, author of *The American Boy* and *Bleeding Heart Square*

VINTAGE BOOKS
London

The Draining Lake

'A beautiful, sad, haunting tale of lost love and lost illusion, regret and betrayal'
The Times

A skeleton is found half-buried in a dried-out lake. The bones have been weighed down with an old Russian radio transmitter: is this a clue to the victim's, and the killer's, identity?

Detective Erlendur is called in to investigate and discovers that there may be a connection with a group of students who were sent to study in East Germany during the Cold War, and with a young man who walked out of his family house one day, never to return. As the mystery deepens Erlendur and his team must unravel a story of international espionage, murder and betrayal.

'Beautifully written and translated, the novel has both a strong sense of place and themes that transcend it; it confirms Indridason as one of those crime writers who rises above genre, combining suspense with moving insights into the human condition'
Sunday Times

'A haunting, compassionate work'
Observer

'Indridason manages to keep the reader guessing . . . right to the last'
Sunday Express

VINTAGE BOOKS
London

Arctic Chill

‘An international literary phenomenon – gripping, authentic,
haunting and lyrical’
Harlan Coben

A dark-skinned young boy is found dead, frozen to the
ground in a pool of his own blood. The boy’s Thai half-
brother is missing; is he implicated, or simply afraid for his
own life? While fears increase that the murder could have
been racially motivated, the police receive reports that a
suspected paedophile has been spotted in the area.

Detective Erlendur’s investigation soon unearths the tensions
simmering beneath the surface of Iceland’s outwardly liberal,
multi-cultural society while the murder forces Erlendur to
confront the tragedy in his own past.

‘An utterly absorbing detective story. In Erlendur – morose,
grouchy, but hugely likeable all the same – Indridason has
created a character in the Morse/Rebus mould who could
stand comparison with either’
Scotsman

‘A highly believable mystery, seamlessly translated’
Independent

‘This novel has great clarity, emotional depth and
resonance’
Sunday Telegraph

VINTAGE BOOKS
London

Hypothermia

'An intelligent, gripping and moody tale with superior
characterisation'
The Times

One cold autumn night, a woman is found hanging from
a beam at her holiday cottage. At first sight, it appears like
a straightforward case of suicide; María had never recovered
from the death of her mother two years previously and she
had a history of depression. But then the friend who found
her body approaches Detective Elendur with a tape of a
séance that María attended before her death and his curiosity
is aroused . . .

Driven by a need to find answers, Erlendur begins an
unofficial investigation into María's death. But he is also
haunted by another unsolved mystery – the disappearance
of two young people thirty years ago – and by his own
quest to find the body of his brother, who died in a blizzard
when he was a boy.

'Chillingly creepy'
Guardian

'*Hypothermia* is one of the most haunting crime novels I've
read in a long time, unsentimental yet informed throughout
by Indridason's extraordinary empathy with human suffering'
Sunday Times

VINTAGE BOOKS
London